UNDER THE LINDEN TREE

UNDER THE LINDEN TREE

Cassandra Krivy Hirsch

encompass
EDITIONS

Published by EnCompass Editions, Kingston, Ontario, Canada.

www.encompasseditions.com

ISBN   978-1-927664-02-5

This second edition is identical to the first edition but newly typeset.

Cataloguing in Publication Program (CIP) information available from

Library and Archives Canada at

www.collectionscanada.gc.ca

Cover art and illustrations by William Ternay

*en**compass***
EDITIONS

Dedication

Colin, my brother always:

1967-2004

"…for an instant he was happy in his dream…"

Chronicle of a Death Foretold
—Gabriel Garcia Marquez

Acknowledgements

Many people and resources over many years contributed to my being able to write this novel, and all of them are important to me, but I'll list them by category (alphabetical within each). Lee Doty, Seena Elbaum, Karen Glick, and Leigh Jackson welcomed me to their summer homes by the sea or in historic (landlocked) surroundings. In 2008, I was awarded a Ragdale Foundation artist residency, which gave me two weeks of uninterrupted time to write in idyllic surroundings, offering me nurturance and the support of other artists at their work.

During my graduate-school years, I encountered gifted writers and professors who gave me time and support by reading and advising: novelist Beth Goldner and poet–writer Anne Kaier were key figures during those years and are still in my life, thank goodness.

Since 1994, I've been part of a stellar group of women rotating in and out of Playpen Writers. They've followed my zig-zag journey toward completion of the book: Sissy Carpey, Joyce Eisenberg (careful reader of the whole manuscript in an earlier draft); Karen Ivory; Lini Kadaba; Nimisha Ladva (encourager and task-setter extraordinaire, I wouldn't have found my publisher without her); Olivia Lehman; Robin Lentz Worgan; Janis Pomerantz; Carol Sabik-Jaffe; Ellen Scolnic; Elise Seyfried, and Ruth Weisberg.

James Rahn is credited with toughening me up in his Rittenhouse Writers Group, which saw my book's earliest pages. James and talented writers in the group held me accountable to craft in early efforts.

Trusted friends Mitchell Cohen, Janis Fine, Denise Gorlechen, Randye Green, Kate Kelsen, Lisa Litt, Tom Novak, Rena Potok, and William Ternay have offered friendship, inspiration, and careful reading over the years. Rochelle and Boris Krivy applied a keen and admirably unbiased eye to my efforts and have encouraged me all along with their confidence in my childhood and adult writing efforts.

In the course of research, I've visited Rockport, MA innumerable times, staying in the Linden Tree Inn, where this story is set (it was once a house, this inn, built c. 1850) and enjoying the nurturing touches of the proprietors, Tobey and John Shepherd. Sometimes I was content just to sit up in the cupola to see what my narrator, Marianne, saw, to talk to Tobey about the house and its hidden corridors, or to walk through Mill Pond Meadow to create my narrator's pathways. There were visits when I was lucky enough to meet with Rockport-born (for generations) women who provided tremendous help. These were the curators at the Sandy Bay Historical Society. They sat with me for several hours, pointing me toward the ideal shelves, and they also led me to Eleanor Parsons (whose surname was a happy coincidence), the local, prolific, nonagenarian historian who welcomed me into her home. It was Eleanor Parsons' book about Hannah Jumper that helped me incorporate that historic Rockport afternoon in July, 1856 into my own narrative. Eleanor asked me to stay true to Miss Jumper's character, and I hope I've done so. Upon her death, Eleanor left a wealth of local history in her many carefully researched and written books about the region.

Early on in my research, I looked to a resource called "The Fishermen's Memorial and Record Book," covering vessels and their crews lost between 1830 and 1873, by George H. Procter. I found the book in the Sawyer Free Library in Gloucester, MA and it provided me the account that inspired me to create the character of Theodore Abel and his heroic tale of survival, in part quoted and paraphrased from pages 89 and 90 of Procter's book. The librarians at Sawyer were invaluable to me in those early days of research.

My children, Ariel, Jonathan, and Ilana, now grown and almost completely fledged, have watched me write this book for so many years that one of them can claim it took *her* lifetime for me to finish. Their encouragement and existence have been essential. Joe Hirsch watched this process as well and was steadfastly supportive.

My brother, Colin Stuart Krivy, is a presence at my shoulder, his own dream to write and teach—his life—cut short by a tragic accident. A thank you for your guidance, Colin, isn't really enough.

May 20, 1994

Steven Hastings
Hastings Literary Agency
P.O. Box 22
Cambridge, MA 02138

Dear Steven,

Thanks for your willingness to look these over. I know we've talked about the journals before but I never got around to showing them to you. I've now sold the old house and my great-grandmother's stuff is about all I've brought to the little condo in Pigeon Cove. You know I don't like my surroundings too busy. These are copies by the way. Seems I'm attached to the originals.

    I understand you think there might be some public interest in these pages. We'll see what you think when you actually read them. Maybe you're right. Maybe people will relate to the idea of life not always turning out the way we think it's going to. My sister Aggie always thought it was sort of wrong, other people reading this stuff, but much as I loved Aggie, she's dead five years now and I guess it's up to me, isn't it? Aunt Amelia definitely would have forbidden it, but she died long before Aggie. My younger brother Charlie could care less what I do with papers and such. As I told you, I'm somebody who's always brooding about just where I came from and I suppose these letters and writings are some sort of sentimental toys for an old man. I take them out now and then, fiddle with them, then stow them. At my age, with no kids to hand them to, I guess stowing means burying but I'm not prepared to do that.

    What do you think, my friend? Do you think my great-grandmother would have hoped people like you and me would read her writing? I'd like to think she wouldn't feel ashamed at us staring into her soul. What do we ever know about what lies ahead after we're gone?

Looking forward to hearing from you, and I hope Linda is well.

Theo Lovell

p.s. That last letter was separate from the journal, maybe never part of it. Aggie found it in aunt Amelia's trunk not long before she died. You'll know best what to do with it.

Part I

Summer Days Ashore, at Sea

JUNE 16, 1855

I have begun this journal in the absence of another I had been keeping and which perhaps will find me once more. It is nowhere I have searched in the house and I suppose it is best to begin a new one before I despair and lose the habit of recording my thoughts. Father has taught me that when something is lost, whether dear or not, giving up the search is sometimes best and often enough the lost article finds its owner. The other notebook contained little more than a recording of daily tasks, shopping lists, and bits of my rambling thoughts. My one regret is that all I have written about our son until now is also lost. I do like to record a word he speaks if it is new, or a thought I have about our Henry, for though he is hardly more than two, he seems to be getting very large very quickly.

I shall enjoy the new notebook James has brought me. It is brown leather, embossed in gold with my initials, M.E.P., and he presented a new quill and bottle of walnut ink with it as well. I make this first entry sitting on the side porch, under the shade of the linden tree, as

Henry takes his nap and James is out at sea. I do long for him when he is away more than just a day or two, but he will be home tomorrow, for this trip is just for two days and it is only mackerel trawls he is setting. I will put an end to my brooding.

JUNE 19, 1855

My son said to me this morning, "Mama, porridge please." It is a thrill to hear him stringing his words together. When he turned two years in March, he was not yet able to make a sentence but could pluck many words from the air to tell us what he wanted, along with a very able pointing finger. In the passing months, though he is not a talkative child, when he speaks his words are carefully chosen. His little brow gathers in concentration and then out pours the sentence! Though Mother would wag her finger, I do enjoy his babble.

JUNE 20, 1855

There is something about going to the milliner that offers renewal. True, it is merely a hat to keep the sun off my brow, nose, and cheeks, though I do have freckles that would belie my ever wearing a hat at all. Yet, each early summer when I go to Mrs. Laughlin's Millinery to commission a new hat for the season, I am a girl all over again, tickled by the choices of ribbons and flowers that will adorn my hat. There are also birds and feathers, things Mrs. Laughlin imports from exotic places. I have chosen this particular milliner since being wed to James, for she is a kindly older woman who always has a little yarn spinning in her head as she takes the things from me that I have chosen. She weaves the yarn around the picture of the hat I will wear when she has completed it and when I return for the hat, she will have written it on a little piece of parchment she rolls and ties with the same ribbon she uses for the hat. It is most delightful.

I will return to her shop three days hence. My hat is to be straw, with a wide brim, wrapped 'round with a petal green ribbon and a little posy of forget-me-nots at the side. James will be as pleased with it as I; of this I am certain.

JUNE 21, 1855

I have told Agatha not to wait so long before she hangs out the linens, for they grow sour smelling. The poor girl tucked her head down and whispered an apology, then hurried away. I do not know if she will last, for she is very sensitive to the slightest reprimand.

Shortly after his nap, Henry jumped into the garden and muddied his shoes, then brought the mess into the house. I have had to take the entranceway carpet outside and beat it harder than a schoolteacher at the slate! It made my boy laugh so that I could not be cross with him and had to laugh, too, at how I must have looked.

JUNE 23, 1855

Oh, my new hat is a beauty! And the tale Mrs. Laughlin wrote and tucked into the inside band is a bittersweet one. She wrote of a girl in a meadow who runs and runs, her hair flying behind her, until she reaches the end of it. There the girl sits at its edge to weave a garland of all the flowers in the meadow until she has used up all but one of each blossom, leaving the meadow bare, a meadow she once loved and wished were her very own. It is a sad-seeming tale and I wonder how it occurred to her, how any of these tales occurs to a woman who fashions hats for ladies, and why she might think them suited to me and my rather more cheerful tastes.

Once, for an autumn hat of mine, she dreamed up a yarn that left me quite melancholy. It was about a boy who loved to fish off the jetty in Rockport Harbor until one day a mermaid beckoned him into the water. He followed, leaving his fishing line and trawl behind. One day, a year later, he was caught in his very own net and could not escape until the mermaid came for him. This happened every year to the boy, who now more resembled a fish, who now longed for the warm, dry rocks on which he once sat, and whose family had long since despaired of finding him.

Dear me, when I think of how forlorn these tales are, I wonder if Mrs. Laughlin herself tends toward melancholy. She seems jovial, yet she is a widow, and has been for nearly twenty years, I have heard. Perhaps she was a woman who wished for more than she possessed and this is the place from which such sad tales come. I say this not with certainty, but with some knowledge of myself, for I have on occasion wanted more than what I have, often in the form of a husband who had not taken so well to fishing for his livelihood, despite his family's lack of need for it. Then I chastise myself for such girlish jealousy. Could it be that this kindly milliner understands my longings?

I do hope I am not as knowable as that.

JUNE 24, 1855

Mother has sent me a note that the visit she and Father planned for July will be put off, for she has a cold. I am disappointed and will instead take Henry to visit his grandparents when Mother is well. She must rest.

JUNE 28, 1855

James speaks very little to me of the fisheries other than to boast of a bountiful trip or to grumble about its disappointing counterpart, certain it is not a subject I will find stimulating. Of course, I would like to know more, and have told him so, yet he insists that I have little to learn that will improve upon my knowledge of the world. Years ago, he told me much about his time at sea, commenting occasionally on the men in his crew. It has been gradual, but he now keeps the fisheries, which he says come with a stench, out of our home. He has assured me that if something ever occurs which merits a conversation between us he will readily share the news.

JUNE 30, 1855

I took tea with Emily McCutcheon at Mrs. Spencer's shop yesterday. She was most distressed as she informed me that her scullery maid, Mary, is to leave her employ and go to the Pringle household— under a very strict supervision, I am sure—to join her own mother there. Because Mary did not get her training in the Pringles' home, Emily expressed hope that the girl will not wither under her new employer. Emily then surprised me with the news that she and her children are to spend some time in Boston this summer where her brother resides. I do worry about my friend, for she is prone to dizzy spells. She has only to turn her head too quickly to bring it on. She is plagued with a delicate constitution.

Wisely, she hires a garden hand for the hotter months when she might thirst quickly in the heat and weaken from her work. Yet, it is all her design that yields such resplendence in her yard. She tells me that the lavender and basil in her herb garden keep invading insects away, so I have followed and planted a patch of each. It is certainly not as robust as hers. This is perhaps why her kitchen garden flourishes with succulent carrots, squash, beans and lettuces and how her flowers bloom with new vitality each spring. Nestled against the house, her garden lends her property a distinction lacked by other homes on her laneway.

My garden is lively enough. Still, I cannot stitch well and it is not likely that I ever will, while Emily produces enviable work. Some of her pillows are for sale in the Bedfords' Mercantile and are quite popular. She can hardly keep up with the requests for her cheerful motifs. While I am not a marvel in the garden or at stitch work, I *can* cook, for Mother has taught me well, even at her own insistence that she do little else in her household. She leaves much to her laundress and scullery maid. She has made certain that I have my own girl, our Agatha. A shy one, she has often made errors that cost me, for she will seldom speak up until well after the damage is done. It is difficult to find something to teach her at which she had not admitted she is inexperienced. I would not think of casting her out, for she is young, hardly sixteen, and I am her first employer. Mother somehow felt it necessary to break her in with me, discovering her through Virginia Pringle's society of women and their maids and maids' daughters who are of age to work. Agatha will learn what she can in my household and one day she will be the very essence of capability, perhaps growing old along with us.

July 5, 1855

It was a festive day here in Rockport on the Fourth and the fireworks display was held on the beach where, each year, we all gather onto our blankets for the brilliance overhead. Henry dislikes the thunder of such a grand show, yet he thrilled at the rainbow bursts that soared and popped above us. I have taught him to press his hands to his ears and I press mine over his to help dull the great boom that one can feel in one's chest. It frightens me as well and I had to bury my own face against my husband's chest. There with my son in my lap and James' arms encircling us both, all was well. We saw many people, just as thrilled and terrified as we were!

JULY 7, 1855

As I looked from the cupola earlier today, James' flag, a proud and lovely blue, sagged at half-mast as they drifted into harbor. I hurried down and out of the house, leaving Henry with Agatha. Dread pooled in my chest as I waited for Mr. Talbot to hitch the horses. We made quick time to the harbor and I nearly leapt before Mr. Talbot brought us to a full stop. An older gentleman, and kind, he looked about to scold me for my foolishness. "Mind, Missus," he said as he came around to help me down. "The Captain isn't going back out today, I'm sure." He was right, of course.

I hardly nodded to Mr. Talbot before dashing down the dock to meet James. He gathered me to him and then pushed me away all-at-once as he told me he had lost two fishermen. "The fools," he spat. "They set out from the vessel on one of the dories just as the fog was coming in. I could not have stopped them, for I was below deck and the men were in cahoots." He could hardly speak further for some moments and I led him back up the dock to our carriage, away from his schooner, from the crew that seemed to be wandering in a daze away from it as well. I will relate here, as close to James' account as I can recall, what he then told me, for I did not write it as he spoke. No, of course, I never meant to either, and did not have my journal, for I do not carry it along with me.

James' head was low, his shoulders heavy with the burden of what horror he imagined his two lost men endured. Too late to stop the men leaving the vessel, James' first mate found him and brought him up to help stop them, spoke to him of the men, already rowed away, who were determined to make a hasty trip to the trawls, thinking they would bring them in and reset them before dark. The fishing had been excellent and the men were set to make more on their catch. Other vessels seemed to be hastening their catch as well, yet James never proceeded this way; it is never his practice to fish more than their days at sea could practically allow, or to go out in a dory in perilous conditions. He is not a greedy man.

Once James was aware of the men's departure, and as it became clear they faced a struggle to make it back to the vessel, James knew the worst was possible. No sooner had the men reached the trawls and hauled them up over their gunwales than they lost sight of his vessel, of its lantern light. Even off its rails, James could see nothing through the thickest fog anyone has seen in years, a fog that had not been there in the hour before. His light bounced back in the swirl of cloud. He could hear the two errant sailors laughing and singing drunkenly in the distance, but how far they were was a grim mystery.

Yes, soon enough he heard them cry out, "Captain Parsons, speak till we find you!" And this he did, yet after a time, no amount of his calling to the men, or they to him, could close the gap between them, for it only widened until each party's cries were swallowed. The seas were rough all night, and all night James stood at wheel and sail worrying and peering into the murky distance, loyal to his compass so that he and his remaining crew should not lose their way as they sailed off course in the search. He listened through a deathly quiet after the water calmed and heard nothing. Late this morning, when the fog lifted, James was back on the course toward home harbor and still had not seen them. He thought perhaps they had made it to shore until, along the way, he saw the empty dory and his heart weighed heavier than stone.

One thing I have tried to tell James is that even as he tried and could not rescue his men, he must not blame himself. He would not hear this, of course, for he is the captain of his vessel and would have prevented the men rowing out in poor conditions for the measly reward of a few extra mackerel. He would also have relieved them *17* from his employ had they survived their foolishness. I sat still through his account, held his wringing hands and asked him if he had had any sense such a fog would come. No, he told me. He repeated that he had been below deck. He went only to fetch a kit to patch a hole in his mainsail, and they were at anchor, readying to sleep for the night, he said. He did not know the two men went out until his first mate told him. It was, he whispered from a tired throat, as if his crew had waited for him to turn his back. He would not have allowed it and cannot think why sense abandoned them all.

James noticed shortly before they made harbor that one of the three demijohns of rum he had stowed in the hold of the vessel was missing. He inquired of all his men, taking a smell of their breath. Sure enough, there was a lingering stench still on them. Then his first mate, whose breath was clean, spoke up and said he was sworn to secrecy when the two men left the vessel, threatened with a dousing of fish oil and a ransack of his possessions if he spoke of their pilfering the rum or of their leaving the vessel before they could make their exit. He had tried to talk them out of such a reckless trip, tried countering their threats with his own, loyal to James' practice of bringing in the trawls next day, and not before to re-set for more bounty, no matter the abundance at sea. His first mate was just as stalwart on this point, which James had once mentioned was the reason he trusted the man to take the helm if he could not. James has no tolerance for greed on his ship, and has sworn his sailors to the same ethic, promising them they will not go hungry sailing with him. He has kept that promise. When the first mate reminded the men of their captain's ethic, they laughed at him, thinking themselves clever to collect and re-set trawls to bring in more catch, and thus more money, before returning to harbor. They said they had done quite enough watching from the rails as other vessels made hasty re-settings.

All the men were promised an extra take from the late night foray, and had been sworn by the now doomed men, Matthias and Caldwell, to be tight lipped. James now fears that this more honest crewman, one Theodore Abel, will be forever tormented by any shipmates he encounters after today. A capable sailor and fisherman, he would like to keep Mr. Abel on his vessel, even knowing the man may suffer worse than ridicule for betraying a foolhardy trust.

I did not ask too many questions of James, letting him tell the story as it occurred to him, afraid he might cease if I were to open my mouth to urge him forward in his telling, for it has been years since he felt free to speak this way. Yet, I had the terrible impulse to inquire after the expression worn by the guiltiest of the deceivers. Liars, my father taught me early in my capacity as employer to a housemaid, even a perfectly guileless one as Agatha if she were to endeavor to lie, look away from those whom they will try to deceive.

Rapt to his tale, I thought still how foolish men can be in tolerable and expected ways, but I do not know how men can watch as their shipmates endanger themselves. I would have told my captain and put an end to the tomfoolery before it began, fish oil or not. What sort of threat is this? Are they not slippery and reeking with fish from wake to sleep? Unable to curb the notion, I said as much to James. For a moment he seemed cross, then offered me a sorrowful smile and said that while it is an admirable quality in a woman to want to avoid trouble, it is more in the nature of men to invite it and that the enjoyment of it is often in the conquering, depending upon the circumstance. Of course, I argued that to invite such trouble is one thing, to be conquered by it as these men were is quite another. I held fast to my opinion, to which he replied, putting an end to the conversation, that while my notions are noble, they would not win me a place on his vessel.

The men's bodies were recovered only a day after some of their clothing and a boot washed ashore, their souls soon after put to rest. All of this within the week of their being lost at sea. Mr. John Caldwell was thirty-eight years of age and leaves an elderly mother and no wife. Mr. Ike Matthias, a younger man of twenty-nine, leaves a wife and three small children, all under the age of ten and no parents who have come to claim him as their drowned son. I will take the women foodstuffs and make it known to all who would care that these families will need assistance. I have already approached ladies from the First Congregational Church and hope to see good works performed as early as to-morrow. I plan to make a visit in the morning. Agatha will watch Henry and I will give her little else to distract her.

I called upon both Mrs. Caldwell and Mrs. Matthias today with bas-
kets of food, though I do think the Matthias family will need a great deal
more. Mrs. Matthias' children are all painfully thin to begin with and
she confided to me through her tears that her late husband often tippled
away his earnings. What a frightful thing for her family to have endured!
I could only sit and place a hand upon her own as she wept. She did not
seem to want me to comfort her at too close a distance.

Mercifully, she is skilled at knitting and with even paltry earnings from
this she has kept a most wretched hunger at bay. She sells her wares at the
Bedfords' Mercantile, too. Since each woman's circumstances vastly differ, I shall ask Emily if she might give some charity to this family from
the proceeds of her wares.

Mrs. Caldwell owned the small house in which she and her son lived
together and seems not to want for much other than company. Perhaps
as long as there are people willing to offer their kindnesses, even in the
form of companionship, we can keep loneliness from encroaching upon
this poor, bereaved woman.

I will return to both households before too long, not knowing what
more I can do, only that I cannot do it all alone and will more vigorously
entreat the charity of others in the community. Even beyond the parish
walls, there will be giving souls.

July 10, 1855

Mother has sent a bundle of new underthings she has sewn for her grandson, thinking he will grow much larger by winter. I believe she thinks I
feed him by the wagonload. Boys do grow more swiftly than girls, or
so I have observed of the children of other families in Rockport.
Emily's daughter, Alice, is the elder of her two children, John the
younger, and now that John is twelve years of age to Alice's fourteen, he is nearly man-size. Of course, my son is two and nearly one
half years of age and I do not believe he will be so large as to wear knickers the size Mother made. They would almost fit me! I have given them
to Agatha for her youngest brother and sisters, for they have little enough

without her or her mother needing to take on more work. Agatha's father is long gone, drowned soon after the last of her mother's children was born, so she will be able to use the extra.

My son will one day be twice the size he is now. She will be making more clothing for him well before then, loving to sew and to knit, so will not miss this batch. Mother would often give my clothing to her maid's family when finished with it, so I am doing what is expected and will wash my hands of any regret. Dear me, that I must even resort to such self-absolution in these pages! I do hope I shall outgrow such nonsense.

July 13, 1855

Emily accompanied me today to bring food to the Matthias home and the widow was most appreciative of our company. We came upon her looking very melancholy with her stitch-work sitting in her lap. We remained a while, speaking very little, for she seemed glad enough to have company without the need of conversation. Her children, all girls, sat quietly in a row, and even lay down in their beds, one by one, to sleep. We then went to Mrs. Caldwell to sit with her for part of an afternoon and we were warmly received. I do hope that before long they might find some happiness in their days. For Mrs. Matthias, it ought to come from her children, when she might seek their sweetness. These three young girls now without their father will have to begin their working life earlier.

Heaven forbid a woman bury her husband or a mother her child. The fisheries are not a kind place to women who are forced to maintain stoicism even in the face of their own fears. Too many of the womenfolk in these coastal parts of the Commonwealth have lost their husbands to the thing that should nourish them. Were James to announce to me today that he has had his fill, I would make a great fuss, glad to have him wholly on land at last. For now, I must wait until he tires of the sea and try not to imagine the worst, putting an end to his inclinations.

JULY 14, 1855

For the past fortnight, but for July fourth, James has been spending far too much time in his study and Henry and I feel it acutely. When I asked him last night after supper, as I took a cordial and he a brandy in the parlor, if he would join us for a stroll into town this morning, he was very distracted, reading the *Gloucester Telegraph*. At first he said, "of course, my darling." Yet, this morning when I told him how delighted we were he would be coming along, he looked at me as if I had heard quite the opposite from his lips only the night before, and then he begged to be excused! I had little choice and turned toward our sweet boy who sat at the breakfast table with an eager smile that fell into his porridge the moment he caught my frown.

When my husband is not working so diligently, his temperament is very pleasing. James makes routine preparations for a voyage and attends to the minding of his own father's estate, which keeps our family robust and is added to with a yearly allowance from my own mother and father. These tasks make up much of my good husband's week and I have adjusted to this part of him that can turn easily away from a more comfortable, land-loving life with his wife and son. I do admire his ethic, yet now that James seems to be even more deeply preoccupied he has grown noticeably distant, delivering words he can scarcely recall after uttering them. At times like this morning, when he forgot the easy promise he had made to us the evening before, it is as if he does not know me.

Of course, I did the unthinkable and voiced my concerns to Mother. She took the opportunity to explain that for James to continue his success, even as he knows our livelihood does not depend upon his seagoing work, I must give him what he needs; that if it be distance from us, his wife and son, even under our own roof, I must accept it with grace; and if it be tenderness, I am to offer myself.

22

After five years married to James, I of course have always known this and it caused an itch at my crown to fight the impulse to hush Mother, an itch that visits me during such moments between us. Yet, overwhelming her words was my own thought that I have forever loved James. For as long as I have known him, my entire life it would seem, and since our first wedded night, I have yielded to his desire for me and for the ocean, the balance of the two seeming to be uneven at times, particularly in summer when he goes out every week. Still, it irks me when he says he will do one thing and does quite another, forgetting his own words.

JULY 15, 1855

Agatha has burned a hole in my best linen tablecloth. She was near weeping when she told me, afraid I would release her from her position. It is true I loved that Irish linen, sent as a wedding gift from the Reynolds, dear friends of Mother and Father's. But it is only a piece of cloth; Agatha need not have wept over it. I suppose I have been short-tempered more recently, no doubt due to James' busier days.

JULY 16, 1855

I am, I must admit here, a scowling, jealous girl. How can one be envious of the ocean? After years of marveling at its powers, I have come to understand that it can soothe and excite a man, vex and beguile him. And yet, a sailor possesses a heart, so must he not also desire a woman to give him what the sea cannot possibly? For, though it sings and whispers, its embrace is never as warm as that of a wife. One might say it is deadly. This brings me back to my fits of unease, though it seems foolish now to see it written here.

Mother would recoil at the sight of me. Did I not marry this man as much for his love of the open waters as for his long understood love for me and mine for him?

JULY 17, 1855

I do enjoy the merriment between father and son and hope sweet Henry will divert his father more often. Today the clever boy led him outside and James went, willingly. I am glad one of us was able to lure him from his tasks. The few moments they spent outside grew into an hour and the sky darkened with an oncoming squall. They came in laughing when the rain began to slap their faces with the wind off the ocean. It was a sight to see my two men together, Henry so like his father in his determination to do something—no doubt growing just as swiftly as James had when he was a boy.

They will one day be a match for each other in strength and speed. I can hardly imagine this, caught between a sadness that I shall lose my small boy, though he is no longer a mewling infant, and a pleasing anticipation that he will grow to be a most admirable man. That my beloved and I will grow old as it happens is quite another matter, rendering me too gloomy even for my own company. When such thoughts as these pass through, they leave just as quickly, for I chase them away as I would a hare plundering the garden.

July 23, 1855

I am worried for my linens! Agatha has injured yet another, this one only muslin and dyed a lovely pale blue, a cloth that did not come with my dowry, but which I chose for my own household soon after marrying. My supply dwindles as she destroys each one with her efforts. I will have to do the ironing myself for now or tutor her further. She is becoming a good and able maid in all other facets of housekeeping, but this is the one task she needs to study or we will be eating our meals on bare tabletops. I can trim away the burned patch of this cloth, baste it in my inept fashion, and hang it as a curtain.

Truly, I do not feel the need for Agatha to do as much as she does. Other girls have come and gone over the preceding five years and have found I gave them too few tasks, at last leaving my employ for busier households. Mother would have me bring in a laundress as she has, but Agatha and I seem to be able to manage. And of course, as Mother continues to push, I continue to push back.

July 24, 1855

When James is attentive to me in the dark of our room, with our son soundly sleeping and Agatha gone home for the day, I forget all my grievances. I am melted like candle wax when he turns to me in our bed and presses his warm mouth onto mine, the lingering flavor of cherry tobacco still present so that I, too, can taste it. When he embraces me in the quiet dark, his hunger wakens mine, and I have learned to love his whiskers rough at my throat as long as they are not newly grown. It worries me that I cannot always match his ardor. I have tried to approach James to begin things, and he refuses me. It is always at his urging that we come together and if I am not immediately of a mind to return his eagerness, distracted as I might be from the day's events, it is my will to please him that moves me forward. His lovingness afterward is wondrous, for he holds my head against his chest, the fingers of one hand tracing my ear, moving through my hair, his other hand making small patterns on my back and shoulders. Before long, I will want to have him all over again and he will turn to me. We have hoped for another child to join Henry and have thus far not been rewarded. Perhaps our boy is to be our only blessing after all.

Perhaps, too, I ought to learn from Mrs. Laughlin's insightful little tales and not want so very much.

July 25, 1855

Emily came to tea today and we sat on the beach, on a blanket, while Henry napped in a corner of shade. She looked very smart in a new pale green dress and simple straw hat, her brown hair gathered loosely at the back. We nibbled at sandwiches Agatha had prepared this morning—something she does particularly well, I am happy to say—and Emily told me of a visit she and her children will make to Boston in the middle part of August. Her brother, Mr. Austin Reed, lives in a grand house with his wife, and they are childless. Emily and her children will stay there for nearly two months! Her own husband, Richard, will not be accompanying her and the children on their journey, for, as she pointed out, who would oversee the bank? It does seem a sad thing for Richard to remain alone, though Emily has pointed out on numerous occasions that her husband and sister-in-law have not managed to befriend one another in quite the way she had hoped. She has also acknowledged that the woman can be belligerent and I have heard her say the same of Richard.

Emily and I do not spend a great deal of time together, for she is often very fatigued. Still, I will miss the only sincere friend I have in Rockport. Fiona Terry and I are ill-matched, for her idea of an afternoon tends toward idle gossip. It is work not to hush her in a way she will not forget.

And who will take care of Emily's garden for her? She has not asked me, for she knows that I let my garden command me and that I may be doom to her patch of Eden. I do not think Fiona is up to the task, for though I avoid her I do know that her gardening skills are poorer than my own. I have told Emily I will look in on her garden as often as I can.

JULY 26, 1855

Today, as Henry played in the yard, I caught sight of my slipshod gardening and began to pull the weeds from the patches of daylilies. Emily's garden has not a single weed as she has taught even her children to remove them as soon as their shoots point to the sun.

As it was very warm, I stood to appraise my sloppy bit of acreage and saw that my daylilies are almost weeds themselves but for their glorious color. They grow in such profusion around the house without any coaxing! I do like the look of them. A burst of strength overtook me and I knelt again to grab at unruly tufts of unwelcome weeds here and there, careful not to disturb the daylilies. Invaders though they are, they have a right to their glory if only because of their vibrancy. It is as if they are paupers dressed for royalty.

It was then my boy cried out! I ran to him, the few steps between us a very great distance, and reached him as a bee was just flying off. Henry would not stop his screaming. I wished the spiteful insect dead and knew its end would come soon now that its poison was used, knowing such a wish was of little use with the harm already done to the child's tender flesh.

His little face turned red and then purple with rage. I carried him into the house and applied a compress to the bee sting but this did not help, so I sent Agatha to Hannah Jumper's home for a salve. Henry was asleep and hiccupping with spent rage in my arms by the time she had returned, flushed and winded, more than a quarter-hour later. I promptly spread the remedy over the wound. Within moments, it looked less angry. The paste Hannah Jumper made is of summer savory, a wonderful little miracle she grows along with many other plants she dries and uses for cures. How perplexing that even the bee that stings produces sweetest honey, a thing we love.

It is a terrible thing to feel that I cannot protect my child even from the smallest villains of this world. He was bitten in the garden and may never again trust a blossom not to harbor such a terrible surprise.

JULY 29, 1855

In the mercantile today, I stopped to speak with Fiona Terry. Oh, she is a haughty thing. I do not understand why she must think herself somehow better than other women of her standing. It prompts the question, has her good husband, Capt. Joshua Terry, ever tried to bring her down a peg? I have the urge to ask him, but of course, will check that before it betrays me. There is no pretense about him, which makes me wonder if he admires it in his wife from whom pretense seeps like an infected wound for which Miss Jumper is unlikely to have a cure. James respects Capt. Terry for his hard work, and they enjoy a good-natured rivalry when they both go out for their catch. I have spied them through the telescope from the cupola to see that they are racing, their bows pointed and swift, almost a match toward their common destination. James has remarked that Capt. Terry is a good helmsman, and often enough moves ahead.

I feel a certain envy of men who can express such things as rivalry in this very straightforward way. For women, it is supposition and suspicion, doubt and jealousies that lead only to pettiness on either part before an understanding is reached. Often enough, it may not be reached at all.

It should not have surprised me then, when I spoke with Fiona, that her words amounted to little more than crowing about her husband's most recent catch, his successes of late, and no well-wishing for me or for my husband's outings. Of course, this presents a further truth I cannot ignore, which is that her husband discusses in detail with her the particulars of his days at sea, while James has grown most reticent on the subject. I will note here the exception of the men he lost from his crew and the generosity of his telling, even as a part of me wished not to have to be told such a dire tale. Yes, Fiona had heard about it and was quick to point out that, while it is a tragedy, her husband has thankfully not suffered such a disastrous loss.

JULY 31, 1855

James is out today setting and bringing in mackerel trawls, a popular and plentiful crop in summer. It is only for a day and a night, more tolerable than his longer trips to Georges Bank. In the past week, when he is home, he spends more time in his study than with us. I have long felt his absence when he is at sea, not enjoying the sounds of our home when he is not about. Yet, even more disquieting is that I will have to grow accustomed to his need to be alone in his study rather than spend time with his family. Of late when I hear his footfalls overhead, he seems as removed from me as if he were not home at all.

It is my habit to watch James from the cupola as he sets sail. Henry was still abed early this morning as I made my way up the cupola steps to catch a glimpse of his father's vessel, named for me. Perhaps my attention was on the final step that would offer that magnificent view of our town and of the ocean stretching beyond it, for as I took the first few steps with the speed and spring of the girl I am no longer, I caught my foot on a loose peg jutting from one of the steps and found myself sprawled across them. Mr. Talbot has already nailed the offending peg flat and my knee is badly bruised, swollen up to a frightful mound. Again relying upon Miss Jumper's herbal tinctures, I have applied a soothing caraway poultice to ease the bruising. She will think my household prone to mishap.

In the faintest evening breeze, I sit here now on the porch with a cup of tea, the pain in my knee still quite persistent, if duller than this morning. I will be moving with great care these next several days, relying more upon Agatha than I have, the sort of reliance Mother would prefer I visit upon the girl more routinely. Overhead, the leaves on the linden tree shake on their branches as if to reprimand me for my foolish haste this morning. My darling boy is asleep and Agatha has finished for the day, solemn after even my gentle reprimand following her last botched ironing this afternoon. She was, I fear, the most convenient target for my upset nerves after the fall, and I will have to make amends. I do not wish to send her scurrying off to another household. It is not my nature to be vindictive, but how many linens must I surrender? I do not have a large collection.

I will content myself with the grand spectacle of a setting sun that has painted bands of rose and lavender across the twilit summer sky. There is no lovelier thing to behold, and I hope that James, now at anchor for the night aboard his vessel, is awash and delighting in the same majesty.

August 4, 1855

My boy has brought me a piece of gooseberry pie straight from the pantry, with little prints on it he made with his fingers, places on the crust where he pressed down on it when we baked it yesterday. Of course, he did not bring it to me himself. James helped him up and swung him onto the bed, the three of us feasting and giggling over the crumbs Henry made on the pillow. It was on his father's side of the bed that he spilled a dollop of gooseberry. What a sorry mess it was, one I will work with Agatha to remove, yet what fun it was to gobble it down and lick our lips afterward!

August 7, 1855

I cannot make sense of James' brooding, nor will he enlighten me. Since returning from his latest trip, he has come to bed halfway through the night and last night, the sixth of his nights home before the next outing, I did the unthinkable, feigning sleep even as his hand moved around my waist, seeking his own comfort before rest, his fingers moving lower to my backside, then close to my sex. I was as still as if frozen. After a moment or two, he loosened his hold in sleep and I too fell away, ashamed of my own refusal to welcome my husband. This morning, we woke to love and tenderness. He beheld me until I opened my eyes, then wrapped his warm, night-shirted form around me and we slept a little longer before he kissed me and rose to begin his day.

AUGUST 8, 1855

I have on occasion wondered how life can rush by as it does. In less than a month I will be twenty-three. That I was ever a child is difficult to imagine, yet I recall with a familiar ache those final few years of waiting to come of age before being wed to James. Those were vexing years that held me very like a firm hand pressing down upon the shoulder of a willful child. I was *that* often enough and sought to wiggle out from under that hand, entreating Mother and Father to let me wed before I turned eieghteen, for was I not long promised to James and he to me? My parents and James' had been friends before I entered this life and James had treated me with great kindness as I grew to be a girl. The day came, when I was fifteen years, as far from being a child as ever; whilst other girls my age seemed very much to be in need of counsel from their elders, still muddying their dresses at play, James and I took our opportunity to pledge to a lifetime together. He was twenty-one and swore that we would be wed following my eighteenth birthday. Our parents wholly approved. Even as I knew in my girlhood that James would one day be mine (for I told him so when I was a child not more than eight years and he agreed, laughing at my girlish notions, and ran to join his friends), the notion of waiting was highly disagreeable to me. James is possessed of greater patience than I. This has always been true and has earned me mild reprimand from my beloved now and again.

I recall that, eager as I was to begin my life with him, I reasoned in my seventeenth year that there would be little difference between the ages of seventeen and eighteen to those whose love is already secure and steadfast. I likened our love to the foundations of a house that holds its dwellers safely, protecting them. Mother and Father rejoined that a hurriedly built house falls to the winds, crushing those within it. They assured me that hastening our lives together would not strengthen promises we had made to one another. Maddening though it was to be rebuked in such a way, and perhaps more so to meet a similar outlook in James, who too keenly sensed that I might ask him to go out on his vessel less often once we were married, I could do nothing but wait.

Time slowed whilst I tried to prod it forward, as James aided his father in managing his schooners from their office, going out on occasion to set trawls and nets and nourish his desire for the sea. He has always longed for more distant ports than those on this length of coastline that beckon the fisherman with their bounty. He seems always to have yearned for more. When his father, upon his death the year before our marriage, left James the titles to his four schooners, James sold all but one and built our home with the profits of his sale. He named the one he kept his *Marianne Elizabeth* for me. He set aside a living wage for us from his father's estate to run our household and enjoy our days, and quickly filled his vessel with a crew of men who work with him all the sailable months of the year. Often, I am moved to remind him that he need not labor so, for we have ample means. It is of little use. My words fall to the wind and drift elsewhere.

I record this history of our love perhaps for a future reader, perhaps for my son. I do believe that it is important for me to gather memories, to take stock of all that has come to pass that has brought me to this most comfortable place. As I sit at my table in our room writing by the flickering light of a taper, James sleeps just a breath away in our bed. He stirs and I do not know where his dreams take him, for I am the one who shares such fancy as the dreams I have, while he is content to make business of his sleep, to rise purposefully with the dawn rather than at leisure. He claims not to dream. Yet, how can a man not be guided elsewhere in slumber?

AUGUST 9, 1855

Today, Emily accompanied me to visit the Matthias and Caldwell women. Others have visited and left their gifts, but it has been too long since our last call.

Having spent this effort this morning, I did not know what to do with myself. James has had to go to Gloucester, informing me that he will be gone the day. So, I wandered from room to room, peering into each as if I were just dropping in for a visit, coming across only Agatha in my travels.

I looked in upon Henry, admired his fair curls pressed to his cheeks, his blanket so twisted around his legs that he had to have been dreaming of a chase. I had to stop myself from gathering him into my arms, for he is so much less a baby each day. To touch him would surely waken him. Content enough with a view of his sweet and peaceful face, I crept out of the room and away. Of course, then he awoke, giving me my wish not to be idle, for he did not sleep again until well past nine this evening and did not settle easily. Now I am very fatigued from a long day.

AUGUST 11, 1855

It is James' twenty-ninth birthday today. Each year on this day, there is a shadow on his brow, for his parents have passed and have not the pleasure of pride in their son. Mr. Parsons has been gone six years and James' mother, Rebecca Parsons, twenty-nine years, for on the very day James was born, his first breath was her last. Mr. Parsons never took another wife.

On a cheerier note, with the help of Mr. Talbot who knew of a litter of pups in Pigeon Cove, and who very kindly journeyed there himself to retrieve a gentle one, my boy and I woke James this morning with a brown Cairn terrier. It is barely weaned, very small, has curious, up-thrust ears and eager brown eyes. He looks more like a cup of warm cocoa than a needy pup. Henry squeals with unbridled delight when the little thing kisses his face with that quick, pink tongue. James and I tossed names back and forth between us this morning as the creature tumbled around over our legs all over the bed, causing Henry to laugh from deep inside his little round belly, a deeper chortle than I have yet heard from my small son.

"We will call him Charles," James said, holding the creature before him and turning him this way and that. "He looks like a Charles, does he not? Certainly, he will one day, when his carriage has steadied and he has better control of all this silliness."

I laughed at what sounded like an old man chiding a little boy who would do anything but his bidding. A pup should remain so to delight his master, if we are fortunate. This is the charm of a small breed in my opinion.

"We cannot call him Charles," I said, taking Henry's hand from the dog's backside. He had begun a tricky journey with his little fingers up under the tail and into the fur of his hindquarters! "He will never grow into it."

"Then, how does the name Nicholas suit him? Or Nestor?"

I shook my head.

"Did you not give him to me? Can I not choose the name?" He tilted his head at me as a small boy might, challenging me, and a forelock fell into his eyes. I brushed it away and he caught my hand and placed the palm of it against his lips. It caused a thrill in me that, if I were not holding our son in my lap, I might have surrendered to in the moment.

"Very well!" I laughed. "You may."

"Then he will be Jackson and we will call him Jack."

"There, my sweet," I said to our son, showing him how to stroke Jack's fur without seizing handfuls of it and pulling. "Meet Jack."

AUGUST 13, 1855

I received an invitation to tea today from Reginald and Virginia Pringle. I understand from Mother that Mrs. Pringle means well and I have accepted her infrequent invitations over the years when I can no longer think of any excuse to refuse. After all, it will not do to use illness as a pretense, for if it should come to pass then I will have gotten nothing less than what I wished for. It may be childish of me, yet I fear I have nothing more to look forward to than her platitudes. Perhaps this latest invitation is an overture in the wake of our husbands' prospective business dealings, for James has only last night shared with me that he and Mr. Pringle have been speaking about James joining him in his granite company. In this spirit, he says that Reginald Pringle wishes to bring James to work for his interests, selling granite up and down the coast. Exactly when and what he will be asked to do James did not mention and I did not press him for answers, glad enough for conversation about something other than Agatha's latest mishap or Henry's newest word. This last, of course, is always news, and Henry is now using his pointing finger less and his speech much more.

I have lately felt light-footed around the subject of James' work, not knowing where I may and may not tread, particularly since he seems somewhat anxious this past week. His birthday the other day was a reprieve from this strange, unuttered preoccupation of his. And knowing of this change in how James will spend his days, accountable to another man's interests, I would now say its relevance is owed to some possible arrangement with Mr. Pringle.

I have exchanged pleasantries with Mr. Reginald Pringle, though not with their son, Thomas. Quite unlike his father, whose color and manner are healthily vigorous, Thomas is more pale and retiring, seeming the quieter around ladies. His age is between James' and mine and, given his discomfiture in mixed company, I am not surprised that he is yet unmarried. Perhaps there is a lady more unassuming than he in this village. I do hope for his happiness one day, though I believe he will need the encouragement of a good friend. James has never taken a social interest in Thomas other than to greet him decorously if they passed each other in town, so I doubt he will be that friend even at my urging. I do wonder if Mrs. Pringle clings to her son as much as he appears to cling to her, not so plainly with his hands as with his demeanor. He may well decide to forgo marriage and remain at his mother's side, though Mr. Pringle's commerce has made this family wealthier than most in Rockport. It does make Thomas very marriageable. I have heard he plays the pianoforte as if born with his fingers upon it, but I have not been present to benefit from this gift.

I will admit that Virginia Pringle is thoughtful in her invitations, although it must only be convention that makes her thus. It was when I lost our first child in the womb that she sent over a meal. I could not stomach it, food being furthest from my notions of healing. But I encouraged James to eat. Mother had done her best to foist Mrs. Pringle's broth on me, but one sip delivered the taste of seawater, over-salted as it was. I chose instead the chamomile tea she sent, grown in Hannah Jumper's garden. Miss Jumper is a woman whose knowledge of herbs I have long sought for the ills which occasionally befall us (her summer savory was heaven sent for that wicked bee sting!) and sipping the tea was a compromise Mother could tolerate, for it was her interest to see me take anything at all, fussy as I was over its source.

That I have thought of that lost child on this day is not by chance, for it would have been her fourth birthday. Had this tiniest life not vanished before breathing her first, for I birthed her three months too soon and she was stillborn, we would not have Henry. We would have a daughter. In her memory, I have gathered a posy of sweet William and forget-me-nots from along the banks of Mill Pond to place in a vase at the southwest facing window of the parlor where the sun bathes our home in its warmest light.

My lost daughter's name, though we could not Christen her, would have been Rebecca, after James' mother. Our son, Henry George Parsons, was named for James' father, Henry Daniel Parsons. I do hope that we have another child one day and that we can name her or him for a living relation who can enjoy the honor.

And finally, before I retire my quill for the night, I must write in these pages that I dearly love our son and would not consider a life without him.

AUGUST 16, 1855

James left today for a short trip to Georges Bank where the crop of bluefish is thick. This season has seen him going down the coast more often, as if there will one day be less time to do so. After all, he will be more involved in granite with Reginald Pringle. He would languish and be disagreeable company if he did not go out often enough in the warmer months and this trip will be for less than a week, leaving me little time to fret. I will simply find things to do.

For one, Agatha might benefit from some tutoring in her ironing, which has not improved. I have taken to pressing my best linens. I will further improve upon my own kitchen garden and my boy and I will take Jack for walks each day. I will read and I will write in this book. There. I have already passed several days.

There was not a stout enough wind when James set out yesterday, so he delayed his departure, professing hope that he would not have to wait much longer. Sure enough, by midday there were healthy gusts that fishermen need to thrust and pull them toward their intended course, far from shore, and later help them in. I watched as my namesake caught the generous breeze in her sails and watched still longer, enjoying, in spite of myself, the spectacle of James' masterful handling of his vessel on his way from harbor. That his absences are difficult to abide is as true as anything else to which I can lay claim about my love for James. Yet, he is a fine sailor and fisherman and I am proud of him as a woman can be. And I am just as proud that he will be more involved in concerns ashore for his business with Mr. Pringle, for there will be fewer trips away, only somewhat longer.

In these five years we have been married, each hour without him continues to smart and for this I chide myself. I long for James even before he leaves, for he puts himself to the task of filling his vessel's galley, stocking it with food for his fishermen. He is out purchasing for a full day or more before his voyages, even stowing rum, a fact over which I have clucked but cannot prevent. That he lost two of his fishermen because of their penchant for spirits does not deter him, though he is not as generous with his demijohns as some of Cape Ann's captains. He saves it for after a trip and now keeps it under lock, he has told me.

Emily McCutcheon departs for Boston tomorrow. She has been wringing her hands over her husband's taste for spirits, though he is a good citizen. The dismay of many of Rockport's women over their husband's fondness for drink when they are not at sea, whether for the months between trips, or even the days, is ever-present. For, many of the fishermen spend their wages on the rum that is so easy to procure. It is no wonder their wives are ready to burst with their outrage! I have heard one or two complain to Hannah Jumper as I have awaited my turn at her nimble fingers when I go to her for tailoring or for the regular collection of her remedies I like to keep in the house. She is a kind woman and listens to all complaints and censures as she pins dresses and prepares herbal cures. She also offers her opinions, and has been heard to say she disapproves of men's tippling as much as the ladies who seek her services.

Thankfully, James does not over-indulge in spirits, though many of his crewmen are drinkers of the highest order. I have implored him to cease providing spirits to them, reminding him of the wretched end met by Misters Caldwell and Mathhias at the hands of rum. His rebuke was that he would have no men to crew his vessel if he had no spirits to offer. He explained that many of the men find companionship within those hours after a good trip out and the rum lends a hand to that and to easing the muscles and the mind. I continue to shake my head in wonder at such a notion and dare not suggest that he lock the demijohns away so the men should not drink while at sea. They would mutiny!

AUGUST 19, 1855

At my urging, in the year before Henry was born, James spent nearly a year sailing less than half the time he had enjoyed before. He was pain-fully idle and we agreed that he should resume his usual outings, though he yielded to me and lessened them some. For a time he honored this.

There is a superstition long at work that a woman on board a fishing vessel is an ill omen. James does not subscribe to this, and I follow his lead. Though there were occasions before we had our son when I boarded the *Marianne Elizabeth* for an afternoon sail, I have not done since being with child, and have been markedly less interested since the boy's birth, thinking it best not to burden Mother and Father with his care in our ab-sence, even for a day.

I have been resolutely bound to land for more than three years and admit that I do miss the sun on my face, the spray from the ocean, and have never much minded my hair coming loose in the wind while on the water. James has adored the faint freckling of my nose and cheeks, for I have fair skin easily sun-kissed. Years ago, as we stood on the deck behind the mainsail of one of his father's schooners, my first time on one of them, I was already very determined to keep James' love for me on course. That day, he told me the pale grey of my eyes would thwart a man's voyage before he reached his intended shore. At this, I yelped with a horrified laugh and he kissed me, not on the hand as he had done all along when we greeted one another with our families, but a kiss upon my eager lips. We were not yet betrothed. I was but sixteen, and felt that first thrill of a more womanly feeling for him.

Since our son turned two, I have occasionally thought of stepping aboard the vessel, imagining a lovely summer afternoon on calm seas, and then, before I can give voice to the idea, I banish it. Still, I will brave the thought that if James and I *were* to perish, Mother and Father would take Henry. They have dismissed the notion of our untimely end, though with an assurance that, of course, they will care for their grandson if such a dark day should be visited upon this family. And, Mother told me, they would bring along Agatha to live with them if this should ever occur. She dwelled far too long on the matter until I reminded her that James and I are very much alive. Though I know my parents would rear and love my son, the possibility of relinquishing him even to those I love, to my parents, hardens my resolve to remain safe upon these shores. To that end, I have not boarded the *Marianne Elizabeth* again.

To cheerier notions: earlier this evening, my son and I took Jack for a stroll along the beach, tugging him lightly on a leather lead Mr. Talbot fashioned for us out of something from the stable. When the pup was not nosing a horseshoe crab's shell or a mound of sea kelp, he nipped at our heels and jumped at our knees until we fell together in a huddle of exhaustion, hardly able to catch our breath for laughter. The air and water were still warm, even with the sun dipping low. We gathered what treasure we could for our little chest at home, and tried to teach the pup to sit, which of course he could not for more than a wing beat. He chased after the flocks of tiny terns scurrying in their earnest determination from the surf and I laughed hard enough to get a stitch.

38 As to the beach's treasures, I am particularly fond of the little purple and white scalloped shells and marvel that such a tiny creature from the sea can create this perfection. I have often wondered at the length of time it takes to fashion this and think it might fascinate me to watch it occur as long as it is not an eternity.

Henry has a puckish nature of late and runs away from me when we are out of doors, his thick little legs not quick enough to outrun me just yet. He giggles as my fingers tag him and then I catch him up in my arms. One day he will outrun even his father.

The sun was finally just a crimson band at the horizon before we returned to the house. It is the same sky I look to each morning that renders my white walls a pale shade of apricot. It is the same horizon that will yield a glimpse of James' vessel tomorrow.

August 21, 1855

In the fall of 1854, I calculated that my monthly course had not come for nearly a half-year. I was no longer feeding Henry at my breast and James and I had hoped for another child, but there were no signs. Most tell tale was that my middle was decidedly not growing. Each month that came and went left me wondering and hoping until I was near despair. I knew I was too young for my courses to end.

I paid a visit to Miss Jumper's home, and was sent away with a powder of motherwort root and instructions to take it with wine in the evening. It has done its work to restore me, and as long as he is ashore when the time is right, James and I continue to hope for a child to result from my rhythms.

August 23, 1855

As I opened to a blank page this night, two cornflower blossoms have fallen to the floor. Here upon the paper is a perfectly formed and ghostly blue reminder of the day I plucked them from Mill Pond Meadow just last week when Emily and I took our last tea of the summer, then pressed them within this book. Now that she is in Boston, and will be away for two months, I will have to make the effort to meet and befriend other women. Mother has scolded me often for being too reliant on James, and on my dear friend Emily for my amusement.

39

Thoughts of untroubled moments and walks in Mill Pond Meadow have not tired my eyes enough. Moments ago, I found myself wandering the hallways once again, first peering in at my darling boy, and then going upstairs with my lamp to guide me. James slept on as he does, enviably.

Once at the threshold of James' study, I stood still as if he were seated just beyond me at his table. I lingered in the shadow and smelled his pipe, strongest up here. Its cherry smoke lingered in the wood, in the blue muslin curtain that was once a tablecloth before Agatha's hand took to it with the iron, and in the books wedged into shelves James built on either side of the bay window. It is not a beautiful room, but is possessed of a stately and masculine quality of which any man might be proud. As a woman who likes small and simple feminine flourishes, I would call it plain but for the gleaming brass telescope, a gift from James' father, perched at the window. The great mahogany table, bestowed upon him by my own father, is in the room's center where James examines his maps and plans his fishing routes, as well as papers accounting for the business his voyages fetch from the fishmongers, and his father's estate. The walls are unpainted pine, with dark, menacing knots that would bite if I touched them, for James did not smooth them. It is a room into which our son, with unrelenting curiosity and interest in touching things, shall not be allowed entrance until his father sees fit to invite him. I, too, do not enter comfortably without a request. Thus far, Henry has not shown an interest, but I will ask James to close the door more often now when he is not up there.

This night, I took a step into the room, holding my lamp before me, and moved with small, measured paces toward the table. I was going to sit at that table and imagine myself a guest, when Henry cried out in his sleep. I ran from the room so quickly I nearly lost my footing and had to grasp at the door handle to keep from falling onto the floor, determined to get downstairs to the child before he woke his father. I would prefer to be invited into James' study than to intrude without his knowledge.

AUGUST 26, 1855

He is gone again and my anxiety plagues me. I must ask Dr. Wainright for a tonic to ease me. Too much worry cannot be good even for the hardiest woman and I am decidedly not that.

Mr. Talbot asked Henry and me to accompany him to town today, perhaps understanding it would be best to leave the usual behind for an afternoon. Dear that he is, he sought a different road for the short journey, a trip we often make on foot when we need only small items, or want to take tea at Mrs. Spencer's shop. He seemed quite intent upon taking us, so we climbed up into the carriage, Henry being handed up to me by Mr. Talbot. As we moved into the road, I found myself looking behind us in the direction we ought to have been going. I questioned him on it and he said, simply, "If it's all right, Missus, I think you and your boy might like this and it won't take much longer."

I judge him most favorably for this in spite of my earlier misgiving, for I did not expect to enjoy the journey. Even as I have lived in Rockport since marrying James, it is not often I venture from the usual path to and from town. As we turned off the main road onto a rougher country way for a while, Henry immediately thrilled at the sight of a hare hopping alongside us as we wheeled along. A moment later, he fairly gasped at a meadow filled with heather and wildflowers. Before long, we were in town, having simply gone a longer way around. I will thank our Mr. Talbot for thinking well enough to show us the things we might otherwise miss when we take the shorter walk in.

I must give up this melancholy that cloaks me of late when my husband sails. It will do my son no good. Though Mother would have me take a tonic made from nasturtium, a remedy by which she swears, seeing Henry today so enchanted by simple, natural pleasures on our outing with Mr. Talbot was, for me, the best tonic of all.

August 27, 1855

My Dearest James,

When you return to us you will read this letter and smile,
perhaps kiss me in your understanding of my love for you and
how I am certain the hours slow when you are away. You may say to me
as you often have that I ought to spend more time taking tea with other
ladies, make other friends to busy me now that Emily is away. Well, I do

enjoy painting now and again, though I cannot claim a talent and this discourages the inclination. I am able to lose myself in a book and in play with our son in the garden and we love to stroll along the water's edge. I am afraid brooding is what I do best when you are away. When you are here, I wish you would join us more often. Henry is not ideal company for my intellectual growth even as I am ideal for his; Fiona Terry is a terrible braggart; and Mrs. Pringle rather a bland companion, a less affable version of Mother.

So, I am back to my pining for you, my love, and I know that it is matched by yours for me. You would chide me for my melancholy. Your more frequent outings in summer have brought it on with a force I cannot harness, so it is fortunate that Mr. Talbot had the sense to lure me from my thoughts today with a ride along country laneways the likes of which we have not traveled even with you. Perhaps you saw them as a boy and then gave them up for the sea. It was a wonderful day and I wish that you had shared it with us.

Forever yours,
Marianne Elizabeth

Now that I have taken a moment to read this note I wrote, I will not share it with James, for it hints at being disagreeable. This is not the way I wish to welcome my husband. It remains tucked into these pages, as I do not like to part with words even if they are not sent to their intended reader. One day, I will look upon it, laugh at the sentimental thing who wrote it, and tender it to the fireplace.

AUGUST 30, 1855

The day after tomorrow is a phrase possessed of an imminence that 'two days hence' lacks. So, I will write here that the day after tomorrow James will sail in and already I feel his nearness. I have set Agatha to the task of washing our bedclothes and they are hanging out to dry, the late summer air filling them with the sweetness of roses and honeysuckle mingled with some of the brine of the sea carried to us on that same breeze. They will not need ironing.

SEPTEMBER 1, 1855

It is late in the evening now and James and his darling, sleepy son dream away in our bed, and wee Jack is a sea-washed, tattered ball of brown fur nestled beside them. I will carry Henry to his own room before long, after I record all of my most pressing thoughts so that I might remember this day for years to come.

James' vessel sailed into harbor early this morning, and it was my birthday today. He was a most welcome gift! His safe return is all I ever pray for, though I cannot say I do pray, not properly as was expected of me when I was a child and attended church with Mother and Father. But when James and I attend the Congregational Church here in Rockport, I do offer supplication perhaps to a God I feel is merciful enough to send all fishermen home to their families. I want very much to feel that this God, particularly one who often enough sends the ocean into a froth that tosses the vessels out further, some of them never recovering, is looking down upon my small family and making a decision about us. Perhaps we are to be spared more tragedy beyond the loss of our firstborn child.

When James walked in the front door, he wore a smile the size of Mill Pond and when I pressed him for the source of his gladness, he said, "we made a bountiful trip, my love, bountiful indeed!" We do occasionally enjoy some of James' catch, though more often, he sails it straight to Gloucester to sell directly to their marketplace.

I steered his broad-shouldered form through the kitchen and into the room behind it we use for washing. Mr. Talbot had pumped water and hauled it in for James' bath, and I had Agatha boil three pots of it to remove the shock of the cold. Henry was clutching my hem, tottering alongside us, and Jack was in a frenzy of sniffing and licking.

As I soaked and soaped his back, James spoke of Georges Bank as more crowded with other fishing vessels than ever, and of the moment when he feared the *Marianne Elizabeth* would surely be dragged onto the shoals before leaving the grounds. He spoke highly of Mr. Abel, his first mate, who handled the violent seas well alongside his captain. James confided (and I kept very quiet, for it is rare that he shares with me these slices of time aboard his vessel) that Mr.

43

Abel has endured some brazen disregard since the loss of James' two fishermen two months ago. I wonder if James will be able to protect Mr. Abel from the force of his crew's dislike and I expressed this concern aloud, unable to help myself. James was able to say only that Mr. Abel was the sort of man who, if he were afraid of his crewmates' retribution, would not have spoken up about their imprudence, though it proved too late to have helped. He seems to feel Mr. Abel can withstand the trials of their scorn, but James wastes no opportunity to reprimand his crew if this scorn rears its head with any deliberate bodily harm.

I stopped washing his back and moved before him, oblivious to the comical image of his hair white with soap and shaped into points by his own hand, an amusing sight for Henry. It might have won a hearty laugh from me as well, had I not been struck again by a horrid thought. "James, if your vessel were ever to be imperiled, you must promise me you will save yourself."

"My dear wife, you cannot ask it of me. I am captain of my vessel and to consider myself first would be cowardly."

For a moment, it seemed, I could not utter a word before I said, "to love you is to ask this very thing! I can only hope you will never be tested." Tears were an utter betrayal.

In the next moment, James leaned out of the tub and took me by the waist, nearly toppling me in! I screamed, terrified and delighted, and our boy cried, and Jack yelped and barked as if the house were afire. Agatha knocked at the kitchen door and called in to see if anyone had come to harm. James called out that all was well and let me go, kissing me with his soapy lips.

After James finished his bath, for he bade me let him do the rest of the washing and I took Henry off to calm and dry us both, we three took ourselves out for a picnic in Mill Pond Meadow.

It was under the great bowing limbs of the largest willow that my good husband withdrew from his pocket the most exquisite mother of pearl locket, with gilt edging and hints of green and pink, lavender, and even pale shadings of gold suggested at every turn in the light. Indeed, its glint caught the keen eye of our boy who reached for it only to have his father take his greedy fingers from the locket and gently admonish him. The boy was mildly put off, and then reached for it again so that his father had to slip the jewel out of reach. Henry climbed in between us where Jack was curled, and sat there waiting for the object to reappear which, of course, it did not. He busied himself playing with the pup's twitchy ears and was licked all over as a reward.

Over our boy's head, James inclined himself to kiss my cheek and just then Mrs. Pringle strolled nearby on the arm of her son, Thomas. Though I have remarked earlier that his age is between mine and James', he has always seemed to me younger than both of us, for his expression is often bemused, as if he were a boy caught in the midst of a daydream. When I spied them I bowed my head away from my husband's open affections as they walked past, steps away. Mrs. Pringle's attention fell square upon us, earning her a nod from James, and Thomas, too, glanced over, tipping his hat. They seemed to want to come nearer, to converse with us, but James then lifted my face to his to offer another kiss, not caring whose gaze we begged.

"I will not do this under her hawkish eye," I whispered. "She will not hide her disapproval." James, like his son, was hardly discouraged from mischief.

"Look, Marianne, they have turned away."

Indeed, they seemed to have changed direction. I told him I was certain we had offended them.

"The woman can hardly know of what she disapproves," laughed James. "Have pity on her kind, my dear."

"How can you mock the wife of your esteemed colleague?"

"He is not yet my colleague and I am only too aware that you do not hold her in very high esteem. I am trying only to humor you, my darling."

45

"And if he becomes your colleague, she will become mine and I will be forced to endure her humorless manner in a regular way! We must always be dining or taking tea or strolling together! James, I cannot bear the thought."

"Marianne, if I should see the benefit of an association between Reginald and myself, I will not demand that you spend a great deal of your time with Virginia Pringle. I dare say she cannot be such a villain if she is married to Reginald and she may find you too youthful for her polite company." I had not thought of this, though doubt intruded upon the happy possibility.

I cannot place my dislike of Virginia Pringle to any one incident. It is only something in her nature that seems to cause an immediate stiffness in my spine. I feel as an animal must feel, its hackles raised when it is threatened.

I need not have worried over the Pringle mother and son any longer, for by then they had climbed the grassy slope out of the park.

I clutched and pulled at a patch of grass and Henry followed suit, gleeful as he threw it at his father. Unable to resist, I, too, raised James' hat and rubbed a handful on the top of his head.

Brushing the blades off, he took the locket out of hiding whilst our boy gave chase to the dog around our blanket. Inside the locket, which now rests just below my throat, hanging from its delicate gold chain, is a lock of James' hair, neatly ribbon-tied with a small and slender band of blue satin. Next to it is a lighter, silkier lock of our son's hair tied with the same. As he fastened it around my neck, I could hardly breathe for a moment, seeing the pains James had taken to secure this treasure and the treasures within. I reached for the baby's crown of curls, wanting to find the place where the one had been shorn. I looked, too, to my husband, whose eyes were on me.

"Now I am next to your heart even when I am far from our home. And the boy will not always be so silky-haired. We will always be happy to have saved this part of him. When we are blessed again, we will add another lock."

This brought to an end the best birthday I can imagine, even with the uncomfortable moment of the Pringles passing us.

September 2, 1855

A note from Mother arrived today.

Dear Daughter,

We have not forgotten you and this special day that held us in thrall twenty-three years ago. I was but a girl then myself and as certain of my place in the world, and in my marriage, as you are. And now, more than twice your years and filled with hope still for a future of watching your son reach his manhood, I must tell you that I am most proud of you, my good and decent Marianne Elizabeth, and of the choices you have made. I confess to doubting once that you might want the life you now have, for you were a headstrong young creature. Father was content to let your notions and tempers dispel themselves on their own and seemed to enjoy, to my own consternation, seeing the steam rise into a cloud above you, boasting that you were a fairer version of him when he was a boy. Of course, I did not think it helpful to your eventual standing that you be allowed to rant on about your own interests and inclinations as if you were bound for suffrage. I wonder, then, having thought and expressed this, if you have taken up any needlework as I once instructed you to do so that the days and weeks without your husband would not be so idle? Your abiding loyalty to your friend Emily leaves you little choice if you are not inclined toward being part of a ladies group or concern as I have tried to encourage.

Father is at the Reynolds' home paying a call to Mrs. Reynolds whose husband passed just three days ago. It was very quick. He fell over at the table during his supper and, I am told, hit his head on the floor. It is said that what stopped his heart was, indeed, his heart and not the injury to his head, for the doctor and his wife were dining with them that evening and saw that poor Mr. Reynolds seemed to sit up abruptly in his seat before he toppled onto the floor. There was nothing to be done. He was only a few years older than your father and I am left wondering after such a horror if your own parents are not closer to their end as well. It is not a matter on which I like to think too long. Forty-seven is not terribly old, but I do feel the ache in my bones now when the air is chill and damp. Only a few years before, this did not plague me so.

With that, I hope you will forgive this tardy greeting and accept our good wishes; that you will take stock of your gifts and cherish those who depend upon you.

With abiding love,
Mother and Father

I must have sighed ten times while reading her letter. It is not Mother's late-coming wishes that trouble me. It is her coolness, as if she were writing to one of the women she knows in her society. Long ago, I came to understand that she is not a woman predisposed to open affection, even in her letters; she prefers to appraise rather than offer praise, and offers a kind word judiciously. I do crave a betraying note that would distinguish her from a woman in the community who might greet me in much the same way.

And Mr. Reynolds! He bounced me on his knee and crooned to me at his table, his Scottish brogue a baritone that came to rest in my heart in my earliest girlhood and never left. When I hear such a voice, though rare, my mind reaches back and stills itself. I have tried just now to summon the memory of his voice and strangely I cannot—perhaps because he has passed?

The setting sun extends its first rays of scarlet and Henry is asleep for the night. James has been up in his study all afternoon into the early evening and has asked for nothing, nor has he seen his son to bed as he often does in between trips on the vessel. I suppose it is best to see to Agatha's final preparations to dinner now that the day is done and hope that it will coax my husband down to join me.

SEPTEMBER 4, 1855
The moonless sky does not offer one blade of light through the curtains. When there is starlight such as there is tonight, James and I lie together, parting the curtains, and peer up at the sky. I have missed this, for he has been away more this summer. Because I am not fool enough to sit here another moment when my husband pats the space beside him in our bed for me to join him there, I will write no more tonight.

48   SEPTEMBER 7, 1855
James and I have come to a place I can neither have foreseen nor reconcile with his gentler nature. His being cross with me is not what is most alarming, for I may have gone a step too far over the threshold of trust. It was what followed that stays with me.

Last night, he came to bed without going to his study. As I drifted to sleep, I felt the bedclothes being slowly pushed aside, and kept perfectly still, listening to James leave my side. I nearly spoke to wonder why he was awake, but something hushed me. It was not that he had been asleep and then awoke, for I had lain awake for nearly an hour before I had begun to drift toward dreams. No, he too had been wakeful, as if awaiting my sleep. I listened to the rustle of his movements as he donned his robe, and lit a taper, watched his opaque form move like shadow through the room and leave it altogether. I heard his journey through the hallway and up one flight to his study. I keened my ears for the creek of floorboards at the entranceway to his study and was satisfied, upon hearing it, that this was his destination.

And then I was utterly perplexed and troubled, for why had he waited to go there? Waited all evening, and then more, sneaking to a place he has every right to inhabit, that I do not approach without invitation, and not at all if he is not there (but for that one instance)? I tossed in the bed and tried to put my thoughts in their place, which is to say, abandon my worry and questions. I could not.

I left our bed, lit my own taper, looked in on Henry who slept so soundly I peered closely at him to see the sweet rise and fall of his chest with every breath he took and released. Then I crept up to the third floor and stood in the shadows, my taper extinguished, and looked at my husband, at his figure, slightly bent toward a large unrolled map on his table. There was a coil of smoke rising from the pipe he held and took away, rhythmically. I smelled the cherry tobacco I have come to love, after finding it distasteful early in our marriage.

I must have grown weary of standing. Perhaps I sighed as I turned to leave, for it was then James turned his head and his eyes sought my form in the darkness of the hallway. I will record the exchange as closely as I can recall it:

"Marianne?"

I said nothing, no better at speaking than a child caught doing no bit of good.

"Speak. Is it you, wife?" His voice was tinged with something close to anger, and accusation. The moniker, wife, though it belongs to me in title, was a new sound on those lips that had nearly disappeared in the shadow cast by his candle.

"Yes," I whispered.

"Come into the light where I can see you."

"James, I will go back to bed and leave you to yourself. Please."

"You must come to me, Marianne."

There was something hard in his voice that I have never heard in my lifetime of knowing him. I did not fear for my safety or for Henry's, yet the shape of things between us had changed in that instant. A note in his voice added distance between us rather than bringing me toward him. I can scarcely believe I stirred such a dark feeling to life in him. I will assure myself that he did not at first know it was I who stood in the shadows or he would not have spoken to me as if to a menacing stranger. Yet, it was my name he spoke and it could have been no one else lurking there. We have never had an intruder in our home.

In one swift motion he came to me, shadows hiding his eyes and deepening the lines at his brow and around his mouth. He placed his hands on my arms, for I had been holding myself. His grip was not so firm as to hurt, but he seemed to be holding me with more of his strength. I knew if I moved to leave, he would not yield.

"What moved you to follow me the way a child sneaks about?"

"James, I was not thinking. Please, let me go down and wait for you. Finish things here and come to me."

He looked hard at me in the poor light and I fought not to look away.

"I did not mean to alarm you, my darling. I could hardly rest before you left the room, and did not so well after. James, your son and I spend too many days and nights alone, even when you are home. You have been far more occupied with matters you will not discuss."

He studied me, his eyes warming again to a place where I have always felt safe and into which I moved with the same ease as ever. He pulled me to him and held me against the cotton of his nightshirt where I breathed, I think, for the first time in an endless moment.

"You must understand, Marianne. I am a man who needs sometimes to be in his own company. How often do I come upstairs to this lonely little room at any time of the day to smoke my pipe or to look through the telescope and you do not come after me? Tell me, what moved you tonight? What notion can you be working up that you had to leave our bed and tiptoe after me?"

His voice was restored to the love that is always there, leaving me little to do but weep. I could not bring myself to tell him that what disturbed me so was that I had never felt so excluded from his thoughts. This man I love, this man I watched even when I was a small child and he a boy, seemed to me part stranger.

He began to move us toward the stairs and then we stopped in the darkest part of an alcove off the landing. His one strong arm around my waist turned me to him and there he held onto me, kissing my face, my tears, entreating me not to weep.

"You think me an insincere wife," I said.

"I do not. I think only that you lacked an understanding. I have given you one now, have I not?" He breathed into my hair, and took the fastening from my braid so that it came apart, spreading across my back at the touch of his fingers.

At once, James pressed me to the wall, his male part hard between us. I wept on as he lifted my nightdress and pressed himself into me, entering my deepest place, moving inside me, supporting my weight with his arms as I wrapped myself around him. The walls outside his study were papered and smooth, yet my spine felt each thrust of his body hard against me. We have not done this in any place other than our bedroom. There was nothing tender in it, yet it was very pleasing. I pushed away my dismay that a loving husband and wife such as we are should behave like two disreputable strangers meeting in an alleyway. I said so, resisting his strength with some of my own as he moved in his *51* masculine rhythm and quickened his breath toward the end for us both. Pressing his hardness to me, moving faster until I gasped, he whispered in my ear, "Oh, but you worry far too much, you silly girl." Perhaps I do, for as my breath caught at the pleasure of our union, I fancied I was, indeed, terribly silly, and smiled into the shadows ahead of me.

SEPTEMBER 9, 1855

James has asked me if we might host the Pringles to dinner. He requested it with great care and allowed me the choice. I need not invite them, he said, disagreeable as I find Virginia Pringle. Nevertheless, I understand too well that with the success of Reginald Pringle's quarry and his interest in my husband as a merchant to the southern states along the eastern seaboard, it would be helpful to make the overture. James tells me he may be working for Reginald as early as the coming spring to travel south and stir some interest in Cape Ann's plentiful granite.

How can I not invite the Pringles? If they are going to be a source of comfort to me by keeping James on land more than at sea, I cannot refuse them. Now I find myself planning a meal for a date three weeks hence that I must force myself to enjoy. Mother will no doubt admonish me if I confide my disinterest. She will tell me that such occasions will strengthen my tolerance for all sorts of people within the world of commerce my husband will enter. This ought to help me regard Virginia Pringle in a kindlier way, for surely there will be many in the world whose qualities are not sterling, whose company is not the most pleasing. Oh, yes, knowing Mother as I do, I am not likely to complain to her now. Having predicted her censure, there is no need to hear it twice.

SEPTEMBER 10, 1855

Mr. Talbot has left us a basket of late summer squash from his Essex friend's farm. He is quite a dear; he takes good care of our horses and our stable is clean. I chided him for giving us a gift when we, his employers, ought to bestow these kindnesses upon him. He is widowed ten years and fathered no children, which has perhaps kept him young in spirit, for he must be approaching sixty years. Around his pleasant grey eyes are deep lines and I would venture that hard labor in bright sunlight, working with the horses, and carrying loads heavier than three times the heft of my own child have been their source. Indeed, he is handsome enough to have won another bride and may yet, though he does not seem moved to do so. He came to James and me directly from Mr. Parsons upon my father-in-law's death. James' father had employed

Mr. Talbot almost from the time he was in business. Really, this is all to say that I am so appreciative of our fine Mr. Talbot!

SEPTEMBER 12, 1855

James is to dine with Mr. Reginald Pringle this night, at his home, even as I am hosting them to dinner near month's end. I am not disappointed that it is just the men meeting, for I will have my fill soon enough. Here in these pages where I am free to complain—for whom will I displease?—I need not muster grace.

I have only met Mr. Pringle in passing on a few occasions, for he had not been to tea in the past when I had chanced, with Mother, to join Mrs. Pringle. Nor had Thomas. It was only Mother and I in the sunroom taking tea with our hostess. It was an unusual room that differed from the darker, austere parlor. The ladies spoke of things that held little interest for me, young as I was. It is Mother and Mrs. Pringle who were acquainted as young ladies and, though our families did not consort while Thomas and I came of age, being from two different towns and seeking our own sexes for companionship, Mother seems always to have held this family in particularly high regard. I must remark that while she has always brooked very little complaint from me about anyone, least of all Virginia Pringle, she is quick enough to make complaint about the ladies who have vexed her, ladies in her Newburyport society with whom I have been acquainted as a girl and who held as little interest for me then as spending an afternoon now with the Pringles and their like.

Now that a partnership between my husband and Reginald is in its earliest works, I will have to assemble my features to affect the faintest hint of welcome to this family. I must do this for James. I have not inherited Mother's pragmatic nature, and she would remind me of it often and with undisguised disappointment. Perhaps when I am her age, I will have attained her stature and ideals.

53

SEPTEMBER 13, 1855

I have received Mother's letter this day and have read it, but promptly misplaced it and can only think it was mixed in among papers. I have not the interest in searching, and so will record what I recall.

She writes of Father's interest in the quarries as an investor, how gratified he is that his son-in-law is to be involved with Reginald, of her further sympathy for the Reynolds widow, and not very much more, but it is good to be in her thoughts. I hope Father will write to me soon. It is mostly Mother who writes for both.

SEPTEMBER 16, 1855

Today Henry uttered an unexpected new word, though his vocabulary has been growing. This word was brought on by pain. He looked at the roses pressing against the house and grasped at a stem before I could snatch his hand away. Oh, but I have cautioned him often not to touch this rosebush! The thorn had already quick bitten the tender flesh of his thumb as I rushed to him. Once again, a lovely thing has yielded him a terrible surprise!

He wept and looked at his bloodied thumb, then at me, the betrayal in his eyes. "Bud!" He cried out in alarm.

"Yes, it was a bud, a rosebud, my darling! Let me have your hand."

He pointed to his wound and said the word again as I bound his injured thumb. It was then I knew he had said "blood," though he might have spoken two words after all.

SEPTEMBER 18, 1855

James is readying for another voyage to Georges Bank. His two lost fishermen are now replaced, for it is the season of frothing seas and gusting winds in the Atlantic and he cannot do without more men at sail. I reminded him, as I always do, to take the cameo on which a painter rendered my likeness when we were first wed, for it rested still at his bedside table last evening. He tucked it into his pocket and said his customary goodbye to me. It is not a farewell, for that is too final. I have never let him take his leave in this way. He always kisses me, covers my face, tells me he will see me in my dreams of him and his of me, and again on the day he sails in. It is never, will never be, goodbye. He promises this more urgently now since my birthday when I pressed him to forsake heroics and think of saving himself in threatening seas. I believe his word that he will return.

Last night James told me what I have longed to hear; that in his new capacity with Reginald Pringle's quarry, he will not wait till spring, but will be commissioned to sail his vessel to Florida as early as October to solicit business for the first shipment of the company's granite to go south, and that he will leave the fisheries. The only fishing he pledged to do thereafter is with our boy, from a small dory on even seas and in shallow waters, or perhaps in Mill Pond. He said this last to tease me, and I knew he meant to ease my anxiety. I know, too, that when he has the opportunity to take the *Marianne Elizabeth* to the water, he will, and that Henry will one day be tutored in how to sail it. For now, I accept that James makes a grand gesture toward me, for our family, and I am grateful.

I am just as grateful to Mr. Pringle for coaxing my husband into business. He will make three trips in the coming year for the quarry, each trip one month long. Yes, it is many weeks at one sail, especially with his trips to Georges Bank lasting not much more than a week, but those are frequent between April and November, so this will be the better situation. With granite his trade, James will be here ashore with me and with our son for much of the year. How can this not gladden me?

James' heat resides still in my most private places. His ardor still hums through me. Somehow, though he has lately favored our unions in places around the house that are not the bedroom, I managed to coax him here last night and the softness yielding beneath us was another pleasure my body yielded to just as greedily as to James. He will be gone before the sun rises, but this trip is among the last of his fishing voyages before he begins his new livelihood with Reginald Pringle.

It is never easy to part, not even as many times as we have had to do over the years. One would think I had grown quite accomplished at being the well-wishing wife, waving from the cupola, standing stalwart with our son, denying my grim imaginings.

SEPTEMBER 20, 1855

Henry cried out in his sleep and I have tried all I can to soothe him, yet he clings so. I have at last placed him where his father sleeps beside me and now Jack, too, is curled there. He fidgets far more than the child. It is a comfort to feel my son's warmth, though I cannot rest. It has, in fact, been an unusually calm season and the Almanac said nothing threatening of the weather, not for weeks, but a stiff wind blows my curtains in and they flap and twist so that I will have to put down my quill and close the window to keep them from coming loose.

Shortly after supper this evening, Mr. Talbot brought Henry a wooden cup and ball, attached by a string. My boy is not yet dexterous enough to master it, but was amused as he swung it every which way. After a time, I had to wrest the toy from his tiny fists lest he come to harm swinging it about, or harm someone else. He did not take kindly to this, and I was beset with the more difficult task of calming him once I gave the toy to Agatha to hide for a while. What a bellow he has for one so young! When I finally settled him in his bed, I took myself off for the same, bringing tea and biscuits with me, and a book of sonnets. Truth be told, I am the one who needs calming.

The room is too warm with the window closed, and I have had to open one side to make sleep more comfortable. Yet, with my son sleeping deeply beside me, the pup nosing around at my feet as he looks for his own place to settle, it may be light before my eyes close and the lark will have gotten more rest than I. Continuing to record my thoughts keeps sleep at bay, so I will close this day with the resolve to sleep.

SEPTEMBER 21, 1855

I have received a letter from Father who writes that he misses us terribly. I, too, miss his quiet presence, his rumbling laughter when his grandson amuses him away from his books. Father has passed his love of reading to me. It is a tonic against worry to lose myself in the tales and thoughts of another.

Mother would be proud to know that I have begun a sampler, but it is the work of a girl, not a woman. My stitching is crooked, and unsightly wisps of thread tuft in places where I have tried and failed to re-stitch. The effect is of a girl who has had a fit and torn her work out, then had a change of heart and tried to salvage it. My inept fingers are a disgrace.

Agatha has just stepped onto the side porch to tell me that Henry has awakened from his afternoon sleep. She will tend to him a moment, but he will want me in short order.

We will venture outdoors and catch some of the refreshing breeze off the water. Though James' vessel is not due for nearly a week, it may be a diversion simply to watch as other schooners make for our harbor, their safe return a good harbinger for the sturdy *Marianne Elizabeth* and its most admirable captain. The air is still again, as it was before last evening's wind blew in.

As the gulls mock from above I am reminded that I really have no troubles, only too much worry.

SEPTEMBER 22, 1855

When I woke this morning, there was a chill, a message that this might be one of the few remaining days left when even a light cape for me and a light coat for my boy are not needed. I knew it would be best not to remain indoors. The sun shone bright and hot as summer by mid-morning, so I took Henry with me to the Bedfords' Mercantile, also intending to go to Mrs. Spencer's shop for tea.

There was much bustle in town today with the usual shopping, though it did seem as if there were more people about than usual. The skies looked clear enough or I would have thought the crowds and extra buggy traffic owing to a coming storm. I do not want to dwell on such dark possibilities. (Even as I read my words over, it is tiresome to me to see that I have often had to remind myself to keep to the optimistic path.)

Once inside the Mercantile, I was warmly greeted by Mrs. Bedford, who busied herself setting large jars of spice on a shelf. She is a dear lady and, with Mr. Bedford, has raised a family in Rockport, coming over from England many years before when Rockport was called Sandy Bay. In fact, Rockport has only been named Rockport since 1840 when I was but a young visitor to these parts with Mother and Father. We came here annually to visit James and his family for the Christmas holiday.

I returned Mrs. Bedford's greeting and she fussed a bit over young Henry as I looked about the store for nothing in particular, for I had only come as a diversion, the walk being the more pressing urge. Though hardly a half-mile, it is always a pleasure as I admire the gardens. Henry kept his fingers away from things in these gardens that might draw his curiosity, remembering, I am sure, the bee sting and that offending rose.

On occasion in Bedfords' Mercantile, I have made an impulsive purchase. Indeed, today my eye moved to a corner near the counter. There was a tiny shelf with small jars of paintbrushes with shiny red handles, their blond bristles fine and smooth, and stacks of canvas beside them.

I took up my son, who had begun to pull at my arms now that Mrs. Bedford's attention had wandered back to her task, and brought him to the display. I knew I would like to have it, even for a time when Henry was older, and thought no harm would be done in encouraging him to paint. I also purchased some flour for biscuits, a book for Father, and another notebook for me so that I am prepared when this one has no more room for my thoughts. The final impulse was a bottle of walnut ink and a new quill, for each of those I use is depleted.

On our way out of the shop I heard the voice of Fiona Terry and looked around to find her about to leave the store just as I was, having tallied and paid for my things. I thought it curious that I had not seen her before, though it seemed she was chatting with Mr. Bedford further back in the store once her purchases were complete. She asked that I wait for her and I agreed. Even as she is not a woman I call a friend, I reasoned that a moment in conversation would do no harm. We walked out onto the street together, my parcel in one hand, my son's small fist clasped in my other. I steeled myself.

"Is your husband out?" She asked as she stepped down from the Mercantile and into the street to join me.

I told her indeed he was out, fishing Georges Bank, and that he would be home in three days. It is, it seems, always two or three days from his homecoming when my worry and longing for James crest.

"Well," she said, as if she were a young girl giving me a delicious secret and I her bosom friend. "I have heard from some of the women in town that a storm is near."

"But this cannot be!" I objected. Fiona moved back, alarmed by my voice. It was then the thicker crowd in town made sense, and a thought I have fought against intruded. I wanted to shake her for her thoughtless offer of ill tidings. Yet, more softly, I said, "Fiona, there is no harbinger of a storm. There has been no hint of anything. If you look, you see not a single cloud above us." Indeed, earlier this morning I had stood before my garden appreciating its startling vibrancy, for my hydrangeas are in joyful, lingering bloom all around the sides of the house and in front. My rose bushes have remained throughout the summer. I have written Emily about my garden's progress, certain she will be proud that anything she taught me has been put to use.

Fiona pursed her lips and tilted up her yellow-bonneted head, as if she would prove me wrong. She did not enjoy my reproach, nor did she have a reply. The sky was indeed a perfect blue and as I looked again from under my bonnet at the brilliant sun, she bent to tickle Henry's chin. He tucked it shyly to his chest.

Of course, she had to speak then, to reclaim her perch. "Yes, blue it is, Marianne, but you and I know that the seas can change at will and we have no say in the matter."

That was quite enough for me.

"Fiona, do consult the Almanac and try to think of something more charitable to do than to deliver harsh reports to those whose husbands are not safely ashore."

Her surprise was genuine, for that is the nature of a thoughtless individual. She takes no care with her words, thinks nothing of their effect on another. I could not bring myself to stay on and educate her or I would raise my voice once more and bring unwanted attention. It is, I have long been taught to believe, not worth the price of a cup of tea to educate a stupid woman.

Clutching my son's hand perhaps a little too firmly so that he whimpered, I bent instead to lift him, nodded to Fiona, and made toward home, so flustered I no longer wanted to stop at Mrs. Spencer's shop for tea.

Perhaps Fiona has nothing better to do than burden others with such gloomy predictions. In fact, I shall not trouble myself any further, for I have spent the evening fussing with trivial things about the house, hardly able to concentrate beyond the refrain of Fiona's smug words. Poor Henry has been bereft of my proper attention all day, even as he played at my feet in the garden before I realized it was time for his supper.

September 22, 1855

Dearest Husband,

You will think me foolish. I think of myself as such, and yet I am unsettled enough to have given into it after an unfortunate exchange with Fiona Terry. I know you will read this upon your return, as you have read so many of my letters to you, and that you and I will have a good chuckle over my needless worry. As I write these words, I am somewhat consoled by the long understood fact that almost as soon as I press my thoughts to the page, I am proven wrong. You always return safely to me. We will resume our lives and enjoy Henry as he grows to an admirable likeness of his father.

James, come home to me. Our son has slept scarcely a night in his own bed this summer. If you do not come home when you promised, he will refuse to return to his room. Of course, this would never do, my darling, even with your preference of late to be amorous with me in alcoves and on the parlor's settee.

I did not finish this note and have, again, tucked my words to James into a pocket of this journal. I will consider at some later date whether he ought to read them.

SEPTEMBER 23, 1855

Resting on the parlor's south-facing windowsill is a picture I have painted and not a very comely one at that. It is a poor likeness of my son sitting at his blocks, his round little fists reaching and placing them until they tower. His gaze is intent on the task. What is most comical about the portrait is the length of his arms, so mismatched to his body that he looks very like one of the primates in the book we have about animals. His nose is somewhat pointier on the canvas than on his face and his shoes are too big. Still, I will not dispose of it. Henry can have it one day and we will enjoy a good laugh over its sloppiness.

SEPTEMBER 24, 1855

As evening gathers, we are forced indoors. The mildest insult is that Fiona was correct in her forecast. While I prefer to imagine she may be concerned for any sailor caught in this tempest, I can only imagine her glee that she had predicted the weather correctly, and her gloating (to anyone who will listen) relief that her husband is not at sea. I know this is most uncharitable of me.

I had thought to call on Emily this morning, under thickening clouds before the wind gathered force. Perhaps she would have been able to offer a soothing word to ease my worry. Then I recalled that she and her children are still in Boston and chided myself for forgetting. I did carry on to her house with somewhat less interest, to extend greeting to her husband, for he has been alone for a considerable time. Richard McCutcheon turned me away with the look of a man who had been drinking. I worried that perhaps he despairs when his wife and children are away and offered to have him to supper when James returns, as much to console myself that his return is foregone as to be a good friend to Emily. I should have extended myself weeks ago, even when Emily tried to dissuade me from the gesture I told her I would make in her absence. She has often complained that her husband is inclined to dine alone and scorns his family's company most days as it is. True to her declaration, he declined my invitation and sent me on my way, rather perfunctorily. As I walked home, the wind nearly took my hat and reminded me that whatever its purpose, I was, and am, powerless to influence its direction.

It is nearly time for supper and I cannot think of food, for the waves now crash over the jetty and their force causes a wall of water to rise that is so great I can see it from the cupola. I can scarcely bring myself to peer through the telescope in that tiny space for a hopeful glimpse of James' vessel. He is to arrive early tomorrow so I would not see him as it is till he is closer to our shores.

SEPTEMBER 25, 1855

Even Henry balled his fists under his chin as, upon waking, I offered up my earnest prayers. My son looked at me and murmured his own plea in a high, worried babble that surely mimicked my own. It was most alarming coming from the child. They were words I could not understand, yet his sweet little voice hinted at a longing he cannot truly know, for how can he fathom what it is I ask or what I would give to ensure his father's safety?

Early this morning, I sent Mr. Talbot with an urgent message to Mother and Father asking them to come. He rode to Newburyport and was back soon after the midday meal which I had Agatha give to Henry but would not take myself. Mother and Father followed, arriving not long after supper, which I saved for them, thinking they had not eaten before leaving home. Still I had not eaten.

It will be for naught, now that they are here. Sending for them was a silly thing, for James will arrive, even a day or two late. Likely, he has docked his vessel at a port along the way to wait out the storm and has sent a message that has not yet reached me. I will not imagine more beyond this.

Their presence is heartening. These next hours, however long they will be until James crosses our threshold, will be in the company of family.

Part II

Despair, Arrivals, and Dreams

OCTOBER 5, 1855

Could James have thought, with even a fleeting regret, about his wife and son? How can he have pushed aside my plea to save himself? It is true that he fought me on it when I admonished him, yet put to the test, I can scarcely believe he did as he said he would without any thought of those he leaves behind.

Mother tells me I have spent the last many days in sleep, hardly waking to eat, unable to care for Henry. It has been a dreamless sleep, induced by the laudanum Father ordered Dr. Wainright to give me. Within a moment of waking, I have understood that I am, as I have dreaded, forever without my beloved James.

It is some kind of cruelty that not only is he lost to me, but that my dreadful anxiety is laid to rest. I want my worry again, for in it resided the possibility that James would return.

Captain Joshua Terry had not been pulled to sea by the good fishing of that dreaded day and now sits living and breathing, at home with Fiona, at table, in their parlor, in her arms.

I wish I had not seen the *Gloucester Telegraph*, for it has confirmed everything, leaving me no hope. Worse, it has told me that James was not far from Rockport's harbor when doom struck. I have pressed the page here, though I am better off casting it to the very wind that precipitated its tale.

T wo schooners, the *Marianne Elizabeth* and the *Abercombie*, both of considerable size and having weathered storms in prior years far out at sea, were taken down with horrifying speed, their men with them, in the terrible gale that moved rapidly up the coast from South Carolina. Captain James Parsons of Rockport and Captain William Bentley of Plymouth, Massachusetts, fought to save their crew before themselves, yet the gale took all but one of the men from both vessels before they were able to swim ashore. The surviving man, of Captain Parsons' crew, is Theodore Ethan Abel, who lived and worked in Gloucester and sailed on Captain Parsons' vessel intermittently for several months as his first mate. Mr. Abel's account of his survival is extraordinary and can be read below as told to the individual to whom it was given:

Mr. Abel reports that 'during the latter part of the forenoon, the weather looked threatening. Later in the afternoon a thick fog set in, which was followed by rain, and the wind increased until it blew a regular hurricane. Both anchors were let go, but the cables parted and the vessel was put under short sail. The gale increased fearfully and the jib was blown clean out of the bolt-ropes. We saw the twin Thatchers Lights, but were too far eastward to strike the channel. There was no help for us now; with both anchors gone, the wind blowing a hurricane, and a tremendous sea running, there was but little doubt that the vessel would go ashore before we landed in Rockport's harbor and, in that event, the chances of being saved were slim indeed. The prospect was a gloomy one, but the crew was resolved to do their best. Captain Parsons stood at his post of duty at the helm to the very last moment, and though I had just spoken with him, made my way to the stern, then tried to return, as I was moving up toward him, I could see that his death blow came from the main boom. He went down fast over the port side and was gone.'

After running some twenty minutes, the thumping of the vessel's bottom gave evidence that the critical time was near at hand. She did not stop her course, but kept moving. Abel went into the forecastle and stripped himself of everything but his shirt and pants for the coming trial. He had hardly done so when the vessel struck heavily, smashing in the bow, instantly killing five persons who were with him. He immediately ran into the hold, when a tremendous sea knocked him clear off the deck and he was swept into the raging waters. With a coolness and a presence of mind hardly creditable, he seemed, as if by intuition, to at once realize his position and, being an expert swimmer, made for the wreck, which he reached and, clinging to it, regained his breath and rested. Seeing an empty barrel floating near, he let go his hold of the wreck, and was fortunate enough to secure it. Placing his breast upon the head, he forced the empty portion under water. This served as a great support, and with it he attempted to affect a landing.

The waves ran fearfully high and as he was borne along he passed George W. Millet and Benjamin Winkle, two of his shipmates, who were clinging to a plank. If ever in his life he desired company, it was at this critical time; but prudence whispered that he must not make himself known, for if he did the chances of escape for all three would be rendered far more hazardous. He heard them each speak of their fearful position, and doubting whether they should be able to hold on. He knew they would have a better chance at survival if they could aid one another. The last words he heard them utter was a promise that if either were saved, they would tell the folks at home the full particulars.

I recognized the name from the day Matthias and Caldwell drowned: Theodore Ethan Abel.

A man who not only survived what other men could not, but who heard the cries of men he saw swept away, and who made a decision to save himself, driven as much by circumstance as by his own strength and will. For he had only just stood with James before the mainsail boom took my beloved. He was the last man to see James alive, this sailor whose powerful stroke led him to safety, and whose sleeping and waking hours must now be filled with the horror of that night when all but he were lost.

He has the gift of waking hours and, though I wish him well, I cannot tell a falsehood; were it James and not Mr. Abel who survived, though a man of whom my husband spoke highly for his morality and toward whom I wish no ill tidings, my life would be very different.

And now, this house, such a big place for my baby boy and me, already large for our small family when James lived, echoes our every sound. Its empty rooms seem to whisper to me of our loneliness, or is that the ocean pounding the surf, spraying pebbles and shells with its force?

OCTOBER 9, 1855

The dead men from both schooners are almost completely accounted for, many of them washed up near Sandy Bay, Pigeon Cove, and other shores not far from ours. It has been a grisly task to collect these men, and with each trip the few brave enough to recover them have made, James has not been among any of the seamen they have found. His coat has turned up and buttoned inside the breast pocket was his compass, engraved with his initials, so that no doubt existed about the coat's ownership. This cruel fact gives me hope that he is alive somewhere, and may yet cross our threshold to reclaim his life. Perhaps he has no memory of who he is, or of who waits for his return? If he survived that ordeal and lays abed in some stranger's home, might he have read Mr. Abel's account? If someone else reads it, and is ministering to his care, would they not identify him as a missing man? I cannot sleep and do not wish to, but exhaustion is more potent than laudanum. When Mother insists I sleep, I simply relent to silence my questions. I might as well be shouting them down into an empty well, for James does not reply and no one dares to tell me what I cannot bear to reconcile with his absence as each day dawns.

OCTOBER 14, 1855

At the Congregational Church's cemetery yesterday, Reverend Pelham gave a sermon that I hardly heard. As he spoke about the many lost sailors from both vessels, whispers found their way to me. I looked toward one elderly woman, her finger pointing somewhere far to the fringe of the gathering. My eyes followed her outstretched hand until I saw a man with dark curls and a face that has seen time in the sun. As I spied him, his keen, hazel eyes found me in the groupings of people there in the cemetery. I could not look long upon him, for to do so would encourage his expressions of regret. Yet, my eyes must have rested on him for more than a moment, for he did take a step toward me. I turned my head to ward off the intention. In turning, I caught the downturn of his mouth. Of course, he might wish to console me, yet to his great credit, he kept a respectful distance. I am grateful, in no hurry to make his acquaintance, knowing little what I might say to offer him any comfort, feeling no inclination toward conversation. Yes, this Mr. Abel, the lone survivor of my husband's vessel, did seem a kindly enough man. It is only that I did not feel up to being kindly myself.

James' remains, that coat, but not the cameo, are buried next to his mother and father on a mound of the cemetery looking out over the inlet.

During the service, Mother and Father stood on either side of me, each holding one of my arms. Henry stood in front of me, my hands on his shoulders to keep him from wandering off to play within and around the markers. I wondered for a moment if releasing him to his desire might be best after all, for I could feel his shoulders twitch even as he seemed just as intent upon remaining with me. I have no doubt he read the solemn expressions on the mourners' faces and knew to keep still.

He does not understand that his father is forever gone and I do not know how to tell him, a boy whose grasp of an adult world is a long way off. Now the boy has no reason to think other than that his father will return as he always does. The regular passing of days means little to Henry. I have been wondering if is not perhaps better to tell him his father has gone on a very long journey, very far away. At the notion, I stop myself. Even if I were to tell my son this falsehood, it is I who may find it easier to believe, my reasoning riper than that of a child hardly three years old. When Henry is older, he will come to wonder why it is that his father has chosen to stay away. What, then, would I offer? Saying he has perished reveals the first truth as a lie, yet the first truth without resolution reveals his father as one who chose to abandon him.

Mother and Father differ on this, Mother telling me I ought 67 to tell my son his father is very far from us and cannot write or visit for a very long time, Father believing it would be better to explain that James is in heaven and that heaven is the place for good people whose lives must end. I cannot possibly utter the words and wish Father would be the one.

OCTOBER 14, 1855

When I awaken each morning I turn to where James slept, always to my left, always with one arm slung across his eyes as if to keep out the insistent light. So soon after losing him, I feel it before I see it, the cool spot where he once pressed himself each evening he spent ashore, warming that place, the smoothness of the bedding he once rumpled and where even in sleep I dare not let myself go.

Each morning I see our wedding photograph on the bedside table next to me and then turn away. I can no longer properly measure time's passing. An hour can seem only moments, while moments linger on, entrapping me in their sloth. James' face in sweet repose, the moustache he wore combed to a perfect shape that curled like a smile at each end, and the eyes within his handsome face that behold me from so far away, sear me anew with every look I steal at that picture each and every morning. I look at it as if I am not in it, for to see us united is too great a reminder that we are to be forever apart. As I busy myself in the bedroom, unbraiding my hair and brushing it loose to coil it up and off my back after I dress, I feel his eyes upon me, following me about the room when I get up from my dressing table, as if he would implore me to look again.

I cannot look any longer without the dreadful understanding that he is gone. I have placed the picture in the small drawer of my bedside table, for the last time holding it to my breast. I am not fool enough to think the warmth of my own flowing blood against the glass of his image will rouse him from what I have come to believe is his permanent sleep. Yes, even as I harbor hope against it, I know he is gone. There have been no notices of a man found matching his description. With every passing day, hope that he has survived, as Mr. Abel was so fortunate to have done, yields further to despair.

OCTOBER 20, 1855

Mother's care of me, and Father's watchfulness as I move about, remind me of when I took ill as a girl. Through childhood fever I felt Mother's cool touch at my forehead, her able hands applying all manner of cure to me. Endearments were not her way, but when I opened my eyes at the end of a long bout of such fever as a child, I saw her relief. As soon as I would see this relief in Mother's lovely blue eyes, the sentiment all but fled and she was restored to her brisk self once again. It is this way now with Mother as she tends to me in my grief.

Longing to rise from my bed and care for my son, I cannot without the world spinning which Father tells me is an effect of the laudanum, though I do not take it nightly. I have refused daily doses of the medicine so that I might move about the house in the mornings without grasping for purchase. Mother warns me not to hurry along, lest I take a fall and be of no use to anyone.

OCTOBER 24, 1855

Emily traveled from Boston to be a friend to me and stayed on three days to make certain her own husband is well. She confided that she is considering an indefinite living arrangement with her brother, schooling her children in Boston where the family lives a decidedly Christian life and does not allow drink in their home. She asked me if I might join her there. I would raise my son in a big city and he would attend a good school when he is of age. Yet, while it pains me that Emily may never return, and I do see the urgency she feels to make the change, for her husband does not appear to be very aware of her or the children, I cannot leave here to take up such a foreign life. I must re-create our lives in this place. It would be hurtful to my parents if I were to follow a friend to Boston after refusing their home for us.

I promised Emily that I would try to visit and she embraced me with all the regret of a friend taking her everlasting leave. I do hope to go to Boston eventually, for I have only been there three times in my life. I tell myself that I am a young woman and there will come a time when I will feel strong enough and brave enough to travel. But on this day, from this moment to some unknowable hour that will find me prepared to venture forth, I cannot predict when I shall feel such daring. I want only to turn back all the days of that last voyage James took and prevent him from ever having gone.

OCTOBER 25, 1855

It is not that I am vain, only distressed at the image that stares back at me from the glass. I do not know who she is, with her shadowed eyes and her dull hair. Were he returned to me, even my beloved husband would not know me.

I will let Mother wash my hair with chamomile tomorrow, for I know that James would be disappointed if he understood that I had let the luster go from the hair he loved so. It is difficult to write those words, for they look now as if I expect him home. His body has not been recovered, nor more of his captain's vestments. No word has come of his well-being. Mother and Father urge me to accept that he has perished so that I may begin to heal and to be a proper mother to Henry. Yet, why should I not hope?

OCTOBER 27, 1855

Mother took one opportunity, in the days before James and I wed, to give me her curt explanation of what a married woman ought to expect from her husband, and ought to give in return. True to her declaration, since the first night of our marriage, James has touched all the places in me I hoped he would; until the night he found me outside his study, I had been timid in my surrender. Often it seemed he needed to draw me from myself, for I could only meet that animal need in him in my demure fashion. At times, I had the sense that he enjoyed this, a kind of chase. Before long, it became a ritual that when his hands reached for me in the dark in our bed, I would at first withdraw, somewhat frightened even of this man I have always loved. It is a rough memory so soon after losing him, yet I dare say I was faintly repelled, too vividly aware in my mind's eye of what he wanted time after time, and what I at first held close, away from him.

The first night of our lives as husband and wife, James called to me softly from across the room where he sat on our bed, in this home he built for us.

We had kissed often, and passionately, against a tree, behind a wall, always where others dwelled, waited for our reappearance, unaware of where we might be or what we pursued. On our wedding night, I was at last before him in a house where other people did not mill about in other rooms. "Come, my heart, at last. I am your love and you are mine. You are with me," he whispered. I went to him, my whole heart his, trembling in my nightgown and gooseflesh skin.

Timid though I could often be in the face of his ardor, nights when James was away I pined for his breath in my ear, strained to hear him come home in the night, perhaps surprising me with an early arrival from his voyages. Because he did this from time to time, I had come to hope for it. This was his cruelest act, offering hope. It was this hope that gave robust life to my dread each time he sailed, and which has left me wondering still if he might surprise me once more, finally, and dwell ashore with me for the rest of our days. I must quell this thought, for each day the hope goes unsatisfied, I feel weaker.

One night toward the end of our first wedded year, I had fallen asleep in a state of longing so very profound it felt like fever. I was with child, my middle not yet swollen with the life of a girl that bloomed and died after a too early birth. James was to be away for a week's time and, as always when he left me for the sea in those earliest years, I was as grim as a woman scorned; he would often tease me for being so dour and then he would simply disregard me for it, sometimes not touching me for days, though we lived companionably through this. It was how we feuded over his need for the sea and my dread of it.

In that fever of longing for my husband so many nights of his absence, my eyes flew open each time my hands sought his warmth and found only the cool, unused surface of his pillow. I would lie awake, staring at an unyielding ceiling.

I recall too clearly one night, the first of those surprise arrivals, my James stole home, his trip done early. He slipped into bed beside me and found me awake, my nightdress parted at the throat, the covers flung to the floor. He reached for the hem of my shift and lifted it slowly.

James' hand moved up the length of my leg, over my hip, stopping at my waist. His hands were large and square, strong hands in which I had always felt safe when he would help me up or down from the coach or hold me against him. That night, he came to me with an urgency I did not understand and his hands had a rougher purpose. That night, he squeezed and breathed in my flesh and moved his hands across my middle, over the growing landscape there, circling it, pressing gently upon it. I held my breath and his hands moved higher, taking my bosoms, again pressing, more roughly, then taking them into his mouth, hungry as if he had been at sea a month with no provisions. The sting of his forceful pull made me cry out.

He came away and moved his face near mine then, his mouth warm, moist, his tongue traveling in and out and around my mouth and across my flesh in a way he had never dared do with me, exploring me the way he might have done with less tenderness if I were not his beloved.

So often, I had recoiled as a virgin might from the thrust of his tongue, but that night it seemed not only had I no choice, but I invited it, slaked my own thirst on that willful part of him. I moved and moaned under him as if his touch were the very source of my life; it was, I felt then, for I carried a life we had created.

I raised my body up to meet his and he rushed in, his face again hovering above mine. I recognized the contours of that face I had always known, the shape of it, until the moon offered a sharp slant of light on his features and I did not recognize him in that moment. I caught my breath at his final push, the pulse of his finish, his breath in the side of my neck as he relaxed while I could not. He had appeared different in that slant of moonlight, a man more interested in himself than in me, in us.

After that night, I tucked away my longing for this aspect of him and for that hunger of my own that had often visited me, that he must have responded to, for he did not reveal it again until those weeks before he was taken from me. Too timid for too long, I had kept my fervor in check when he bedded me after that night in our first year. Now I no longer have either aspect of him; his tender nature nor its counterpart.

Writing this I am aware of how peculiar it is to me that I can recall this one night nearly four years ago, yet (excepting the night he found me outside his study) of the many we shared, before or afterward, no others are as clear to me. My skin does not react with the memory of those other nights in or out of our marriage bed as it does with this one, with the thrilling alarm of it. Writing it here is difficult, for I want only to recall of my beloved the aspects of him that made me feel tenderly loved. Had his love resided in the violence of that union as much as in his gentler attentions? I must believe it did, for even the pain of his hungry mouth was pleasurable. Recalling that night, I believe I have been many different women; once a lovesick girl, then a young married woman who lived dutifully for her husband, and lastly a wanton wife, only with James, in the dark alcoves and parlor of our home. Now I am his widow and utterly unable to reconcile these women into the one that sits writing by her taper, longing for the man who will never again belong to her.

OCTOBER 28, 1855

How can I think of living anywhere but in this house? I will not go back to Newburyport and live with Mother and Father, though they have strengthened their campaign to have me go. Certainly Mother has. They would like to give my son a home that is, at the very least, presided over by two parents, though they are his grandparents. And what does this make me? Shall I be a child once again, subject to the laws my parents raised me with until I married James?

This morning, as Father played with his round-cheeked grandson, I sat with Mother in the parlor. She was knitting a scarf for Henry, clucking over it as she lost stitches and then found them again, looping them quickly back into the robin's egg blue wool that had begun to form her gift to him.

She found me watching her work and spoke with the quiet, stern voice I have not heard in many years.

"You must be the one to put it on him, to wrap it loosely, securely around his small shoulders and neck and be sure not to let it dangle as he runs," she warned. She is filled with such admonitions. I pursed my lips to hear her tone, her instructions to me, as if I were still a child, and stifled any protest. It would surely have drawn a frown. And, yet, she would go on!

"It is all very well now, my good daughter, that we can help you here as you need it. We want you to take your rest so that these most difficult days are behind you. We are here to help restore you to yourself. Soon we will all go back to Newburyport to live as a family."

It was not the first such mention, but it was the first of a declarative nature, the others before it a gentle inquiry, a testing of the idea. This time, the curve of her lips warned me that she had thoroughly made up her mind. And still, the words before this lingered. "Restore me to myself, Mother?"

"My darling girl, I do not presume to think it will take so brief a time to learn how you will live your life without your husband. He was your beloved. If his parents were alive to witness his end, they would want your comfort, the reliability of your son's well-being. James would also approve of such an arrangement. No doubt, they might all have suggested it themselves." The satisfaction of her assumption, the accuracy of it, weighed upon me and I rested my head in Mother's lap. I expected she would not tolerate it for long. It seems to me I was a girl only yesterday. And yet, yesterday, it feels, too, as if I had my James here, the aroma of his cherry tobacco coiling up from the small, round oak table in our parlor on which he rested his pipe on its porcelain tray. Mother took me by the shoulders, her grip firm. I recalled in that steady blue gaze a need I once had for her comfort, and knew that now, as then, I would benefit from it in the only way she could offer it to me, in gestures of efficiency and strength.

"You will need to stand straighter for your son, Marianne, and for yourself. You cannot dwell too long in your grief."

I opened my lips to speak and she lifted a hand, halting me. "You are not alone in this world. You have your son. He is small, but mighty enough to prop you up with his need for you at his tender age. And we are not hastening to leave. There is also the Pringle family and they will want to show their kindness to you. You must permit it."

As has always been my way with Mother, I let her have her soliloquies, particularly when I wished most to rebuff them.

We returned to our former states, she busying her hands at the needles, I with Elizabeth Barrett Browning's *Songs from the Portuguese* which contains lines that, when James lived, were swollen with all of their intent. James had given the book to me now three birthdays past and I loved to read aloud to him those years, and he to me:

If God choose, I shall but love thee better after death.

Is a heavenly love greater than an earthly one? How can I love him more now that he is gone? How might I have loved him more in life?

OCTOBER 29, 1855

They mean well. They are my parents and want what is left of my family to live well. Yet, I am determined to do so under my own roof, the shelter James built for us.

OCTOBER 30, 1855

Only fifty pages remain in this volume that was James' gift to me and then I will begin the one I purchased the day I met Fiona Terry at Bedfords' Mercantile.

A small chest sits beneath my bed. Inside its single compartment is a small collection of glass shards rubbed smooth by the ocean waves, and of exquisitely imperfect shells. I have taken the chest out and poured its contents on the bed, sifting through the gems within, remembering the moments attached to the day James found them, recalling the broad, expectant smile that came with the giving, the girl who held her palm out to receive them. She is now a widow.

NOVEMBER 2, 1855

The gesture Mother has anticipated arrived at my home today, its messenger Mary, once the scullery maid in Emily's household. Her presence is a reminder of Emily's absence and I kept her there in the vestibule, tried to coax her in for a bit of tea and cake. She would not stay, for her new employer, Mrs. Pringle, was awaiting her return and, she said, a reply from me. On pretty lavender-scented linen stationery that belied its author's austerity, herein is pressed her note:

Dear Mrs. Parsons,

Doubtless you are weary from grief. I have only the deepest sympathy for you and hope to provide comfort in some manner as the days swell to weeks and to months, and with them your loneliness. I invite you and your son to spend some time in my home with Mr. Pringle, our son, Thomas, and me. While not a suitable playmate for your boy, Thomas is an affable associate for you.

The thought of raising your boy without his father will deprive you of the rest you need, particularly in these earliest and most shocking weeks since your husband's passing. I will not be surprised if you need assistance and hope you will recognize that we can offer you more than you might expect from, dare I say, lesser known citizens of Rockport.

Now that colder nights are upon us, you would be wise to consider my offer.

> With kindness,
> Virginia Pringle

I felt the first stirrings in many weeks of a familiar indignation and sent Mary away with an indefinite reply, an "I will of course accept your invitation at some point in the future" and with thanks, hastily written on my own scentless card. She looked uneasy at the prospect of returning to her employer bereft of any certain word from me. Hoping to ease her worry, I explained to Mary that I was too weary to compose even a shopping list for Agatha or chores for Mr. Talbot and that I would reply specifically before too long. She departed with a worried frown. I could not concern myself further with her worry and once she turned heel, she left my mind altogether except for the moments I spent recording it here.

It vexed me these many hours later as I combed out my braids before the mirror. Recalling the temerity of Virginia Pringle's presumptuous words, I wanted to cry out, but Mother and Father were just below me in the parlor. I do not wish for Mother to know about this invitation or she will press me to accept and I will find myself in the Pringle household as soon as a week. I would sooner have had the dinner with the Pringles those weeks ago, for it would have meant James lives; that he does, in fact, wake and sleep in this house with me.

Yes, it is true, as Mrs. Pringle was moved to mention, sleep does not come easily now that dread of our future is more certain than what our future holds. Yet how dare she presume she can see into my flayed heart and know how the night plagues me? And how dare she push her spittle-lipped son at me when I am newly a widow?

NOVEMBER 4, 1855

In his sleep, Henry whimpers like his pup. When I look at that boy, recalling his father so easily in the child's eyes, I feel it fresh. Each day stretches taut until it would snap. I can only close my eyes in the moments before the lark opens its throat. I do not want a sleep remedy any longer despite this hardship and have reduced my dose to half and then to a quarter of its original volume, despite Mother's urgings to keep it at full dose. Even on so little of the remedy, I am foggy for hours. It is a good thing to have both Mother and Father here to help me with my son and assist Agatha with the household. Even as it is unreal, even as I want Mother and Father to leave us to our dismal days, it is good.

NOVEMBER 5, 1855

Mother woke me this morning with tea and biscuits she made in the hour before the sun rose. She is an early riser, as James was, and has always chided me for my tendency to linger under the quilts, particularly in cooler months. When I was a girl, I ignored her rebuke often in favor of the warmth of my bedclothes. James liked to rise early, too, and often coaxed me out of bed with him. In warm weather, if he was not sailing, we would take our breakfast under the linden tree. This past summer, we had not indulged in the ritual. I had missed it and been too reticent on the subject, deferring to his preoccupation with work matters.

It is not luxury and dreaminess that holds me still now. It is moving through and beyond each moment. My son feels the absence of his mother and if I continue in this way, Mother and Father will surely remove my choice in the matter of where to raise him.

NOVEMBER 8, 1855

Tonight, the quiet presses upon me. The utter lack of expectation that my husband will later join me is my only companion.

I cannot bear it, yet in writing it, I give it voice and its darkest feature: truth.

NOVEMBER 9, 1855

Henry touched my tears with his small hands this morning. He had wandered from his bed across the hall to my own, as I knew he would despite my best efforts to encourage him to start his sleep in his room. Many nights I do not expend the effort.

He touched my face as I clung to the darkness behind my eyes with morning's insistent light pressing upon me. It was to the soft trail of his fingertips across my cheeks that I surrendered and brought him up and under the quilt with me.

"Kying, Mama?" He asked me, his sweet voice a clear, tinkling bell around us.

"No," I lied to my son and, bless him, he did not persist, choosing to press his sweet smelling head to my neck.

How not to weep through my dreams? How not to feel James here with me, unreachable, cold to the touch, seeming alive and as far away as he could be? It is this recurring sense, this anguished wish that has me weeping behind closed eyes.

Finally, it was the smell of Mother's biscuits that stirred first Henry and, with unwilling limbs, his mother to begin the day, to make a friend of it.

NOVEMBER 10, 1855

Mother has arranged for her first cousin, Lucy Milgram, to live as my helpmate. She will arrive tomorrow, and Mother has brooked no protest. I do not know why I should need her with Agatha staying on, but Mother has already made it a firm plan and Lucy travels here as I write this. For now, I shall simply make her comfortable and let her be, to please Mother. It will be a brief stay. I will make certain of it.

NOVEMBER 11, 1855

Lucy arrived within moments of Mother and Father's departure today. They ought to have stayed on to welcome her, but Mother assured me Lucy did not need it, that she is a capable woman and that it would do me good to govern my home once more. She urged me to consider Lucy as not simply a companion, but my helpmate.

Hardly an hour after her arrival, my elder cousin had already stoked the fire and was preparing our supper for later in the day; this, with no guidance from me. I do not wish to have her serve me, though by the looks of her I imagine she would as soon serve as be served; she is very comfortable in the kitchen. I believe Mother has given her very pointed instructions and this does not surprise as much as irritate me.

I perched on a bench in my own kitchen to watch her move from cupboard to cupboard. So little at work in my home, I felt more like a shiftless child as I watched Lucy busy herself. I asked her if she had eaten. She turned her broad, flushed face on me, and smiled in a kindly way.

"I took some breakfast just before you came in here, Mrs. Parsons. A piece of bread pudding and hot water with lemon," she said in a voice so low I had to lean forward to hear her and I nearly toppled from the bench.

My last interactions beyond the household were in the days before James perished. Yes, it was at the Bedfords' Mercantile. Now the title of *Mrs.* chaffed at my heart. "Lucy, we are family. Please address me by name. I am not your employer. It is Agatha who is my housemaid."

"No," Lucy said quietly. "Your mother has sent Agatha to another family who needed her."

That Mother would presume to govern my household in this way is an affront! She did not consult me, nor did Agatha make mention of her dismissal. Perhaps she did not see it coming, or was warned against saying as much? I have not been terribly attentive to domestic matters, even caring little for the supply of linens as they dwindled, for they have even more without a word from me in response. Of course, Mother must have relieved her of that chore when she saw the damage. It is too wearying even to consider a contest of wills with Mother, yet I will inquire whether she gave my girl an extra sum in parting.

All my trouble must have been etched upon my face, for Lucy spoke her next words as if she were trying to appease, though whom I am uncertain.

"Your mother has told me to be sure you nourish yourself and that you have a child who…"

I am no better than my son, for I do tend to pick at my food when troubled, much as I did when I was a girl. Of late, my tendency has been to rearrange it on my plate. The looser fit of my skirts is telltale.

"That may be," I interrupted her. "But you are to be my companion, not a servant."

"Your good mother instructed me to tend to the boy whenever possible," she added, as if to convince me otherwise of her status. Mother had told me only that Lucy had been in service with other families before coming to me.

I explained to this kindly woman that I do not mind fussing in the kitchen, and that the bread pudding was something I had made only the day before, my very own recipe. Mother has taught me a little something that keeps my sleeves rolled for part of a day. It was important to me that Lucy know this much.

I told Lucy that I am grateful for her but that I wished to share the household work as I had done with Agatha. I told her of our agreeable arrangement, how I would tend to my son and even do some cooking while Agatha saw to it that the house was kept neat and helped with the washing. Though much of it is drudgery and I have done little in the past many weeks, it will be a welcome preoccupation.

So, we have struck an agreement of our own, Lucy and I, though I think Lucy will try to do more to help than I may require of her. She is clearly very capable, perhaps even headstrong.

And, yet, I do not know a thing about her. She is my grandmother's niece, by a brother, and both of them are long gone. She has been delivered from within the folds of Mother's family, yet does not feel like kin to me.

I must be ungrateful for not relishing company in these weeks. If Lucy were not here I would have to make do; my son and I would be alone and Agatha would come to tend to things, then leave at each day's end, as would our steadfast Mr. Talbot. But the worst of this feeling must surely pass. The shadows on the walls, the reminder of James in the smell of his coat and hat, his shirts and the warm sandalwood smell of his side of the bed I cannot bear to move from at night; all of this will fade. And what shall my boy and I be left with after?

It must be Lucy.

NOVEMBER 15, 1855

It is difficult to reconcile Lucy as a close relation to my mother, who is of good height and does not reserve her wisdom for quiet reflection. No, Lucy is a small, doughy woman, quiet and pale, her brow arched as if in permanent surprise, her spectacles perched on the end of her small, straight nose. Henry is tentative toward her and when he dares to approach her, he likes to touch her tightly coiled brown and silver hair. Dear that I think she is, she allows it.

Mother says Lucy's age is a few years more than her own. I asked Mother, before she and Father left, if she and Lucy played together when they were children. She told me that Lucy's mother and father, Mother's uncle Edward Milgram and his wife, Laney, had moved far from Newburyport, taking Lucy with them when Lucy was barely a young lady. Mother and Lucy were unable to correspond thereafter. She mentioned this as if someone had willed their separation. I found this peculiar, for Mother's will is a great deal mightier than most, and when she was a girl she had to have practiced it on someone to refine it. Yet, it seems that someone was not her slightly elder cousin.

I know Mother and Father are not far, that Newburyport is hardly a half-morning in the carriage, but their absence smarts as a pin to my finger when I mend Henry's night shirt.

It is supper now and the sun is nearly set below the horizon. A scarlet rim rests where the ocean meets the sky and the last of the terns are having a banquet in the surf, their heads bent low as they scurry from the advancing waves. It is not a scene I tire of, yet the last time I remarked upon it, it was a day of laughter that seems part of the life of another woman.

81

NOVEMBER 16, 1855

The other day, before Mother and Father went home to Newburyport, Father found me in the parlor and gave me a pouch filled with coins and banknotes. Mr. Talbot had Henry in the stable, letting him watch as he groomed both the horses and finished shoeing, feeding, and grooming

Father's two for their journey. Looking from the side window of the parlor out toward the stable door, I had been thinking how lucky it is that my son can still be in the company of a man, though it is not nearly the blessing of having his father watch him grow. It was then my own dear father entered the room. Recalling our exchange, I feel fresh tenderness toward him.

"There, my Lass," Father said. Hearing my childhood name brought me to the brink. "Be sure to use what I give you for yourself and Henry. Not a penny to Lucy since we have taken care of her. I know your husband has not left you destitute, but it would make me happy if you will accept it. We will always be of help to you." Matters of money and business were always between James and Father; this was most unaccustomed and I thought to refuse it, but Father pressed it into my hands with a plea in his eyes like that of my son when I refuse him a sweet before supper. I beheld his melancholy smile, the sweetness in his aging face, and closed my hands around the pouch. Father, releasing the heft of coin and the crinkle of banknotes to me, embraced me and left the room, and then the house, to see to their carriage as Mr. Talbot was hitching their horses to it. Mother and I had said our farewells.

I suspect Mother was unaware that Father had given me this gift. At the time, she was upstairs fussing about with her saddlebag and Agatha, who had not yet left, but who would not return after that day, was assisting her. Mother's difficulty accepting that I will remain rather than bring my son to live with them was evident in the briskness with which she has lately tended to me. Henry and I will stay on in this house James built for us. I will raise our son under this roof. I do not come into this resolve by any accident.

Following dinner on their last night with me, when Mother tried once more to make the case for bringing Henry and me back to Newburyport, it was Father who spoke up and instructed her to have faith that my son and I would do well, for there is no one so very far away that I would be deprived of companionship, assistance with my son, whatever the need. And, of course, now there would be Lucy. Mother looked chagrined at being even gently scolded by him. I do not believe I have witnessed this between them, for she has always been a strong presence. Father has been mostly content to defer to her nature and we have lived (during my girlhood, and now) peacefully enough, even with my long held disinterest in her often irksome ideas about how I ought to spend my time (at stitching, idle conversation, parlor games). In the moment before they pulled away from the house, Mother offered a quick, firm embrace and took up her cape, then allowed Mr. Talbot to assist her into the carriage. Her cheeks were flushed pink and her eyes were blue pools ready to spill over, a spectacle she could not have intended to reveal.

I have stowed the money pouch deep inside a drawer for safekeeping. Yes, we are well provided for; this house James should have lived in till his old age will remain my house now that the title belongs to Father. Money is the least of my worries, even as the cause of its plenty is at the height of reasons for my grief.

NOVEMBER 19, 1855

I have at last written to Virginia Pringle to thank her for her offer to help my son and me and took the opportunity to mention that Mother's cousin Lucy has been enlisted as my helpmate (I chose these words carefully for Mrs. Pringle's benefit and for mine, to deflect scrutiny) at Mother's insistence. I concluded with another vague promise that I will make time for Mrs. Pringle before too long.

I believe I have done what is expected and earnestly hope she will not make further overtures. The time for us to dine as two families has come and gone and I see no pressing reason for our coming together.

It is true that James mocked Virginia Pringle in Mill Pond Meadow when we picnicked there on my birthday, yet, he would counsel me to take her up on her offer. So eventually I must, if only to show gratitude for her husband's intended generosity toward James. If Reginald Pringle's plans for him had come to pass, James would have known a different kind of life; a life sometimes at sea, less imperiled than a fisherman who sails often in stormier seas and for many months of the year.

The thought does persist that with two mentions of her son, Thomas, in her letter I can only think that she means to pair me off. I did not address Thomas, or any companionship between us, in my letter to Mrs. Pringle, for I am not in want of a male friend.

November 22, 1855

My Dearest Henry,

You are such a small version of yourself, the man you will grow to be. I have at last told myself that your father has gone away on a very long journey, an important one that he cannot discuss, and that he will not be heard from. I have not yet spoken to you of this, and when you call out for your father, which you do less often now than even the week before, I can hardly form a word around it. Then your anguish passes and my relief of this comes in its wake. Sitting near me, you busy yourself now with little blocks of wood your father made for you to build with and you look up at me with your wide grey eyes, flecks of green in them that remind me of the ocean when the sun is glinting off it in midday. You give me your toothy grin. I want to rush backward to when you were brand new and all we three knew was that the sun would set at night and rise after your father who would be up before the larks and the jays.

I can hardly hold you when I feel this way, the truth weakening me. The reminder often assaults me that you are the only real part of James that I have left and that I must hold onto you until you refuse to let me, and even then for just a little longer after that.

I am ever,

Your Loving Mother (M.E.P.)

NOVEMBER 23, 1855

Yesterday I took my son for a walk along the path in Mill Pond Meadow and came across a tree. It is not just one of the many trees, each almost indistinguishable from the other, in that small park; it is the tree under which James and I stood when he asked me to marry him. And, though I knew—had long known—that he and I would one day be together, I made a little sound, a kind of cough, and he took it for doubt. The look on his face was of pure horror.

"Marianne?" He had asked me, all of his own instant anguish bundled into my name.

84

In fact, it was my only wish to have him belong to me, but there was also a flutter that traveled up from my chest and brushed against my throat causing that cough.

Perhaps it was fear. I have to wonder now; fear of what?

"My darling, doubt is not even a possibility," I told him. And he kissed me for that first time as a man kisses the woman who belongs to him. I was sixteen.

NOVEMBER 25, 1855

A letter has arrived that I cannot touch now that I have read it. It sits folded on my dressing table, rebuking me with its presence. I have hidden it behind one of my bottles of perfume, and now peer at it not knowing what to do. If I should burn it or cast it upon the surf, its truth would not vanish, for the man still lives and I have known of it since we buried the other members of the crew along with James' remains. Of course I would not wish this surviving fisherman ill, nor am I fool enough to think banishing his words causes him to vanish from the earth.

It is a letter from Theodore Abel. I had put his survival out of mind after seeing him at the funeral. Like James, a few of the coffins of his doomed seamen were filled with only a shirt, a hat, a pair of waders whose ownership could only be a guess based on who had not returned. And as I read Mr. Abel's letter, the memory assailed me of this man standing among the mourners, his eyes downturned in the moment before he lifted them to me. His letter's date is only a half-week old and its mark is from Gloucester.

November 21, 1855

Dear Mrs. Parsons,

Please accept my apology for being the lone and unworthy survivor of the doomed *Marianne Elizabeth* and the *Abercrombie* two months ago. I know it took your beloved from you, the entire crew but for me, and those I never knew on the other vessel. My survival will cause you to question: if your husband couldn't outwit this disaster, why should it be this man?

I, too, have asked, Why me?

I have no wife or children, no mother or father and not a soul awaited my return each time I sailed into harbor, nor sent me off when I left. This isn't to win your pity, dear Mrs. Parsons, only to further show you the truth that there's not a reason I can think of why I ought to have lived through such horror. I'm alive, and for reasons I don't know.

The only comfort I can offer is that the wave that claimed your husband to the sea was singular and forceful and he met his Creator swift and sure.

Your husband will remain fixed on a lofty perch in memory, as he was in life.

Humbly,
Theodore Ethan Abel

I will write to Mr. Abel and admonish him for forsaking his good luck. Life chose him! I will counsel him to use his renewed life in the best way that occurs to him. I will tell him in this note that if he wishes to visit Henry and me, that we will welcome him. Perhaps it will be an unexpected balm to see and speak with the man who was the last to see my beloved breathing, standing, living.

NOVEMBER 26, 1855

Last night, sleep delivered me to the depths of the ocean where I was able to breathe in the water as if it were air. I found James clinging to a part of his splintered vessel and he beseeched me to release him. I pulled his clothes loose from the wreck, yet he still could not move. He pointed to his legs, which I then saw were pinned beneath the anchor. I lifted the great piece of iron made almost weightless in the water, though even in my dreaming I knew this could never have been the case. Still he could not move. He then thrust his hands out to me and opened his mouth in the shape of an "oh." I did not know what he was telling me. I held fast to him, but he pushed me away and up toward the surface.

When I opened my eyes this morning, the word, "go" was on my lips. Was it the sound of my own voice pleading with my husband to let me remain with him at the bottom of the ocean? In the dream, the words came from his mouth and not mine. Could he have been imploring me to leave him be? Dreams are a cruel visit, for his face is as clear as if pressed close to mine, and when I open my eyes, there is nothing but a white ceiling.

NOVEMBER 30, 1855

Today Mr. Abel paid a visit, unannounced, bearing a humble smile that perfectly matched his letter to me.

He was dressed in a brown wool suit, worn at the collar, and a clean shirt, threadbare at the cuffs. His shoes were polished to a dull sheen and scuffed miserably around the toes. All of his clothing, including his cap, seemed chosen with care for the occasion of coming to call. I must have been staring at some aspect of him, having forgotten myself, for he startled me when he spoke, identifying himself in a peculiar way.

"Mrs. Parsons, I'm Theodore Abel," he said to me. "From your good husband's vessel." He looked down, intent on his feet. Those last words had come slowly, as if they resisted utterance.

I must have betrayed my surprise, for I had not expected him to call, nor had he sent word. Seeing him, I knew it would not have been his way to do this and he seemed to know my thought.

"You replied to my letter, Madam. You said I should come."

Had I? Yes, I had.

He continued. "I couldn't wait any longer. I regret that I didn't send word of my visit, but I didn't plan to call until just this day. I have no prospects for work and no certainty that I'll be in Rockport even another day, so I took my opportunity this day to see you and I hope it doesn't cause you trouble."

He began to step back as if to leave. I called toward him. "Mr. Abel, please let me offer you tea. I have not been overly attentive to common courtesy these past months, or had occasion to offer it." Even as I spoke the words, I wondered what has kept this man until now, so long since James' death. Having brought all of his humility to my doorstep, Mr. Abel must have sensed this, too. And, in that very moment, I searched myself for a shred of pity for this man who felt he did not deserve to live, and I found a lack of it.

He spoke up and said he had sailed with James before on many occasions, though not all of them consecutive after the incident with the Messrs. Mathias and Caldwell. I did not know what I should offer in reply. He could not have known I was unaware of James' crew in easier times, and less so after those two men were lost.

We stood just inside the vestibule, Mr. Abel barely beyond its threshold. A column of dust glinted and swirled in the wedge of light offered through the window next to him. That same light landed on his crown, so that his curls appeared not brown, but nearly bronze. He looks nothing like James, whose ruddy complexion after a voyage brought out the light in his grey eyes and reddened his lips from the wind, whose darker hair fell straight across his brow except for one untamed forelock. Closer to me than the day at the cemetery, I could see that Mr. Abel has perhaps a few years on James, and that they have worn deeper on him. Two lines run on either side of his mouth, and are more pronounced with even the slightest inclination toward a smile, faint as it was when he offered it in that first moment in my doorway.

My son awoke then. Perhaps the rumble of a man's voice roused him, but I was relieved, for Henry's dreams worry me, dreams that make him twitch and fret in his sleep.

He must have let himself out of his little bed, the thud of his determined feet taking him from his room to the edge of the stairway. I imagined him at the top of the second floor landing teetering, unsteady, still hazy from sleep. I turned from Mr. Abel and rushed up the stairs, leaving my guest quite alarmed by my departure. Luck visited me as I caught my boy whose first step down would have doomed him.

Briefly annoyed that Lucy was nowhere in sight, I have since learned she had gone out to greet him when she saw Mr. Abel approach, asked him who he was and the reason for his visit. When he satisfied her questions, she later told me, she was so astonished that she slipped in through the side porch, letting him ring the bell himself, and placed herself in the kitchen in case she was needed. She said she busied herself so as not to overhear what was not her business. I have expressed to her that she might be best within sight when a man comes to call, though I do not expect gentleman callers, nor do I desire them.

Clutching my son to me, relief caused my legs to quake as we came downstairs to Mr. Abel. He looked down at the boy and seemed overcome even before the child spoke.

"Pa-pa?" My son said, coming fully awake. "Pa-Pa!" He wriggled free of me and went to Mr. Abel, throwing his little body at my guest's legs and clinging hard, as if his slight frame could anchor the man in place. Mr. Abel looked at me, helpless. I, too, was surprised, for as I described, the two men did not share a likeness. I believe my son was delirious, so fresh from sleep.

I bent down to pry him loose and when I stood straight again, my face was warm from the effort, from being beaten and pushed at by Henry's little fists as he fought to be let down. Of course, I was not about to lower him or he would only pester Mr. Abel again. Desperate to quiet the child, I began to croon a lullaby in his ear until he was calm.

Mr. Abel did not clear his throat or shuffle his feet, so it was a long moment before I looked toward him again, remembering myself. Yet, he had not turned to leave. He stood before the two of us, his hands at his sides. Embarrassed by my poor manners, I repeated my request that Mr. Abel come in to take tea.

I have briefly thought to write to Mother and Father of his visit, and then thought better of it. For what would I say about him that would not cause them worry? Surely, Mother would disapprove of Mr. Abel's undeclared visit and even more so, his later intention to return. I cannot even tell them that this stranger was charmed by their grandson.

I cannot write to them that the man who survived what my husband and so many others did not is a kind man and less fortunate in his circumstances than we are, and that I look forward in a peculiar way to having him return, for he was the last to see my beloved standing, and there is some need in me to cling to some notion of another man's favorable view of my husband, even if he does not spend many words on it.

No. Such a letter will not find its way to Mother and Father. Rather, I will paint them a little portrait with words, a tender scene in which Henry plays with the curtain of my hair when I sometimes uncoil it in the parlor in the evenings. I will write that Lucy feeds a fire in the hearth each afternoon to keep the house from cooling too quickly before evening now that winter is near. I will tell them that Mr. Talbot has taken to giving Henry sugar cubes and apples for the horses, giving him a brush to help in their grooming, and that he lifts Henry high to keep him safe from their shifting hooves.

They will enjoy a newsy letter of enjoyable moments, for I want for them to imagine my days as not so very dark.

Part III

Doubt and Good Intentions

DECEMBER 1, 1855

Mr. Talbot asks when I would like to go to town to replenish any food stuffs before the weather turns, for we have already had some severe rains and I expect snow will follow soon, and hard. He has been good enough to fill my lists, sometimes bringing Lucy, often going alone. I see that he enjoys the company, and that in Lucy he finds a worthy seatmate, though a shy one.

DECEMBER 2, 1855

An outing to town today proved useful. The air was bracing in a pleasing way for a first day in months beyond my home's garden path. Mr. and Mrs. Bedford greeted me warmly and as I basked in their kind attentions, I recalled they had visited the house in the earliest days of my grief. How many other kind visitors have come and gone that I have forgotten? How many did I receive through the haze of that laudanum? Mrs. Bedford admonished me not to fret over formalities such as remembering people who call in sympathy. It is the sort of propriety reserved for exacting folk, she said. She and her husband do not keep company with such types if they can help it, she clucked.

All in all, the outing was livelier than I expected. I managed to give my attention to the list I had made, scouring the pantry as if it were the first time I would go to the store. Once there, Mr. Talbot was near at hand to bring the purchased items to the carriage. My relief at not running into Fiona Terry was nothing less than mountainous. All in all, it was a good day.

DECEMBER 4, 1855

Lucy has begun to read to me from my book of Shakespeare's sonnets and it surprises me how expressive she is with these verses, yet how retiring she is when going about ordinary business. Our conversations have mainly to do with meals we will prepare, the care of my son, or the needs of the household. I do not imagine I will require her help for much longer, for I believe my son and I can manage quite well enough on our own. I will want Agatha to return if she has not found employment elsewhere. I wrote to her mother on the matter and heard no word other than that the poor girl has been unemployed since Mother gave her leave. Rather than have Agatha languish during Lucy's first days with me, I sent the girl a basket of items to mend and it has come back to me untouched. Mother has done harm here; Agatha seems a proud girl who will sooner be a chambermaid at an inn than a housemaid to a good family. The note is enclosed here:

> Dear Missus Parsons,
>
> It's not your fawlt that I am unhappy with the cirkumstances of my unemploymint. Your mother, though a good woomin, releasd me without word of why or promiss of later summons by you. You were in no state to help me, so I didn't ask. I will not come back to your home if theres a place with you, though it's not your fawlt, as I sed. I am sorry for your linens, all those I rooned. And most of all sorry for your lost husband.
>
> Agatha

Her pride sticks, even so young. I reassure Lucy often that I will soon be strong enough not to need her help and I think to myself that I will coax Agatha back. Lucy offers a patient gaze, yet something in her expression tells me she takes my words and places them on a shelf as if they were butter or sugar, to be used at some more opportune time.

November 30, 1855

Mrs. Parsons,

Thank you for allowing me to visit with you on what would have been one more dark day in a miserable collection following me since the ships went down. You raised my spirits with your kindnesses, your tasty teacakes, and your son who's definitely the image of his father. I hope for the privilege of another visit with you both again. If this is too forward a thing, I'll understand your need to refuse.

Most sincerely,
Theodore E. Abel

DECEMBER 5, 1855

During our visit, I observed that in spite of the horror he endured, Mr. Abel seems to regard the world around him with an optimism that must reflect his temperament. This is enviable, for while he did not lose a loved one, he lost a livelihood for the foreseeable future. He reported to me that he is finding it difficult to get more work on another fishing vessel and will leave Cape Ann if he must.

Mr. Abel and I sat in my parlor five days ago, with tea and lemon cakes between us, a small boy tapping at his knees and playing with his large rope-bitten hands. James' hands were not quite as carved with markings, for he spent fewer years at sea and more at wheel than sail. Henry traced the deep scars and calluses etched across Mr. Abel's palms and on the looser skin webbed between the thumb and forefinger of each hand. All at once, Mr. Abel lifted him up and over his head and gazed up into my son's face. For just an instant, the child looked down at me from the firm grip of Mr. Abel's hands, as if unsure, though not at all frightened, and I was going to tell the man to put my son down. But then Henry laughed! I was glad indeed, for I have become more

93

accustomed to the boy's moods matching my own and confess that I, too, was not frightened for my son's safety.

I will never forget Mr. Abel's words as he put my son on the floor at his feet and looked at him. "You're a fine young man, small Mr. Parsons," he said softly, though Henry had resumed his intent examination and was picking his way along the buttons of Mr. Abel's coat. "Brave as your father was and gentle like your mother."

At that, I ended our visit, too ashamed to have Mr. Abel see my face. No doubt he would have tolerated my tears, understanding their cause. Yet, the true intent of his visit was, I believe, to cheer us both, not to summon melancholy all over again. Oh, dear, perhaps I know nothing about what he intended.

December 8, 1855

It is not that my Henry understands his father's passing—for how could a child not quite three years fathom such a thing? There are days when he might spy me in the grips of sadness, with my shoulders rounded and my chin tucked to my chest. At such times, it is the fatherless years weighing upon me that lie ahead of my son. I have begun to observe myself as if from the outside so that when I catch these slips into melancholy, I might coax myself away from them for brief spells. But I cannot always do so, and the child is a keen observer of his surroundings and the people in them.

December 12, 1855

The weather is warm today, an unexpected lull between the seasons. I stepped onto the side porch into a mild afternoon under a pale blue sky with no threat of snow or rain. Now I write in my book whilst on a blanket on the cool sand. Henry is napping indoors where Lucy tends to supper, and there is not much afternoon light remaining.

The tide is coming up. Wavelets lifting, advancing, and retreating like a child outrunning his mother. It is no wonder I make such comparisons, with Henry already so quick he will outpace me when he is not much older than his very nearly three years.

This warmth in the air belies the nearness of winter. The wind off the bay is not so kind as it was only a few weeks before, but even the slight chill in the air will not keep us indoors now that we have finally ventured out more this week. My boy and I have walked along the beach during one outing and the way he plucks stones from the sand as if he were picking flowers (which I hope he will next year, forgetting the bee sting) is very dear.

DECEMBER 13, 1855

Mr. Abel has come back for another visit. This time he sent a note ahead requesting an opportune day and time. I had replied that today would suit us. As nothing is really pressing, for Emily has no plans to visit Rockport till spring and I have no thoughts of venturing to a bustling city or to town, it seems we have too much time to idle. (I will have to call upon the Misses Caldwell and Matthias, for even though they receive food and some companionship from a number of women I had earlier enlisted, I know I have neglected them since James' death.)

When Mr. Abel came today, yet another mild day, we took a walk. Henry tottered just ahead, bundled well in his woolens, and Jack darted about and sniffed all around. When Henry thought to dash away, Mr. Abel ran after him and caught him up. It is a good thing my son likes to be lifted high in the air and apparent that Mr. Abel enjoys children. Perhaps he has experienced them before? No, he did say he has no one left but himself and this would include children. It was heartening to see the two of them so at home with one another after just the one visit before this. My boy has needed to match his energy and growing strength to someone and I am unworthy of it.

Looking back up the street toward the house, I could still see Lucy on the porch, a thick, bright blue woolen shawl gathered tight around her plump form. I had pressed her to keep the brown quilt resting across her lap to ward off further chill and thought perhaps she would retreat into the house as we ventured farther, but she held her place, her bright gaze turned our way, as if to look elsewhere would be unforgivable. I believe she has recalled my earlier words to her that it is improper for a lady to keep company with a man without another trusted person nearby, though we made more and more steps away from her. The impropriety of our first visit, with Lucy hidden away in the kitchen, would infuriate Mother, yet a walk as easy as the one we took today would hardly be objectionable.

I cannot fathom my elder cousin yet, but will make a point of understanding her better as our days together continue. She has not given me a date of departure, nor am I lately moved to request one, despite recent comments I have made here. Her company has been more of a balm to me than an inconvenience of late; as I feel more like myself in her company. I have grown accustomed, even very fond, of Lucy.

As I turned my eyes from the house and Lucy's perch, Virginia Pringle was bustling toward us from the other direction, from town, taking the path toward the water. It was too late for me to steer us away. We all came to the same place and greeted one another. She smiled at my son and me rather curtly, her lips hardly moving. At Mr. Abel she drew her mouth into a small, tight greeting. Her small brown eyes were level and hard on him for a moment before she addressed me. He held his ground and greeted her with a slight bow, lifting his cap, and excusing himself to tend to Henry's curious nature, for the boy tugged at his britches.

Mrs. Pringle and I stood to watch them and I called out to both of them to stay out of the water. The woman frowned before turning her precise gaze to me. She commended me for being out in the air and expressed her hope that I was managing well enough. She announced that she would be sending her son around to call at week's end and that she had hoped I would consent to a visit to her home, as her invitations have indicated and my responses have not. I knew I should be embarrassed, perhaps mortified, but I could not summon such humility.

Still, not knowing how to refuse her in this more intimate moment, I consented to receive her son.

Her voice is surprisingly handsome; rich and deep, almost masculine but for a higher timbre behind it that graces her notes, but does not soften them. This voice and her height are her only attractive aspects. She is almost as tall as Mr. Abel who stands close to six feet, somewhat taller than James had been. (I noticed today that he must lower his head to enter my doorway.)

As she looked again at Mr. Abel from under a hand shielding her brow, there was, I think, surprise in her gaze, to see that Henry sat comfortably astride the man's shoulders. Virginia Pringle flinched, as if something smarted under that dull brown wool mantelet. Then she said "good day" and turned away from the beach toward her coach and its driver. She has rather a brisk pace for a woman her age.

I caught up with Mr. Abel and Henry, who placed his hand upon my head. From where he sat up high, the child bellowed, "Lookameee!"

"Oh, darling, you are very high indeed! Hold tight to Mr. Abel!" And he did, squeezing his legs more snugly around the poor man's ears for better purchase. His beast, as Mr. Abel would seem to be in this capacity, did not so much as wince.

Mrs. Pringle had somehow turned the bright day very cloudy and cool, and I thought to make mention of this, then thought better of it. Decidedly less interested in continuing the walk, I suggested we turn for home. Mr. Abel was disappointed, and my boy was, too.

Beginning to move in that direction, I found myself alone for several paces before turning to see the two of them bent over an anthill on the path. Each of them peered at it with great intent. I wandered back to them and knelt to see that one of the insects was dragging a piece of another ant twice its size, never staggering or losing its way. As I beheld this feat of strength, I realized I have a very great distance to travel toward a sense of my own strength and that I have barely gone a step.

December 14, 1855

Dear Mrs. Parsons,

It wasn't easy coming to your door and not truly a kind thing, after all, even to pay my respects. I fear I may only be causing you more grief. Thank you again for an afternoon I won't soon put out of mind.

I remain your friend,
Theodore E. Abel

DECEMBER 15, 1855

It is no mystery to me that Mr. Abel's connection to James is what prompted me to offer tea the first time he called. As that first afternoon passed in his company, there was something not as apparent which has remained with me; it was a demeanor of confession which arose with thoughts Mr. Abel did not voice, yet seemed on the verge of expressing.

As he has now twice spoken of leaving the region in search of work on another vessel, I offered my friendly hope that he will find a situation here, for I have observed that while he seems to have come from little means, he expresses himself well and could perhaps be employed in another capacity. Nevertheless, if what James said was true of the other men on his ship, they would not have let Mr. Abel be easy following the tragedy of the Messrs. Caldwell and Matthias. They would have punished him for his truth-telling and spread word to other fishermen throughout Rockport and Gloucester. I imagine since then, such word has compromised Mr. Abel's chances of employment on other schooners.

Here I confess to a hope that Mr. Abel does not estrange himself. Of course, the Pringles of the world will look askance at my friendship with a man not my husband, but I have been well enough brought up to know that Lucy's presence ought to prevent gossip mongering, even among the most disagreeable of the sort who will stir it up. And of course, we do nothing to stir people to gossip.

But why should I be preoccupied with the Pringles? Yes, Mother and Father would have me be mindful of that family's interests, for they are meant in some fashion to reflect mine. Unhappily, they are far more interested in me than I am in them. I simply want to forget quotidian formalities, the sticking points of being a widow; I wish to live my days quietly with my son and with my memories of a too short life with James.

DECEMBER 17, 1855

I have at last, and rather late, commissioned a hat for winter. Mrs. Laughlin promised it would be ready for me three days hence. I marvel at her nimble hands, for she must have many such orders for the season.

In the past week I have had that cheering visit from Mr. Abel and good company with Lucy. Henry has added more words to his speech, and there is now a lovely garland upon my door from our Mr. Talbot. He brings cheer to me with his thoughtful gestures, to Henry with his kindly attentions, and, I have noticed, to Lucy who grows lovelier with a flush when he is near.

December 18, 1855

It was Lucy's birthday today and I surprised her with a lemon meringue pie, a treat for us all. Wanting very much to have her out of the house this morning so that I could make it, I sent Lucy with Mr. Talbot, with a list to replenish the larder. Off they went, pleased to do the errand, Lucy clutching her cape around her, her genial escort doing his best to help her up into the carriage. She does not climb well, round as she is. I had to smile from where I looked on from the parlor window.

December 19, 1855

I will relate a letter from Mother which I cannot press here after a spill from an errant boy's elbow this morning at breakfast:

Mother does enjoy a regular word or two about her grandson and continues to hope for a visit before the snow makes roads impassable. She fears a difficult journey for whichever one of us makes the trip, yet has asked me to come for Christmas, certain that my son and I ought not to consider spending this holiday in solitude. I, in turn, have requested that she and Father come to us. Even as it is unthinkable to celebrate any sort of occasion when my beloved will never again know merriment, I am not up to traveling, not even to such a lovely home as the one in which I was born. There are rooms for Henry, for Lucy, and for me, and though it is not as grand as the Pringles' house, a house too grand for me, it is far bigger than my own, and boasts an ample yard. It is not as near the ocean. How did I spend so many years unable to hear *99* the whisper and roar of the sea until I came to know it here in Rockport? I cannot imagine a life without it, particularly now that James has not been returned to me. One might think I would prefer to be away from the vast body that swallowed James. One would be much mistaken in this. It is not as if I imagine it might yield him again one day, alive and whole; it is only my need to be near where he rests.

It is here I must stay, in the house James and I shared. If it will be a melancholy holiday, it is only to be expected. Henceforth, I will do my very best to give my son the cheer he deserves and in this Lucy will be my aid. The air I breathe here is accustomed, for though my husband's body is absent, does not have a place in the earth, but has dissolved somewhere on the ocean floor, things to which his scent clings are all about the house. I have not been able to face opening his armoire, but it is a comfort to know his clothing resides behind its cedar doors. One day I will have to make work of the removal of his clothing, offer it to less fortunate folk. For now, I cannot. So, Lucy and I, Mother and Father all sit stalemate in our homes, unprepared to make a journey that would no doubt bring us all some cheer. James would urge us into the carriage and onto Newburyport with Mr. Talbot at the reins, but my once even vaguely intrepid spirit is not up to bundling us all up and away.

DECEMBER 23, 1855

Of late, Lucy has taken to sitting by the fire each night with Henry and me, reading to him. After he is abed, we read to one another. It is these hours after supper when my good cousin seems at her liveliest, though it is quite the contrary for me. I continue to dread the onset of night and it does come so quickly now. Staying up very late has caused me to sleep later in the morning, well past the lark that seems to chide me. I must put a pillow over my ears to mute its incessant rebuke! I am of little use to Lucy on such days.

As we sat before the fire this afternoon, Henry clutched charcoal nubs, dragging them around on paper I had thought to use for gifts, but have until now abandoned. My interest in fussing over such things lies limp as untied ribbons, the vigor drained from the tasks surrounding this once happy time.

I looked at Lucy who was absently purling with wool that seemed intent upon wrapping itself around her; from the corner of my eye I spied her continually unraveling it from her wrist and elbows. I smiled at her mess.

"You are at the mercy of your wool," I commented. She peered up at me and suddenly dropped it all in her lap, prying the loops from her hands in frustration.

Knowing Mother and Father would have us on their terms, it has been James crowding my thoughts and that somehow he is now three months gone. On the heels of this unsettling fact came a picture of Mr. Abel quite alone. Then came the realization that it would be monstrous of me not to invite him. James might have made the gesture himself were he here. With this consideration, how might I have resisted?

Lucy divined my thoughts as if they were a hidden spring. She did not waste words. "Cousin, it would be a kindness to invite a less fortunate soul for this holiday. I ask for myself, too."

Until now, I had not let myself think of it, not once, disavowing any thought of our ill-gotten new friend.

"It is late to be offering invitations, Lucy. He will already have his plans, I am sure."

Her blue eyes, clear again and now bright with new determination, settled on me as if to tell me I ought to know better. How could I not laugh? Under that gaze, feeling by turns resolute and pleased with myself, I stood to gather my son to take him to bed. Henry bade Lucy a sweet, shy good night. I told her I would think on the suggestion and speak with her in the morning.

DECEMBER 25, 1855

This morning, I awoke resolutely against a widow's colors. There must not be any black on my shoulders or at my waist today, came the first thought as I lay warm in my bed. Each day I don a widow's dress is a declaration that I cling to my husband's memory every waking moment. Indeed, but for an occasional bit of color in my hair of late as a nod to the season, an attempt at festive comportment for all of our sakes, I have worn black, loyal to its truth and custom. Today I did not. Even now as I write late into this evening, I remain wrapped in the festive colors of the holiday. To remove them would be to relinquish a certain feeling that has come with the holiday and which I did not expect. I shall write about these feelings without elaborating upon any conclusions I may have drawn.

After a dreary Christmas Eve that Lucy attempted to make somewhat cheerier with sweets, baking to fill the house with ginger and plum, and even dear Mr. Talbot singing some carols with her to Henry and me (my son is quite the warbler himself, though his words are comically mispronounced and his melody wanders), we all turned into bed.

I slept as if someone had given me a strong brew of black tea without the cream and sugar I love, so that my eyes remained open most of the night until finally fatigue won me over. Henry, who has just begun to sleep more nights in his own bed, jostled me out of vague dreams and a heavy sleep before first light, so I gathered him into my bed and let him complete his rest with me. Though he is too young to know the days of the week or month, he has been running into my bedroom and opening my eyes with his own fingers since the smell of Christmas baking began earlier in the week and Lucy's fuss over garlanding and wreathing the house inside and out began with it.

Almost immediately after I dressed this morning, Henry led me down the stairs toward the parlor where he saw a collection of parcels by the hearth, all prettily trussed in colorful ribbon and plain paper. Lucy must also have prepared these. He trotted toward the spectacle and toward Lucy who had set our dining table with plates filled with currant biscuits, bowls of porridge, raspberry preserves and a big pot of tea. I hugged my shawl, already feeling a winter chill coming from under the door to the vestibule, and stopped. There was a shadow beyond the glass. It was a man's figure. I could just see his pale outline against a grey morning sky that promised snow. I approached the door and peered through the curtain. There was Mr. Abel, his hands stuffed inside the shallow pockets of a too thin coat, his head down. Before parting the curtain, I knew; yes, I could just make out the now more familiar profile of his long, straight nose, slightly crooked at the bridge, his high, broad cheekbones. And when I glimpsed him fully, I observed that a lock of brown hair strayed from his wool cap and that he had grown whiskers.

I opened the door and we stood, saying nothing, the cold air rushing into and throughout the house, eager as an unruly child. Lucy came around the corner clucking about keeping out the cold and stopped short at the sight of us.

"Dearie," she chided me. "Let the poor man in! You can see he's ill clad!"

I did and we stood still in the hallway, Mr. Abel trying, I believe, to measure my reception of him.

I stepped back and let my cousin take the lead. She brought Mr. Abel in and closed the inner door against the icy air.

"Mr. Abel, it's good to see you," she said, her voice deeper with the pleasure of seeing a friend, though he is really still so new to us all. "It feels like years since you were last here." She was speaking thoughts I dared not. "Let me take your coat and you can come and have a Christmas breakfast with us. I know a little boy who will leap at the sight of you."

As Lucy predicted, when my son caught sight of Mr. Abel, he went running to the man who lifted him so that they were face to face.

"Hello, small Mr. Parsons. You might have grown since we last met."

Henry clapped Mr. Abel's shoulders, my son's small hands landing square and firm on him. It was easy to see that the two enjoyed each other and within this moment I felt a calm I have not for some time, a feeling that chased away the persistent ache that had kept me wakeful.

DECEMBER 27, 1855

Since Lucy's arrival, I have carried few assumptions about her with me, hardly thinking of what little I know of her other, as my fondness for her has grown, than the spare details Mother shared with me. Mother had told me only that Lucy was employed as a housemaid most of her life, that it is this role as well as companion to any employer, that she would carry on here.

I see now that it has been my error to suppose that Lucy has not harbored her own sorrows. I have underestimated my elder cousin. True, she is unmarried, but I have learned that she is not without a child somewhere in the world!

Lucy asked me if, after supper and getting Henry off to sleep, she might have a few moments with me. It was then she told me of Rose as we sat in the parlor, she with her stitching, and I with my book. As soon as she sat, she stood, and her needlework dropped to the floor at her feet.

She explained to me that she was barely seventeen when she birthed Rose. "I haven't had the pleasure of watching my grandchild grow. My daughter's husband, Timothy, doesn't yield to me." These words brought a flame to her cheeks, for in the next difficult breath, she told me she has seen her granddaughter Hannah four times in her young life.

"Philadelphia is a great distance from here," I offered.

"It's not the distance that separates us. People travel, cousin. They hire coaches. There are steam engines."

"Can you not visit with them?" I knew as I said it that it was far more troublesome than Lucy's ability to journey south to her family.

"Timothy won't have it."

"Does my mother know any of this?"

"Cousin, she knows more than she ought, but she was hardly a woman herself when my daughter was born. Once it was certain I was with child and no father in sight, your Mother's interest in me, or in our companionship, wasn't helped along by our elders. We left Newburyport. I'm sure your grandmother, my auntie, wouldn't have wanted us to be bosom friends given my disgrace."

Hearing her, I felt a heat in my own cheeks and forehead. At last I understand the expression Mother wore when she told me that she and Lucy had not consorted as young ladies. She must have been taught to be ashamed, forbidden to have associations with her cousin. Surely, such a friendship might have blossomed but for the appearance of a child without an accountable father. It must have caused a terrible shifting of loyalties. Hearing of it, I felt at once indignation on Lucy's behalf. Yet, knowing Mother was not yet a woman herself when Lucy gave birth, how can I not feel a shred of pity for her that she should have been tutored in her feeling? I credit her for bringing Lucy into her family's midst, the very thick of it, and I will not confess to Mother that Lucy has confided in me, for she would see it as a flaw in Lucy's conduct to have made the admission. It would reinforce all Mother has been taught of how to judge Lucy unfavorably.

When my cousin left the parlor, I watched her mount the steps, listened to her progress toward her bedroom where I have no doubt she took up the comfort of her cross-stitching. The sampler she sewed not long after her arrival, the image of my house with its garden drifting as if unsure of where it truly belongs, hangs framed on a wall in my bedroom, right over my writing desk. As I sit here recording Lucy's confidence to me, it is upon this lovely little picture that I gaze now, with waves of blue behind it to mark the ocean and little bits of white stitching to mark the froth of it. I do not know how she creates such work so quickly. One day I will watch her, with a book in my hand so that I will appear to be reading. I fancy she does not like people peering too closely, though she has a keen, watchful eye herself.

DECEMBER 29, 1855

As his mother warned me he would, Thomas Pringle has sent word that he would like to call. It has taken longer than her original suggestion, and I thought, hopefully, that it was forgotten. I have asked that Lucy be very present when he comes, not simply busy in the kitchen or elsewhere in the house, for it is my certainty that his mother would like to have us better acquainted. I do hope she does not accompany her son. He will come tomorrow afternoon.

DECEMBER 30, 1855

Thomas Pringle is a smartly dressed man, well-mannered, and smiles very little, though when he does, his countenance takes to it far more readily than I had imagined it might, given his mother's taut features and his inheritance of them (though his are still an improvement). James and he crossed paths often, but had not formed a friendship. It had perhaps more to do with the two men's disparate natures—Thomas tends toward reticence and my husband was more forthcoming among male company. Yet, during his visit today Thomas did express regret that he and James had not made a proper acquaintance and he kindly conveyed deeper regret for my loss.

Mrs. Pringle, who of course kept us company, affected a false gaiety that I will never reconcile to her otherwise tart demeanor. Unfortunately, with her there, Lucy's presence was little needed. Instead, my good cousin simply bustled in and out with a cart, poured our tea, and served our sandwiches, then slipped away as if borne on the wind. The visit idled for well over an hour with very little conversation other than the weather, which is unerringly predictable in this season. As one might imagine, talk of it proved a struggle.

When my guests took their leave, Thomas sent his mother on a few steps ahead of him, and turned to me to speak in a low voice.

"You are quite lovely, you know, and if you will let me be your friend so that we might please my mother, I will ask nothing more of you." He kissed my hand and bowed, and then was gone. My relief was great, both in his words and his mother's leave-taking.

I may have judged him harshly in the past. Perhaps he favors his father. Should he choose to call again, I will welcome him as my friend and hope his actions are not at his mother's prompting or in her company. Lucy is a sufficient presence to put Virginia Pringle's mind at ease, I am sure, and I will promote this to bring it about.

DECEMBER 31, 1855

To acknowledge the New Year, we five—Lucy, Henry, Mr. Abel, Mr. Talbot, and I—dined together this evening at my table for an early supper in the waning afternoon light. Of course, I do have my misgivings; Mrs. Pringle's disapproval of Mr. Abel is fresh for me still.

So, here I will confess that I allow his visits in opposition to her displeasing nature, often despite such a barb, and that I have come to find him so engaging. Certainly, I am aware that she intends for her son to be my suitor. (She mistakes Mr. Abel for his competitor!) Though she has no hope of realizing this, as confirmed in her son's parting words to me that were out of her earshot, I do enjoy getting her to bristle at the notion that Thomas might be edged out of contention. There is, I should also record, no contention, for I have come to think there is no use in remarrying.

106

During our New Year supper, Mr. Abel asked me to call him Theodore. I thought it a joke at first, for I had been asking him to pass this and pass that at the table, beginning or ending each request with "Mr. Abel" until I, too, thought it sounded ridiculous. Lucy had begun to stifle her own amusement. Finally, he cleared his throat.

"Mrs. Parsons, I can't answer you any longer if you talk to me as if I were your teacher or some other professional." He adjusted his waistcoat and the good-humored look he gave me belied his discomfort. He seemed, in fact, quite amused, even a touch eager.

I am not yet ready to give up my surname for my first in discourse with him, or to use his given name, though I imagine it would eventually feel quite natural. Theodore. Yes, even writing his name does feel oddly sweet, as he is, but I will refrain from overusing it here.

After an evening with the people who put me most at ease, I will complete the day's recording with this: Mr. Abel's most winning feature is his patience, after the smile that broadens and lights his face.

JANUARY 1, 1856

With a new year comes the promise of spring in just a few months. The prospect helped me get out of bed in the new light of morning on this first day of the year, cold as it is and well enough into winter as we are now. Henry, awakened by his own dreams in the middle of the past three nights, has taken to my bed once again. His tiny toes warm mine if I curl my feet up to my chest and wee Jack nestles against the boy. I do miss James the most when his son is in my arms or playing peacefully, unaware of me and of the ache in my life where his father used to be. Henry has a charming way of looking at me from the side in a manner his father had. Such reminders bring home my melancholy in the same heartbeat as gladdening me with the promise of his father living well in him.

JANUARY 4, 1856

Another visit from Mr. Abel who cautiously occasions a conversation about his captain, watching me as he does; perhaps he looks for how I will react in some way befitting a recent widow. I am detached at such times, preferring not to lose my composure. Mr. Abel sees me, I think, as a woman not easily undone and I shall keep it this way.

JANUARY 7, 1856

Today, much of my afternoon was spent sorting Henry's clothing, separating the things he wore when he was very small from the things he can wear now. He is growing by the week and I now wish that I had not let go the undergarments Mother sent me. I do not want my boy to fall ill because I did not clothe him amply.

My head feels light when I give it the slightest turn, so I will rest and hope that when I close my eyes, my sleep will be free of trouble.

Tomorrow I will go into town with Lucy and choose some fabric. She has offered to sew some well-fitted britches and warm shirts for Henry. She is, as I mentioned the other day, handy indeed with needle and thread. I have already written to tell Mother to send less of her own efforts so that Lucy feels as useful as Mother would have her be, despite my interest in working alongside her at many tasks. Sewing, of course, has long ceased to be one of them.

Now, I shall retire earlier for a change.

JANUARY 17, 1856

I have not written for many days, too weak to record my thoughts, hardly possessed of a thought at all. Lucy has been a source of strength and steadiness, as I lay not very useful to anyone for close to a week. I felt Lucy press cool cloths to my forehead and heard her gentle reassurances that Henry was in her care. How he must have fretted so when I was unable to go to him!

She tells me that I spoke my husband's name often and that she nearly called for Mother in the first two days. Then my fever broke almost as soon as the thought stirred her to act and since then, most of what I have done is sleep, with just the past day and night a more wakeful time. Dr. Wainright has, she tells me, been to visit twice, staying a particularly long time when his worry was greatest, and then leaving my care to Lucy.

The first day I felt somewhat restored was yesterday. With some urging from Lucy and her sturdy palm beneath my back, I sat up only to lie down again. I will record as closely as I can the exchange we had, having heard from Lucy things I shall piece together here. I learned, too, something that troubles me still and has stirred me to act.

When I first sat up in bed, I cried out, "The room is tilted!" and held fast to her soft arms, their surprising strength when wrapped around my shoulders a force I knew to be my safety.

"It's still and straight as you are, Cousin. Take your time with getting up."

"But I want to see James," I told her, pushing her arms aside as I tried again to rise and then fell back to my pillows.

"Cousin..." she began, the tremor in her voice betraying her uncertainty and terrifying me. "Your husband is..." Worry lifted her generous brow and I admit to being cross with myself for being so absent of mind as to think James still lived. I had thought it was Henry's name I spoke.

"No, no. It is my son I want, Lucy. Where is he?"

"Sleeping. Mr. Abel is with him. He's also sleeping, on the chair next to the boy's bed. He looks uncomfortable." I could imagine Mr. Abel's larger frame occupying the sturdy wooden chair next to Henry's bed and that he would awaken with sore bones from draping himself uncomfortably within it. I wondered, too, in my own drowsy state, how long he had been in the house that he felt moved to sleep and in such a place. Nothing about his being present alarmed me in that moment.

Lucy explained that Mr. Abel had called each day begging a report of my health.

"That was very kind," I said. "Still, I am just as glad that it was you at my bedside."

In a rush she confessed to me that early on when she had to tend to my son and to me, when Dr. Wainright had given me laudanum and Hannah Jumper's remedies had proven of little use, Mr. Abel had availed himself to help Lucy on an evening when he had sent a note around for a next day visit. He had come immediately upon her reply that the visit would not be for pleasure, but to tend to the infirm, to me.

"I spent very little thought on it, Cousin, and you'll wish to thank Mr. Abel when you see clearly."

She said that upon relinquishing some of her vigil to him, knowing he would be ill-suited to caring for a small boy's needs, she was grateful for his help.

"Do you tell me that while I lay in my fever, completely unaware, that a man I hardly know saw me in this vulnerable state, that he sat here alone with me?"

She blushed, a different shade of pink than that reserved for Mr. Talbot, but did not turn her gaze from me.

My honor has been compromised. In this Lucy bore the force of my dismay, for her judgment was very poor indeed and I am worried about people's opinions for whom I care not, but whose word can make life here in this community and in my household very different.

"Lucy, you ought to have sent for Mother after all or, loathe though I am to suggest it even after the fact, Virginia Pringle," I chided, for though I do not relish that woman's company, in my delirium I could hardly have known it was her care if I was so far gone that I did not sense Mr. Abel so near. I can only hope she has not discovered this gross impropriety and I said as much to my cousin.

And then I had a memory, as if a waking dream revisited me. Yes.

"Lucy, each time my eyes opened, I saw *you* and there were times I was certain my James sat with me." She looked upon me with concern and moved toward me with a compress, but I stopped her. Yes, it *was* so! The weight and presence of my husband pressed on the edge of my bedside. I recall his touch, his callused hand at my cheek, a spoon in his hand lifting broth to my lips. My thought came hard that it should have been James and not Mr. Abel! Let the truth have changed to a waking dream! Even a ghostly presence is better than an unsuitable one.

During this conversation with Lucy, I sat up and my head felt ill-secured. I lay down again, limp as a tea towel.

My dear cousin looked at her two round hands, one still clutching a damp, cool cloth, and let my words sit unanswered between us. It was then I recalled with startling clarity a change in their guard when Mr.

Abel sat where she did and I could not form the words to tell him to go. Unbidden, came a shred of memory from those hours; Mr. Abel sat beside me, in a chair, and read aloud, softly. I cannot recall the words or their origin, only that he was their reader and that he paused now and then to look at me. My eyes must have been open, for I now have a clearer picture of his eyes resting upon my face before he bowed his head into the text again and continued.

Oh, I do not want to imagine that I lay in the most intimate of places, in my bedclothes, my hair pasted to my head and cheeks, and that a man whose acquaintance is still very new, a man who is not my husband saw me in this shape, as helpless as a baby, perhaps as inarticulate as a lunatic. I lamented this to Lucy who told me I uttered nothing but the occasional plaintive cry for James.

I know as I scratch these words apace with my frantic disquiet that it will haunt me later to have had a man not my husband in my home late into the evening hours, and with some regularity, these past many days.

With this realization I have since made a decision: Even as I believe that Mr. Abel did what his kindly nature and concern for me moved him to do, I announced to Lucy that I cannot permit him further visits until he is summoned, and that this may not be for a very long time. He will have to understand my reasons.

For the first time since her arrival, I saw something other than a lingering serenity in my cousin's face. Her pale cheeks flamed, for she has come to know my thoughts on the subject of propriety—that I do, of course, adhere to it, but that it is also a hindrance to enjoyment at times, such as when Henry attempts to make bubbles of his broth and we cannot help ourselves, laughing until we are breathless. She tried to tell me that I would be the more aggrieved by my actions, but I took the opportunity to make it clear that Mr. Abel's presence would only draw unwanted scrutiny and that I have no choice.

His presence in my chamber cannot be compared to a child's blissful ignorance of decorum; no, I am too well aware that Mr. Abel committed a far worse indiscretion, one to which Lucy should have been sensitive in her own experiences. Yes, I do understand that it is her unfortunate circumstance as a girl that is to be blamed, for what can a girl in her situation have known about propriety?

She fought me on the point.

"A blight on what the neighbors think, Cousin, if you'll forgive me for saying so. I believe you might even agree with me about Ms. Pringle. They can't possibly know Mr. Abel's goodness or how he helped you and me so well."

"And they will not, Lucy. They will never understand what you so easily believe. It would have been so much better had you sent for Mother."

"Perhaps, but I was here a great deal, Cousin! And Mr. Abel was an angel. It was he who fetched the doctor, and when I could not, he fed you a curing broth sent over by the very ladies you have these past months nursed and helped yourself, the Misses Mathias and Caldwell. Many nights, your good, unfortunate friend slept on the settee in the parlor in case you called out so that I could tend to Henry if he, too, should cry out. And he did often, your boy, missing you so much. We didn't permit your son near you until your fever broke."

I lay there a moment to absorb what she had told me, hardly daring to imagine my son's suffering in being deprived of me. The moonlight over the ocean spilled into my bedroom through the parted curtains; in that column of light there seemed to tower questions with no answers. Just this made me fierce on the matter; no, I would not relent in disallowing Mr. Abel's unannounced, uninvited visits here. Even now, I feel my decision is sound.

"Lucy, please ask him to leave. Tell him I will write to him and explain my reasoning. If he is a thinking man himself, he will understand without explanation."

Without a word, she did as I asked but not before leveling a very critical pair of eyes on me that I could not bring myself to meet full on.

JANUARY 18, 1856

Mr. Abel left without protest. Lucy reported that his smile was forlorn, that she reassured him I would soften over time and he would soon be a guest at our home again. It is true, I will. And yet, I suspect that as disappointed as our friend confessed (to Lucy) to have been, he knew how improper it would be to stay now that I am well, and he must have felt some misgiving for having remained so indecorously in my company. A dear to help, he was foolish not to consider the consequences.

Oh, I am torn! For rough as his upbringing must have been, it speaks of his goodness that he remained in support of Lucy and of me while I lay feverish. Not for a moment do I imagine that he would choose to linger any longer than was necessary, bringing harm to my standing in the community. Yet, the unkind thought weighs upon me that if Mr. Abel were to take ill, I do not know if I would have surrendered myself to care for him. Dear me, I hardly know this man and now worry that he feels too soon a fondness for me that I cannot say is matched for him.

I have written to Mr. Abel to thank him on both Lucy's and my own behalf, adding what he must already understand, that for the sake of my husband's good name he must not come to visit for the foreseeable future, for tongues would certainly wag if they are not set to doing so already. After Lucy's correct reassurances to him, I expressed as well the truth that he is pleasant company and that before too long I will ask him to tea and hope that he will accept.

JANUARY 21, 1856

Virginia Pringle's censure regarding Mr. Abel was delivered by her maid, Mary, formerly in the employ of the McCutcheon household. Her tidings were most uncharitable, the sort I have long known reside in her unseeing heart. I wonder at times if she is a relation of Fiona Terry's and, if so, do they sit in one or the other's parlor and exchange a scarcity of pleasantries?

Yes, Mother and Father have elected the Pringles as my surrogates and I suppose they felt it was their duty to enlist a vigilant eye, even as there is little in my quiet life that would be the cause of disquiet. After all, it was of my own volition that I sent Mr. Abel away, understanding without being reminded of it that his intimate presence was improper. For that matter, if Virginia Pringle were paying closer mind, she would have insisted upon coming to my bedside herself or pressing Mother or Father to come to my aid. Being a nursemaid to the infirm, even those in whom she professes to have an interest, is clearly not her strength.

It is a wonder to me that Mother and Father did not come. Perhaps they did not know of my illness, for I have not yet written to them, wishing to keep them from worry.

The unpleasant Pringle letter is folded herein. Though it sullies these pages, I will keep it here as a reminder of what vexes me about this woman.

January 20, 1856

My Dear Mrs. Parsons,

It is clear to me that Mr. Abel has no one to represent him. He is of insufficient means and has no ties to the community, except perhaps you, of late. What respectful man—a gentleman if he aspires to keep company with you, but only by wish, not upbringing—visits a woman in her home in the evening hours and does not leave? I am aware that you were ill, that you are not a wanton woman, and I am glad that you have your cousin to keep company, yet I question her sense that she allowed this man across your threshold as you lay in your feverish state, vulnerable to his advances. When Thomas called upon you, I saw fit to accompany him, lacking the confidence that your cousinly companion understood her obligation to you. This, mind you, was before you took ill; since then, your cousin has vindicated my lack of trust. I blame myself for not properly attending to you whilst you lay ill, yet I was feeling the onset of a cold myself and thought it best not to aggravate it, nor spread the incipient malaise.

I hope you enjoyed the broth I sent and that it helped restore you to yourself. Please convey my regards to your cousin. With the exception of her lapse in judgment during your illness, I believe you are in excellent hands, for she clearly nursed you capably.

I remain your concerned neighbor,
Virginia Pringle

JANUARY 25, 1856

Mother's short note to me, which I cannot seem to find, has explained that Lucy reassured them of her ability to care for me and would send for them if the situation became truly grave. The worst, she knew, had passed. I cannot imagine Lucy mentioning that Mr. Abel was her helpmate, but have no need to imagine, for Virginia Pringle will have done the telling and I have only to wait for Mother's rebuke in another note.

JANUARY 26, 1856

Fiona Terry and I arrived at Mrs. Spencer's teashop at the same time this afternoon. I could not bring myself to greet her. I tried to appear as if I were just passing the shop, but that was unconvincing, for I had already begun to take the steps up from the wide porch and could not turn aside. And then Fiona was suddenly at my elbow. My task had been to purchase some Ceylon and Chamomile teas, not linger over a cup and a biscuit with anyone, least of all Fiona.

She placed her hand upon my arm. To my surprise, she offered an apology, very sincere, that she had been blind to my worry the day we met just before James was taken from me. Quietly I told her not to fret over something she could hardly control, and that she cannot have foreseen my tragedy. I longed to get out of the shop and Mrs. Spencer was standing at the tea boxes ready to assist me.

Fiona's eyes filled with tears. She expressed further misgivings that she had not come to call upon me in my hour of need, during those earliest days and weeks of mourning. As the months passed, she felt worse over it, and finally too ashamed to call. It was this shame, she confessed, that also caused her to think she had brought my loss upon me. Here, I nearly scoffed that she should think herself powerful enough to have such an effect, but I kept my temper even.

When I returned home, I was in an ill humor and Lucy bore its effect. I asked her why she allowed Virginia Pringle's food into my home, and demanded to know if Mr. Abel knew it before feeding it to me.

"He didn't, Cousin," she insisted, puzzled by my mood. I believed her, and made my apology before going up to my bed to rest. Before drifting to sleep, I reasoned that if Mr. Abel had understood the full range of my feelings toward Virginia Pringle, her soup, or anything else she bestowed upon me for a cure, would not have passed my lips. It is also safe to assume that if Lucy was earlier unaware of my disinterest in that woman, she is well versed in it now.

FEBRUARY 1, 1856

Lucy, clearly troubled by Mr. Abel's banishment, has left me a note:

> Dear Cousin,
>
> Mr. Abel insisted that if the moment to do me one charity after what you've suffered were put before him, I must let him do what he could in aid. He left me no choice, though did not force himself into the house. I had the chance to turn him away, but I could hardly do that, not with what you were going through, not with my need for help with both you and your boy. Agatha, your prior girl, didn't answer to my note, and Mary, Mrs. Pringle's girl, came and went with soup or stew, as did the Misses Caldwell and Matthias, but no one of them could stay long. When a man wants to do good for others, one ought not to stand in his way. It was because of his great good will that I didn't see further need to summon your good parents. Had your ague worsened, I wouldn't have wasted another hour, and Mr. Talbot would have fetched them here.
>
> Ever your loyal cousin,
> Lucy

Upon reading it, I offered her a note of my own in which I thanked her for all she has done these months, and that I would be in a sorry state without her. She is a gift. When we sat down to dinner, she approached and offered me a strong, motherly embrace, different from those Mother sometimes offers, with far greater warmth. It is I who should have offered the embrace, asking for her understanding.

It is a day of notes, for Lucy then handed me another, on a bit of my own notepaper. Upon it were words written in another's hand, which I knew to be that of Mr. Abel. I have read it several times this evening before pressing it here.

January 18, 1856

Mrs. Parsons,

Your face, when you're in a state of sleepy, feverish confusion, is very dear. I'll say only that about my thinking as you fought your way back from a fever that I confess left me fearful one night.

 Should you be restored to ease in my company, I'll call again.

Theodore E. Abel

Lucy had been holding it for me and would have given it over sooner, she said, for he had asked that she give me the note upon his leave taking. Yet, she realized as he left, seeing the melancholy in his eyes, that she knew something of the nature of the letter and thought it best to hold it awhile. She smiled as she watched me read the words and then assured me, when I said that I could not possibly answer his letter, that she was certain he did not expect a reply.

Mr. Abel's note is really far too easy a telling of his heart.

And there is something very knowing indeed in Lucy's calm blue gaze that, in these few months with her, I have come to value.

FEBRUARY 4, 1856

I will not be ruled by convention. Many would say a year for a bride to mourn her husband, and that may suit some. What if it must be more than a year? Might I be scorned if I feel that within a half year I cannot bear to wear another black petticoat? The likes of Virginia Pringle and Fiona Terry would be quick with their criticisms, yet it is all very easy for them to offer rebuke when they have not experienced such a loss.

Henry distracts me from my gloom when it visits. He is forever inquisitive and gamboling about the house and yard in search of mischief. His activity and constant chatter are my deliverance.

So many mornings I awake with an aching head, for with each dawn comes the reminder of what my son and I have lost. Some mornings still find me huddled under my bedclothes and even wee Jack cannot warm my feet or cheer me then, for my grief and its accompanying chill press in upon me.

But today dawned with the brightness of an opal and I did sleep more soundly than usual. It is a rare thing to have the sun shine so insistently in February, as if it would warm flowers enough to coax them up from their sleep. As I rose and stretched, warmth moved through me into my limbs. I felt something else, too, and moved with more purpose through my dressing. After Lucy tied my corset, and I hers, and left me to finish my washing, as I do each morning, I fastened my locket around my neck, the very locket James presented to me on my birthday last summer, and today peered inside it. I have not looked at its contents since he gave it to me. The blue ribbon around each lock of hair is a bright reminder of that day nearly six months gone. I touched each treasure and closed the locket, holding it a moment. Coiling my hair for a bun, I decided to tie it with a bit of color. Sensibly, it was a blue ribbon I chose. It is the color of a hazy summer sky, almost matching that which ties my son's and his father's locks inside this filigreed opal piece that rests at my throat.

At the breakfast table, Lucy smiled in greeting. She seemed not to be able to account for what it was that drew her eye, suggesting it might be a better night's sleep. It was the proper guess. She nodded her approval, just one of her many gestures that I have lately observed, and that I have come to understand and appreciate.

February 7, 1856

In winter, the ocean's surface is a steely, unyielding grey. When one steps out of doors, one is hit hard in the face by a snap in the air.

I have not gone to the cupola these days for fear it will give me only an empty space where James used to be, the ghostly memory of his sails full as he headed out into open waters. Now there is nothing of him promised there, though schooners drift each day across my panes, coming home and sailing out. There are far fewer now in this season, but I had forgotten the pleasure of watching from high above the rooftops how the ducks slide as they land. They frolic as if they were children, sliding on the frozen pond. I hear their babble as they congregate and imagine I hear can the clamor of their wings as they try to slow themselves on landing.

As my son gains confidence in his stride, I cannot begin to imagine what he will do without his father. Perhaps it is not something I should imagine. Not now. Winter's mournful whistle at my window is frightening enough. In the quiet and early dark of winter, grim thoughts will set upon me like wild forest creatures. I am best keeping busy, though there is little to do with Lucy minding the house more than I had let Agatha take on.

Mr. Talbot has been a dear with Henry who enjoys visits to the stable. They give the horses apples and carrots, and he lets my boy place the shoes on their feet whilst Mr. Talbot holds it still, then takes on the more dangerous work of nailing it in place. Of course, the heft of the horseshoe is too much for Henry to do with a steady hand, so Mr. Talbot is most helpful and gentle with him. In the absence of James and of my own father, I believe he does fill a need in small spaces that mean a great deal to a young boy's mother.

FEBRUARY 8, 1856

Last night, I heard my boy cry out and ran across the landing to his room where he lay slumbering and quite alone. But of course, it was I who had been dreaming, waking in my own bed to the memory of that dream and my own cry. Too awake to sleep again, I sat in the chair beside my son's little bed, wondering as I moved toward it, what I would find. What did I expect? Warmth, perhaps. But the chair was cold, as if James could not possibly have warmed it with his presence. Or perhaps it was cold because of him? Yes, I confess that I did hope for a telling sign, even as I dreaded it. Yet, what would I do with such a sign but mourn my inability to touch him, to reach him?

Oh, it is folly! I will not allow such nuisance to crowd my thoughts, waking or asleep.

February 10, 1856

Dear Cousin,

My daughter Rose will be visiting with her husband and their daughter. They'll have attended the wedding of her sister-in-law in New London and it suits them to come a little farther on to see me.

Will you help me make arrangements for her family's lodgings? Do you

know of an inn or a woman who takes in boarders?
She's due within the week.

Yours,
Lucy

FEBRUARY 10, 1856

Lucy is a shy one, writing to me when we live under the same roof!

I cannot wait to meet Rose and her family. These frigid, darkening afternoons wear upon us all and three new faces will be welcome. Lucy is a grandmother and should enjoy the nearness of her grandchild! I told her I should not have it otherwise and so it is settled. Rose, Timothy, and their daughter, Hannah, will lodge here. Readying the house will occupy my mind.

February 11, 1856

Dear Mrs. Parsons,

Once again, I invite you to come to my home for tea. While I understand that the earliest weeks after your loss made it difficult for you to move about and that soon after you were beset by illness, I hope you will accept this invitation. My son, Thomas, asks after you and I can only reply that without a visit from you, my answers are pure conjecture.

I trust this finds you fit and I will look forward to a prompt and favorable reply.

Mrs. Virginia Pringle

FEBRUARY 12, 1856

Prompt reply indeed. I will have to summon all of the good will and courtesy Mother taught me, bundle it onto a saddlebag, and lay it at the old crow's feet.

As for Thomas, I am content to keep our transactions brief and civil. I simply do not wish to entertain any new friendships.

Fortunately, he does not expect me to pander to his mother's wishes, and has implied as much. I should not judge him harshly, except that I am uneasy even with our alliance, and his professed resistance to his mother's wishes.

He is tethered to his mother, his daily comings and goings closely watched. An odd thing; so different is he from his father who appears stalwart and jovial. Though a full-grown man, Thomas' affect is more that of a younger child, eager to be with other children, yet others are not drawn to him. My son was not particularly charmed during Thomas' visit with his mother. Still, he is a decent sort, if not the sort of man whose favor I would curry.

I know I cannot avoid her for very much longer. In my mind is every possible scheme to forestall accepting her invitation—knowing that the day I finally relent will protract into other afternoons if she has her way, if I bend easily to it. But if I continue to refuse, she will continue to pester me with requests. Perhaps there is no point in postponing this most unbearable task. I shall have to yield. Accepting his mother's invitation may satisfy her a while and then I can be left alone. I will do just that to win this result. Mother and Father have always held the Pringles in high regard, so it is really to my parents that I defer.

FEBRUARY 15, 1856

Since my dream that James was in the house, I awaken more often again in the middle of sleep. My body's timekeeping betrays me in this way; I would much rather sleep past dawn until the sun is risen enough to stir me, until the birds themselves crow and warble. Yet, the stubborn aspect of me that clings to the insufficient warmth of my half-empty bed presses me where I lie, imagining all that I cannot during the busiest waking hours of the day. I wonder such unanswerable things as, what must heaven be like? Has James a perch up there from which he can see all that was once his to enjoy? Does he know how vexed I am by that Pringle woman's interest in me?

Beloved, you miss far too much being so far from us. Your son's softness is yielding to the muscle of an active boy; the dimples in his knees disappearing so that they grow more square and solid; his elbows are pointier. What, my love, were your final thoughts when you were swallowed whole by the hungry, raging sea?

Tonight Lucy's daughter and her family arrived. It was near nine o'clock when they knocked at my door and Lucy bustled in from the kitchen where she had been making bread and preparing tomorrow's supper. She had already put biscuits in the oven to offer the travelers, and had mulled wine ready to pour. She had earlier said she wished to warm Timothy's unfriendly nature before he could bring it to my hearth.

Rose is several years older than I, near thirty, and bears an astonishing resemblance to her mother around the eyes and mouth, her forehead just as high and broad. She is slim and the flush in her cheeks seems a permanent and radiant part of her aspect. I hope we will be friendly cousins.

She arrived at my home with her child, Hannah, who is hardly eleven if she is that, standing just behind her, a timid blue eye all I could make of her peeking around the swell of Rose's skirt. Hannah seems small for her age, proportioned like a China doll.

Timothy came up behind them, satchels clutched in both hands, and loomed very large over his wife and young daughter. I had to tilt my head far back to catch a good look at him, not an easy task in the dim vestibule. He is tall and lean, his eyes a flinty grey, his mouth a grim line not much softened by his cordial greeting. I now feared for Lucy's ease in his presence, though she delivered as cold a gaze upon him in return before she seemed to remember herself.

She was earlier to the door than I, and did not offer so easily to move and let me help her family in, for she stood looking at her daughter and granddaughter as if seeing them for the first time. Indeed, after what she explained to me, it is quite as if it *were* the first, for Lucy's excitement, simmering beneath her corseted girth, was infectious. It became necessary to touch her shoulder and move her aside so that we might let them all through the chilly vestibule.

Timothy took the first opportunity to speak and, setting down the satchels inside the foyer, bowed and took my hand to kiss it. Lucy stepped behind me then, as if to retreat further into the house, but when I peered back at her, she was looking at Timothy as if to wish him away. Yes, I am sure she would have preferred the exclusive company of her daughter and grandchild.

Timothy gruffly addressed his mother-in-law, thanking her for making the arrangement with me for their comfort. Then he addressed me. "Mrs. Parsons, I am so sorry for the loss you have suffered. We do not mean to take advantage of your weakened state by staying here. You will not even hear us." At this, he sought his daughter forward with a commanding stare. She crept out from behind her mother and met his gaze full on before she turned to me, as if to say she understood what was expected of her and understood as well the penalty of her disregard should she reconsider.

"Yes, Mrs. Parsons, we will be quiet as…as…" Rose began before Hannah could speak.

"Ants," Hannah put in. This earned her a proper glare from her father that sewed her lips shut. But I had to laugh and held out a hand to the child who came to me as if instructed by the hours of propriety learned at her parents' knee. When a hostess beckons, you come, they would have tutored her.

Hannah wore a calico-print dress, all blue cornflowers and daisies that brightened the blue of her eyes. Her hair was one long pale red plait down her back, its color her father's. Lucy could hardly contain herself, hugging her granddaughter tightly to her bosom, holding her out with extended arms to beam at her, then clutching her close again. The wordlessness of the exchange was fitting, knowing Lucy as I do now. She does not spend words thriftlessly; her language seems to reside in her eyes.

She quietly passed the child to me and began to bustle Rose and Timothy up the stairs to one of my unused rooms at the rear of the house on the second floor, prattling as she does when agitated or excited, explaining to them all they might expect in my spacious home, such as when meals are served and how easy it is to get to town, how Mr. Talbot would show Timothy the smithy where he goes to hone his tools for the horses. While Lucy took the lead from the top of the stairs, she held her daughter's long-fingered hand from behind. Timothy followed along behind them with their belongings.

As we showed them their rooms, Hannah spoke again and I feared Timothy might take a paddle to her. He looks the type.

"Mother says you have a child. I do like small children," Hannah said to me. Her voice was barely a breath in the air before her.

"He turns three very soon," I told her. "Your grandmother has trimmed his curls and he has two new teeth, so he hardly looks like the baby he was even last month!"

The haircut had been Lucy's idea and I had fought it at the start, but she was daily vexed each time his longer locks dangled in his porridge. As she clipped away at his crown, I could not watch and so left it to my cousin. Lucy had charmed him through the entire ordeal, singing to him in a tremulous, sweet voice. When Henry had emerged from the kitchen and bounded into my arms, he looked years older. Silly thing that I am, I wept for his lost curls, later gathering them into a small box.

Hannah tapped my arm. "May I see him before I go to sleep? Where is he?" Her voice was so delicate I almost missed her words.

"Asleep."

"May I please see him?"

"Hannah, that is quite enough," came Timothy's warning, his voice deep. I feared he would be the one to waken my son.

Avoiding any punishment he might impose, I spirited Hannah out of the rearmost bedroom where her parents would sleep and back down the hall into Henry's room. We stood there in the dark and peered at him. He stirred, so I moved us away and back and took her to the bedroom I had chosen for her.

It is tucked away, down a stout hallway to the left and just behind the main one. Within the room there is a pretty little vanity table, a porthole window that overlooks the back garden, although there is nothing to draw the eye now, and another window that offers a view of the jetty and the houses spread around us, with laneways that lead toward town. I had placed some writing paper and a bottle of ink at the small desk that sat just under the window and on her bed is the coverlet Mother sewed for me when I was a girl near Hannah's age, white quilting, soft as clouds, threaded with blue and green ribbons at its edging.

Hannah's mouth formed a little "o" and she went immediately to the desk and then to the bed and the vanity and back to the desk where she peered out the window only to cast the reflection of her gladness back at the two of us, for the lamplight shone brightly on the glass. She turned to me, her eyes round.

"Thank you, Mrs. Parsons."

"Dear girl, I am your cousin. You must always call me Marianne," I told her. I hope she will.

February 18, 1856

I have written a newsy letter to Mother and Father, telling them of our visitors. This may not have been in Lucy's best interests, given what divided our families when Mother and Lucy were girls. I ought to have thought harder before giving them too detailed an account. Well, I did not speak of Timothy's demeanor. It is Hannah who inspired me to write, for though only a single day has passed, already she is a wonderful companion to Henry, more patient than I with his little messes left about the house as he goes exploring in cupboards and clears shelves of things I really must remove altogether until he is old enough to know better. Throughout the day, Hannah talked to him about his discoveries, and put everything back in order when he went down for his afternoon rest. I cannot imagine her doing any ill.

I have also written that I lately look to Lucy for company by the fire in the evenings and that I am grateful for her presence. She has proven herself steady. I feel as if I have known her all my life. In closing my note, I thanked Mother for her and hope her response will be favorable.

I have, as usual, raced ahead of myself, for I would prefer to start at the beginning of our Hannah's first day with us. Perhaps because they are traveling and have some time to rest, Hannah was up before her parents who slept until it was nearly time to think of preparing dinner, a meal I like to take at noon. When she awoke this morning, her first in my home, the girl knocked gently on my door.

I welcomed her and she drifted to my bed where there is a small settee on which she perched herself as prettily as if she wore a party dress rather than a nightgown. The embroidery on her gown is of enviable precision—I have hardly mastered a needle and thread without making a pincushion of my fingers, much to Mother's distaste—and I reached toward it, tracing the miniature rose petals and leaves twining around tiny trellises all up and down her pale green shift.

"My mother made it for me," she whispered. I had yet to hear her speak the way I have heard other children her age do. She may be so fearful of a scolding that she has fixed her voice at a permanent whisper. I leaned in, the better to hear her. "She's a seamstress."

"I cannot even pretend to darn a sock," I told her, laughing at my own ineptitude. Her smile was sweet, quite uncertain whether to laugh with me. She has been well brought up, I can see.

"I'll teach you, Mrs. Parsons, if you like, if you feel that learning from a child is the right thing." Again I laughed. This time, Hannah turned her eyes down.

"Oh, Hannah, I am not laughing at your expense, but mine, at how pitiful it is that I can hardly do what you and your mother and grandmother do quite naturally. Now I am reduced to mocking myself. I would be delighted if you would teach me to thread the needle without wounding every finger. You will have accomplished much if in your short visit you teach me even this small thing."

"Mrs. Parsons, I know you can do it better than you think." Then she corrected herself. "I mean to say, Marianne."

She seems a wise child. I wondered how a girl so young should seem so old.

"Do you think your boy will be up soon?" She asked, eager for a playmate. "I would very much like to see him."

So we tiptoed across the hall and stood over him. We watched him for a moment until he first began to stir. He does not waste his time with preambles to waking. No long stretches or cooing in his bed until I wander into him. Sensing us, he awakened and sat up straight. Hannah put a hand to his head and stroked his short curls. He rubbed his eyes and reached for me, his eyes on Hannah, this new face he did not recognize. He looked from me to the girl.

"Mama," came his gruff little voice, fresh from sleep. I lifted him up, but he has become such a bundle of muscle and growing boy that I do not carry him about these days, fearing a fall or an errant twist of my back.

"Darling, I have a new friend for you. This is Hannah."

"Hello, Henry," she said to him. I rather liked her use of his name, and I think he did too, for at once it seemed to give him a new ownership of it and he wriggled to be put down. She held out her hand and he took it. I believe he was grateful to have such a pleasant face to greet him after the daily sameness of Lucy and me. Hannah turned to me. "Does he like to be read stories? I'm a very good reader."

This could not have been greater news. What other surprises could Lucy, in her circumspect nature, have for me after a daughter and a precocious granddaughter?

"I have just the thing," I told her and dashed into his closet where there was a stack of books I have been keeping for him for when he is of age. Lately, reading to my son was more than I cared to undertake, ambition being in short supply. James seldom read to his son, but would often sit nearby and listen. I am sure he enjoyed the portrait of mother and son cozy with a book as much as I enjoyed the look of father and son in the garden.

When I turned around to hand one of the books to Hannah, the two were not there. I heard my son's voice in the hallway, words that often made little sense to me, but that I liked to answer as if I understood. It has always been this way between us. As his mother, I do not want him to think I cannot fathom the thoughts he chooses to share with me.

"Yes," Hannah said to him importantly by way of a response to something I doubt she fully understood. "I feel the same way. Shall we go downstairs?"

"Down-airs," came his enthusiastic reply. I watched them go and felt such a surge of relief and sorrow, for she could not be a better sister to him than if she were born to me instead of Rose. As it is, they are cousins, my son and her daughter, distant at that, and living too far apart to make their friendship anything more than bouts of childish longing for the next reunion. My heart has already begun to break for the two of them, anticipating a tearful goodbye, particularly for my son, smitten so young.

"Do you smell what I do?" I asked the children and they turned to me, their cheeks pressed together, for Hannah had knelt next to him, and he embraced her!

"Griddle cakes?" Hannah ventured.

"Gribble cape!" Henry parroted and she giggled.

So we three tiptoed down the hall, rounding the newel post and down the stairs to the kitchen where Lucy was busy making breakfast enough for a feast. I dare not imagine the passing of days that will bring an end to Lucy's cheer and Hannah's delightful presence.

FEBRUARY 19, 1856

Lucy has intercepted a letter at the door, delivered whilst the children and I were taking Jack for a stroll. I was glad to have received it.

> February 16, 1856
>
> Dear Mrs. Parsons,
>
> It's a singular life I lead these days. Work is in short supply for now, as vessel owners are less inclined to take on more men for the scant days they do go out.
>
> What fills your days as winter crawls on its belly, in no hurry to leave? I hope you have a stack of wood at the ready and that your Mr. Talbot is in aid of this need.
>
> Please write to me if you will. I won't be at this address much longer as I will be moving to another rooming house deeper inland. The proprietress of this one is selling out from under me as she moves further south to be closer to her daughter and grandchildren.
>
> > Yours with hopes for a future visit in your warm surroundings,
> >
> > Theodore E. Abel

I wonder if Mr. Abel supposes he might actually receive a letter from me. I confess that I do not mind his letters in the least. When I am caught unawares, my thoughts wander to him as well, to what he must be doing to stay warm. It has not been my habit to respond to each of them, for I cannot have him think my thoughts go to him as often as his to me. But tonight I will write him a brief note inquiring after his health, for even such a friendly inquiry cannot be misconstrued. Of course, I do not imagine it will.

As for Lucy and her family, I see that Timothy's very presence abrades her nerves, though he otherwise has every appearance of trying hard to please. Yes, it is difficult to escape his stern gaze, made more so by a muscle that leaps to attention at his jaw; perhaps he grinds his teeth.

Funny, too, and preferable to what I expected after her account of him, Timothy has been only polite toward Lucy, as if they were meeting for the first time. My cousin scoffs when his back is turned and has told me that he goes too far beyond normal courtesy to ingratiate himself. My observation is that he is in every obvious way responsible, and he is helpful with the child.

During a conversation we had over dinner after our first full day, he revealed that he is a blacksmith. In this, I think he is a fair provider; Rose, too, with her work as a seamstress, earns a wage. My single criticism of him is that when he perceives impertinence in Hannah and even Rose, he is harsher than I believe is necessary, for there is not a brazen note on the lips of his wife and daughter.

All in all, Lucy's complete disdain for her son-in-law mystifies me. At the sound of Timothy's voice, she stiffens. She has confided out of his hearing that she is relieved at least to see he loves his wife and daughter. Her main complaint, I grant, has been less about his temperament, more to do with his seeming lack of interest in Rose's visits to her mother.

Toward his wife, Rose, he is often amorous even when we are about. She cheerfully rebuffs his hand-holding, the little kisses on her cheek, the ardor of his gaze by turning her face or taking her hand away before he can take it from her. It is a game, perhaps; they behave as *129* newlyweds. I have wondered if Lucy suffers from a rash of jealousy that her daughter's affections have been all but appropriated by this capable man. I do see that it pains her to have less time with Rose than she would have hoped now that she is here with her family.

They have all settled in well and Lucy, a woman who prides herself on efficiency and speed in her tasks, has let things pile on a bit. Since I have not been comfortable with her as my maid in the first place and she has gladly done far more than I would enlist her to do, I do not mind taking things on myself. I would like her to enjoy her family. Of course, when she sees me wiping down the scullery, she takes the cloth from me and shoos me off.

There is a ghostly aspect to the spectacle of Rose and her family living under my roof, as if James had lived and I were beholding my own little clutch, years down the way, and with our son rather than a girl. The workings of this family have me spellbound.

FEBRUARY 20, 1856
This letter was placed upon my vanity table this afternoon.

February 18, 1856

Dearest Mrs. Parsons,

I've continued to busy myself with making inquiries after new employment and continue to have no luck. I know the reason for it, and here I confess to a crime I don't believe I have committed. Still, it sticks and follows.

No captain knowingly wants a Jonah on board.

There. It is said. I've been troubled, unsure how to tell you that this unfortunate reputation followed me all my months on board the Marianne Elizabeth even without my knowing it, that in fact it was a trick played on me at first and that we all laughed over it, my shipmates and your husband, too. On your husband's vessel my name was always mine, Theodore. Theo, they called me often, but when my back was turned, I heard some of the men whisper that I was a Jonah, that we were doomed, all of us doomed because of me. Thankfully, my captain was an educated man and did not fall victim to the belief in this.

I prefer to tell you with spoken words, to see your face as you hear my telling the story of such a name and how it came to me, but don't know when that will be my privilege. I've hoped all this time that you would dismiss the myth of it upon my telling it, but I know that you may now think me the cause of your grief. There's nothing I can do to change it or your thought on it, or to reverse the circumstances of the disaster itself.

Please think of me when you can and do so with charity.
Kindest regards,
Theodore Ethan Abel

I have shown the letter to Lucy.

"What can he mean?" Lucy asked me after she read it, her finely arched brows drawn together. "Can he mean that he thinks it was he brought her down?"

I clutched the letter in both hands, nearly crushing it. Lucy rescued it from my clenched fist.

"Wait!" She said, her voice too loud for her, startling me.

She need not have worried, for Rose and Timothy were in town taking tea and Hannah was in the parlor entertaining Henry. Jack has taken to curling up in a corner of the parlor settee where James used to sit reading. With all three young ones happily engaged, I had walked into the kitchen under the pretense of helping Lucy, one hand in the pocket of my skirt grasping the letter. Henry was so enthralled by the pictures Hannah was sketching for him that he did not see me leave his side or he would have come whimpering after me, much like tiny, incorrigible Jack. He, too, stayed in place for once.

"You must keep this, Cousin," she remonstrated, unfolding Mr. Abel's letter when I held it toward her. She smoothed out its creases with her small hands, round as a child's and lightly freckled. She pressed the paper to the sideboard and placed a hefty book atop it for good measure.

"I shall not keep it! It is as good as a farewell, and from an accursed man," I said. It is odd that I uttered these words before I had fully made up my mind. I wonder now if perhaps I am looking for a reason to end a particular longing for Mr. Abel's friendship, for his company. If so, this is as good as any reason, though I do not need one. Knowing what I do now, how can I welcome him back again? I wonder, too, if it is simply that I want to lay blame. After all, was James not snatched from me? A great wave or a swinging boom is as good as a murderer, and the force that compels either no less savage. Was he not robbed of his life, his wife and son, and even the silly little creature I cannot allow to sleep on the floor, for he is James' pup and will sleep nowhere but on James' pillow?

"You believe in such nonsense?" Lucy reproved me. "I didn't know your husband and still I think he would chide you for your doubt and harsh judgment." She shook her head with a vehemence that was less strange to me now in the wake of her response to my dismay over Mr. Abel remaining in my home during my illness. She is right, of course. I have my own education to back me up, to fend off such superstitious nonsense as ill omen. I can see James as Mr. Abel described him, laughing it all away, feeling invulnerable to any ill harbingers. He would have reproved me too, for he held no belief that the elements themselves are governed by anything but the pull of the earth and what the clouds themselves contained. The way a man lays a hatchet on deck, an act I have heard sailors believe can invite bad luck, meant nothing to my husband; Mr. Abel was a man he trusted. I shall follow James' example, heeding my good feeling toward this, his first mate.

Honoring James, I know it is best to write back to Mr. Abel and put his mind at ease. Yet I keep awake this night wondering if, by making such a gesture, and further soliciting his attention, I finally do dishonor to my good husband in a different way.

There in the kitchen with Lucy today, I held my hand out for the letter. The anxious lines at Lucy's eyes smoothed as her face relaxed. She placed her hands over mine and turned my hands up, restoring the letter to the warmth of my palm.

"You won't regret your decision," she said, and I wondered how she could possibly know just what it was, truly, I had come to conclude about Mr. Abel's unfortunate admission. Even now my mind roils as violently as any gale-whipped sea.

132   February 21, 1856

Soon after supper this evening, Rose and Timothy went for a stroll. The moonlight is generous in clear skies and it is warmer than most winter nights on our little piece of shoreline. Lucy urged them out the door, perhaps thinking I might need the quiet. They are very little trouble to have about, and Timothy says little to me or to Lucy. He spends a good bit of time walking about the village and has spent some hours with Mr. Talbot keeping the stables. I can see our guest is not a man who likes to be at rest for longer than sleep commands.

Knowing Lucy pines for time with Rose, it was a surprise to see her urging them out of doors for their own time alone. As the door closed behind them, she turned to me with a grin that suited my mischief-making son more than it did her.

"I have something to show you," she said. "Hannah and your boy will want to see it." Her eyes darted about and she crooked her finger at me as she strode toward the stairs and up. How could I refuse her?

I peeked in on the children. Hannah was reading to Henry in the parlor, their favorite pastime, and the fire warmed them enough to pinken their cheeks. The logs Timothy had toted in from the shed as effortlessly as if they were kindling crackled and hissed. I did not wish to intrude on such a perfect picture and turned to leave them in their sweet tableau.

It was then my son turned his head and caught my eye with his own pair of sleepy grey ones. He stretched fully in Hannah's lap, then slid off like a cat and raised his arms to be lifted.

"Your grandmother would like us to come to her room. She has something to show us," I said to Hannah. She looked just as sleepy and it was not even half-past six.

Obedient child that she is, she came along. Henry wriggled to be let down and slipped his little fist into Hannah's hand. It is a constant delight to see this tenderness between them, distant though they are in years.

When we reached the top, I heard Lucy call quietly from her bedroom. It is perfect space for Lucy, with a bed, a cutaway space for her to sit and sew, and still another space opposite her bed that contains a rocking chair once used by James' mother when she was in confinement with child. Here, I have seen Lucy rock quietly and look down at the bare forsythia bushes and frozen rhododendron hugging the sides of the house. The flowerbeds are dormant, and I have not asked Mr. Talbot to plant the usual hardy crop of geraniums. Lucy has told me she will plant it full in the spring with perennials that will cheer the place.

(My, but I do digress often as I record events! I do so in speech often as well and James would tease me about this regularly. Lucy has said she finds it a charming aspect of how I voice my thoughts.)

We three arrived at Lucy's bedroom's threshold to find her sitting in her rocking chair with a thick book in her lap, its pages poking out at corners, its cloth binding shriveled as if laid once upon a fire and then quickly snatched away in the moment before burning. Lucy's wink coaxed Hannah forward. Henry climbed into Lucy's lap, while I moved behind them and peered over her shoulder. She opened the book to the first page and Hannah took in a breath and held it. She let it go and breathed, "Mother."

"Yes, these are pictures of your mother, drawings of when she was very young." She watched her granddaughter's face.

And then, of course, came a question even I wanted to ask.

"Who painted this, and who painted the others, too?"

"Her father was the painter."

As Hannah's finger traced the coarse, aged brushstrokes of the watercolor and ink etchings of her mother, I marveled at such revelations. Lucy felt my eyes upon her and she chose to avert her own, a game we have nearly perfected of late when there is a question or a matter of some challenge between us, though of course we must ultimately confront it.

"My grandfather draws?" Hannah asked. "My mother hasn't spoken of him. Where is he?"

I was struck by how odd the question was, for if she did not know where her grandfather resided, it was clear he had never been spoken of to her. Lucy seemed unprepared for this but she did not reveal this in her reply.

"Oh, he's long since gone to his Maker. Your mother wouldn't likely speak of him, with hardly a memory but from her youngest years. He wasn't a father to her in the way your father is to you, dearie."

Hannah was visibly perplexed. How can Lucy have opened this subject in so casual a fashion?

"You see, he wasn't given…"

And here, Lucy trailed away as if she might stop speaking altogether, but Hannah pulled gently at her sleeve, coaxing her.

"Grandmother?"

"I have said far too much. He was her father, but not her guardian. This is all you need know for now, child."

The girl was disappointed, and I was relieved. Hannah is far too young to hear the facts of her mother's origins.

"This book is our secret, Hannah. I want you to see that your grandfather had a gift and someday I'll leave this record to you. By the looks of it you're more than half-grown so it won't be long!" Lucy gave the girl a small squeeze around her slender waist with a free arm.

"Why aren't I to show it to my mother and father?"

"Shall I tell you truly why?" Hannah nodded solemnly. "It's my own fault and to have you keep a secret because of my foolishness is undeserved. Your grandfather died before your mother grew to be a woman. He didn't even know her, didn't ever hold her to his cheek."

My own look of dismay must have mirrored the same in Hannah's stricken eyes. "Then how could he have made these drawings of her?" she asked.

"He wasn't permitted near your mother after she was born. It was my own father's decree. Your grandfather was a very poor man, an artist as you can see in these pages, but unskilled to do much else, and uneducated. He was a student of the world, Hannah, and as gifted in drawing as with a paint-brush. I'll say no more, but while you're here and any other time you come to visit, you may look in the pages of this book as often as you wish." And then she whispered this last in her ear, though I could hear her well enough. "I hope you'll come again before you're too big a girl to sit on my lap." Too lucky for Lucy, her granddaughter did not question her further about her mother's origins. I imagine she itched to do so, and I, too, felt my curiosity swell. Lucy is a treasure chest of mysteries, it would seem.

She removed her granddaughter from her broad lap and stood, smoothing out her skirt and hugging her own plump middle. I noticed a small shiver travel through her shoulders. She turned to leave and I stood still behind the rocker as Hannah took her own seat there and opened the book to begin her acquaintance with her grandfather. I have learned by looking closely at the signature of each piece of art, that his name was Matthew Hennessey. And, on the very first page, before the very first picture of Rose, is a line in this man's uneven hand that reads, "For my child, the gerl I know in my hart even thow not in lyfe." There are, too, drawings here and there of Lucy as a young lady, though her face is less distinct than Rose's in the pictures that Matthew Hennessey created of the two together.

Hannah sat silent, turning pages until Henry reached down from me toward the fragile bundle of pages, barely held together with twine, and said, "My book!"

"Indeed, it is a book," I told him quietly, moving back a step and tickling his ear with the breath of my voice so that he brushed me away, wriggling to free himself. I had to put him down, but my words held warning. "And it is Hannah's book. You have many books, too."

"No! Me! Dat book!"

He fairly leapt toward it, knocking it halfway down the other side of Hannah's lap, but she caught it in its descent and clutched it to her.

"Henry, I will read you a story. I promise you." And she looked up at me, beseeching.

"Come, my little reader," I said and scooped him up, kissing his sweet, soft belly. "We shall go in search of the best book for Hannah to read to you." And we left the room where Hannah sat peering at the pages, turning each one as slowly as if she might sit there a year. My son was giggling past his distraction as I continued to enjoy his belly.

February 22, 1856

136

Today was the last for Lucy to spend with her family and I feel I must be out of the way, yet they have become part of my household in this very brief time. True, the time I spend with them amounts more to observation than shared occasions, except when we sit around the table or when I can charm the young ones outside on milder afternoons. They seem content to play in either of their bedrooms near the window where they are bathed in afternoon warmth, or in the parlor where Mr. Talbot may have built a fire in the hearth. Jack, true to his loyal nature, follows them everywhere and Hannah often simply totes him under her arm where he is quite content, his little legs dangling under a portly middle. Lucy has been feeding him leavings from supper and I will have to ask her to shrink her portions or he will be waking me through the night to be let out.

Hannah has taught Henry better than I how to stroke his back and muzzle without pulling at his wiry fur. Of course, there are moments when the impish boy seizes the pup's tail and Jack lets out a yelp and flees to safer havens, such as under my skirt or beneath the dining room china cupboard.

It has been just the right kind of visit. Rose, Timothy and Hannah have made themselves perfectly at home here and without trouble. I have yet to see anything truly vexing pass between Lucy and Timothy, yet there is little interaction between them other than the passing niceties of a "good day" and a "how was your breakfast." I suppose Lucy is being prudent here, for if her criticism of Timothy is to be believed—and I am wont to believe everything Lucy tells me even as I reserve my harshest judgment about Timothy—remaining detached is the best thing for her.

The wind tonight is shrill at my windows, rattling them in their panes, and the fire Timothy had built with such care and a bounty of the silver maple logs I favor died to embers long before I ventured up to bed. Still, I kept my feet propped toward it and drew what warmth I could from the faint glow before folding the blanket Mother and Father sent last week and retiring. (The note Mother clipped to the blanket read, *"Darling Daughter, Keep yourselves warm and comfortable and think of us as you do."* It is a most affectionate note for her. The blanket is a richly woven blue and gold angora to which the lavender scent of my childhood home clings from little sachets Mother sews and places in the trunks in which she stores things out of season.)

I knew that sleep would visit me if I were quick getting up to my room.

It was just as I stepped on the final stair at the top post of the second landing, the weakest plank in the floor betraying me, that I heard Rose's quiet laughter and stopped there.

"Hush, Tim! She will hear everything!"

"No, no, lovely, not if she is trying not to hear."

Such carefully chosen words from a man who does not know me! How must I appear to him? It sent a smarting reminder of my birthday picnic in the park when James and I embraced in sight of Mrs. Pringle and, to me, how he ridiculed her for what he presumed was her ignorance of romantic love.

I took myself quickly to my own room and met my pillow, breathing deep in the hope of any lingering trace of my husband, wishing for him until my eyes closed upon wet cheeks.

FEBRUARY 23, 1856

They have left and Lucy has spent the day in her room, refusing tea, refusing to come out of her room the entire day.

Henry is beyond confusion over this turn in Lucy's mood and has been asking after Hannah, peeking around corners as if she were hiding in her usual places when they played. I have had to take him away from Lucy's door often as he pounds it with his solid little fists. "Looshee! Looshee!" He calls and she refuses to answer. It is quite a melancholy household.

I know her heart is cracked in two over her family's leave taking. It cannot be easy or even tolerable. Yet, I did implore her, once Henry had gone to his nap, to let me in. I hoped to comfort her as she has done for me. Hers has been an entirely practical approach that can wrench me from darker days; I do not know how I can allay her suffering other than to let time do its work, as it will for me. Perhaps in the meantime she will let me sit with her, for our misery is not so terribly different. We long for those we love, but whom we cannot have in our midst.

At last, well into the evening after Henry had been up, played the rest of the afternoon, taken supper with me, and already been to bed for an hour, Lucy bade me come in. She opened her door and waved me wordlessly to her sewing chair in the alcove.

Her usually pink cheeks were pale. Her eyes, always clear and bright, were a darker shade of blue, and red around their rims. I wondered, as I sat beside her at the edge of her bed, if I ought to summon Dr. Wainright for a tonic.

"I don't know if I shall see my granddaughter again before she's fully a woman. It may sound foolish to you, that I'd think Rose would keep the child from me for so long, but she's done so until now. The last time I saw that lovely girl she was but seven years and did not recognize me then because the last visit before that had been when she was five years. The time before that still, when she was three years old, just a mite older than your son. Cousin, what reason can Rose have to keep that child from me? I did not do this with her. I shared her with my mother, each and every dawning day."

I began to answer, to offer some logical reason, though it was not likely I could summon anything, knowing little of Lucy's history as a young mother. Then Lucy answered herself and her conclusion seemed long considered. Her voice, too, rasped across each word.

"It's Timothy. That man keeps his daughter from me because he does not approve of me, or of the way Rose came into the world. He'd have it that we see none of each other and that he be their sole guide. I'm grateful for the little bit of fight Rose must have in her to have convinced him of this visit."

"But how can he presume?"

"He can presume mightily because he comes from a family of judges. They're not judges of the court or of the ministry. But they have long stood in judgment of me, oh yes! I've had to beg Rose to work on Timothy for this last visit and I'm not above begging for another before summer. Rose would have me thinking that she's the one to hold herself back, not wanting me to lower my regard for Timothy, but he has made clear to her that his for me is very low indeed. No, if she feels shame about her birth, it wasn't me taught her that."

I could say nothing. Her tirade was unaccustomed and I feared she might send me out if I were to voice my thoughts. She might have forgotten I was nearby; I had moved nearer to her side, perching the edge of her bed, and she stared hard ahead, past me.

And in the next instant, she fully invited me into those miserable eyes of hers. "I should have been forthright with you from the beginning of my stay. But I took you for an innocent, much like I was, and I did not want you to think ill of me for my foolishness as a young woman. I've never been a lady like your mother. Mine married less well. You, Cousin, are quite a lady."

I gathered her to me, felt her stiff back yield until she folded her shoulders in upon themselves and began to quiver with her weeping. "Lucy, my dear, dear cousin and friend, you have only to trust me from this day forward. I will not betray that trust. And I will remind you to send weekly letters to invite your family to stay here, so that after a little while, Timothy must give up his obstinacy and send his wife and daughter even if he chooses to stay behind with his anvil."

Here she laughed and pulled away from me, wiping at her glistening face with a kerchief she had clutched and wrung the entire time we sat together.

"Anvil indeed," she chuckled through drying tears. And we both began to laugh heartily enough that it woke my son.

FEBRUARY 25, 1856

Why can dreams not be hand-picked like wildflowers or penny candy? Last night an unsettling one woke me to the sound of my own voice. In my sleep Mr. Abel appeared as if from across a great distance, further even than the Gloucester rooming house where he last wrote that he lives. His lips moved and no words escaped from them. He seemed to be saying, *forgive me* and when I opened my eyes this morning, the words on my lips were *come back*.

FEBRUARY 27, 1856

It has happened and I have allowed it. We went to visit with the Pringles yesterday, without the treat I had thought to bring, for I am simply not up to indulging her. I had been too busy to bake with Lucy's family visiting and could not bear to burden my cousin with such things. The visit was a deed I could not put off any longer, for soon after the one note came another that sat under a stone on my front step. It read simply, *"I look forward to your company tomorrow. T. Pringle."* His was not the usual perfect cursive, but somewhat wayward, the tails of letters wandering away from the letters themselves. How disquieting is the thought that Thomas may indeed be pining for me after he had earlier disavowed his own mother's intentions! Could he be so ill-mannered as to make his intention a half-year after I am widowed, duplicitous enough to have lied to me when he professed to want only my friendship? He seemed perfectly content to masquerade a friendship to placate his mother, and want nothing more. Of course, Mother would happily have me consorting with the Pringles at every opportunity; her urgings resound even from Newburyport.

Yet, it is strange that Thomas was never presented to me as a suitor, for he does not strike me as entirely unpleasant company for part of an afternoon. There must be a young lady in the Commonwealth who would be charmed by his odd brand of youthful energy.

So, today, I put on my best dutiful daughter and neighbor face and bundled my son into his wool coat, hat, mittens and scarf. Only his grey eyes peered out at me from the brown wool; eyes so filled with expectancy that, quite without meaning to, I felt a certain hope well in my own chest that this outing might prove pleasurable, for we had not paid anyone a visit for such a long time. In going, I felt it was doing Lucy a good turn, for she could use the quiet to rest. I handed her a novel and hope she will read it. She was set to refuse it, saying she reads very slowly. This can aid her, too, for perhaps it will make her sleepy to labor through the pages. If I were the one fortunate enough to stay home, I would devote myself to the entertainment of a good read for the afternoon and evening.

When we reached the Pringles' home, I drew back before the walkway leading to their imposing front door, a great entryway with granite pillars on either side. It made my own front door look more like the threshold to a tiny cottage. The Pringle home sits back on a rise off School Street that overlooks the lower lying main roads of Mount Pleasant and Main Streets where daily commerce strolls back and forth. It is as big as two houses the size of my own.

I set Henry down, having scooped him into my arms on the way along the cobbled path, where Mr. Talbot let us off. Holding my son shielded me momentarily against the house's looming presence and the inhabitants within.

The moment I set him on his sturdy feet, he scrambled over to a great, elegant vessel filled with chrysanthemums and began to pluck them, one at a time, from their stalks.

"Henry!" I scolded. My son turned a bewildered gaze my way, as if to say, "Mama, these are flowers and I must pick them!"

"These are not our flowers, Henry," I admonished him, but more mildly. He stopped his picking in that instant, but presented me the one he did pull from its pot and my irritation dissolved.

I had not knocked, yet the door opened. It was Mary, of course, and she greeted me with a small, guarded smile, as if she did not know me quite as well as she had when she was in her previous employ. Who had taken her sweet grin away? Even when she delivered notes to me from Mrs. Pringle, she seemed ill-at-ease. She took one long look at my son and then at me, turned around and, with scarcely a crook of her finger, bade us follow her into the house. I could see she had been hard schooled by her employer. We followed.

The polished wood along the corridor gleamed under the weak light of wall sconces. Though it was daylight, I could not see much beyond the girl who strode just ahead of me to a small room where she told us to please sit and then took our over-things.

"Mr. Pringle, Mrs. Pringle, and Master Thomas will be in presently, Mrs. Parsons. They are expecting you." Her stiff manner was decidedly wrong for one so young, the words rehearsed. If she had been raised in another sort of household, she would be preening for tea socials and dances at her age. Or if Emily were still in town, and she has ceased writing to me in recent months, this girl would be more relaxed in keeping with her employer's ways. She is eighteen, and acts like an old, seasoned servant.

My musings about Mary are nonsense, a waste of time. I do not know why it is I paint such pictures in my head of people I do not know, will never know, truly. It is a habit of fancy I have had since girlhood and for which Mother often chided me while Father would wink and encourage me to go further. He did enjoy my imagination.

I tried quietly to move Mary's eyes to my face, but she let her gaze remain fixed on the cameo at my throat. It had been a gift from James when we were to be wed; a miniature painting of a meadow, with a child sitting under a lone linden tree, reading. It was the linden in this tiny picture that caught James' eye and moved him to choose the plot of land on which he built our home in 1850, the year we were wed.

After Mary left, I turned my son to me and whispered, "Well, I should think we are expected!"

"Mama, I want to see Looshee!" was his reply. I told him we would leave after we had some cake, his favorite treat in the afternoon, and he was again distracted for the moment.

The Pringles' house less resembles a home than a museum. Henry looked around the small room in which we sat awaiting our hosts, and I too made my appraisal. Its contents were a testament to wealth I have never known, though I was born to some comfort. Without needing to stand and peer closely, I spied crystal decanters and ornate silver, gold inlay in many of the wood surfaces, paintings of men with sober expressions and women whose faint smiles betrayed sadness, even in the lap of such opulence as that which surrounded us in the Pringle household. I noticed there were no flowers or bright colors, not even in the drapery or wall covering. It was, by my measure, a cheerless room.

And then I heard a rustling. My head turned to see a figure obscured in shadow as he neared the room. His voice preceded him and I did not immediately recognize the source.

"What a young man he is becoming! You have done well by him these fatherless months." Of course, it was Thomas. He spoke like his mother and I was unprepared for the assault of the same haughty tone so that even the praise he offered left me hollow of the appreciation I know would have been proper to offer in return. When he was in my home, he had been quite reserved. The contrast was at once striking and off-putting.

I stood and smoothed my dress, black taffeta but for a lavender sash tied at the waist. I chose it to enliven what promised to be a gloomy day, but in that home it felt like too loud a comment in defiance of my mourning. I knew as I chose it that it is not mourning I defy; it is Virginia Pringle, but my bravery remained in my home. Still, having made the error, I held myself proudly as Mother taught me, for while she might not approve of my blaze of color today, she would reason that since it was done, I ought not to wear it with regret.

Thomas took my hand and placed his moist lips to the back of it. When he turned his attention to my son, I pressed that hand against my skirt to wipe his drying kiss away. His attention returned to me in an instant, for Henry had hidden behind me.

"Mrs. Parsons, you look well indeed. I worried that it might be too soon after your illness for you to come to visit. I told Mother, in fact, and she disagreed, calling you a hardy girl."

This surprised me and I hope Thomas did not see my eyes grow at the compliment, unaccustomed as I was to its source. I have never sought her endorsement.

"I have had time to rest, Mr. Pringle, and I thank your mother for her encouragement. I was raised not to languish if I was fit enough to walk."

"Your son is the image of you, with your kind smile," Thomas continued, unfurling his own ribbon of praises, though the fact that my son had yet to smile at anything but my mention of cake—and this before Thomas' arrival—seemed to escape our host's attention. I took Thomas for less than astute, perhaps even approaching false, for when my son smiles, he is not the image of me, but of his father in every way. It is what everyone sees. Had Thomas not seen James up close?

"Mrs. Parsons." He cleared his throat, clasping his hands behind him. A pale red forelock leapt to attention on his head and he seemed to be waging a quiet battle over whether to press it back into place or let it rest sprung halfway up. In the end, he puffed a bit of air upward and it moved aside. "I am aware that we have not become well-acquainted over the years since you came to Rockport from Newburyport. I did have the greatest respect for your late husband and I am sorry for your tragic loss." He spoke the words as if reading them from a card, his inflection somewhat more pronounced than seemed natural. "I hope to close this distance between us. I hope," he coughed lightly into his hand. "I hope you will call me Thomas and that you will allow me to call you Marianne." I wanted to warm toward him for his effort, especially since he had made a point during his visit to me of rejecting his mother's wish to court me. Could we not then be friends after all? Yet, with his phrasing and this suggestion of using our given names, my mind quickly turned away from anything like the urge to thank him. I felt decidedly put off in a way I had not experienced when Mr. Abel had asked me to use his given name without expectation of using mine. I knew this reaction to be unfair to Thomas, but could not prevent it.

For, how could I not cringe at this, how it bespoke a brazen intention, so plain in his mother's frequent entreaties and her foisting of her son's company upon me? His earlier protestation of that very same intention now rang as insincere.

"Mr. Pringle." He frowned at my address.

"Thomas," I corrected. "Yes, I will use your name, but I do ask that you do not presume…" And I could not finish my request.

"In my home, no one presumes," boomed his father from around the corner. Reginald Pringle's hearing was acute indeed and his voice echoed along the corridor. Thomas unclasped his hands and something in his manner changed, seemed to retreat as his father entered the room and came toward us.

I had seen Reginald Pringle from afar, and when I was younger had occasion to meet him in the street whenever my parents brought me to Rockport to visit with the Parsons or other families. However, here in front of me he was a large man. His girth was impressive, although his face was slim and pleasantly ruddy, his legs long, his hands so solid they swallowed my two. My son peered up at our elder host, his own eyes larger with wonder.

"Well now, what a tiny gentleman we have here. I have not seen you since you were puckered in the mouth," Mr. Pringle boomed and I realized, too late, that he referred to a baby suckling at his mother's breast, something I did only in the privacy of my bedroom but that he would not have known, assuming I would take a wet nurse. Mother had encouraged, even insisted upon it, and I had refused. Of course, Mr. Pringle was not present while I had fed my infant, but it revealed a playful nature in him I could not imagine was tolerated by his wife. I checked myself against blushing by bringing my boy to me and bowing my head into his. Mr. Pringle quieted, sensing my discomfort, and said, "Yes, he has grown well. Mrs. Pringle is just dressing from her rest. When she joins us, she will be restored to herself by the young lad's presence."

I did not know what he meant by referring to his wife as needing in some way to be restored, but I did like him immediately. I decided his hint at my keeping my son at my breast was simply part of a peculiar, candid nature in him. His friendliness was undisguised. He wore a smile for its own sake and it was infectious. It was then Henry grew a smile of his own, the first since we had approached the house and he had spied the flowers.

Even as I write these thoughts, I realize I have been unfair to Thomas, for he bore a friendly demeanor toward me. Perhaps familiarity with his affect will make me more accepting of his companionship. Yes, perhaps I can grow accustomed to this part of his nature and accept it as I have accepted his father's easy disposition.

Now, I must return to my account of the afternoon, or I will lose my thoughts. I feel moved to share it in great detail as well as I can recall.

Mr. Pringle bade us follow him.

"Shall we move out to the terrace? It is closed in, and there is generous sun there in midday. I have managed admirably to keep some things alive in this room."

Yes, there were small, thriving fruit trees in large pots, some of them dripping with tiny orange globes that I recognized as the one that sits on my kitchen's west facing sill drinking up the light. There were others, more tree-like, with darker, misshapen fruit. A sharp sweetness clung to the air.

Mr. Pringle explained its origin to me. "These are kumquats and figs," he said, his fingers reaching for each fruit, touching them gently with his large hands. "They grow in eastern climes, and I had the pleasure last year of visiting the Far East. I may be the only American owner of such a strange fruit. You can see this corner of paradise in such a dark house works well for them. They hardly complain except to wither a little when the air becomes too dry for their delicate nature. Would you like one? Thomas, please pick one of each for Mrs. Parsons and her son." I could not have refused even if I wanted to.

As Thomas moved toward the fruit, Virginia Pringle herself entered. Bright sunlight splashed itself without regard all over her dark clothing, bringing out the pattern of the red and black print in her wool dress and the silver in her hair pale red hair, a shade she has passed on to her son.

In that moment she entered, I reconciled her with her image in one of the many paintings I had spotted hanging in a room we had passed on the way to the terrace. It was a far younger Mrs. Pringle, perhaps even before she was wed. I hoped to go and sneak another look before the afternoon was over. In that painting was a woman whose gaze was lighter, though still not enjoying the youth that was hers.

As the much older woman before me, I thought she looked more favorable in this light, surrounded by greenery and by her belongings, than in harsh daylight out of doors. She came toward me and took my hands in hers. Her palms were warm, a surprise.

"I am glad to finally have you," she said, her words an odd combination that implied both gratitude and possession. "I have asked Mary to bring our tea here to the terrace."

Mrs. Pringle sat with her back to the sun, patting the seat beside her. Her gesture conveyed an insistence I was not in a position to refuse so that I took my place there. I beckoned my son to my lap, but he would have none of that. He insisted upon getting a closer look at Mr. Pringle and was quickly rewarded. Our host lifted him up with a jolly pretense of effort and put him on his knee so that they faced one another.

Mary scurried into the room pushing a tea cart ahead of her. On the table she placed perfect little sandwiches, some with deviled eggs, ham or cucumber in between their slender crusts, and tea.

She began by pouring tea for me into a delicate primrose-patterned cup and did so with my hosts as well. Looking more closely at the girl, I could see a furrow in her forehead, as if she were pained; her earlier command was gone. Mrs. Pringle eyed her closely and the girl did not meet her gaze. "Come, Mary. Be quick about it," her employer said in a voice I imagine she used only for her household help, though it was barely a notch below her usual. And then she turned to me.

"Mrs. Parsons. You have had a difficult time and yet you look even more flushed with youth than I could expect. You are sleeping well?"

"As well as winter will allow," I told her. There was nothing behind our words. She knew I had banished Mr. Abel. She had, the following day, sent me a short note I can hardly bring myself to record (and had quite deliberately put it out of mind until just now) in which she commended me for the deed. Were he still spending time in my home, she might be fishing for such an admission on my part, words or not, that a man was responsible for my healthy looks, but she gave nothing of herself away. There was nothing to give. In fact, just the other day, Lucy had remarked with pleasure, that the shadows beneath my eyes were gone.

"Having my cousin near is indeed a comfort," I said, wanting them to know how well I had come to need and adore Lucy.

With great interest, we all watched my son play with Mr. Pringle's thick, grizzled beard. I felt Thomas watching me. He had kept quiet since his father came upon us and I was glad for it, though I felt sorry that he seemed to lose something of his earlier confidence in the company of this great-sized man.

"Yes, your Mother and Father did well to send her. I trust she enjoyed her visit with her family?"

"Very much," was all I could summon, for I did not wish to relate even one moment of the experience. She and Mother must surely speak of my household's visitors and this displeases me. I hope Mother is more diplomatic than to spread what amounts to idle gossip to a woman like Virginia Pringle. Is it possible that the two women are not so very different? It chills me to consider this.

148

"I understand her granddaughter is quite precocious," my hostess persisted. This was my answer to whether they spoke of Lucy's family. It is one thing for me to write of the innocence of the visit to the woman who sent Lucy to me, yet quite another to have her parade my accounts. I could only confirm and extol, for I did not wish to enter into other territory. No words regarding Lucy's anguish would pass my quill when writing to Mother or from my lips in the Pringle household.

"Hannah has a quiet way about her, yes. In some ways, she is wise beyond her years, yet in all the ways that count she is still a child. She was a marvelous playmate for my son. Their parting was tearful for them both."

Mrs. Pringle clucked her tongue perhaps in sympathy and turned to her husband who was chortling behind his beard as Henry tickled his chin, his small, deft fingers creeping toward the kindly man's neck.

Mr. Pringle then looked up at me and said, as if he were deaf to any disapproval his wife has expressed about Mr. Abel, "I was in Gloucester Tuesday last doing some business at the post office and chanced to meet a Theodore Abel who asked if I knew of you. I replied that I most certainly do know of your fine family, that I had begun to work with your excellent husband before the tragedy. I knew him to have been associated with your husband and was glad at last to meet the man. He asked to be remembered to you, Mrs. Parsons. He is a remarkable man if he survived that terrible gale that cost you so much, but I believe he was particularly melancholy. When I inquired, he explained that he has been unable to find suitable employment, feeling deprived of sleep and of the companionship of sailors he once knew. I told him I recalled the account of his survival in the *Gloucester Telegraph*. As a matter of fact," Mr. Pringle fairly twinkled and I can feel now the same blush that overwhelmed me at his next words. "He confided to me that his despondency was owed in part to being unable to see his new friend, the small Mr. Parsons, was the way he put it, I believe."

I mustered a smile and nodded in thanks as his wife stiffened beside me. Mr. Pringle returned his attentions to my son. I do believe now that he is ignorant of his wife's contempt for Mr. Abel and that he meant to convey kindly the greeting sent to me as well as his respect for the heroism of Mr. Abel's survival. I believe, too, that Mr. Abel recalled the day he was so coldly greeted by Mrs. Pringle only last autumn when he and I walked the beach with Henry and wee Jack, and that he quickly understood Mr. Pringle to have received him differently than his wife had done. I am glad he acted to convey his wishes to me, particularly in view of the tirade that followed.

For, when she was quite sure her husband had finished his speech, my hostess let her true feelings be known to her husband. "Well, I cannot begin to think of an individual less worthy of your attention or company, Mrs. Parsons. You have been brought up to understand that there are some people with whom we must not consort. I applaud you for your impeccable judgment in forbidding him to cross your threshold." I could not help singling out the "we" from her lecture. She was very much mistaken in including me in her society.

It was then, as my son sat contentedly against the soft belly of our host and Thomas sat somewhat huddled into himself, with one knee tapping, that I knew I could not brook this woman's ill-considered appraisal of Mr. Abel any longer.

"Mrs. Pringle," I began, rising from my seat beside her and turning to face her. "Please allow me to correct you. Mr. Abel, a man whom you insist upon eyeing as a villain, is nothing but good. He came to me in his own hour of need, mindful only of my sorrow, and alone in the world. He became a friend to me, to my son, and to my cousin as he aided her during my brief illness. It was a fever which, if it struck you, I daresay it might knock something upright in your unjust conviction of Mr. Abel." Here Virginia Pringle drew in a breath, rose abruptly from her chair and stood her ground, seeming taller. Regrettably, it was I who took a step back.

But I was not finished. "I will ask that you refrain from belittling this man, a stranger it is true, but a man who means no ill and requires a livelihood to build himself up respectably after losing everything." Here I said nothing of his being haunted with the name Jonah and its effect on his pursuit of work. "I ask only this of you and no more. I thank you and you, Mr. Pringle, and Thomas, and offer my apology for having to take my leave before we have finished."

I took my boy from Mr. Pringle's lap and was met with some struggle! Yes, Henry had, without my noticing, tucked himself in there comfortably. He set his mouth firmly, tightened his body, and would not move. Mercifully, Mr. Pringle stood and eased the boy down, reassuring him that they would meet again. Kind as he is, I fear I have offended him with my own tirade, for I certainly left his wife slack-jawed and befuddled as I left.

Their son hurried after us to retrieve our coats from Mary. He entreated us to stay on. Of course, I demurred, suddenly terribly weary.

"I am afraid I have done too much damage, Thomas."

The look on his face bespoke the opposite. I believe now that he may come to call quite free of his mother's determined will.

February 27, 1856

Dear Mrs. Parsons,

I hope you will forgive my wife. She has not yet learned that not all of her intuition is laudable, that not everything over which she holds a conviction is something to be shared in gentle company. I did not at first understand why you spoke so angrily until my wife set me straight, explaining her understanding of Mr. Abel's visits to your home, that you and he had formed an acquaintance she feared would grow to friendship, and that she wholly disapproves of this. It is true that we are not your parents and that you are a grown woman. Yet, while I do not condemn such an alliance myself as that which has formed between you and Mr. Abel, I do caution you not to nurture it.

First and foremost, you are a lady of some means and education; means left you by your husband in the event of his untimely death, and provided you by your parents in the form of allowance. Yes, parents do have occasion to converse about their children and while I do not wish to bother or offend you, it has been expressed by your parents that we take some measure of care where you are concerned, ask after you now and again, and invite you to tea or supper if you will come.

Secondly, though not less worthy of your consideration, is that the younger of our society looks to its elders to set the example. If you are seen consorting intimately with a man within your period of mourning, there will be gossip and perhaps you will be shunned. (Of course, I will always go out of my way to greet and be pleasant toward you. Knowing your family as I do, I would not follow such scornful suit even if my wife sets the precedent for it.)

Finally, I must add that, although I do not sanction Mr. Abel's returning to your home any time soon to keep private company with you, meeting him in Gloucester I did feel that he was a good sort, a man who took care, a man I would be happy to call a friend were he to come this way again. I did not say it the other day during your regrettably brief visit, but on the afternoon in Gloucester that I saw him, I came away feeling that it would be a pity not to be able to help in some way and so I took the liberty of making arrangements to aid Mr. Abel in finding suitable employment.

Thank you for coming to visit our home, for doing what you visibly could to tolerate my wife's disposition. I do hope you will come again. Your son is a delight, after his mother.

Kindest regards,
Reginald Pringle

MARCH 4, 1856

Even as my letter to Mother and Father was newsy, I decided to adopt a contrite, confessional tone in the account of my tirade at the Pringles, an episode that still leaves me shaken as much from the memory of my own indignation as that it has brought home a feeling about Mr. Abel that I fear may have been too transparent to my hosts, specifically to the lady of the house. I am not prepared to make apology to Virginia Pringle, so perhaps this conveyance to Mother will do well enough, for the two women clearly write to one another.

In my letter, I recounted her friend's comments about my private home life that sparked my anger. Though it is already done, I do not relish the admission of my behavior to Mother, but I had rather be the one to deliver it than to have her learn from the Pringle woman. I inquired as well whether she had mentioned to Virginia Pringle Lucy's circumstances as a young woman and implored her to say as little on the matter as possible, for Lucy is a fine woman despite earlier mistakes. And how can Rose be called a mistake, or Hannah by association? To think it is to cast a shroud of regret upon their very lives.

Mother's reply arrived just yesterday and was rather tart, which did not surprise me. She confirmed my supposition that she has been corresponding with Virginia Pringle more often since James' death, informing her of the comings and goings in my home—based upon my accounts to her!—just as Mrs. Pringle has informed her, surely, that Mr. Abel visited me. Mother wrote that she has no regret about sharing details of Lucy's life, for Lucy is my companion and therefore directly relates to concerns about me, though why she did not consider such things before sending for Lucy is quite beyond my reckoning. As if she would read my mind, for I did not include that question, she even had the temerity to suggest that perhaps Lucy was not such a wise choice after all if her actions were drawing criticism from such a prominent family.

I replied to her letter this morning, stating that not only is Lucy a fine companion and helpmate, she has come to be as dear a friend as any and exercises great care in my household. She does not possess a mean or duplicitous spirit and can iron expertly, a task on which she insists (I know Mother would be pleased with this). Finally, I wrote to Mother that whatever Lucy's imprudence as a girl, she is the mother of a fine woman and grandmother to a wonderful girl, both of sterling character doubtless inherited from her.

All of this correspondence has left me rather winded and I must finally sleep.

MARCH 5, 1856

Mr. Abel lives in Rockport now. Mr. Pringle has secured him a place in his very own granite quarry after he too found there was little progress to be made in the fisheries. I believe he said he would like to see this young man gain a fresh start. He made candid mention of the fact that he was not in the habit of confiding to his wife all of the men he hired and that this fell well into that category. Mr. Pringle had told Mr. Abel, I am sure with great diplomacy, that Mrs. Pringle would not have taken kindly to it.

I have written to Mr. Abel and invited him to join us for tea this week, but cautioned that he must curtail his visits from this point, which I hope he will understand as my care with Virginia Pringle's too careful vigil over all that I do, no matter how ordinary. Lucy's presence will reassure everyone, of this, I am fairly confident. She seems to have weathered any hints of disapproval well enough and is not as faint of heart as I imagine anyone thinks her at first glance.

Even as I write vaguely of decorum to Mr. Abel, I cannot help the flood of relief that comes with knowing he is situated, that he has a roof of his own, however modest. I will chance to write it here that I am glad he has returned, for I did worry for his welfare. When he comes to us, I shall offer him a small picture I painted of Henry when the boy was sleeping one afternoon, curled upon the hearthrug. It is very oddly proportioned, though my son's features are true enough.

March 5, 1856

Dear Marianne,

I hope you will forgive my mother and her insinuations, as well as the tardiness of this note to you. I confess to being ignorant of your friendship with this Mr. Abel, but when I think of it, and of my mother's sharpened dislike of him, I am of two minds: one, that he cannot be such a bad sort for befriending you, as this indicates impeccable taste, and two, that he is a cad for keeping such devoted company with you so soon after you have lost your beloved husband. Please allow me to invite you back to make up for the unpleasantness of the previous visit. I would be honored to be your host and my Mother will comport herself more agreeably.

Yours most truly,
Thomas

March 7, 1856

As long as I can forestall a return to that household, I shall. Of course, I will have to send off a reply, but it will be a brief and polite refusal.

Mr. Abel had replied to my note and came to tea today. He looked quite the gentlemanly figure, with new trousers, a new hat and coat, and still sporting his whiskers, now grown thicker, but well-trimmed. To hear him speak of his anticipation of working for Mr. Pringle is nothing less than gratifying for us in this household. We have all missed him. Henry spent a good while watching Mr. Abel before dropping his guard and tottering over to play at our guest's knee. Mr. Abel was only too happy to win the boy's favor once again, for when he first called, Henry did not seem immediately pleased to see him and stayed behind my skirt. Lucy hardly disguised her own delight and Mr. Talbot, too, coming upon him outside the house, seemed very glad to have Mr. Abel return. They spoke a while on events about town, and if I did not know better, I would say Mr. Abel looked as if he had never been away for so many weeks. When he arrived and had been greeted by everyone, he sought me out. His warm eyes held me in place inside the entrance hall a moment longer before he took my hand and placed a warm cheek to the back of it, then a kiss upon that same hand. He has not done this before and I do not know what to make of the warmth I felt at his touch. I could not linger in that appreciative gaze another moment. Lucky for me, Lucy turned my guest's shoulders to face the parlor so that all of us moved in that direction. Mr. Abel let go a low, mirthful chuckle at her insistence.

Before leaving this afternoon, Mr. Abel presented me with a cloth-bound book in which to write. Its cover is the color of midnight and has no embossed letters upon it, but a painting of a tiny window with a garden box of flowers hanging from its sill. It looks like a window I have seen before. Yes, it is reminiscent of so many of the garden boxes that sit outside the windows of homes in Rockport.

MARCH 10, 1856

My boy has caught a fever and has thrashed in his bed with it two nights now. I have moved into his room, though Lucy tried to convince me that she would keep an eye, at the very least to take turns. No, I must be by him, to catch him when he wriggles so far down the bed his legs almost pitch him onto the floor, as happened the first night of his fever. Sleep would not be mine if I were to remain in my own bed and let Lucy be nursemaid. Even Mother, despite her aloof efficiency, nursed me to health herself when I was a child.

Henry often likes to be rocked well into the night before I can put him into his own little bed. Now he stirs and fusses, reaching for me until he is assured that I am there asleep beside him on the floor. He is happy to have Jack curled up in the crook of his knees. Lucy made me a palette of my own bedclothes, layering it with more blankets from the other beds in the house so that I will not be so far below my son's bed or have too hard a floor for a night's sleep.

The third day of his fever, today, he has cheered some and the shocking scarlet lashes that inflamed his round cheeks are faded to pink. He has almost his own pleasing color restored to him and now asks for Mr. Abel whom he calls easily, "Teeder." It has been an easy restoration to the affection they shared on first meeting months ago. Since his recent return to Rockport, Mr. Abel has been to visit twice now. On both occasions, Lucy has attended us, though even as I record her efforts, I have to laugh aloud, for we are as well-behaved as two people ever were, given our circumstances.

Of course, Lucy has decided to place all her faith in Mr. Abel's healing presence as a companion to my son, and yesterday walked down our very own King Street to Beach Street, over to Main and up to his address on High Street to tell him herself that small Mr. Parsons demanded the pleasure of his company. Today is a particularly good day to appease Henry, for it is his third birthday! This morning, when he woke, looking more alert, I knew he was well on the mend, and it could not have been a more perfectly timed a recovery.

Poor luck for us; by Lucy's later account to me, Mr. Abel was not at his home when she went to call. She left him the note she had penned herself, but as she was readying to leave, a woman answered the door to the little house.

Lucy was so flustered by the surprise of the woman's presence that she could not speak, only stare and sputter and then turn to come home, thinking all the way that Mr. Abel was a mysterious man indeed. That conviction changed soon to a darker one.

Devoted to Henry, our friend appeared at our threshold before sunset this afternoon, a basket in his hand. I had come down the stairs from my son's bedroom where I had been putting down fresh bedding. As I reached the middle step on my way down the stairs, out of sight of Mr. Abel and Lucy as she answered the door, I heard her greet him with a chill in her voice that made the vestibule seem balmy in comparison. He did not understand her cool greeting, and stepped in, though just in and no further, before Lucy stopped him.

"I don't know who you think you are, Mr. Abel, or where you think you are when you come to my cousin's house to spend time, but if you've any decency, sir, you'll make your choice and be done with it. It is either my good, kind cousin or that…that strumpet who greeted me at your door today."

There was a brief silence and then Mr. Abel burst with laughter. It was a deep-in-the-belly chortle I had not heard from him before and it brought me all the way downstairs to the door where I took my place beside Lucy. I must have been as pallid as she was flushed, for she had embarrassed us both.

"What is so amusing?" I demanded, already uneasy about what I had heard earlier from her about her errand to his quarters, now the more so about what she presumed exists between Mr. Abel and me. She looked from me to Mr. Abel, two angry lines between her eyes.

"Perhaps Mr. Abel should explain," she said, leaving him little choice even as he wiped at eyes wet from mirth. I was caught between indignation that he should take his behavior so lightly and guarded pleasure in his obvious delight. I did not know what to make of Lucy's outrage at his presence, for she had asked for this very thing for my son, and had been given my consent to do so.

"It's nothing, I think," he said, composed now. Of course, this only inflamed my cousin more and I began to wonder myself just how genuine a man stood before us.

"How can you say it's nothing and seem uncertain in saying so?" She demanded of him, speaking more for herself than for me, I think, for I cannot profess to claim any true jealousy. It would be improper for me to do so without an understanding between us, and no such thing exists. "You have cad written all over you!" Lucy said quite plainly.

It was then, of course, that Thomas' letter and Mrs. Pringle's censure and warnings came back to me in a cold and bitter tide. I could picture them wagging their knowing heads and I felt myself begin to heat with the disgrace, grateful that I had not made an utter fool of myself with Mr. Abel.

He turned to me, suddenly quite earnest.

"Mrs. Parsons, there's no duplicity, I assure you, not of the sort Lucy might be suggesting. It's only my landlady."

Lucy bridled. "Well, then you two are made for each other!"

"Oh, but this is all she is, Lucy, and she was tidying up. It's an arrangement she made as part of my lodging in exchange for some help from me around the place. She keeps my quarters from looking like those of a slovenly quarryman and charges me very little rent. In return, I fix the chimney on the house and perform other such tasks for her. I didn't mean to alarm you, Lucy," he said, before turning a beseeching pair of brown eyes on me.

Lucy seemed to retreat then. And though I had only just walked into this odd moment between them, I felt removed from harm; in fact, my relief was immense. We later learned that Mr. Abel's landlady is Mrs. Allison, the wife of a merchant, and that the two of them came from Beverly last summer.

Mr. Abel did not stay to supper. He played with Henry a while, doling out all manner of goodies from his basket, trinkets he said he bought at the store his landlady's husband owns. A wooden toy soldier, an India rubber ball, and a doll made of straw with a knit cap and britches all widened my boy's eyes. We had a wonderful time bringing the laughter out of him, for I have not heard this most glorious sound in too many days.

Had I gone to the Allisons' mercantile on Main Street, Mr. Abel inquired. I had not. Lucy, for her part, looked stolidly opposed to entertaining the idea of going there and I found her loyalty—to me, I had already surmised—comical and touching.

The proprietors of the mercantile on Main Street have always welcomed me, old Mr. and Mrs. Bedford brightening when I have brought Henry into the store to see what new fabrics and preserves, books or little toys they have, my boy and I so enjoying the gleam of new things. I have not been there in too long. I would pay them a visit soon.

Mr. Abel left us before dark, and I walked him to the door, leaving Lucy to entertain Henry who was beginning to yawn, his energy quite depleted.

As I moved to hand our guest his wool cap, then his coat, he took my hand. It startled me enough that I took it back and, with it, his coat. He smiled, a sadness thwarting the progress of his very fine and generous mouth. His gaze forced mine down to my own feet.

"Mrs. Parsons, your cousin was right to scold me. I hope you'll forgive me for the earlier misunderstanding. I hadn't written to you yet of my new living arrangement. Had I, your cousin would not have been..." At this we both smiled a little at the memory of her temper, so quick to flare, another new aspect of Lucy.

"It is the best kind of arrangement," I said. "How can it not be?" I was very aware of my hand in his palm, how warm were his own hands. When he took his leave, I brought my two hands together and felt how cold was the one he had not held.

It is late now. Both Henry and Lucy are asleep, but I must give voice to a thought, if this can be thought any kind of "voice," muted as my words are in these pages:

I confess to feeling relief that Mrs. Allison is only fulfilling her end of an arrangement as landlady and that she has a husband. Yet, unease tugs at me like an annoying schoolboy at a girl's hair. If she were to exact favors from Mr. Abel—but no, she is the wife of a merchant, a public figure in her own right whose virtue must weigh on her as surely as expectations weigh upon me regarding the way I lead my life as a widow. She would not dare.

March 10, 1856

Dear Daughter,

You know I am not much of a hand with the pen, that I am not much more inclined to spoken word, but I thought of you the other day as I walked along a path that you used to take to school and admired the pond that freezes over to a perfect, smooth pane of ice on which you skated as a girl. My grandson will enjoy that when he grows older. Your mother and I hope you will bring him here, and that you will stay for as long as you like. Perhaps now you are not inclined to venture far from home, but when you do, bring cousin Lucy to ease your travel burden.

I must conclude here as your Mother is calling from some room of this house and I cannot imagine what she wants. She is always after me for

something these days, as if an old man has nothing better to do (aside from
reading his books and smoking his hickory pipe).

With affection,
Your Father

MARCH 12, 1856

Mr. Abel has sent a note asking to call tomorrow if it is not too much
trouble to prepare, as he has something to tell me. I am caught between
wondering and not wanting to know. Lucy peers at me with a secret sense
all her own and I am suddenly ill-at-ease with her girlish nonsense. I
must attend to my son, feed him before he falls asleep, for the dim skies
portend a storm before the day is over. With shadows following us about
the house, we are all a bit sleepy in these ill-lit rooms. Perhaps I will bake
a pound cake this evening.

MARCH 13, 1856

Not only has Mr. Abel repeated words I have forced myself to forget,
those dwelling on his reputation as an ill omen, a Jonah, on board my
husband's vessel, he has confided that his only comfort will be in my forgiveness. I will do my best, as I have done throughout these pages, to recall the conversation.

We had just sat down in the parlor and I was lifting a piece of lemon
cake onto a plate to hand to him. "But I have nothing to forgive," I told
him as he began to present his request. I could not meet his eyes, grave as
they were, searching me out.

"Yes, you do. Captain Parsons didn't approve of such lore as omens and
harbingers of ill luck except by the stars themselves, and only through the
lens of his own education and the maps he used to guide us. You
did say you don't put stock in it. But you said so in a letter and now
you and I are here. I must see it in your eyes, Mrs. Parsons, to be
convinced of your forgiveness."

I flinched at this, for he could read me well. It was not that I had
bumped up against a notion that forgiving Mr. Abel was a wrongdoing;
I could not blame him, truly, for what attached itself to him before he was

fully aware, and I did think it nonsense before James' vessel went down. All I had ever heard about Jonahs was from James, that they were victims themselves of a sort. (Mr. Abel does not seem the victim, nor has he yet in my estimation, if only because of his remarkable survival.) I had heard of insufficient hauls because of them, or near disasters. Yet, since this man had confided his curse, I could not keep the thought away that if he had not joined James' crew, the *Marianne Elizabeth,* the *Abercrombie,* the crews from both, and my husband might be here.

So, our teatime was somber and ended hastily, with Mr. Abel claiming he needed to attend to his landlady's chimney before dusk. When he left, Lucy and Henry came downstairs from Lucy's room where she let him play with his new toys and blocks while she knitted. My son did not sense that Mr. Abel had been present only moments before and for this I was grateful, for he is a sensitive child and would surely have had a fit of temper if he had any notion of the visitor he had missed. Today's visit was not to include him.

Lucy was altogether another matter. Seeing the tea things spread out and hardly touched, she lifted her brow and then went to gather it all up. I bade her stop and sit to help me finish what was left. We ate the entire cake, every last crumb, and downed the pot of tea. She seemed to be waiting for me to speak and when I did not, she did not press. It is an aspect of Lucy for which I am most grateful.

MARCH 17, 1856

Mr. Abel has not called since he asked for my forgiveness and I could not offer it the way he would accept. Lucy finally implored me to summon him, to take a walk into town and stroll near his street. I refused, for that is a girl's behavior, not that of a lady, and she is frustrated with both of us. Yet she will not go either, respecting my choice.

MARCH 19, 1856

Lucy has heard from Hannah! She read me her granddaughter's letter, which I will not copy here, for it is not mine, but can almost rhyme off by heart. Hannah says she is earning all the highest marks, both in reading and mathematics, the two most difficult subjects. Her teacher has told her that she is teacher material herself and this thrills the child. She would like to visit and tells Lucy she is working on her father to soften him toward the idea that she might come alone, on a coach with a family bound for these parts next month. She is now twelve years old, and very independent. Lucy glowed with pride for her granddaughter when she told me that as a girl, she herself could hardly walk to town alone, fearing strangers. I cannot imagine my cousin in this way, yet she has taken on many years and experiences since that time, all of them helping to make her the strong woman she appears to be.

I had to give Lucy my kerchief, as hers is not yet dry from the washing she did. She was not fit to talk for several moments after reading me the letter. Then she stood, smoothed her skirt, and said she was not about to get her hopes up, as Timothy had been hard-nosed until now, and why should that change?

I told her I hoped she was wrong and let my own hopes swell.

MARCH 22, 1856

The Pringles are having a party. I had been prepared to wear a black satin gown and just this morning, rediscovered a dress made for me before James and I were wed. I had worn it to parties in the months leading up to the wedding, months filled with merrymaking and curtsies and gratitude to those who had bestowed their blessing on our love. It is a gown of green velvet, the shade like spring, its neckline not so low as to reveal the bosom I have developed since giving birth, yet not so high as to brand me a matron. I shall wear my hair up with the matching clip made for the gown and the shawl, in a pale shade of blue silk. I am putting the widow's frock away for an evening, and will face Virginia Pringle head-on in colors to make her eyes smart.

162

MARCH 23, 1856

The Bedfords have been very good to us, sending an extra sweet home with Lucy now and again for which they do not want payment. Thinking it best to thank them myself at long last, for I really do not venture any further than my own stretch of beach (and even then, not since fairer days), I wrapped myself in my wool cape and shawl and Mr. Talbot drove me into town. It is such a short distance I could have walked and perhaps enjoyed the feeling of my limbs getting their due. Yet now as I recall it, I am the better for having ridden, for when I arrived at the mercantile and walked inside to greet the Bedfords—Mrs. Bedford was folding linens and Mr. Bedford replenishing the penny candy jars—the first person my eyes found was Fiona Terry. I do not understand how it is that my encounters with her seem always to be at this store. Immediately, I regretted my decision to go. Luck being what it is, she found me just as I noticed her and she strode toward me so quickly I had no chance to move to any other part of the shop or out the door.

She began by embracing me as if we were friends long apart. This has always struck me as peculiar. Whatever urge drives her to do so, and in public, she appears to think I would welcome the gesture.

I moved apart from her and could say nothing. I did see, however, that she was with child; my duty, then, was simple.

"Fiona, I hope you are keeping well."

"I do not feel as well as I might some days and Captain Terry has been my knight." At this, she must have seen something in my face, for she took a step back and then came forward once again to grasp my hands in hers. "Marianne, do forgive me." I knew she would speak of that dreaded day in September and not of the revelation that she carried her husband's child; that in my eyes as I beheld her middle, she must have seen my own reminder that this will nevermore be a hope to have with James.

"Oh, no, do not speak of it," I said. "For if you were not the one to say so, I would have seen it myself or I would have heard a report another way. You did not bring about a tempest, Fiona." Yes, I realized as I spoke those words that for all her puffed-up certainty about just what was in the air that terrible week, she could no more have caused my grief than Mr. Abel could have done as a Jonah. I moved forward and gave her a quick embrace once again, bade her farewell, and left before she could say another word. My step did feel lighter, for there had at last been some good in an encounter with Fiona.

163

It was on my way to the stable across the road where Mr. Talbot was waiting that my tears came and I could not have seen my way home on foot, which is why having Mr. Talbot and the carriage were a godsend after all. Of course, the poor, bewildered Bedfords did not benefit from my purchases, for I had left without making them and without even a word of greeting! I shall go again in a day or two or send Lucy in my stead.

MARCH 26, 1856

Lucy could not speak when I presented myself to her before leaving to go to the party last evening. She stood before me, her hands ghostly pale with the flour she was sifting for bread (for she loves to bake; confirming this, she says it quiets her mind). A tear traced a path through the flour smudged on her cheek and she expressed some concern that my vivid colors would stir the room to gossip, even as she knows how little I care to think about the prospect, for I have shared my view often with her lately. Perhaps she was very sentimental before she came to live with us, but I do believe she might have grown more so.

I was grateful that Henry slept through my departure. When James and I would go out of an evening, it would more often be when Mother or Father were visiting and the boy, so small and devoted to his grandparents, less mindful of our comings and goings, did not fuss. He would do so mightily now.

Mr. Talbot greeted me as I stepped outside. He dipped his head in a rather silly bow, something I have never thought necessary, and helped me up into the carriage. Dear that he is, warmed blankets were folded at the ready for me against the chill of evening and he draped them over my knees before taking his position and getting us started on the short journey to the Pringles.

I wished all the way there to be greeted by Mr. Pringle himself, but it was Thomas who took me by the waist and brought me down to earth, to the solid stone walkway that led to his parents' home, tiny lamps lighting the way.

"My dear Marianne," he said in that same fawning way he greeted me that regrettable afternoon of my outburst. "You look radiant and shame even the exotic flowers that Mother has ordered for the party. I more than anyone am so glad you came to my Father's birthday. He was asking if your son would be a guest as well, but Mother reminded him that tonight's company was of a certain sophistication that your young man had not quite attained. Father was almost pouting when he said he is the birthday boy and would rather have your boy in his company, but Mother set him straight."

Wiping a droplet of spittle that had landed squarely on my nose, I feigned at dabbing my cheeks with my kerchief. I tried to look away from Thomas, even as he faced me directly, his hands still at my waist. His familiarity sickened me. If he were to re-claim the shyness I detected when he and his mother visited me and he confided that it was only for her that he was my new bosom friend, I would be more at ease. It would seem instead that he counters those earlier words with his actions, as if to be my suitor!

Virginia Pringle swept toward me then and took me away from her son. I wondered if I had been in better, gentler, hands before.

She did not seem vexed by my attire, and I admit to being disappointed. "Mrs. Parsons, you look lovely, and I know there are people inside who are eager to make themselves part of your circle. Come," she beckoned. It was a transformation that took me so off my guard that I let myself drift alongside my hostess toward the main hall which, unlike the day when my son and I had visited, was now glowing with firelight from wall sconces, very soft and welcoming.

Mrs. Pringle moved me into the room where we waited during our last visit not so very long ago. There were many people already gathered there and as I was about to find something to occupy myself, such as admire the paintings over the fireplace, I heard a voice I know as well as my own and turned to its source. There, very smartly dressed themselves, in a circle of people I did not know, were Mother and Father!

I flew toward them and then checked myself, but I need not have done, for Father was already moving quickly toward me as well and had me in his elegantly suited arms. "It was very difficult not to let you in on this one," he said. "But your Mother would have tarred me if I had."

"That settles it then," I said into his shoulder, my eyes stinging, a lump in my throat that made it difficult to say anything more. I felt the eyes of a few watching us, detected a faint smile on the faces of what must have been some more tolerant guests. Mrs. Pringle herself stood aside, patient and polite. Mother was at my side and kissing both my cheeks, once each, perfunctorily. Her display would have been little more in private. And yet, I have always understood she loves me as a mother should love a child, however private her feeling is. Father's embrace was a delight in its snug warmth, but Mother does not venture further to convey her affections. A great deal of the time, I do not begrudge her, knowing that her mother, too, was more aloof. I do enjoy a boisterous show of love toward my son wherever we are, for one day he will grow past his interest in having his doting mother cuddle him.

"We arrived this morning and are staying here," Mother said.

"You must stay with us, with Henry, Lucy and me!" She looked at Father, her eyes sending him a thought I could almost read. It must also have more to do with Mother's comfort, for she does like to spread her things a bit and have the freedom to move about with little worry over a small child getting underfoot. While she does cherish her grandson, I have detected the same impatience in her when he behaves willfully as she showed me when I was a child.

After stepping out of Father's embrace, it was clear that he was regretful that they have opted for the Pringle household. My home is so much warmer for him. He enjoys the evenings most, I think, as I see him relax in the parlor with his pipe and a book, his feet propped before him. Still, I chided him and Mother, who excused their absence in my home.

"You have more than you can abide for a woman newly widowed, my darling girl. We will stop and see you tomorrow on our way home." I envisioned Mother and Virginia Pringle talking about my well-being over tea and it caused a pinprick of discomfort in my temples.

A laugh boomed behind me. "Well, Daniel, it is a surprise, indeed!" Mr. Pringle said to my father. "And Helen, this is a treat for an old man like me!" He stepped forward to kiss Mother's hand, which she gave him. She withdrew it too soon, this error unusual for her, leaving him for an instant still slightly bent over an empty space, holding a hand that had vanished. She seemed genuinely bashful at his display, for father is not nearly as effusive a greeter, and certainly not after nearly twenty-five years.

The evening was spent dining and talking among the people of Rockport and Gloucester who held the Pringles in very high esteem. I had one conversation with a Mrs. Stevenson, older than Mother and Virginia Pringle by many years. She is married to one of Mr. Pringle's business associates and allied herself with many women in the town against the fishermen's over-indulging in spirits, particularly in the off-season months. With vehement conviction, she remarked to anyone who would hear it how the enjoyment of drink depleted family economy. I have learned that numerous women complain to Hannah Jumper (and the women in the circle around us who heard the name agreed that Miss Jumper is an indispensable asset to Rockport for her knowledge of medicinal plants and her nimble sewing fingers) of their husbands' tippling. She has become the women's great sympathizer and given her own voice in complaint, though she is not married to anyone.

The more Mrs. Stevenson spoke of the townswomen's discontent over the demijohns sailors toted and filled and refilled, the redder her mottled cheeks grew. She concluded by telling me to make certain my son does not take to whiskey and rum, that he confine his interest in the drink to after dinner in refined surroundings. Lucy and I do enjoy a glass of Port many nights before bed. It has had the effect of softening me after a day of mood managing. Of course, that is our circumstance, and not something the fishermen that the townswomen complain about can choose as we do. They take their liquor more roughly and live more roughly too.

Mrs. Stevenson had the look of a woman who might have taken me across her knee, so irate was she at the merest notion of excessive drink. She would not have approved of my husband, for though he did not overindulge, he regularly provided his crew their demijohns of spirits. Some of those men tippled throughout the fishing months, he had let me know, and a few would be found useless enough for James to dismiss. I will admit that the tragedy of the Mathias and Caldwell men is directly owing to their intemperance. As a consequence, privy to this woman's tirade, how could I not offer my assent?

I was relieved when the woman's attention was moved away from me by the summons of a similarly aged dowager friend of hers, for I could then sit and watch the guests mill about the rooms. Thomas was strangely absent during this time.

In the moments before the dinner bell chimed and the servants came to usher us into the grandly appointed dining room, it was Father who kept me company. Now and then, he would press a hand to my arm and move me through the room, nodding to those who offered a greeting, stopping now and again to introduce me to couples whose association, I remain certain even now, he hoped I would make.

There was one woman in particular whose name I readily recalled after our first introduction: Irene Jamieson. She stood quite alone as Father brought me near. I admired her dark hair coiled at the back of her head, and her handsome, high forehead. She appraised me with quite the roundest light brown eyes I have seen and held out her hand to greet me. She wore a wedding band, though for some time I saw no man in the room that might look about to claim her. When I did, later at dinner, his presence seemed to diminish her and it made me less favorably inclined toward him, a too-quick and childish judgment perhaps.

"I have heard of you," she said. This startled me, for I have neither heard of Mrs. Jamieson nor seen her. I am sure I blushed like one shamed, for I do not enjoy the thought of being discussed, particularly in circles with which I have no connection. But the way she spoke this fact was simple and filled with understanding. In fact, she did not, it seems, have anything disparaging to go on where I was concerned.

Whatever she had heard, unless she was of the Virginia Pringle way of thinking, she had come to a more favorable conclusion. Still, I must have shown my confusion. "Oh, no, I should not have said such a thing," she corrected herself.

"It is not at all for you to worry."

"I would worry if it were up to me. I cannot think how you have managed through these months. If it were me, well…" She did not finish the thought, but her eyes did the job for her. She seemed to have great compassion toward me and we had only just met. Although I did not want her pity, I liked her instantly.

"Do not think of it," I reproved her, and now in my memory of our exchange, she hid a sadness of her own, I think.

"Forgive me, but I do not know why we have never met before this evening," I confessed.

She laughed. "I do keep to myself more than I ought," she said. "My husband works long weeks in Boston and I am mostly alone with our daughters, so we enjoy our gardens more than we have moving beyond them."

We chatted in a friendly way for a few moments and I learned she has two daughters, Eleanor and Pauline. Father remained nearby speaking in a most animated way to Mr. Pringle and Mother stood off in a quieter part of the room in conversation with the hostess. Other people milled about, now unseen to me, though the blurry spectacle of the Pringles' servants doing their best to make all of the guests comfortable was impressive. They glided to and fro, offering up trays of delicious treats and aperitifs to whet our appetites.

Among them was Mary, the maid who served us when Henry and I came to tea the previous month, and the very same girl who led me from the front door when I arrived at Mr. Pringle's party. She looked markedly changed this evening, and I could not pinpoint the difference. She moved about the room with an older woman who looked very like her but for a bonier frame and a gaunter complexion, and I realized this was her own mother, long in the Pringles' employ. They were both vested in the smooth, snug frocks with thin blue stripes. I am sure not *169* a wrinkle would be abided. My own Agatha had worn a frock of her own, with a full skirt, and I had provided her an apron. Lucy hardly donned an apron and wore her own skirts and blouses too, perhaps to maintain what I preferred, a decidedly un-servant like affect.

A tiny bell rang out summoning the guests to the dining room.

Thomas, gliding in himself from I know not where, immediately took my elbow, while Father moved toward Mother to escort her. I watched, baffled, as Mr. Pringle whispered in his wife's ear and she smiled up at him so that I nearly lost my footing and had to grasp at Thomas's arm for support. Thank goodness, he brought me up quick enough so that no one would have seen me stumble. Then he bent his mouth to my ear.

"If Mrs. Stevenson had seen you take a fall, she would have you pegged a tippler. You are lucky I caught you." I knew he was right in this. I will be careful not to cross paths with her too soon. For his part, Thomas was only doing what he must where I am concerned, both of us aware of his mother's friendlier approval, preferring it to her grim scrutiny.

I managed a small smile and wrapped my shawl about me with my free hand, for it had slipped when I had almost fallen.

As we took our seats at the long dining table, the hosts at either end, my parents to my right, Thomas to my left, I looked around the table and thought how festive it all was. Then, Mr. Pringle raised his glass and stood to speak.

"My friends, my son, and my dear wife," he said, looking down the table at his wife so that again I was struck by a softness in her that I had not thought she possessed. She looked happy to have these people around her, happiest most of all to bask in her husband's devotion. I had not imagined her susceptible to any tenderness.

He continued. "Tonight, I am one year older, though not so much wiser." He chuckled and we joined him. "And if you look about you, you will see that the people you do not know have in common with you the connection to me and to my wife and son. I mean only to say that I feel more fortunate to enjoy your friendship, your expertise," and here, he nodded to two gentleman, one older than he, the other closer to my age, "than you can possibly feel to have suffered me in your lives for these many years." Again, we had to laugh at the ridiculous notion that Mr. Pringle could be anything like a nuisance or a hardship. We all, I could feel with certainty, enjoyed him. "I implore you then to eat, drink and be merry!" I heard the smallest gasp from the other end of the table just as I saw Mr. Pringle wink there, where Mrs. Stevenson sat with her back pressed against the chair, her hands folded primly in her lap, her pink-nosed husband nodding to the steward as he poured a lovely pale pink liquid into his glass and then moved to pour the same into hers (before she placed her palm in the way of progress) and all around the table.

"To sixty more years of friendship!" The guest of honor bellowed. We all raised our glasses of champagne and clinked before drinking, some of the guests taking the sweet bubbles in only two draughts and singing a wobbly well-wishing chorus.

The first course came. As I ate my broth, Thomas regaled me with the story of his days working at the quarry, though with his fine-boned hands I could no more imagine him lifting heavy rocks than I could imagine those hands not being scarred after such labor. And, of course, they were not, leaving me to wonder if he was telling me the truth. I could fasten my attention on him for only a moment, aware as I was of Mother's head bent toward Father's and the way they spoke to one another, intent on hearing the words each spoke to the other. I recalled a dinner party James and I had attended and my sense of James' steadfast presence, his hand at my waist or my elbow, how he stayed within smiling distance even if he moved just a little off to speak with someone. I recalled the safe feeling of having my husband near and felt his absence during this gathering as an acute pain in my eyes.

"Excuse me, please, Thomas," I said, forcing it back. "Would you mind if we spoke after I finish my broth? I do not wish for it to get cold and I do not want to be rude to you by eating it when you want my attention."

He looked only mildly affronted, but then his mouth, set in that narrow face, with high cheekbones that have always struck me as more feminine, rose in acceptance.

As I ate my broth, taking each spoonful slowly, Irene Jamieson, right across from me, began to involve me in conversation. Her husband was seated next to her, his hand rested on her own. I sensed the weight of it and that it seemed she dared not move her hand from under his.

Even as she and I spoke, I knew it was not much time before I would have to turn to Thomas again and listen to his endless outpouring, but this woman was divinely sent. Irene told me she and her husband had left both her feverish daughters in the care of their governess. Her concern was evident in the lack of interest she showed in her food. She was re-arranging it most of the evening.

I suggested that perhaps she might send a messenger to find out how they fare, certain there must have been someone, one of the servants, who would be willing to make the small ride to her home in Pigeon Cove, as I learned early on. I could not imagine her having to worry the evening away and said as much.

She lifted her shoulders and began to leave her chair when her husband turned to her, lifting his face in a question marked with a stern brow. She pressed herself back into her chair and inclined her head toward me.

"Who might be able to go?" She asked.

I turned then to Thomas, and his expression betrayed his gratitude. He must know my feelings for him do not match what is becoming more apparent in his for me. Yet, all I wanted of him was to enlist a servant to send on an errand for poor Mrs. Jamieson.

"I will send my own coachman for you," Thomas said to her and she nearly wept with relief.

"This is most heroic of you, Thomas," I said, meaning it and touching his hand in spite of knowing better. He looked at my hand resting upon his, even just the feather light touch I offered, and quickly took his away. I wonder if I made too encouraging a gesture.

"Did I hear someone say 'heroic?'" Mr. Pringle asked me from his seat. He had been spending much of the time talking to the elder of his two solicitors. Mother had turned her attention from Father and wore a smile that I recall from my childhood bespoke contentment in the bustle around her.

"I was only telling Thomas that his helping your guest is an act worthy of the praise," I said. Under his father's favorably appraising eye, Thomas bowed his head. He was, in that moment, the humblest man I have yet known in my life. It grazed my heart to realize that Thomas was a man intent on pleasing his father. A son should want to please his father above all else before he marries, of course, if indeed Thomas aims to marry.

Mr. Pringle's summons to his coachman was made and Mrs. Jamieson was given the news thirty minutes later. She quickly shared it with me. "The children ate a meal of beef stew and now sleep well," she said. She took my hand across the finery on the table to convey her thanks.

At the end of the evening she asked me to bring Henry to visit her and her children following their recovery, which she assured me would be soon, and I accepted. At last my son and I will go on an outing that suits us, for I have been very remiss in this way and now will make a point of pursuing some company other than my own and Lucy's. I have relied on her far more than I intended to, and she must need some time to herself now and again.

"That man is quite intolerable," my mother whispered to me as we later strolled toward the conservatory where dessert would be served.

I rebuffed her and for this she was unprepared. "I quite disagree, Mother. He shows only kindness in his actions." It was not a gentle hint, yet it drew only a puzzled look.

"If you mean the man who continues to call on you in your very own home, I fail to understand how, bereft as you are of your husband, you tolerate even a moment in his company."

Now it was I who was caught unguarded. "No, Mother! I am speaking of Thomas." I darted a quick look over my shoulder and lowered my voice. "*I* do not fancy him, but he would make someone a fine husband. As for Mr. Abel, he is very good company for all of us, and does no harm. He is quite alone and we do him a service in friendship."

"His sort is not worthy of you, Marianne, in any capacity."

"Worthy? And who might be?" I could not keep the challenge from my voice. Were I a child, I would have been banished to my room for the night or soundly thrashed, perhaps both. Mother did use her hand, while Father's discipline always dwelled in the stern down-turn of his mouth and could wither me on the spot.

"I shall not even speak of it. You are in mourning and we cannot consider a suitor until the period is done."

"I have no interest in considering anyone a suitor," I said, seething. I could not look at her, but did not want anyone to understand our conflict.

I put my arm through the crook of hers and steered her away from those moving up behind us. We stopped in the conservatory. "Mother, I have the impression that you and Mrs. Pringle would have me married off to her son before a year is up."

She stopped and turned to me then, her expression one of utter consternation and surprise.

"My dear child, I loved James as much as if he were my own son. I cannot, any more than you, dishonor him by pushing you into another marriage before you feel at ease. Yes, yes, you will one day feel prepared to share your life with another, yet waiting longer than this coming autumn to open yourself to it will do you no good. You have a son to consider, and a household you can hardly manage between you and Lucy."

I could not speak to contradict her presumption, but held fast to my own truth that we two women, Lucy and I, were doing a fine job of managing my household. I wished for Mother to stop her nattering, but as is her habit, she carried on. "Your conduct, the very indiscretion of inviting that other man into your home as a companion, is something your father and I will not tolerate. You not only dishonor your husband's name, you bring disgrace upon your family. I will do what I must as your Mother, asking the Pringles to take an interest in your pursuits. If you insist upon making fools of all of us, of yourself, of your late husband, I will wash my hands of you."

At this, she turned from me with squared shoulders and faced Father who had come upon us. His smile faded when he saw what must have been the same tears in her eyes glistening in mine and he reached for her, as well he should have. It is good that she has Father's calming influence, even if she has already had her fit.

At last in my own room, I can hear the ocean outside my window, a distant thunder and hiss on this clear, cold night. I am too tired to feel any lingering indignation, for Mother will do what Mother must and it is for me to be mindful of every step I take. I will simply look forward to a visit with Irene.

Lucy has been taking Henry for afternoon strolls before his nap, running his little legs until he nearly collapses with exhaustion. She is looking more trim for her forty-seven years. She has never admitted her age to me, but I confess to seeing the inscription of it on one of the etchings in the book she showed us when Hannah visited. It means, after the numbers I tallied, that she was no more than a girl when she gave birth to Rose and that Rose was hardly older than she when she birthed Hannah.

During Lucy and Henry's outing, I wrote to Irene and invited her to tea. The distraction of other women with children will prove most helpful, though Fiona Terry has since sent me a note asking me to join her for a more conciliatory afternoon. I cannot lift my hand to respond to her. It is not that I harbor further ill will toward her, but I am not eager to sit in her parlor and feel the absence in my life of a completeness she still claims.

It is much later now, near midnight, but I feel it is imperative to record the events of today before I try to sleep. It has been quite remarkable.

Today, as I sat at the small oak desk in the little room off the kitchen where I chose to do my letters, the inkwell yielding little but drops of the walnut ink I have been buying off the shelves of Bedfords' Mercantile, there was a knock at the door that I almost did not hear, so absorbed was I in my letter to Irene. When I finally reached the vestibule, I heard the door chime and realized that it had not come from the front entrance, but from the side of the house, the other door that leads from the side porch entrance and where our milk and eggs are delivered. It is through that door I pass in fair weather so that I might sit and write under the linden tree.

On my way to answer the bell, I nearly bumped straight into Lucy. She was flushed and breathless and my son, whom she had taken for a stroll through Mill Pond Meadow not an hour before, was not with her.

Her voice came in a gust. "Cousin, I ran into Thomas Pringle on the way with the boy, along the lane that leads toward the pond, and he wasn't at all himself. He was at the pond's edge and seemed about to plunge his entire self into the frigid water, when your boy rushed to him and they both tumbled in!"

For a moment, I did not know if I had heard correctly, but the distress

175

on Lucy's face and in her wringing hands set me straight and I had to assume that if something were amiss with Henry, she would speak if it. She must have put him to bed, I surmised, and I would not have heard them, so absorbed was I in writing my letter. Dismissing the concern, I inquired whether Thomas was well.

She was stunned. "Cousin, your son fell in with him!"

I can hardly steady my hand now to think of it! She turned heel and hurried out the door, calling behind her, "he is coming, Cousin, with Mr. Abel!" I grabbed at the doorframe and reached for a chair, unable to hold myself up. My one remaining treasure could very well perish from the cold against his soaked skin. I imagined him fading in my arms and hardly heard Lucy's account until she was before me again, grasping my arms.

"Did you not hear me, Marianne? It was Mr. Abel happened along the laneway just a moment after, a miracle for which I can thank only the heavens, and got the two out of the pond. They are steps from the house. We must feed the fire and warm the blankets."

It was too late to do this, for in that instant they arrived and I sprung up, a dizzy rush nearly taking me down again. Mr. Abel came first, clutching my son to him, his own coat wrapped snugly twice around Henry, big as it was on the tiny frame of a child of three. Thomas shuffled along behind them, his head bowed low in shame or disappointment I could not be sure. But if he had meant to jump into the pond and, as Lucy said, was then helped along by my son and then the two of them fished out, his plan was foiled. He now had to face himself and our questions.

Upon entering the room, Mr. Abel moved quickly toward the hearth and began to strip my boy of his wet, frozen clothing, all the while rubbing his limbs, speaking softly to him. He turned his head to Thomas and told him, very firmly, to take his clothing off and sit by the fire to dry in his underthings. My throat was dry as kindling, my eyes filled with the vision of having nearly lost my son. I knelt by Henry and Mr. Abel, and took my boy who was not whimpering, but grinning through his chattering teeth. Ignoring poor Thomas, I am sorry to say, I held my son's shivering body to me. Mr. Abel moved aside and then stood to go into the kitchen.

The fire raging, Lucy had gone into the kitchen before and had returned again, wheeling a cart topped with brimming cups of coffee and a mug of warmed milk and honey for my boy. She placed them in each of our hands. She whispered to me with the certainty of a medical nurse that my son's milk had a dash of mead in it to calm his trembling body. I held him near, curled in my lap, as he drank from the cup, growing calm. Within a quarter hour, he fell to sleep in my arms. He looked as if he'd simply had an afternoon of vigorous play in the winter air, not a terrible plunge into a half-frozen pond.

We all sat quietly before the fire, each with our own thoughts until, nearly dry, Thomas began to pull on his still wet trousers. He begged his leave so that he might go home and rest. I had an old coat of Father's in the closet that I have always kept on hand for when he visits and knew that he would not begrudge Thomas using it for a time. As he pulled it on, all of us still in a kind of reverie, I turned to him. He looked to me as well and it could not have been easy, for the shame I had seen drift near the surface at his father's birthday celebration when we sat at table now resided openly in his eyes, carving lines around his mouth that aged him.

"Thomas, if there is something you cannot face, if you have trouble that you cannot bring to the threshold of your own house, will you consider me your confidante?" It was all I could think to say.

He looked away once more. "It is not a burden I can bring to your threshold any more than to my own family, good lady. I thank you for your generosity. I think most highly of you and I do believe my mother does as well." I would not allow myself to discuss that sore point, that the source of my vexation for the past many months has been his mother's open disapproval of me and of the company I keep or do not keep. I need hardly wonder what her point of view would be if she could behold this scene. Furthermore, I did not understand why she might continue to consider me a possible relation in the wake of Mr. Abel's impropriety and my enabling it. Clearly, I am not to be trusted, if I regard myself as she must regard me—quite unreliable in my judgment.

177

This has yielded the truth that that no matter what his interests or his or our mothers' campaign, I could never marry a man for whom my pity was the prevailing sentiment.

Mr. Abel was still warming himself by the fire and I had not even thought that he must have been half-frozen as well, having gone into the water to pull everyone out. He had about him an air of strength so at odds to Thomas' huddled form that I had not even considered Mr. Abel's discomfort. At once, I was contrite.

I offered both men clothes and only Mr. Abel accepted them, though I knew I would fetch them for Thomas as well. I placed my now sleeping son beside him on the settee. Mr. Abel tucked the woolen blanket more snugly around him.

The clothes I gave the two men came from a closet in my bedroom, a closet I have not had occasion or nerve of late to visit, for I cannot move them from their proper place just yet. I found two warm shirts, some knickers and wool britches and placed one pile folded beside Mr. Abel and another by Thomas. In the kitchen was the comforting sound of Lucy moving about and gathering ingredients for the beef stew she was driven to prepare after such a harrowing afternoon.

"These are my husband's older clothes, but they have worn well."

Mr. Abel regarded me uncertainly. In his eyes were many questions he would not dare ask any more than I could bear to hear them or form their answers.

To Thomas I said, "You must at least choose wisely enough to be warm. If you leave here in your damp clothes and catch a fever or worse, it will be on your head for refusing my offer." I know I seemed to chide, yet it was all I could do to urge him. He simply sat wrapped in the blanket and said nothing but to thank me.

Mr. Abel stood to his full height, more than a head taller than I with my shoes on, and gathered the bundle of clothes with him to go upstairs. I pointed him toward the bedroom at the top of the landing so that he might change.

I imagined he would fill the clothes out well enough, if snugly, for he is a little taller and broader than James had been, more muscular perhaps because of the work he has lately done in the quarry and the work at sea that he had for what I imagine has been most of his life.

Within a few moments, he was downstairs again, clothed in what James would have worn on a quiet, resting Sunday. I bit my lip almost to bleeding. He looked as different from my husband as he might ever have done, his hair a different color, lighter, with curls close to his head, his eyes, too, a light brown. He looked, in that moment, ill-at-ease under my gaze, but did not break it. It was I who could not let my eyes linger.

For his deed at the pond, I could hardly manage a thank you.

"If you had not been there, I cannot think. I will not."

"And you mustn't spend a moment's thought on it, Mrs. Parsons. I was there. It's all that matters and now it's best forgotten."

Henry was still deeply sleeping, his breathing even, the flesh of his round cheeks pink at last with restored warmth. Jack was curled up in the crook of his body and this must surely have quickened the warming of my boy who will likely regard the day as an adventure if he recalls any of it.

I wanted very much to ask Mr. Abel if it frightened him to go into the pond after my son and Thomas, if it brought on the memory of that terrible day in September. Imagining the scene over and over throughout the rest of the afternoon and into the evening, I shiver now as I sit writing by a newly kindled fire. Henry is put to bed, his stalwart savior and Thomas long gone from the house in the carriage Mr. Talbot insisted he hitch to take them home.

MARCH 30, 1856

I have written to Mother and Father in bold terms, telling them how Mr. Abel has performed the work of a hero in rescuing their grandson and Thomas Pringle from the icy waters of Mill Pond. I described my relief as both Thomas and Mr. Abel, the latter clutching my son, came through my side door in an icy vapor and that Henry is unscathed because of Mr. Abel's quick action. My gratitude to Mr. Abel is boundless and I wished for them to understand plainly that regardless of his upbringing, his seeming lack of origin, he has performed the highest imaginable good.

APRIL 2, 1856

Henry has not suffered any ill effect from his fall into the pond and I have been in a state of prayerful thanks with each glance I steal of my healthy

son at play. I suppose I am of two minds on prayer, which is that it suits
me to offer it when I am in distress or grateful, and that I can live without
it when life moves at its more relaxed, uneventful pace.

I have received an invitation to dinner at the Jamiesons and I have accepted. It could be that the several years between us—for I think she is past
thirty—have given her a more confident affect, though not haughty like
that of Fiona Terry. No, this advantage of years seems to prop Irene above
uncertainties that plague me almost daily. Things such as, am I seeing to
my son's needs adequately enough as a husbandless woman, or have I instructed Mr. Talbot sufficiently in the haying down of the horse's stalls,
given Lucy the correct amount of coin to do her twice weekly errand to
the Mercantile, said the proper *thank yous* to those who came to pay their
respects in those darkest days after losing James. (I can hardly recall who
came and went to and from the house.)

Being in Irene's company will, I hope, bring some of her self-posses-
sion along to me.

Virginia Pringle was already in the Jamiesons' parlor when I arrived with
my son and was shown there to await my hostess. I did not know she was
also to be a guest and the light spirit that had accompanied me to the
Jamieson home fell quite at my feet.

Mrs. Pringle surprised me first with a smile that was remarkably ordinary. On sight, I braced myself for her eagle-eyed appraisal, for again I
had elected not to don entirely black dress. My skirt was navy, my blouse
lavender. She seemed, at least on this day, not to care. Her capricious nature has me on edge of late as I wait for her to spring should I fall
out of her favor.

Even more shocking was her warmth with Henry. "Why, young
man," she said, bending low to face him. "I have heard the tale of your
little misadventure." He batted his hand at her shoulder, a gesture I tried
to stop as he took aim. It was playful, but a surprise to her and she made
a small sound, a tiny shriek that I took for dismay. It may have been how

she expresses delight, for she wore an uncertain smile. She recovered quickly and spoke to me. "You must be very relieved your son is safe."

"In equal measure relieved and glad to be rid of the thought that harm would have come to anyone that day. How is your son?" I inquired, wondering with more warmth than she usually inspired in me. I meant it as a gesture for Thomas and it encouraged his mother. Of course it did.

"Mrs. Parsons, you cannot know how it gladdens me to have you ask. In fact, he is quite despondent since the day at the pond, and I believe this to have been true for days before the occurrence. I cannot think how I missed such melancholy before. I need hardly tell you, it would be a tonic to have you visit."

I am proud of myself, for I said only that, yes, I would be glad to oblige her. I longed to say more. I longed to ask her what made her son so unhappy that it would seem he tried to take his own life, and so pathetically, in a pond barely deep enough to reach his shoulders were he to wade to its depths. It would swallow a child whole, of course. I knew that exposure to the cold alone could end a life.

She shifted in her chair, as if her dress were ill-fit to her pointy form, and then our hosts arrived, along with Mr. Pringle who had, it was understood, arrived late due to a meeting with his quarrymen. He took my hand and kissed it, his whiskers scraping a little, and then swung Henry up in the air as men are wont to do with children—a habit that makes me somewhat nervous for their little heads—and then put him down on the floor as gently as if he floated there.

Mr. Peter Jamieson was a man of considerable size now that he stood before me. He was taller than my husband had been, of greater girth than Mr. Pringle, and a good many years older than his wife, nearer Father's age. He bowed to me. "Mrs. Parsons, I had not the pleasure of greeting you at the Pringles' home last week, but allow me to say *181* that you are a most welcome guest in my home. I knew your husband through commerce. In fact, I purchased a schooner from him and his fine father some years ago and it has proven sturdy for the fishermen to whom I sold it in turn. Your husband was honorable where others I have dealt with since have not been. I am deeply sorry for your loss." Mr.

Jamieson then bent, with visible difficulty as if he had hurt his back, to look Henry in the eye. Henry looked directly back at our host, his bright eyes unblinking for that instant. "This boy's likeness to his father will be a comfort to you, I hope," remarked my host.

"Yes," I replied. "When I look at my son, I do enjoy his father's memory."

My son has never averted an adult's gaze before and this was no exception. His calm, gray eyes seemed to ease our host into another state of mind.

"There, now," Mr. Jamieson said, shifting back to being the host as he pulled at his waistcoat and took hold of one point of his mustache to pinch it into place. He addressed us all. "Will you accompany my wife and me to the dining room?" His question was polite, his authority clear.

I peered down at Henry who scowled up at me with a fistful of my skirt in his hand. I loosened his fingers and led him along behind the men, behind Mrs. Pringle and Irene who, when she came into the room, looked as if all I had concluded about her from the previous visit had taken its leave and left nothing but the shell of a handsome woman. I could not even make her meet my eyes.

As we took our places around the oval table, I asked Irene if her children would be joining us.

She confided that her daughters were not in the house. "They are now recovering under the care of Mr. Jamieson's older sister."

"They are being expertly cared for," Mr. Jamieson corrected. His tone seemed meant to rebuke her. "And, in fact, as of yesterday, they are not staying with my sister, but have been taken to a facility where there are several nurses and a doctor who will see to their needs. My sister could not withstand the exposure to their illness any more than we are able and asked me to find a proper place for them to take cures and convalesce." This was clearly news to Irene, who blanched.

"But, Peter, they are too young to be away, without the attention of a loving hand…"

"They are surrounded by loving hands, my dear, who will bestow care with a professional touch. That will be all on the matter. We have guests."

One look around the table revealed that all of us were uncomfortable and bewildered. What could have been so dire a germ as to have the children removed from the safety of their home and the warm nurturance of their mother, then of their aunt?

"There, my dear, your daughters will see good health much more quickly in such capable hands," Mrs. Pringle offered with a pat of Irene's hand. To her credit, Irene gave her thanks.

"Mrs. Parsons!" Mr. Pringle bellowed, startling me almost out of my seat so that when the serving maid was ladling soup into my bowl, it went nearly into Mrs. Pringle's lap. "It seems a mutual acquaintance of ours, in fact a quarryman in my employ, is to be commended for his brave deed the other afternoon."

His wife looked at him, curiosity bending her lips into a small frown. Perhaps this was her first understanding that Mr. Abel is her husband's employee. It might also have been news to her that the man she can scarcely honor with a glance had come to the aid of her son the day he rescued Henry from Thomas' failure to end his own life. This is what I have come to believe about Thomas' intention, though to have attempted it in so public a manner was quite another kind of act that suggested the opposite intention, for how could he not have thought he would be saved?

Mr. Jamieson piped up then. "Ah, yes, that Abel fellow. He is oddly quiet and I would not have supposed he had a bold nature." He chuckled and turned to Mr. Pringle. "How is your Thomas then, Reginald?"

"He seems well enough. He attends to the usual daily grind, and then takes his meals alone after Virginia and myself. Not as talkative as usual," he said, and as he did, seemed to wonder about it.

I could hold my tongue no longer. "That Thomas is despondent may have something to do with his inability to confide his deepest truths, whatever they may be, to his father. The tonic would bet- 183 ter be provided, I believe, with an offer of confidence lest he take another dip and not be so fortunate as to be plucked out of the water before the cold takes him."

Oh, I had done it again! Gone and spoken entirely out of turn and to a man I admire as much as I do my own father. Poor Mr. Pringle, all the mirth and flush gone out of him as he turned in mute surprise to his wife who now glared in my direction, and with proper cause this time.

I fled her gaze, preferring to fuss with my soup and to help my mercifully quiet son with his. Of course, he was content to blow bubbles into the bowl with each mouthful and everyone was being careful not to mention it. I knew I should have left him with Lucy; she had told me it was foolish to bring a little boy to a dinner for adults even if he had been invited, an unusual thing in itself. I now see that Irene must have yearned for the company of a child in her midst. Yet even I was divided now that I sensed his presence was a reminder to my hostess of her own children's absence. My small son is a shield behind which I continue to hide every time I am invited out. After my outburst, a wardrobe would have been the better hiding place, yet there was none in sight.

In the uncomfortable moment that followed, Mrs. Pringle grew intent upon her own soup, and her husband engaged my son, coaxing the boy away from his noisy play with the spoon and gently instructing him how to eat properly. Peter Jamieson called to his manservant and whispered something to him.

"I do like to walk," Irene said to me, at last intruding upon the uneasy quiet. "I tend to favor it most when the evening approaches if you would ever care to join me."

"Well, I do not like the cold," I admitted. "But I am glad you asked. Lucy has said I ought to get out more, even in the chill, so I will join you on your next stroll."

She placed her warm, pale hand on mine and smiled as if I had just removed a barb from her flesh. "I will call on you tomorrow, then."

Before long, the servants had surrounded us and were filling our plates, the host and Mr. Pringle had engaged in talk of commerce, and Mrs. Pringle was affably discussing the weather with Irene. The older woman liked the cold, she said. It was not a surprising fact, though I was cheered myself, if a little wary, seeing this new aspect of Virginia Pringle, this attempt at sociability, apparently for its own sake.

The rest of supper passed without incident and I could not leave without apology to my hosts for my outburst, and particularly to dear Mr.

Pringle. In response, Mrs. Pringle sniffed dismissively and her husband had the grace to bow and offer me a conciliatory smile. I could have expected nothing less really.

Irene came to my door in the hour before twilight this evening and we walked the circumference of Mill Pond Meadow, bundled against the cold, picking our steps carefully, and watched a scarlet sky begin to darken through the budding branches. I had left Henry in Lucy's care for this stroll and cannot recall the last time I felt so free to express myself to another person since my husband passed, for I do check myself with Lucy often, mistaking her for one of Mother's confidantes because of her advanced years. Of course, that is ridiculous, for Lucy is my companion and helpmate, not Mother's.

I told Irene about my sense that James is sometimes near, that often I awaken in the early morning, before any light comes through the curtain, and hear his breath, smell the tobacco as if it floats up from a lit pipe in his hand. This feeling lasts only as long as it takes to fully open my eyes and when I do, my surroundings are cold, the pipe in its resting place, untouched as I knew it would be.

"Your dreams fool you," she said, drawing my arm through hers. "I have had such dreams of my daughters and they are living! But they are so far away from me, it is as if…" she could not finish the thought, nor did she need to. "Mr. Abel is garnering much favor in Reginald's eye," she remarked. "He seems to have come from nowhere, or anywhere. Do you know of him?"

Here I did not know whether to admit that not only do I know him, but that he has become a friend whose company I enjoy, who visits my thoughts more often than it would be wise to admit. I peered at her in the half-light to see if a secret knowledge was there, but there was none, so I confided that I did know him as an acquaintance, for *185* he had been James' first mate and, as the one survivor, had introduced himself some weeks after the vessels went down. It was all I felt free to mention in that moment.

We moved on to talk of the peculiar Mrs. Stevenson and we both laughed at her earnestness, but not far enough back in my mind was the thought that I had not heard of or seen Mr. Abel since he plucked Henry and Thomas from the pond. I have even taken up needlepoint to distract myself and my fingers ache from the pinpricks meant for the fabric. Writing, I can hardly press the quill so my words are fainter upon the page.

Several moments into our walk, Irene confided to me that her husband does not allow their children to cry. "It is true, they are getting older. Pauline is eleven and her sister, Eleanor, is not much younger at nearly ten years. Yet, he persists in forcing them into a stoicism that is not in their nature. It is habit for a child to cry when she is ill, natural for her to want her mother. I do not think I have seen him react so harshly to the children before and now they are without both of us, far away until they are healthy enough to come home. It may be weeks!"

"What is their illness?"

"They have pneumonia. My own mother nursed me through it when I was but five years old. My younger brother lost his life to it only two years ago. But without a loving hand, how can their health be restored?"

"Can you not go to them?"

"Peter will not allow it."

I could not believe that the woman I had thought so confident upon first meeting her would not balk at this edict.

"Forgive me," I began, measuring my words. "But what would your good husband do if you were to suggest what you have just said to me?"

She turned to me and reached for my hands. "I have said all of this and more to Peter. He will not consider it. He does not want me to risk the contagion and says there is a perfectly capable nurse tending to them in the hospital that his sister has selected. It is among the best," she said, and then dropped her gaze, belying any conviction. In the next breath, she held fast to the truth she knew best, that nothing could be better than a mother nursing her own children back to health, and I had to agree. Taking her arm and steering her back along the path, I knew that my new friend might need me as much as I needed her.

Lucy has been peering at me lately with a funny half-smile that I do not pretend to fathom but which leaves me with the thought that while she can be a sly creature she means no ill.

This morning, I received a note from Irene on pages with flowers pressed into them. They must be from last summer and it pleased me that she would take blossoms she had preserved and pass them to me.

> Marianne,
>
> *You brought me no end of good with our stroll and your concern. I know that in the years to come, we will always be friends and that if ever you have a care, grave or trifling, you must share it with me.*
>
> Your friend,
> Irene Jamieson

It pains me that her suffering seems perpetrated by her husband's unrelenting conviction that her children belong elsewhere in their illness. I will call on her the day after tomorrow.

April 10, 1856

Lucy urged me to send a note to Mr. Abel inviting him to a meal. "Respect to your good parents, Cousin, but your neighbors be damned," she said when I told her that I risk Mother's censure and Mrs. Pringle's condemnation, even after this man aided her son. I have wanted to invite Mr. Abel, but have stayed my hand, unsure of a reason why I ought not to invite him, and brought up short by the truth that I want too much to invite him. While Lucy's rebuke took me by surprise, if I am to be honest with myself I care little for the neighbors' disapproval. This is my home, Mr. Abel is my friend, and my son and I should enjoy his company. It is time I behaved as mistress of my own household. I must overcome this childish fear of my elders' reproach, for what *187* am I doing that is worthy of their worst criticisms? I am guilty of no indiscretion, nor do I seek such a thing. I want only to bring a smile to my boy's lips and some cheer to a man who has no one to call a friend.

The difficulty, much as I am gratified by their presence, is that Mother and Father arrived last night and will remain for a week. This, at Mother's insistence, particularly since our last reunion was so unsatisfying and she and Father left the morning after Mr. Pringle's fete rather than stay and visit. They have lately become tethered to home and I cannot account for it. Perhaps one of them is not well? Father did look a little pale.

Now that they are here, it is as if Mother and I never had words when we spoke at the Pringles' party. Perhaps she is more favorably disposed, having learned of Theodore's good deed at the pond. And in spite of my house being smaller than what she is accustomed to, she does enjoy it here. I sometimes think she enjoys it too much and is too at home in it during her visits, for now that I am widowed, she seems to feel that she is my mother in the way she was as I came of age and it is simply not the case. In my own right, I am a mother with a child to usher into his formative years, and I will not allow her to bustle around here as if she were mistress. Yesterday not five moments after her arrival, she ordered Lucy about as if she were a common servant—her very own cousin! I had to take Mother aside and silence that high-handed nature of hers. What follows is a faithful account:

Mother was busying herself with her grandson, trying to engage him in drawing a picture. Of course, what he most wanted was to plunge his little fists into the batter I was stirring. I urged them both out of doors and Lucy offered to make tea for her and Father since they had just arrived. Mother's response was to refuse Lucy's offer and to tell her to see to supper preparations. Then she turned to me and said that she did not wish to amuse her grandson out of doors, but that Lucy ought to do so, even as she had just ordered her to prepare our meal. I am only glad that my cousin was out of earshot for that remark, for she had turned on her heel and left the room. I heard her ascend the stairs.

Really, I do not understand how Father can bear it. The older Mother grows, so grows her arrogance! If she levels that attitude at Mr. Abel, or even Mr. Talbot—who is a paid servant with nothing but respect for my family!—fear of impropriety in my own home will not quiet me.

Oh, I am getting far too rattled over something I might not have to suffer. If I am to endure her visit, I will have to make every effort to distract and accommodate her as a daughter does her mother. When she is at peace, she is a most congenial presence!

I will leave off with the thought that if she should misstep—such as telling me how to care for my boy—I shall nip her fast in the bud and she will feel it acutely!

April 11, 1856

Mother finally leveled her particular scorn at Mr. Abel last night at supper to which he graciously came. I had my misgiving about inviting him when Mother and Father were visiting, yet they ought to be able to see the true nature of the man whose might saved not only his own life when the vessel went down, but that of my son in the pond. It ought to change Mother's blind opinion, and perhaps this will carry over to her imperious friend, Virginia Pringle.

Mr. Abel showed up with his hat in hand, a little parcel for Henry, and a humble smile. Before he entered the parlor where I introduced him to Mother and Father, I took the opportunity, before my parents, to tell him properly how glad I am for him that he has found employment with Reginald Pringle. He confided that he found the days more taxing than being aboard a ship, that he missed the groundswell of the ocean and would still trade it for the unyielding stillness of a granite floor, but that he was indeed grateful for the employment. It has, of course, robbed him of the time he once devoted to visiting us, though this was prior to my illness and the months when he kept away. Yet it is my notion that Virginia Pringle, now aware of her husband's sympathy and perhaps respect for the man, has made it plain to Mr. Abel that he must not entertain hopes of a friendship with me and he has obliged by keeping some distance.

His acceptance of my invitation to supper flies against my suspicion—would he risk the security of his new employment? But I *189* have no way of confirming it other than to ask him outright.

How can I? It would put him ill at ease. Inquiring suggests I would welcome more time in his company.

And I do, but this is not at all the point.

He does look well, if tired around the eyes. Yes, now that I think of it, this fatigue would go further to support his reasons for being less heard from of late, and rescues him from my inquiry.

Entering the parlor, I felt Mother's cool appraisal settle on him even before we were fully before them for introductions. They went well enough, with Father standing to shake Mr. Abel's hand and, visibly pleased, receiving as firm a grip as he gave. Mr. Abel bowed his head to Mother who, with less obvious pleasure, offered her hand. He took it with grace, but did not bend to kiss it, perhaps sensing she would not welcome such a gesture. Not unlike my first reaction to Thomas, Mother placed that hand at her back as if to wipe it clean even without the touch of his lips against it. It was an altogether different reaction than that which I observed when Mr. Pringle kissed her hand in greeting last month. Mr. Abel turned to me, with a smile, but evident in his gaze was his understanding of Mother's lack of regard for him.

I know asking him to join us might have proved a great risk to his pride, yet as I earlier prepared the meal with Lucy in the way Mother taught me, the thought teased me that perhaps she might show some kindness toward my guest. This first greeting was not a hopeful sign.

Lucy and I had prepared Beef Wellington and bread pudding, sweet green peas, and a delicious chocolate pie that, in fact, was James' mother's recipe and which I know Father likes. We were all at the table, enjoying the coffee Mother had made, when she addressed Mr. Abel. I believe it was the first thing she said to him after the unfortunate greeting they exchanged when he had arrived. Father, in sharp contrast, had been very sporting all evening and seemed taken with my guest, regaling him with tales of his own career in commerce.

Mother interrupted them without preamble.

"Mr. Abel, where is your family? Perhaps your mother and father are nearby?" Mr. Abel revealed no surprise at the question, though I had hoped it would not arise. How I imagined this could be avoided is a mark of my foolish optimism.

Immediately, Father placed a hand on her sleeve, its meaning, I took, to quiet her or to steer her off this path. She would have none of it.

Mr. Abel smiled at her, his gaze utterly without resentment of the meaning in her question, and for just the one moment, I felt pity dampen my regard for him. Surely he must have sensed her condescension and his rebuttal would follow! Yet, if my opinion was momentarily diminished, I am more admiring of him now for his reply.

"My family is myself," he said simply, parting his hands so that his palms showed, as if he would offer himself whole to her beastly intent. Mr. Abel's upturned hands revealed the rope-bite scars for all to behold. Old lines etched by hard work revealed a difficult life, not at all the life of a man Mother would ever consider adequate company; not for her, not for me. It does not matter that my husband had spent some years at sea, and that he preferred it. For Mother it is all to do with standing and the origin of that standing. James was the son of a wealthy businessman; my friend Theodore Ethan Abel is the son of no one who matters to Mother or to Mrs. Pringle. He can claim nothing of distinction in his line.

"Do you mean, there are no other Abels but you?" She asked, leaning toward him, not at all sympathetic to whatever his sad story might be. I had the urge to pull her back in her seat as if she were a child leaning too far past a ledge, when it was really my friend I ought to have warned. After all, what could be so difficult for her to believe? Many a man walks the earth with no family, though I have not met one until Mr. Abel who would readily reveal the sad truth of his life to a harsh judge of such things. It would be a different question from me and my not asking it has more to do with my disinterest in the matter of standing. Mother's friendly tone masked the reek of her disdain.

"None," he replied to Mother's query. "And there haven't been others since I was sixteen and my parents were taken from me. Their parents died long before I came into the world and I have no brothers and no sisters. There's a cluster of cousins in England, but I've never heard from them."

Oh, dear! Why has he never shared this with me? It is true that since meeting him I have let myself believe a false, if unspoken, tale, that his provenance was a result of his brush with death on board James' vessel. That only makes me the fool and not Mother, who has thought to ask.

This is, of course, the prerogative of any parent. My own omission drives hard the point that I am after all more like the child I was until not so very long ago. Forgive her though I cannot for her tone and motive, she has asked the proper thing. Had I a daughter, I would do the same. And when Henry is of an age, I will also have certain curiosities and a duty to explore them.

"What was it that your father did to make his way?" Mother persisted after receiving an answer to the first query and showing little but a momentary frown when he revealed the loss of his parents. Here Mr. Abel looked to me once more, perhaps wanting me to intervene, but I could not. Again, I recognized that it was not a question a mother or father knew not to ask. In fact, it was the very question I should have expected, except that Mr. Abel is not a suitor, not in my estimation, and I am sure they do not consider him thus. Yet, they posed such questions to other suitors who thought to tread over my early-blooming love for James. (I recall, too, that they asked it of James when he first began to court me, although then it was a light-hearted joke because James' father and mine were lifelong friends).

In the instant before Mother engaged him, Mr. Abel was almost at ease, telling me about his work at the Pringles' quarry, that he is learning much at the urging of Mr. Pringle, despite the trial of such grueling work.

Mr. Abel straightened his posture even more and this broadened his already impressive shoulders. "He was a fishmonger, Mrs. Laramie. Proud to be so until the day he died." Quietly, I cheered my friend for rising above his humiliation.

"Yes, pride is an admirable trait if not carried too far," Mother said. I still cannot fathom her meaning; it seemed at once to be faint praise and warning, the first surprising me, and my friend did seem to relax. However, there was harsh judgment in her words, in her demeanor with him, from the moment she met him.

I was desperate to steer the talk elsewhere. "Mother, will you help me in the pantry please? There is something else I need you to carry out."

She looked at me, and then at Lucy, who eats with us always. Mother was clearly puzzled. Still, she came, with a reluctant step that near-ly matched Henry's when he is bound for his daily nap, and when we reached the kitchen, I cornered her.

"How dare you? You have no place, Mother, with your own father once a miller's hand, not the proprietor of a mill at all." She kept herself half-turned. "And if Theodore's father was a fishmonger, then Theodore himself chose a profession that honored his father. He was first mate on James' schooner, loyal to him before anyone. You do him a great disser-vice." I recall now as I write this that I referred to him as Theodore when speaking to Mother, yet had avoided doing so, even to the man himself. And yet, I write it easily here now. She noticed it and remarked upon it. "He has asked me to address him by his first name," I told her. "I have not yet."

"Does he address you by yours?"

"He does not. If he did, I would welcome it."

At this, she offered me her disapproval and I rejected it.

"He is my friend, Mother, and you might not enjoy this. You might even ask your good friend Virginia to keep a keener eye lest he steal into my windows as we sleep."

She was shocked at my nerve, but contrite in the moment afterward. The reversal of our roles quieted us both, for I was perhaps too harsh in my censure. I filled the tea cart with the pie and plates and wheeled it out to the dining room, Mother at my side. She must have thought me mad pushing my own tea cart, still clinging to her belief that even her own cousin was meant to replace Agatha and in far greater capacity, but I cared little for her suppositions. In fact, I had earlier told Lucy I wanted her to sit more and that I would take care of our dessert serving. I did it as much to give her the rest as to try Mother's patience.

"Mother, I must admonish you to keep from insulting my guest further," I said to her in the moment before we reached the dining room.

She did not reply but joined the others, sitting quietly next to Father who now held Henry on his lap. The two were at play in a spirited game of peek-a-boo. Theodore, a name I will now use confidently in these pages, was also engaged in the game.

Eventually, Mother relaxed enough to laugh at their antics and I joined in. As we ate our pie and Father made a jovial show of spooning it into first his and then his grandson's mouth, and Theodore and I spoke of my plans for the garden, Lucy rose to clear our dessert plates. Despite my urging her to wait until I could help her, she begged the task for herself and I relented, understanding she might also be uncomfortable around her high-handed cousin.

No one entering for the first time would have guessed that moments before Mother had not only affronted Theodore, but that I had scolded her as if she were a naughty child. The palest light of the deepening evening slipped though the curtains of the parlor where we had moved after dinner and in that light, I was relieved to see that Mother was somewhat less narrow-eyed when she looked up at Theodore as he played with my boy. In fact, I am sure a corner of her mouth lifted which, when she saw me catch it, she quickly turned downward in concentration on her cross-stitch.

After a time, as it was getting late, Lucy lifted my sleepy boy and coaxed him to bed, for he was half-asleep. Father, too, took himself off to bed. Theodore and I sat by the fire, he seeming to push himself into its corner very far away from me. Mother, sitting opposite us in the rocking chair she gave James and me when I had Henry, feigned reading. She had made it her task to remain.

Theodore seemed hardly able to speak let alone move.

Before long, Mother looked close to dozing over her stitching. She woke with a start every few minutes and finally called to Lucy who came bustling in, looking as if she had been interrupted at an important task.

She whispered in Lucy's ear and then left the room with a kiss to my forehead and her apologies to all of us for her sleepiness.

Lucy sat in Mother's seat and sent me a look of such exasperation as Mother left the room and headed upstairs for bed that I nearly laughed aloud. I hid my smile behind my hand, rising to poke at the embers so that Theodore would not see. I am sure he knew, too, what Mother was up to in her fortress of propriety—my home, her duty—but I did not want to see it in his eyes. To seek this mutual understanding did feel too intimate.

After Mother left the room, Lucy left briefly to retrieve the quill and letter she had been writing to her granddaughter. In that moment, I whispered to Theodore if he had been insulted by Mother's pointed questions. He said that he had not, but that somehow he had expected her to be more like me.

I giggled. "Oh, my dear Theodore, you could not have been more incorrect!" His smile was broad indeed and it was in that instant I heard my own use of his name and knew the source of his gladness.

APRIL 13, 1856

Irene Jamieson called on me today as I have been unable to take much time to spend with her since Mother and Father arrived. They urged me out the door.

In truth, it is a return to melancholy that has rooted me to home these past days. I fear I am cheerless company for Irene who needs someone to lift her spirits, not drag them down as if weighted with stone.

I have again been spending long hours staring into the dark, fighting a growing understanding that James is forever lost to me. Then I scold myself, as Mother would do, whispering that I am no use without sleep. I can almost hear her voice escape my throat, a troubling notion, though perhaps inevitable, for we do sound similar when Mother is in good spirits. And when I am in bad spirits or scolding Henry, I hear the edge she can take on in her voice.

I had Mr. Talbot hitch up the horses so Irene and I might take a proper ride. Mother smiled and waved us out the door, happy to be entrusted with her grandson's well-being for part of an afternoon. She would have me spend all of my days with Irene as my bosom friend.

"You would do well to model yourself after such a woman," Mother told me this evening as we were turning down her bedclothes and placing the sack of warm stones at the bottom. Though it is less chilly now that spring has begun to take hold, even in summer Mother's feet are uncomfortably cold while Father's, she complains, are so warm that they cause an odor beneath the quilt. Of course, I had to quiet her on this remark about Father's feet. There are some things a daughter does not need to understand.

Her remark about Irene was not untrue. I have seen that my friend holds herself in a way that belies her troubles while I may not always be so adept at concealing mine. If Mother were to learn of how Irene suffers in the absence of her children, holding herself erect under the weight of an edict from her husband that she cannot see them before they are well, she would faint with disbelief and admiration. I thought to confide this about my new friend and then reconsidered. Mother no doubt would agree with Peter Jamieson and I would be left to wallow in my own dismay. Again, I must remark that she is too similar to Virginia Pringle in her thinking! It is a wonder I can tolerate Mother as well as I do, but this comes from my overall love and esteem, for she is a fine woman even so. Mrs. Pringle has yet to convince me of any winsome qualities.

Mr. Talbot offered to take the reins so we could chat amiably without worrying about our direction, but I decided it might not be a bad notion to take up the reins myself as I used to do now and then. And where did we go? Somehow, I found myself steering us to Mrs. Allison's shop, the very lady who boards Theodore. I felt a distinct unease heading there, even as Theodore would be away at the quarry, but Irene wanted very much to buy her daughters some hair ribbons and candy sticks to send with a young couple leaving soon from Gloucester for Clifton Springs, New York where the Sanitarium is situated. I thought that seeing Mrs. Alison's shop could do no harm. On the way, Irene explained that sending her daughters these pretty, sweet things they adore and that might reach them by week's end, lifted her spirits just to speak of it. She would bundle the trinkets with a series of letters she had written. The mails, she complained, are too, too slow.

196   "It has been nearly a month since the girls left and I cannot abide it much longer, Marianne. In due course, I will have to go there myself and risk Peter's harsh disapproval."

"Do you know how much longer they will need to stay?" I wrung my hands through the words. The very thought of being apart from my son for more than an afternoon ran through me like a blade and with it came afresh the memory of that day he toppled into the pond.

"I do not," she said, and turned away from me. She could not have understood my gesture and I have yet to tell her of Theodore and his deed.

"Irene, is there no way for you to visit with them, no one who will convey you and your husband to where they are so that you might reside closer to them?"

"I have proposed this to my husband and no sooner was it on my lips than he told me that our children were too attached to their mother—to me, Marianne!—and that they would grow stronger not only in their convalescence but in their independence as long as we remained here."

I was struck dumb. How could a man deny his children their mother? How could he suppose that they would recover more speedily away from their parents? I thought of Timothy and the brittle civility that existed between him and Lucy, and in that instant knew that he was of the same ilk. Somehow, even in the few days they had spent with us, I knew that Lucy's son-in-law was a forceful man, yet hearing Irene's account of her husband made this all the more unpleasant a revelation.

Mrs. Allison was in the shop and regarded me with a kind look, telling me that her tenant, Mr. Abel as she referred to him, was a fine helper and that her husband has appreciated his extra hand. It was then Mr. Allison came up from a storeroom and greeted Irene and me. Without prompting from his wife, he repeated much the same praise for Theodore and I left feeling a balm had been applied to some of the less favorable thoughts certain people have expressed about him. I knew I would like to visit their mercantile again.

We headed over to Mrs. Spencer's little shop for tea after Irene chose her gifts and were warmly greeted by the proprietress who asked after my son and gave me a warm hug. She said she was glad to see me more about town, that the outdoor time agreed with me. She sat us at a little table by the window where we could watch people *197* bustle through their afternoon activity.

There in the quiet of Mrs. Spencer's shop, I spoke to Irene with more candor than I planned. I spoke frankly of my despair over losing James. Yet, speaking of it, I did not feel its weight as had been visited upon me in the past months, or even last night.

I told her of my disapproval of Mrs. Pringle, and hers of Theodore, how it vexes me even though I do not consider him beyond friendship. There is, I told her, a feeling that he is a part of my life now because of James, and that I must always, and will always, be good to him, for he was good to James. She was moved to pose a most unfortunate question for which I cannot fault her, feeling the need to protect my thoughts, but the relief of spilling them before her left me lighter afterward.

"Marianne, do you feel that this man is good to you, that he will always be no matter what his role?" It was very much to the point.

"We are well provided for by James' trust. I do not want for money and certainly I do not wish to be courted."

She lifted my chin to read me better.

"You are a troubled woman, and I see it as clearly as if looking in the mirror. You question your privilege, to be drawn to a man of whom no one seems to have a high opinion because he is borne of tragedy and has no apparent history. You ask yourself if it is unwise to place your trust in him, and worry this fondness has affected your son as well, and always there is doubt. You doubt yourself so very much."

"How do you know me so well, Irene?"

She beheld me a moment, and smiled.

"I have felt this as you do. My husband came to Rockport as a man of mediocre station and my family was unwilling to accept him. He is a good man, steadfast in his religious beliefs and devoted to his family, though I think you doubt this now. I clung to the goodness in him, and still do, as I feel that my own faith in him will surpass the disapproval my family now expresses all over again because of his harsh stance on our daughters' placement away from home."

I hope my friend did not see in me the same disapproval of her husband who, I felt, had at heart his own sense of what is right where his children and their mother are concerned. Perhaps Irene would prevail, if not in the way she hoped, then by way of believing that her husband was doing the best thing for their daughters. Yes, it will, I think, be her optimism that wins her an anguished victory over her suffering.

Yet, like a magpie's constant querulous reminder of its presence, something nagged.

"Irene, I cannot accept your comparison of our two lives in this way. If I were to allow a friendship to further flourish between Theodore and me, I risk disgrace. True, I would have the means to live well and we could remain in our home and go about our daily rhythms as long as my family allowed it, and I am certain they would after a good while, even if it would be strained. Yet we would be doing so without a soul to call a friend other than Theodore and my cousin. Yes, I know you would remain a friend, though your husband might forbid it. I do not say this in disdain, but because I understand that his word carries great weight with you and you risk his disapproval if you argue it. I am sorry to put it so plainly." Irene turned to the window. "I have a prediction for you, then, dear and sensible friend," I said. "You will decide to travel to Clifton Springs and be near your daughters, in spite of your husband's refusal to allow it. In time he will forgive you this, and you and he will live your lives together, having made your peace."

"You say it as if it were foregone," Irene whispered, tears brimming in her warm brown eyes.

"Indeed. We are alike this way. But if I were to surrender to my own will, a will I have not confronted until now, to allow Theodore to become a significant part of my life, I could not recover so easily. Perhaps I might never recover from the loss of this community. It fears acceptance of those whose fiber does not match their own, yet they hardly look past the outer fiber to see the inner. Sometimes I wonder how it is that I am the daughter of a woman who reminds me of some of the least pleasant aspects of being born into privilege. I only hope some of my father resides in me."

Irene took one of her hands in my two and squeezed it gently, then let go. It was our promise of mutual understanding. We did not speak for the rest of the time it took to drink our tea and nibble at our plate of butter cookies. As we took our seats on the carriage a short time later, Irene turned to me and said, as if confessing a secret, "you have allowed me some hope, Marianne. I had not anticipated hope, entertaining only worry."

She was flushed with something more that I could not divine beyond the hope she professed. For the rest of the ride to her home, from where I proceeded home on my own, she was amiably quiet. I thought it best to leave her to her own thoughts, for perhaps they were about her children, and I tried in vain to fend off my own about Theodore who had crept into my thoughts and would not leave.

APRIL 18, 1856

Today, the sky goes on forever. If it were just a little bit bluer, I would think it unreal, a color from a child's book of pictures. Even the gulls soaring high are visible by their shape; aimless, drifting dark arrows against a blue pallet. The forsythia along the path's edge of Mill Pond Meadow is visible from the cupola where I have come this afternoon to pen a few thoughts.

For days now, Henry has wandered to the surf's edge and touched it slowly and with some hesitancy as his fingers draw near. Then, he snaps them back as soon as the cold touches them, surprised and terrified, laughing, his eyes round with wonder.

"What is it, Henry?"

"Fish?"

"Yes! Fish swim in the ocean!"

"Me!"

"No," I said, shivering with my arms about my shoulders, pulling my cape close around me. "Too cold. You would not do well in there, love. You should know that now." I could not yet laugh at the memory of his dip in the pond, and here we were at the ocean's edge. I recall even now the shudder that traveled through me those hours ago at Henry's interest in the water.

Yet, he sat down on the sand and began to tug at his little shoes and coat, as if he were hot and needed to take them off. Laughing at last through my protestation, I bent down to scoop him into my arms. We were whirling around, he with his giggle like the sound of a brook in the spring, when a voice stopped me.

"Mrs. Parsons, it is lovely to see you and your son out on this particularly cheerful day."

I stood before her, teetering slightly, Henry clinging to me with his strong little legs because he, too, must have felt the world spinning. My laughter disappeared in a vapor before me, and the smile I wore fell at my feet.

"Mrs. Pringle," I said. "Thank you. It is good to see you as well."

She cleared her throat and straightened her fur muff around her hands. The cold air puffing from her beakish nose nearly set me to laughing again, for she looked more like a mythical fire-breathing creature than a gentlewoman, but I kept my mirth in check and waited.

"I called at the house, but found there was no one there. As I was walking, I heard you and your boy, so I have come to greet you."

It is odd how her words, so ordinary and friendly in anyone else, belie what I have come to believe is her truer nature. Odd, too, that she would approach me as if she meant nothing but civility—or her brand of it.

"Welcome, then. May I offer you tea? Lucy is out today, but I can prepare it easily enough," I said, in spite of myself. To my relief, she refused.

"Of course, I do hope you will come to my home again soon. Your son is a delight to us, and your company is good for my own son."

Oh, yes, the delight was plain in her pallid cheeks and hard, gray eyes. What could I do but tell her I would be delighted myself? How much insincere delight can be shared between us? Well, if only for Thomas' sake, I will need to make a call soon, so I told her I would make a point to visit.

APRIL 20, 1856

Hannah is due to arrive in a fortnight. A happy day it was to receive that letter from Rose. I have already made the child's bedroom, putting little dolls and books on the windowsills and placing on her bed a new nightdress I saw at the Allisons' mercantile when I was there with Irene, and made a note to myself to return for it. It is made from Irish linen and woven through with tiny satin posies and green ribbon at the bodice. A most lovely thing for a lovely girl.

I was graced by a visit from Theodore today and his presence was a tonic. We sat indoors on the sun porch, warmest in the early afternoon even this early in the spring, and watched the gusting wind sway the linden. So rapt was I to the tree's motion that when my friend began to speak, I did not hear him. He was well into it before I noticed his lips moving and that his smile was forlorn. I could not imagine why, when we were enjoying this time simply sitting and letting the peacefulness of a warm house surround us. Lucy was in the parlor, hardly a room away, busy with her stitching, and Henry was napping after a hard morning's work with Mr. Talbot in the stables. I am more grateful than ever for Mr. Talbot's indulgence of my son who is more active than ever.

"I've spent weeks preparing these words in my head," Theodore was saying.

I turned to him in confusion and immediately had it in my own head to say, "no. You must not say it," for I realized I knew precisely what he intended to say.

Instead, I spoke of time. "You understand it has not been a year, that I am still in mourning. If you are a friend to me, you will care about this." He looked away from me and then back, his bravery restored.

"I don't wish to care," came his reply, with an edge of frustration.

"Which means you do," I said.

"Well," he said, "do you?"

"I care about what it will mean to my son later in his life when the truth is brought to him that his mother was still in mourning…"

"Please," he said. "Stop."

"It is not only other people," I said, indicating with the arc of my hand this accursed village and their concern for every citizen's well-being. "I must be at peace with my choices…" I recalled the other day with Irene, and that as long as she is not with her children, or near enough to them, she cannot be at peace, that she faces a most unpopular decision, and that I as much as encouraged her to make it. And, again, I chased away any likening of our situations.

Theodore's brow gathered and he leaned back, as if to create a gulf between us. "Am I a poor choice?"

"Theodore," I said, my hands on my face. "It is not as simple as you hope." I looked at him through parted hands and wished to touch his face, to smooth the whiskers he had grown over the winter, and, yes, to smell them, imagining they held the breath of whatever is borne on spring breezes. "I still grieve for my husband. And, yes, though it may smart to hear me say so, it is also true that I still long for him to return. Oh, dear," I said, seeing his face. "I know how ridiculous it is to speak of that aloud, how impossible an outcome after so complete a tragedy."

He stood then, very quickly, and asked me to understand that he could not come to call for a period that even he could not decide was right, and he took my hand and kissed it. It is this hand that I pressed to my own lips after Theodore left the house by the porch entrance, pulling at a low-draping branch of the linden that snapped back as if in defiance as he walked away.

As soon as the door closed, Lucy came to me and put her hand on my shoulder. In her touch I felt her loyal friendship, now and for years to come.

APRIL 22, 1856

It is a preposterous thought that Theodore was delivered from those frothing seas in my husband's stead, but of late this thought has occurred to me. I will not think of it again, for it is James who should be here and whom I will never again hold. I do long for my husband's return despite knowing it will never be. Dread of a future without him is still more present in the dead of night and in the earliest waking moment.

And yet, for weeks now, though I have not recorded their instances, it has been Theodore's face that passes before my eyes when I close them at night. Contrary to a playful nature I have come to know in him, when I close my eyes, I see him as at once so very tender and serious. In the dark, I feel his unuttered plea to allow him into my heart, and I feel my hand reach beyond me, the thought willing it forward. In the dark of my bedroom, there is no one to touch but myself.

And I have done so only last night, feeling the heat beneath my nightdress, pressing there and lifting it higher so that my fingers found the heat source I have not touched since before I was a married woman. Moving my hand back and forth over it, I allowed the rhythm of my fingers to bring me to the edge, then over, over, and up to a place so perfectly sweet and wild that when I came down, back to my life, to the cool spot of my bed I never inhabit, I wept for the shame of this longing, the empty space of it.

Theodore is in my thoughts more and more. I feel his need but can do nothing. To have written of it here leaves me wanting to shred the words and exalt in them. He cannot know how deeply he has come to affect me.

APRIL 24, 1856

James surfaced again in my dreams, just last night, his features indistinct at times, and at others so vivid that even in the dream I turned away in shame. And it was shame, not the lark, which woke me. I pulled the quilt over my head so that Jack began to root around with his wet nose in search of me. Finding me, he sopped my face with his wet nose and tongue until I put him on the floor and sternly told him, "No, Jack. Go!" He whimpered, leaned forward on his paws, and lay upon the floor with a sigh.

I have not heard from Theodore for nearly a week and learned from Lucy who heard from Mr. Talbot who overheard from someone working at Mr. Pringle's quarry that Theodore has been sent on an errand to New York, to the great city where surely a man more accustomed to life in a village and at sea would be lost.

It is unlike him not to write. Even when it was I who asked him not to come after my illness, fearing the impropriety of his campaign for my friendship (that I see now was not at all thus; it was devotion); even then, he wrote to me once.

APRIL 27, 1856

Today the sun did not waken me, for it had barely risen. What did was the sound of a man's voice. "There now, Lucy. It is best to sleep. I will mind the boy."

I recognized the voice, gentle and respectful, a quiet rumble within it, yet could not place it. I slipped from my bed, wrapping my gown tight around me, and crossed to Henry's room. He was fast asleep. Then I walked quickly to the stairs and down. At the entrance to the parlor, I spied Lucy and, moving further into the room, saw that she was

sitting in a chair in the parlor, her head back, her face flushed and shin-
ing. Mr. Talbot sat on the settee at a respectful distance, though he was
perched as if to leap toward her should she need him. There was urgency
in his eyes as he beheld my cousin. My concern betrayed me before I
spoke and he stood as I entered.

"Missus, I hope you'll forgive me for taking too much time away from
my work this morning. Lucy's taken ill."

"No, Cousin, I'm not ill!" Lucy protested and popped up from her
chair to prove it, then had to sit back down, her hand to her forehead. I
moved toward her, reaching for a blanket from the settee. One look at the
worry in Mr. Talbot's face brought home the truth. He wished to be the
one who comforted her.

"What brought you in here to Lucy's side, Mr. Talbot?"

"I believe it was the sound of Lucy at the open window, Missus, in the
side room. I heard the window open as I was entering the stable, then she
started to cough and could not seem to get hold of herself."

"It's nothing, Cousin," she said, as I pressed the back of my hand to her
cheek and, as sure as we were all sitting there, she was feverish, though
I could not say for certain if some of her heat was due to the presence of
Mr. Talbot. I dare say she had him quite alarmed and that he had his effect on her. Still, there was no doubt she needed her rest.

I looked to Mr. Talbot and understood his thoughts. How long has he
held Lucy's interests in his heart?

"Well, if it is nothing, then why do you look feverish? You feel it too.
Yes, quite!" I said, my hand pressed to her brow. "Come with me to your
room, Lucy. I will not hear otherwise, with your granddaughter's arrival
hardly a week away. If you will not listen to me, you are of no more use to
me than a child." Of course, I was not altogether serious. I could
not do without her, my cousin, my friend and she knows it well   205
now. I could not scold her with any conviction.

She looked at me then, weariness and gratitude crowding into her eyes,
and it felt good to have made a decision about something for a change,
about someone other than my son for whom I could care openly and with
purpose.

April 28, 1856

At last, a letter from Theodore. It nearly stopped my heart to read it.

Marianne,

It's not my nature to be forward, yet it's all I can do to keep myself in check when we occupy the same place. You'll forgive me, I hope, when I explain myself.

It's time for me to tell you that your husband, my Captain, showed me your photograph. It was the one time, and it was moments before we even set sail for what would be our last voyage together to Georges Bank or anywhere. I can't think why he chose to show me who you are but that he was speaking of his family, and of his dear Marianne, as we were setting the compass. He pulled your photograph from his breast pocket. It was a very small picture that, when he looked upon it, seemed to radiate the same love for him that he felt for you, and he brought it to my eyes. I'm only a sailor, a fisherman, and I wasn't his bosom friend. But he trusted me, and seemed to think I was fit to look. He may have been wrong, for afterward I was chiding myself for thinking of you once too often—which is to say, for even one moment. What I mean by this is that you were familiar to me before I came to your door that first time. I didn't intend it, this familiar feeling, but couldn't chase it away anymore than I've been able to shed the curse of being thought a Jonah.

I came to you honorably, the first day and the many days since. I did not have designs on my Captain's wife, nor did I think myself even worthy of your company. That you welcomed me so easily then caused a reversal and I left your home that day feeling lighter than I should have given your suffering.

Please don't hold me in contempt for feelings I didn't go looking for. I have tried to dodge every thought of spending more time with you and your son, and stayed away as much as I could bear to achieve this, thinking that absence would dull the need.

Being human is my worst fault, if it can be called that. Being guilty of enjoying your company is not far behind.

I hope this finds you suitably comfortable in spite of the chill as the new season takes its time arriving.

I am ever your friend,
Theodore Ethan Abel

I have penned a response I am not certain will find its way to him, and if it should, it is written here too, for I wish to recall my thoughts in this circumstance.

April 28, 1856

Theodore,

I feel as if I have told you once before not to consider yourself unworthy; then, it was regarding your survival. When you first came to me, I thought for an instant your resemblance to James quite dazzling. I think I might have been looking for James in you, or in any man who would have come to pay his respects so soon after losing my husband. I soon realized my error, for as I have come to know you, I understand that your features and compassionate manner are all your own.

My spirited son is quite taken with you, and often has your name on his lips. He chirps, "Teeder" and I am reminded of your delight in it when he does. I have seen the way your face warms and grows rosy with affection in Henry's company.

When you came to my door that first day, so forlorn over your own miracle, I saw in your face something I could not be sure was real. The glass is beveled but when I recall it now, I see the shape of your face through that blurry pane and recall the smile, which disappeared the moment we truly faced one another for the first time.

I now understand from your letter that you must have been readying yourself to meet me, though by then you would have recognized me in the street were we to pass in our travels.

A smile is far from suitable when calling upon a bereaved woman. If I were another, harder sort of woman, our paths might never have crossed after that day. For weeks afterward, the effort of a smile hurt, though I attempted it often for my son, for Lucy, my parents, and for you.

And, yet, here we are, friends of an odd sort: a grieving widow and a lone survivor of an unthinkable tragedy that has made a wreck of my family. What are we to do?

207

In the earliest days and weeks, I was unable to imagine a life without my husband. Yet, each day passing and taking me with it has forced me to do just this. And now that you have laid your heart at my threshold and even confessed what you believe was a lack of decorum, I must tell you that your affections are not in vain; they are only confessed too soon.

With warmth,

Marianne

MAY 2, 1856

It is late now and everyone sleeps but me. It is so often this way, though I do like the quiet, the sound of my quill scratching in its travels across the page, the wax sizzling in a puddle around the wick of my candle and traveling down to its holder. It is a candle I particularly like, giving off a lavender scent.

Today I awakened to the sound of Lucy's knitting needles tapping and looked to the window seat to see her there, rocking in my chair, smiling at me. She looked remarkably well, though she had refused any fussing and ministrations from me, only sleep and some beef broth and tea these past four days. I have done more about the house than Mother and even Lucy would approve of, so have slept more thoroughly at the end of each day. I hope she does not decide to take issue with the tasks she usually reserves for herself. She is well aware of my appreciation for her willingness to do them, and if I know her well enough by now, her pride would be bruised at the notion of being idle, sickness being her last excuse for it (and a feeble one by the standards she has set for herself).

"Forgive me, Cousin, but I couldn't keep myself away. Today Hannah comes to us and I haven't closed my eyes but for an hour. Will you not rise now?" I pressed my palms to my eyes, still reluctant to open them to daylight.

"Lucy, we have already prepared Hannah's room. You made the dinner last night, against my counsel, for you should have rested more. You laid out the frocks you made for her. What more can we do but wait?"

She leapt to her feet then and I was impressed to see that she is sprier than I knew. "I can't wait!" She said, as if she were a child and I had denied her pudding before supper.

"Well," I whispered to show her that Henry was still asleep across the hall, and I rose to gather myself into the warmth of my dressing gown. "It is our lot to wait out the morning and the afternoon will come soon enough," I chided, hearing my mother's voice escape my lips, though more gently. At that, Lucy sat down and took up her knitting again, wrapping her shawl more tightly around her and tucking her chin into the ruffle of her blouse.

"As you say, Cousin. And when do you suppose the young man will be up?"

There was indeed a stirring and a murmur across the hall. "I hear him now," I told her and moved across to his room to collect my son.

"Mama," he said, his voice gruff and sweet with sleep. He reached for me and I gathered him up and held him, breathing in the smell of his boyhood, understanding in a part of my most unwilling heart that he will one day grow too old to receive my tenderness or to return it in the way he rushes to do now.

"Lucy will make us biscuits and eggs," I whispered in his ear.

"Tasty for me!" he cooed. His words are coming in new ways every day now. We went downstairs and Lucy prepared a most delicious breakfast. I did not tell him of Hannah's impending visit, wishing to surprise him and to be careful, lest he need his sleep before she arrives. The rest of the day, Lucy fretted and wrung her hands and put herself to all manner of busy work until at last I stopped her from plumping pillows and smoothing beds in every room for what must have been the fourth time in an afternoon.

Hannah arrived late in the afternoon right before dark. The poor child had been traveling since dawn and her companion, a woman from her community who had been commissioned to care for Hannah on her journey, was no better off. She was a girl of seventeen who had a destination and went right to it, to an elderly aunt whom it was her yearly time to visit.

Lucy bundled Hannah into the house, put her in front of the fire she had been stoking for the past hour, and brought her a bowl of thick beef barley soup.

Hannah has grown since her last visit! She now wears her hair in braids bound close to her pretty head rather than laying across her shoulders and she is still quite shy. Yet, she possesses an admirable calm, as if she has left behind the girl and taken on the poise and gravity of a young woman. When Henry caught her eye as she rested in the settee by the fire and he stood at my side, perhaps making up his mind if it would be wise to approach her (for he is a shy one with the ladies), she winked at him and reached to tickle him under his arms. He wriggled away and then up to her, close to her, and at last into her lap. It was, for Lucy and me, a moment that belonged only to the children.

Hannah fell asleep there after a time and Lucy, again surprising me with her strength, lifted her granddaughter to stand and guided her sleepy form up the stairs to bed.

May 3, 1856

As Hannah ate her first breakfast with us this morning, she was filled with news.

"Mother has taken on a very important lady who asks her to sew everything for her. She is a judge's wife and very kind."

Lucy nodded her approval. "And what of you, Hannah, how's your schooling?"

Hannah frowned and waved the thought away. "It's the very same, Grandmother, but for the teacher, who is a bore. We all yawn through the day and it's a wonder we can learn anything."

"Come now, Hannah," I said, laughing in spite of myself. "You are a quick wit. You must be learning something in school."

"What I learn, I learn from reading books the teacher doesn't command us to read. And Mother tells me things."

Lucy's brow rose over her wide blue eyes.

"Things? What things?"

Hannah brought a spoon of oatmeal to her lips and fiddled with the next spoonful.

"Cousin Marianne, might we take Henry for a walk today?"

Lucy turned to me and then to her granddaughter.

"I'll come along, Hannah," she declared and rose to begin clearing things to the pantry.

When they returned, Lucy confided that Hannah did not revisit the subject of conversations Rose had had with her daughter and she did not press for details. This is in character for Lucy who does not tread where she feels she is unwelcome. But I do think Hannah would let us in on her education at her mother's knee if we were to inquire. I am not sure it is my business to do so, so will leave it to Lucy.

May 4, 1856

Theodore arrived today, shadowed some under the eyes. With Lucy and the children out, it was I who opened the door and stood before him, then regarded his still, broad frame filling my doorway, his rueful gaze regarding me. We stood very near one another and I felt the warmth of him. He lifted a hand as if to put it on my cheek, then took his hand back. I reached for it myself, brought his palm to my face. He did not move.

"Lucy," I whispered.

"Do I look like Lucy?" he queried. How could I not smile when I understood how he knew my meaning and found the humor in it?

"She and the children are out walking. They are due back. She will be happy to see you, but you must leave for now and come back later, when they have returned."

"It's you I came to see. You're the woman who is happy to see me. Please, you're moving away from me."

"Yes."

I did not wish him gone, for the impression of his hand had done its work, had sealed in me the thoughts and feelings I have tried wishing away. There was nothing for it but to lead him into the parlor by the fire and sit, though across from him, and for a long while with little to say. It was not the companionable quiet we shared the week before, in those moments before he left me unsure of when he would return. No, today we two sat for perhaps a quarter hour looking into the fire, exchanging a few words about Hannah's visit and his work for Mr. Pringle. As I spoke, he searched my face for its truth, and I, determined to be unknowable even as my whole being was a house whose doors were flung open for curious trespassers, hid that truth anywhere I could think to hide it.

211

Yet, Theodore is not trespassing. I have allowed him in, and though I am not ready for visitors who would peer into and then cavort in these rooms in my heart and head, rooms I have shrouded in dustcovers, I want so to welcome him.

I rose quickly as Lucy, Hannah, and Henry entered through the front door, laughing from the happy time they had enjoyed outside. The noise of the their chatter startled me. I must have reached out for something to steady me, for there was Theodore now risen from the settee and at my side, hand half around my waist so that I let the veil of my lids close to everything in the room but the warmth of his palm.

"Why, Theodore," I heard Lucy say, the delight in her voice plain, "We'd thought you gone for good!" He dropped his hand, but his gaze held mine for that instant before he turned to Lucy, smiled, took his polite leave, promising he would return another day. Lucy was clearly puzzled until she noticed my expression, which must have sent its message. Before she could protest Theodore's leaving, or properly introduce a very curious, beaming Hannah, and before Henry could begin to play with Theodore, our friend was gone.

I feel his smile on me still.

May 5, 1856

In my dream last night, James was by my side, right here in the bed we shared, and where I now sit propped to write. His face was close to mine, his breath warm on my forehead. I felt him, yet I could not open my eyes nor could I smell him. I awoke to the new day and Jack's cold, wet nose on my face as my eyes let in the grey light. Dreams of James continue to leave me shaken by the new memory of his absence each morning, yet more and more as I fall to sleep, I think of other things, other people: those who live. During the day, I may encounter a memory, yet it is easier now to let it drift away after dwelling in it a moment. I am not prey to daily despair.

May 7, 1856

Earlier today, Lucy's voice called down the hall, inviting me to her room as I was poised to go downstairs. She was sitting in her rocking chair, her silver-brown hair a braid down her back.

I had thought she might want to speak of Theodore's visit, his hasty leave. "I cannot stay long, Lucy," I said, just stepping into her room. "Henry will want his dinner soon. And your granddaughter will be asking for you." It is best, I know, to keep busy, to busy my mind. Speaking of Theodore is not where I want to dwell, try as I have done to move through my days without the interference of my sense of him.

"It concerns Mr. Talbot."

She had my attention. I do not think she understood what I had seen that day in the parlor, the devotion in Mr. Talbot's eyes. I sat on her bed, alert to her interest.

"He's in service to you, as I am."

"Lucy," I began in protest. "You are not."

"No, Cousin, whatever you say, I'm dedicated to your well-being and to the boy's. Don't contradict me on this," she admonished quite as if she were my mother. I had to smile, for if she were truly in service, she would not speak to me in this way. I enjoyed the contradiction.

"Go on, then."

"What sort of man is he?" She asked.

"What sort do you take him to be?" I asked her.

"I do believe he's good through and through. Where was he, before he joined your household?"

"He was employed by my father-in-law as a jack-of-all trades. He began service for the Parsons when he was twenty-five and is now nearly sixty. Before that, I believe he was a carpenter with is own father until that business died with the elder Mr. Talbot. He is the best sort, Lucy."

"He's been a great help to me lately, offering me a ride to town when I've no tasks to perform, laying a blanket on the path out the door and into the carriage when the path is sodden, as if I were his employer. I hardly know what to do with his attentions."

"What do you imagine doing?" I knew this was a question weighted with meaning that Lucy might consider improper, but I could not resist, feeling as I did. As I do.

"I imagine as little as possible," she offered with a sly smile, delight flickering in her blue eyes.

May 8, 1856

Dear Marianne,

I must leave Rockport for a month on the instruction of my employer,
Reginald Pringle, who has assigned me a task. I'll be traveling by sea to
England at week's end and would be pleased if I could call on you before
that day as I have something to show you. Please accept my apology for my
behavior of the other day. I don't know what possessed me.
    Oh, hang it, perhaps I do.

Yours,
T. Abel

MAY 9, 1856

Theodore has given me what I never imagined, what I should never have
thought to see again. He came to tea as planned and Hannah and Henry
joined us. Lucy set out the tea things and retreated to the pantry where
she claimed dough for a piecrust awaited her attention.

Henry played with Theodore, robbing him of any opportunity to
drink his tea. Hannah engaged him as well, reading to the lot of us from
Shakespeare's *Midsummer Night's Dream* and acting the parts to perfection. I had not thought her a performer!

Presently, Lucy emerged and summoned the children to the upper
floors where she told them it was time for a lesson. Hannah's lip curled
in a mockery of her own scorn and Theodore laughed at her display, but
Lucy, stern and purposeful, patted her granddaughter's rump and bustled them up. Though I knew she had to attend to the children, that it was
best done upstairs, I found my hands trembling, and hoped she would
return soon.

It was then Theodore turned to me and cleared his throat. In fact,
he began to cough in a fit and I thought he might have choked on a
biscuit. His brown eyes brimmed and he stood to collect himself. It last-
ed only a moment, but I felt quite helpless and was going to call for Lucy
when Theodore, his eyes brimming from the cough, sat down again and
looked at me as if he were going to say something very grave indeed. I

214

could not contain myself.

"Theodore, you frighten me. What is troubling you?"

He stroked what had become a handsome, neatly kept beard and peered down at his folded hands.

"Are you anxious about going out to sea again? If you are, I might have a book of poems…"

"No, it's not anything like this. Yes, of course, I'm not rejoicing that I must be away for such a stretch. It troubles me. I hadn't imagined heading for such distant shores."

My face grew warm and now it was I who could not keep from staring at my hands.

And then, into my palm he placed my very own cameo, the very one that had belonged to James and which bore my likeness.

Questions fought their way to my lips and the ones most pressing were the ones I held back.

"Perhaps you wish to keep it," I said. I held my open palm to him, looked at his face and saw the answer there.

"It doesn't belong to me any more than…"

I placed it in his upturned hand. "You must hold it for me," I urged him. "It will be your talisman. Perhaps it can protect you more than it did your Captain. Of course, it was not meant as protection, only…" and then I could not speak.

"I'll write to you from England and I'll bring home a treasure for your boy."

"Bring yourself home," I whispered and stood thinking to leave him there so I would not have to watch him go, but he reached for my wrist and held me there a moment, looking up at me, gratitude and resolution, grief and joy, all the feelings that welled in me telling the story in his face. He then rose and pressed his lips upon mine, a warm, firm touch and for only the briefest moment, then lifted my palm to his cheek and kissed it. He was gone before Lucy came back.

And now I will air my thoughts. I have come to believe that James gave Theodore the cameo and asked him to give it to me should he be lucky enough to survive what seemed unsurvivable. I am not affronted that

Theodore let all these months pass before returning it. What plagues me is the feeling I have that Theodore will return with feelings made stronger by absence. I have been a foolish woman to lead him this way, despite my own feelings. He will be the better for it if he does not harbor hope. Mother and Father and the Pringles will have their justifications about me; in fact, Virginia Pringle is being far too quiet for my comfort.

An image assaults me. My husband, a man who knew he would soon be dragged to the depths of the ocean he loved, turned to his first mate in a desperate act and thrust this piece at him. "Take it!" He must have told him. "Take this and give it to my wife and do not fail me. Tell her I loved her, that I will always love her. Remember me to my son." It is these words, or words like them, that I cannot bear to have Theodore confirm.

Oh, yes, I could imagine that it happened in just this horrible way. And then I ask myself, if this truly was my husband's final earthly request, why did Theodore wait so long to do as he was asked. Can I fault him, feeling as I do now?

May 10, 1856

Hannah has made a home with us. She tells me when she sits in my room at night with Lucy and we three talk as girls, that her Mother has asked that she stay here for as long as she might, as often as I will have her, for her father has made it clear that when she reaches the age of thirteen she must apprentice her mother in tailoring and give up her schooling.

"But you're such a smart young lady, Hannah! How can you idle your days at a needle and thread?" Her grandmother asked, not bothering to hide her dismay. And, though I would agree that Hannah is terribly clever, and has a knack with a paintbrush, too, she could make her sewing work a success and command considerable business. But I held my tongue, for she is not my child or grandchild. She is a gift to be enjoyed only for as long as her mother allows or, more to the point, her stern father.

The child placed her round, blue eyes on me and all of the inquiry she would not, could not, give voice to was delivered in that gaze. Her eyes are so like Lucy's.

"Hannah, if you are not sent for, you may stay for as many days and weeks as you like!" I told her. Yes, to promise such a thing, or lend hope to it, might be cruel, but her face opened into the grandest smile I have yet seen claim her. No more was said on the matter this evening.

And now, later into the evening, I am anxious reflecting upon our conversation, for what if Timothy does send for her very soon? Might she be defiant? I think not, if the last visit is anything by which to judge. She is far too deferential a child to plant her feet in refusal of her father's wishes.

May 13, 1856

The seas are rough today and I can only hope that Theodore is well beyond this ocean and closer to English shores. I refuse to dwell in my worry. I have even, after a stern talking to I have given myself, veered sharply away from contemplating anything beyond his safe return.

And this is not difficult with such goings on as have occurred this week. First, as I wrote the other day, Hannah has asked to stay on, which makes me very glad and has undone her grandmother with delight. Lucy cannot stop wringing her hands in anticipation of either this wonderful notion or the thought that Timothy will summon his daughter home at any moment. I have had to calm her with whatever I can grasp. I even gave her my painting kit so that she and Hannah could sit on the porch and do portraits of one another, which took the length of the afternoon. But this is only one thing to busy Lucy for a brief spell; I am not so full of ideas to entertain a mature woman and a now twelve-year-old girl. My strength is in diverting my son, a boy easily pleased by my occasional antics or a story I read to him.

Thomas showed his face this afternoon, without the benefit of his mother to see to our time together. His, I do admit, was not an unwelcome visit. I have worried about him, for I have seen so little of him these months since he pitched himself into Mill Pond, but I have been disinclined to call, which has been my weakness, based entirely upon my reluctance to see Virginia. I will have to work on this selfish aspect of my nature, but not today. Today, I will credit Thomas with a genuine, open nature all his own.

With Lucy nearby, we had tea, Thomas and I, and he was very candid with me, sharing a surprising truth about his mother.

"Mrs. Parsons," he began, reverting to an earlier formality between us, and I worried that he might be about to confess the nature of his truest feelings for me, as Theodore had. I would be forced to refuse him. "I am ashamed," he offered instead.

I filled his cup almost to the brim and laid some of Lucy's coconut cookies on his plate, but he did not reach for any of it. With his discomfort I could not enjoy my own refreshment and so sat back and folded my hands in my lap.

"What can possibly shame you?" This was not what I expected.

"My behavior, first of all. I have not been the friend to you that you need. Hardly could I have been such a friend with my mother prodding me at every turn to act against my nature."

His words, every one of them, were weighted with all he did not say, all I could not fathom. And I found myself wondering if I might have accepted his friendship with less reservation had he offered it on his own terms. Yet I could not have known those terms and did not pretend to know as we sat there in my parlor, the afternoon light warming us both.

"What is your nature, Thomas? That is, what might you have done?" The question was too direct. It had the effect of prying him open, and he looked overjoyed too, as if he had waited for someone to ask.

And then he began to speak.

"Marianne, I hope you will forgive my candor. I will look at our meeting here today as a token of your good will toward me, which I understand you might not always have felt. Doubtless, you once quaked at the notion that I might have elicited your friendship through pity…"

"Thomas," I began but he kept on, not even hearing his name.

218 "…and then I leapt into Mill Pond without thinking beyond the ridiculous, which was how it must have appeared to you and anyone who could bring themselves to look on it with a smirk. And there was your most esteemed friend, Mr. Abel, whom I confess to having doubted, infected by Mother's opinion of him, until he came into that frigid water after me to save a life that can bring no possible benefit to him, for

my mother does find fault with every trait of his. I half-understood this disdain of hers prior to that day he fished me out, but now I cannot grasp any of it and see that she is the one at fault for her harsh judgment. Do you realize," he continued and I heard a rustling in the hallway, turned to find nothing out of the ordinary but Jack poking his nose into Thomas' hanging cloak, looking for something he would never find, a morsel or a toy to gnash his growing teeth on, and turned again to face Thomas who had not recently taken a breath. "That it dawned upon me that day, drying out in front of your hearth, that if Mr. Abel had fallen into the water and I had been a passerby, given the attitude in which I had been steeped since childhood and my inclination toward mother's flagrant dislike for this man or any like him, I am reprehensible to myself in knowing that I would have made somewhat less of an effort to pull him out."

Here he took a breath and I did as well, for to hear him speak in such a rush left me with need of it. I managed to say something during his short rest.

"Thomas, you must not be harsh with yourself. You are acting strange, if I may say so. And who is to say what you might have done given different circumstances? You cannot possibly know this."

"Oh, but Marianne, I do know it too well. I am Virginia Pringle's son and have felt the sting of her disapproval before. It has sent me into such a fit of grief that I still wonder how it is that I can ever please her."

"But you are a good son! You are! I see it in the way you walk with her and listen to her. You are a reverent, doting son and she could hardly ask for better. You must also take after your father."

"Your indignation on my behalf is touching. I have seen the way the two of you chaff when you occupy the same room even with many people between you. Well, you have my friendship no matter what your feelings are for my most difficult, beloved mother."

It was odd comfort, yet I am at last happy to accept his friendship on such terms as these; both his genuine respect and affection for me, and his acceptance of Theodore despite his mother's disapproval. Virginia has raised Thomas to be so devoted to her that he would feel ashamed to contradict her. Though I love my own mother, I like to keep to my own path now that I am a woman in my own right. I feel no inclination to behave or think as she does, even as it may sometimes be what divides us. I am aware, too, that her voice has slipped from me now and then, and that I carry her voice with me more than I would like.

I had to know something that Thomas was not delivering. "Please forgive the question or disregard it, but I am moved to ask you. What makes your mother so very…" I searched for the least damning word and found none. Thomas, bless him, understood my half-formed question.

"It is grief, Marianne, nothing more remarkable than that, and nothing less. You and she share this, yet you seem as different in aspect and sensibility as two women can be."

Yes, of course. Grief.

"She has lost someone, Thomas?" I had not thought of this, had never entertained for a single moment that Virginia Pringle was anything but a dour old queen with nothing better to do than berate her subjects. How can grief not have occurred to me?

He looked perplexed by my own surprise. "She lost her husband when they were married but five years, Marianne, and I was a child. I thought perhaps your mother might have let you in on something of her girlhood friend."

"My mother," I sighed. "No. I am afraid she left this most important piece of information out of our conversations."

"He was not my father, not in the way a father should be to a child. Reginald is my truer father. Her first husband is my father only in that he is my blood relation. And he did not perish at sea the way your husband did, but ran off with a woman from Boston, a senator's eighteen-year-old daughter. I know this to be true, though my mother has always told me he perished in a quarry accident."

"And how did you come to know differently?"

"I was a small boy at my mother's knee, not much older than your son, when a strange woman came visiting, a woman my mother called a friend whom I have not seen since that day. At no more than three or four years of age I had a penchant for the ladies' company even then, enamored of their chatter and their perfumes. Their very affect made me a happy child, enveloped in this sweetness. But this visitor had a very grim message for my mother and I heard it, though I could not have understood. My mother did all she could to undo the truth I heard after she bustled this woman away, and she succeeded for a while, for in truth, it was a memory that only came to me in later childhood when the meaning was clearer." I came to understand in that moment of Thomas revealing his mother's tragedy that, undeniably, Virginia and I share an almost identical grief: each married five years, with a young son, our husbands have been lost to us.

Thomas, I believe, was enjoying my attention to his every word. In fact, I had to lean back in the settee when I realized how much nearer I had inclined toward him, transfixed by his tale. "My father," he went on, ill-at-ease with the word, "the one whom I would be told was dead, was in fact alive and living in Boston in the lap of luxury with a woman to whom he was unmarried. This voice that carried this terrible truth —my mother's voice—struck my young ears with such a ringing clarity and nothing my mother told me could purge it. As a young child, I heard her sorrow without understanding it, but later, a young man, I understood the betrayal and her loss with it. After her circumstances improved from her marriage to Reginald Pringle, I tried mightily to put her first husband out of my mind, as I am sure my mother did. But it has made a lasting stain upon her happiness, even as she loves her husband, the man I now call my father. I fear it strains her affectionate nature, a nature I have seen when she is unguarded. Such moments are rare, as I am sure you surmised early on in your dealings with her."

"I cannot imagine your confusion, Thomas, when you were a boy." I poured him more tea and he drank deeply, as if it were ale or water after a long thirst.

"There was no confusion, Marianne, only certainty that as I grew older, I would offer her comfort simply by being a man very different from the one she first married. The man I ought to call a father has been Reginald Pringle and has raised me to be a far better man than my scoundrel of a father might have done. On this there is no confusion, though I am occasionally more under Mother's powerful influence. Even as you now know that I began with one father, when I use that word now and for all these years, it refers to Reginald."

"Thomas, you have told me much and I have taken advantage of your good nature. Perhaps you should go home. It is getting toward supper. I must tend to my son and to Hannah and get my son to bed soon after."

Thomas stood to leave, yet he stood still and earnestly took both my hands in his for what I was certain was the moment I had come to forget and now feared again in a rush, a moment that, as I recall it now in my writings, makes me smile at my own foolishness.

"Now you know what makes my mother cool, what she might even be suspecting of your friend, Mr. Abel. And you know for certain that I harbor no ill will against him, nor do I pretend that you and I will ever be suited, or, to be more precise, that I could *be* your suitor."

And in this last he had me, for it was the opposite of what I imagined he would say in this regard. "Do you mean that your mother does not have designs on the two of us?"

He laughed. It was a sad, bitter laugh from a man whose true feelings for me have not, until today, been as apparent. "She may very well, my dear, dear Marianne, but she would be terribly inaccurate in her supposition. I have not the heart to tell her, but I think you, with your feelings about Mr. Abel—oh, you cannot hide them from those eyes of yours when you hear his name spoken—will let her know in your own time. I will worry about myself."

And with that he took his cloak and hat and let himself from the house, leaving me to my surprise and relief.

MAY 14, 1856

Hannah has brought me the most beautiful piece of embroidery, a stitching of a girl sitting beneath the linden tree in the front yard. I will cherish it always. I have a little wooden box frame and will hang it in the front hall for us all to admire as we come and go.

MAY 16, 1856

This morning, I awoke smelling James' cherry tobacco and felt a great ache when I touched the empty place beside me. It was warm from my traveling sleep, for I do now use all of the bed. Yet, it should have been cool, for I was on one side when I woke, and had likely been for a good while. It was as if someone had been there and left. I could not while away another moment there, knowing my head was foggy from sleep and a lack of reason that comes with the first few moments after waking. I crept across the hall and looked in on Henry who has been sleeping in his bed once again for a fortnight. It seems to be the rhythm of his sleep now, between my bed and his for stretches of two weeks. He was not in it. Just as my heart began to race, I heard his voice and Hannah's drifting down from upstairs. Wrapping my dressing gown around me, I followed their voices and knew before I reached them that they were in the cupola, though for a moment I feared they were playing in James' study. I have not been since he passed and cannot bring myself to go in there. I have asked Lucy to keep it clean and intact.

When I reached the cupola, I found Hannah and my boy huddled together with a blanket over their knees and a book in Hannah's hands held open between them. She had brought up a little collection of pillows for them to sit upon and Henry rested his head against her arm. She looked up to me when I reached the top, my breath a little cloud before me, for it was still quite chilly for a May morning, and the sun hadn't fully risen to warm the small space.

"I hope you aren't cross with me," Hannah said. "He could not sleep past dawn and came into my own bed but wouldn't be still, so here we are. He chose this Mother Goose book and Henry is a wonderful reader!" Yes, it appeared he was reading, for he has memorized it entirely.

The teacher is there in this child and I could not have been angry that they had climbed up and burrowed into this little place, for Hannah was taking such good care with my son. But it was too cold to remain into the morning, even as the clear sky promised a warmer day within the hour, so I told them to follow me down to breakfast where I made them some oatcakes and sausage. Even Lucy had not stirred yet.

Or, perhaps I should say she did not stir until she smelled the breakfast.

I write on and on and in doing so, I try to forestall thoughts of Theodore's absence and his return. There. I cannot say it enough, for it is all that I will allow. All that I can allow.

May 18, 1856

Dearest Marianne,

Don't fault me for reaching out to you across the Atlantic simply to tell you that thoughts of you help me see beyond each day. True, you don't say that you wish for my hasty return, yet you didn't disregard my affections those weeks ago. With this memory, I'm encouraged to write to you. Your picture, the tiny likeness set in filigree, has been a beacon.

My time here has been spent visiting wealthy landowners who would build banks and offices and with whom Reginald Pringle has an interest. He's sent me to learn about the commerce of such an enterprise. I can't truly believe that he's chosen me to represent him, except that he assures me I'm up to the task. For so long I've felt the lower man, the one suited to menial tasks. But I was blessed in younger years with a mother who read to me often, a father who didn't decry it even as he prodded me toward a practical living, and a feeling that this association with Mr. Pringle, though I don't relish the company of his wife any more than you do, bodes well for my future prospects.

I hope I will visit with you upon my return.

Truly,
Theodore

MAY 18, 1856

Theodore's giddy confusion about how to proceed with me matches mine regarding my manner toward him. I have a mind to take the letter and bury it in the sand, but I will tuck it away with the others he has penned and when he returns, I hope I can offer him the kind of friendship that promotes ease between us.

Mr. Talbot has asked to take Lucy for a stroll. I cannot deny her this pleasure, for whenever he is near, her cheeks flush crimson and she begins to chatter to me as if someone had wound her from behind. And Mr. Talbot, too, has been courtly in her presence, bowing to her as she passes which brings a little, embarrassed giggle from her chest. I imagine that when they go on their stroll they will have to take a moment to talk to one another without the blushing and bowing. It is lovely to see these two dear people so mutually fond.

May 23, 1856

Temperate days beckon me from the house for many hours at a time so that by day's end, I am too tired to write in these pages. I shall make a better effort again, though often I feel it is better to live outside my mind than too much within it as I am here. Daily, I take Hannah, Henry, Lucy, and even Jack along the beach and we gather shells and smoothed glass, stretch our legs, wade up to our ankles in the cold surf and run from the waves. Then we go to Mrs. Spencer's teashop. We have become accustomed patrons this last week and Mrs. Spencer has teased that she will place a sign at the table we favor that says, "Reserved for Mrs. Marianne Parsons and companions."

Hannah has been reading to Henry each morning and evening and she has been painting pictures with her grandmother. I see that Hannah has a talent and imagine it has come from her grandfather. I will always wonder about this union that produced Hannah's mother, Rose. I will always feel a certain sadness for Lucy. The man she first loved, even though he was considered unsuitable and she might, in a more highly placed society, have been exiled, was the sacrifice she was forced to make. That he seems to live on in Hannah is a miracle of sorts.

May 27, 1856

I am undone! Theodore has sent me a package, small and neat, my name etched in his own uneven script. It is the cameo I gave him. With it, a note I press here.

225

Marianne,

I wish not to cling to you as a hope for my life's happiness, but thoughts of you are truly my only comfort. It's true that this treasure is a talisman to me, but you're the more so and I send it to you as a token of my faith that I'll return on the second day of June.

Yours,

Theodore Ethan Abel

JUNE 1, 1856

It is nearly nine months since James left this life, left me and his son, and I long for the company of the man whom James admired for his integrity. He would not admire his first mate as one who seeks my heart's favor, and who has found it. There. I have said it and now that it is here in these pages, I must tuck the thought away and go to sleep.

I have tried for nearly an hour, stowing this book and climbing into bed, snuffing the lamp. But I cannot sleep. I cannot even sit on my bed, or lie in it this night. It is Jack's bed now, for he takes it over. Never have I seen a dog thrash about more and I laugh at the sight of him walking this quilted landscape, and at the press of his paws upon my back, his nose in my ear, tickling. I have tried to put him out of the room, but he is accustomed to the warmth with me and yelps and scratches enough to waken the household the moment I close the door. I am glad Henry does not carry on so, yet my will is weak with him, too, when he protests sleeping in his room.

Yet, neither boy nor dog keeps me wakeful. It is that I harbor far too much hope for Theodore's safe return, his smile behind his beard shy and welcoming, his eyes searching me for signs of friendship without the constraints that propriety imposes. When I close my eyes and try to conjure my husband, it is Theodore's face I see. I cannot abide this, cannot allow my husband's memory to be supplanted. I still don the widow's dress and feel false with each day I do so. I must banish my shame, yet the only way I can think to do so is to banish Theodore, but I have no reason to do such a thing.

I brushed my hair for well over one hundred strokes, losing count soon after that; it gave purpose to this late hour. Strands came away in the

226

bristles. If I continue, I fear I may lose it all. The only thing to do, then, is read, even as I write of the intention to do so. Yes, I will read some of Henry's books. No, I will read a letter from Mother that I received today. She announces that she and Father will visit mid-month and gives news of the Reynolds family and of the McGlinns whose daughter is to marry the Reynolds' son and is it not a terrible pity that Mr. Reynolds has passed on and cannot be at his son's wedding. And she mentions that she and Father are happy to be coming as they have not seen their grandson in far too long, and why do I not visit? Why must I stay close to home now that the weather is turning fair? It would be a cure to get beyond the confines of Rockport and visit my first home, she admonishes. I had to take a breath after reading the letter, a letter that irked me so that I will not press it here.

I do not need a cure from what she calls the confines of this village. It is my home. From what do I need a cure?

She, of course, will persist on this one, and perhaps I will go there with Henry one day soon, though I feel most comfortable staying here, living my quiet life with my son, with Hannah, Lucy and Jack.

As I prepare to close this entry, my hope for Theodore's safe return beats soundly in my chest.

JUNE 3, 1856

Theodore has come home. He called on us this morning, his whiskers trimmed, his clothes newer than anything I have yet seen on him. They looked spun from finer cloth and had to have been purchased and tailored for him in England. This new suit spoke of dividends on his journey, yet even more than what must have been gratifying commerce was what shone from his gaze. There was in his eyes pride and humility, a brightness that invited me in and held me still. His dark hair was tightly curled against his head and I had the urge, which I quelled by gathering my skirt in my fists, to push my hands through those curls.

I stood looking at him, at this man I had thought of besides little else in spite of my efforts to keep busy for the past month, and tried to speak.

Tears came and I had to look away, my shame too plain. He spoke my name, and then Lucy was coming down the stairs, as she does, uncannily, when Theodore and I find ourselves in a peculiar moment. She stopped, astonishment lifting her brow before she beamed a most generous smile expressly at Theodore.

She beckoned him further in. "It's a particular pleasure to have you back!" My good cousin spoke for us both. I have come to see over these many months that she is very fond of Theodore. "Come have some breakfast with us, will you?"

I did not look at Lucy then, for I did not want her to see my joy and tried to stuff it into my collar.

We sat around the table, Lucy next to Hannah who sat next to Henry, who was thrilled to sit by Theodore, who sat by me. Suddenly we were very quiet. The children, perplexed by the adults surrounding them with unaccustomed silence, soon engaged Theodore in a game of hide-the-salt-and-pepper and within a moment, my son was astride the man's back.

Lucy soon rose and began clearing the breakfast dishes. "Hannah, mind you bring the child with you when you go outside. But stay in the yard. Don't go down to the water until I go out. I'll be along." Hannah nodded to her grandmother and to me and off they went, my devoted son clutching her most capable hand and waving goodbye to us all as he chirped, "Teeder, g'bye!"

With Lucy in the kitchen and the children out of doors, Theodore and I were quite alone, he staring at his mostly untouched plate of eggs as I fiddled with my teacup until it nearly toppled. Righting it made a terrible clatter and stopping the teacup from falling off its saucer made more of it. I looked up at my friend.

He smiled and I had to look away again, finding it very difficult to meet his gaze.

"Theodore," I said as I regained my resolve and looked at him again. I would not waver, I thought to myself.

"Why are you whispering?"

"Because I do like the sound of your name and whispering it seems proper now."

"Well, then, whisper," he said and moved his chair just a little nearer mine.

"It is…I am…" I lifted my face then and in that one moment of foolish bravery, I let him have the full view of any and all the feelings I wore.

"Yes. I see. I too have difficulty with what's between us, what isn't, with my having revealed my heart to you too soon. I've troubled you. I shouldn't have spoken." And here, he turned away from me, quite an unbearable thing, but he did not leave his chair.

"Theodore, do you know what I thought whilst you were so far from these shores? Do you know what I feared and what kept me awake many nights?"

He faced me again, his chair inching nearer still, and I played with my own fingers in my lap.

"Will you make me say it, then?" I smiled, and every nesting bird came to roost in my stomach.

"Say it only if not saying it is more painful," he replied.

I let out a bellyful of air. "Oh, both alternatives smart! I am most out of sorts. It is just that after losing my husband I must now worry when you go to sea that you will never return." My hands twined furiously around the bow on my skirt. "I have learned how weakening it is to my family, to my son, when I am in such a state, and I cannot allow myself to know weakness. Perhaps if I were of the sort Virginia Pringle has become, I could weather it—this, this…"

Theodore reached across the small space now left between us and took hold of my busy hands.

"Why think your feeling a weakness? Why imagine that to feel tenderness robs one of strength? Marianne, when I think of you, and when I imagine that one day you might grow to love me, I feel stronger than any man, as if I could lift a dry-docked schooner with my own hands." *229*

I looked at Theodore's face and saw in it all the truth of what I would not let myself confront until now, until that first moment in his presence this morning when my heart exalted upon his safe return.

"I do not know how it can be that having spent a lifetime knowing my husband, knowing and understanding his every breath and mood, that I can have begun to move toward you as swiftly as I have. It does not feel like something a good woman should acknowledge, much less act upon, within the first year after being widowed."

He looked upon me a long moment and I willed my eyes to stay upon his. Then he spoke of the heart. "Marianne, I once read in a book of anatomy that the heart is a muscle filled with vessels of the blood that sustains it. The poets know as well that the heart is responsible for so much more than the beat it makes to keep us alive. The heart keeps us moving along on our own vast seas, Marianne. If we deny it, we capsize it."

Theodore was now flushed with his own revelation and had lowered himself onto the floor on his knees. I reached for his hands as easily as if they were my own, enjoying their roughness, their strength, and then, almost without a moment's thought, I lifted his hands to my lips and there we sat, my head bowed to his head resting in my lap. There we sat for a long while. When I heard Lucy breeze past the parlor, I felt her hesitation at the entranceway before she whistled her way up the stairs to make the beds, but not before she called out to the children that she would be there in short order and would bring Theodore and me along for the fun.

June 5, 1856

Hannah and Henry are inseparable and Theodore calls at the house each early evening after the quarry closes its office. He stays only to supper and hardly lingers, though it is long enough, and hardly a visit at all, ending far too soon.

I am not surprised to have received an invitation to dine from Mrs. Pringle, only more surprised that a note has not come admonishing me to keep Theodore at a distance. Those notes have stopped coming, and so have the same from Mother. I prefer to think it is owing to their acceptance of Theodore as a fixed presence, a dear friend to all of us—to me, to Henry, and to Lucy. I hope I am not mistaken in my optimism.

230

Yes, I shall join the Pringle family for dinner tomorrow evening. I will leave my son at home with Lucy and Hannah, and I will try my very best to behave the way a lady ought who does not wish to earn the scrutiny of her hostess. Theodore will be present, I have learned, and this pleases me. Now that he works more closely with Mr. Pringle in a business capacity, it is sensible that he be thought an associate worthy of their company, I should think. I am gratified by his ties to Reginald Pringle who, it would seem, knew to look inside Theodore to find what neither his wife nor my Mother wished to see. Yet, even with the support of his employer, I suspect Virginia Pringle has consented to invite Theodore only as a means to watch me closely when I am in his presence, to satisfy herself that I am too soon distracted by what her conviction and upbringing tell her is the wrong sort of man. She will then waste no time in reporting to Mother. In short order I will receive a reprimand, and perhaps even a grim visit before we can make our way to visit them. I am determined to conduct myself in a way that will not invite reproach.

Theodore has told me that his employer forewarned him of Virginia Pringle's possible cold shoulder, but that he will brook no disrespect from her toward his protégé. Even as I clutch at my belly with worry, I am more than a little curious about how the evening will go. Lucy has advised me to keep cool no matter what nastiness escapes Mrs. Pringle's lips. At all costs, I am to appear unperturbed. My cousin knows me well.

JUNE 6, 1856

When I arrived at the Pringles' last evening, Mary brought us into the parlor to wait and Thomas strode in soon afterward, greeting me with the warmth of our recent conversation. He offered a sly wink that made me laugh. Indeed, his charm has nearly eclipsed the smugness he affected when I first came to their home at the earliest part of the year. Perhaps that demeanor was put on for his mother's sake. Never mind, for the warmth of our growing friendship has finally and completely displaced my earlier uncertainty about Thomas.

Just as I rose to place my arm through his, his mother entered the parlor.

"Now, you two, what can be so amusing?" She looked as if she had caught two children being naughty and was the loftier for it and, yes, within that superior gleam in her eye was the triumphant assumption that her son had charmed me at last. He has done, yes, but not in the way she would hope. I looked to Thomas for rescue, but he had begun to turn away, my cloak over his arm to pass on to Mary who had arrived too late and earned a dark stare from her mistress and a contrasting smile from Thomas which he quickly snuffed out when he turned to face his mother.

"Thomas, please take our lovely guest to the sun room. Your father and I will join you presently and then we will all go into dinner," Mrs. Pringle all but crooned. I did not feel any particular threat of being alone with Thomas now that I knew he pined for me no more than I for him. Mrs. Pringle did not mention Theodore. In truth, I hoped he had arrived before me and that I would discover that somewhere in the great house, perhaps in the library, he was already in conversation with Mr. Pringle.

We left the parlor and turned into the front hall. I tried not to look behind me, for Mrs. Pringle had cornered Mary and was snarling at her for being too slow. As if wound from behind, Thomas guided me away more swiftly. I stole a look at him, at the furrow in his high, handsome brow.

"Ah, poor Mary. Mother has found her wanting." He was looking at Mary, had in fact stopped us in our progress to watch her unabashedly. And he did sound concerned. Yet, almost in the same instant, he turned his attention away from the young housemaid, as if he had been caught at something, and whispered to me. "Now, are you going to be able to maintain your pretty composure this evening? You will be challenged by the company, I believe."

I turned to him and not very gently poked him in the rib for his impertinence. Yet, I did feel safe in knowing that perhaps Thomas was now more a friend to Theodore, particularly after the now pointedly unmentioned day at Mill Pond Meadow. He pulled my arm more snugly through his own, and with his long stride bustled me ahead of his mother. The sound of Mrs. Pringle hissing her reprimand at her young servant had ceased before we left the front hall.

Once in the sunroom, we sat, Thomas at the pianoforte, his mother soon next to me on the settee. I did not feel especially interested in listening to music, but I knew that the moments before Theodore's arrival had to be spent thinking of anything else.

Thomas laid his long fingers upon the keys and from them flowed a rhapsody that closed my eyes. I listened to Chopin and felt as if someone had borne me across a great expanse of water to a figure that stood alone and still until I reached him. I was certain it was James, with his captain's hat and britches. The music spoke of him, its rush and roar, and then the thrilling upsurge that pushed me faster toward James on that blue, blue ocean until I felt arms around me, taking me down into the bluest heaven I have ever known. When I opened my eyes, Mr. Pringle stood before me. He was smiling down at what must have appeared to him to be a woman in a swoon. It was a great embarrassment and I can only be grateful that it was my host and not his cantankerous wife, for though she sat beside me, she seemed as intent on the music as I had been. And as clear now in my recording of the image as it was when Thomas played, I recall that in the instant before I opened my eyes I saw Theodore, not James; it was Theodore's arms keeping me afloat.

"Now, Mrs. Parsons, you do look as though something has taken firm hold of you," my host said, though he cannot possibly have understood how correct he was in this. He held his great hand down toward me and I put my hand upon it to rise. By this time, Thomas had ceased his playing and was escorting his mother to the dining room ahead of us.

When we arrived, I looked about, confused, and Virginia Pringle smiled with a certain satisfaction at my curiosity. If there is one thing about me I would change, it is that my feelings are too apparent for all who care to notice, and often at inopportune moments.

"We are one gentleman short this evening," Mr. Pringle interceded before his wife could issue what must have been favorable news for her. And, yes, it was plain on her thin, curled lips as she confirmed it.

"Yes, well, that is a generous station you bestow upon him…"

"Virginia, there will be none of that," Mr. Pringle admonished her to my delight and lasting surprise, a wagging finger in his words. I still cannot recall anything like it between them before this evening and can only hope this kindly man who had thought to protect Theodore from her scorn would set his wife straight again if need be. She did seem put in her place, if only for a moment. Theodore, despite his earlier life as a ship's mate on fishing vessels, is more a gentleman than many and it is to Mr. Pringle's credit that he defended him.

I tried not to inquire after Theodore's absence, tried not to fret over what must have kept him, but could not contain my question for very long.

After the soup course was cleared, as Thomas was amusing his mother with a tale involving a young girl from church flirting with the pastor's son, I turned to Mr. Pringle.

"Why is it that Mr. Abel could not join us this evening?"

"I am afraid, my young friend, that he has taken to his bed. It is not of any urgency. His note spoke of some headache and fatigue. Surely, it is this shift in the winds and some delayed effect of a long journey recently undertaken. The air is colder than it has been in weeks."

"I wonder if he might need a doctor?" I tried, oh, how I did try to say this without betraying my worry, without grabbing hold of my volition and marching from the house and straight to Theodore to tend to him myself.

Mr. Pringle patted my hand, offering a kindly smile. "I will see to it that my young apprentice receives the attention he needs, Mrs. Parsons. Worry not. Straightaway, after supper, I will send Dr. Wainright there to see after him."

This put me at ease enough so I was not unnerved when Mrs. Pringle, having heard her husband's promise, said, "Oh, I hardly think the good doctor ought to be troubled. He will have placed himself before his own fire and called it a day. Do not disturb him for this, Reginald."

And up went his hand, halting her! I looked at Thomas who was moving his fork handle in minute patterns on the cloth. He lifted one brow at me. Mary hovered not far behind him, awaiting orders from the Pringles, and seeming most discomfited when she looked upon Thomas, even at the back of his head.

234

As the evening progressed, Mr. Pringle charitably engaged me in talk of my son, a subject I found refreshing. I found it difficult not to notice that every few moments, Mary would let her eyes rest upon Thomas, follow his movements, listening most attentively to his speech as if she would measure its cadence. When she was busy at her work, Thomas often turned his eyes to her. They never let their eyes meet and soon enough I knew it to be a game.

The meal progressed quickly, for there was little to keep us all too absorbed after I spoke of Henry and our sweet cousin Hannah. Thomas had grown quiet, as he does the more so in his father's presence, and I felt it my task to keep the conversation away from Theodore. This was not difficult, for Mr. Pringle did not speak of him again, perhaps sensing his wife's challenge as well.

Virginia Pringle took my hands as I stood to take my leave.

"It was a pleasure to have you here, dear," she said, her voice approaching an attempt at maternal affection, though not near enough to warm me.

"Yes," I agreed and then, ignoring prudent judgment, I added to Mr. Pringle, "I hope to return and that Mr. Abel will be well once again so that he might join us."

My hostess's expression immediately soured, but she recovered with admirable speed. "I will leave that entirely to my husband," came her reply. It was clever, indeed. I felt a certain admiration for the understanding she and Mr. Pringle had arrived at this evening, with hardly a word to express it.

Thomas gave my arm a faint tug as I called out my last goodbyes to my hosts. In the entranceway, I took my chance.

"Has your mother's maid caught your fancy?" I knew the answer too well, and worried for him. Perhaps in understanding whether it was true, I hoped to offer him the protection of my friendship, if it can be called protection given his mother's views. Thomas looked at me as if to ask if it were that plain. "Oh, yes, my friend. I can hardly imagine your hawk-eyed mother has missed it."

He frowned at me, and confided, "It is hardly that easy a fancy, my dear." My surprise, despite what I had already concluded, was great, yet my parting words bespoke otherwise. "Thomas, take care. Take the best care." I was thinking of the formidable adversary that his mother would be to a union between her son and a housemaid. He knew this better than I, than anyone in his midst. Mary stood not far away, half in shadow, as if waiting for Thomas or someone to give her a task, and I looked toward her. Her chin was tucked down and I could not see if she wept or smiled at what I had discovered, for she must have heard.

I left the Pringle household and said to Mr. Talbot on the way home that I would like it very much if people might show their love to those truly deserving and not fear the scorn of those who would consider the object of their love less deserving. I was thinking then only of Thomas and the quandary he must now be in, sweet on Mary. She is but seventeen and hardly in the household a year, still learning. If he does not have true intentions toward her, he must forswear them, but it is not for me to instruct his heart. Mr. Talbot replied with, "that might be so, Missus," but only, I think, because I employ him.

Then I closed my eyes and, except to walk into the house and up to bed, I did not have another thought until now, so early in the morning that I am the first to stir. It is the perfect time to write and I do not do so often, choosing the nighttime ritual, or the times when I cannot sleep. Now I have already slept as well as I could manage. Lucy's breakfast smells will not lure me away, for she still rests herself.

June 6, 1856

It is evening, but I record the date once more to keep this entry separate.

Theodore is unwell. He has an inflamed throat and a fever and he hardly recognized my presence. How I came to this discovery follows:

This morning, immediately after breakfast, I left Hannah and Henry with Lucy and went straightaway by Mr. Talbot to Theodore's little room in Mrs. Allison's house. She had been hovering over a pot of broth in her kitchen and I, too, had brought some sustenance to offer Theodore for when he could sit and take it from me.

Mrs. Allison had come to the door with her apron on, a large serving spoon clasped in one hand and a look of such surprise to see me that I realized that she truly did not know why I had come. I had come unescorted to see a man who was not my husband nor, to anyone's eye, my suitor, and had planned to spend time at his bedside. In point of fact, I was wearing mostly black—my skirt, shawl, and hat. In my haste to reach Theodore, I had not sent a note ahead, so she had every reason to be surprised.

When I told the good landlady my purpose, clutching the basketful of my own offerings with the determination of a child, she held open the door for me, her brow gathered in concern, perhaps for her boarder or for the bold visit I was to make. I could not be sure. It left me with a feeling of renewed disquiet, as I recall visited me when Lucy first discovered Theodore's living quarters. For, though Theodore was indeed only her boarder, had a sentiment for him grown in Mrs. Allison, a married woman?

She nodded a respectful acknowledgement and held the door open more generously. Relief was mine, for it seemed to suggest she bore me no ill tidings, at least for the moment. This would have to suffice, for to beg any more curiosity of a woman I did not know well enough to call a friend would no doubt travel beyond this threshold and invite more than Virginia Pringle's scrutiny. Despite Mr. Pringle managing to keep his wife's scorn at bay last night, this has become of late a persistent worry of mine and I can, as I write of it, hear Lucy chide that I am pandering to an old woman's self-importance.

"Is he much better?" I asked the good landlady. "Has Dr. Wainright been to see him?"

As we moved out of the little entranceway and toward her kitchen, she talked freely.

"Yes, the doctor was here last night, sent by Mr. Pringle. That man's better than most, excepting my own husband of course."

"Was it quite late when the Doctor arrived?"

"No, Mrs. Parsons, it was nigh on eight. The evening had just come on."

Yes, Mr. Pringle would have told his wife one thing and done another in the case of a person needing care. Alarmed as I was when he had told Virginia of his intention to send the Doctor to Theodore after dinner, he did excuse himself briefly. Perhaps he took that opportunity to send for Doctor Wainright. In this way, he appeased his critical wife and saw to the possible gravity of the matter of a sick man, a man who must mean something to him, for he could not know what

Theodore means to me. I should say, he *cannot* know.

Mrs. Allison continued her narration, telling me the Doctor gave Mr. Abel, as she called him, a proper going over before he came down to instruct her. "Said I must do all I could to see to it Mr. Abel recovered before his fever rose back up and took him down. He left just an hour before dawn. The entire night has seen me over the broth on my stove, up and down the stairs to try to get some into the poor thing who's not in much of a mood to take it. I've had no time to tend to my shop with my husband, but he was sporting about it, bringing in extra water for me to boil and making the breakfast. There's a bit more oatmeal in the pot if you've an appetite for it. You're a godsend, Ma'am. D'you think you might take it up to him? He could use a bit of company and I think mine is not what he pines for. Perhaps it's a woman who left him behind, though now one woman's company may be good as the next to give him the healing touch."

Oh, but I was grateful for this outburst! It made me realize I had nursed a small, persistent suspicion about Mrs. Allison and, by implication, I suppose that meant I did not fully trust Theodore in this living situation, though I must say I have no right to entertain suspicion. It makes me feel foolish to record the admission here.

In an instant, this well-meaning woman had snuffed it all out. Her relief was plain, in her speech and in her posture, easy from the moment she realized I had come to help. And though I know it was very lucky that I came, who would have sent for me, truly? Would Theodore have asked for me in his delirium? He had not so far, it would seem, and I attribute this to his protection of my name even in his febrile state. Or perhaps he truly does not want my company and so has not asked for me. When one is ill, possessed of little other than the thoughts and needs that come rushing from an unguarded tongue, his true wishes are uttered. That Mrs. Allison presumes he pines for someone may just be her fancy and I am attaching meaning where there is none.

Pressed into service by Dr. Wainright and by an abundant compassion Mrs. Allison clearly possesses, she would do a fair job of caring for Theodore without my help. I stood in her kitchen wondering if I ought simply to leave her to care for him and went so far as to take a step toward the entranceway. I cannot pretend that my thoughts did not go to worrying over what trouble I would stir by visiting here as often as Theodore had when I was ill. Of course, Theodore took up residence in my parlor whilst I fought my illness, and I will not follow suit in Mrs. Allison's home, for there is no need.

She looked up from her stovetop and reached a hand toward my arm.

"Do you need to go so soon, Mrs. Parsons? You might stay awhile so I can fix my husband's dinner and take it to him at the store. I hope you will." Her words were pointed, her voice kind. She did not understand what it meant for me to stay on without her present somewhere in the house and I did not set her straight. I simply nodded and let her know she could rely on my help. How could I leave? There were now two reasons to remain, one of them Theodore, the other relieving his landlady.

The broth she handed me was filled with beef and vegetables, meant more for a healthy man than one whose throat will resist anything passing through it. I had brought clear consommé and with less salt, so I fancied it would not hurt to have her stew-like soup for myself and let her believe Theodore had made short work of it. That is, if he could waken long enough to take anything.

Mrs. Allison led me upstairs to his little room, a proper square, with a carved out nook and a window seat that looked upon streets perched well above the harbor. Beside that window, Theodore had placed a crude shelf that bent under the weight of his books. He professed to have been a reader and, looking through the titles, I was newly taken by his interests. There were tomes by Nathaniel Hawthorne, Charles Dickens, Percy Byshe Shelley, Mary Shelley, and all of Shakespeare's plays. Within the rows were books filled with etchings of ships at sea, the natural world, celestial bodies, and one small green book with no title that I pulled from in between a volume of sonnets and an old ledger.

It was Theodore's cursive, his angular letters standing apart from one another even as he managed to connect them with a little curve in between, traveling on for pages and pages. I had thought at first it was a ship's log, yet the date on the first page was October 1, 1855, after the ships had sunk. We had not met yet; the vessels, James, and everyone on them were gone. I opened the notebook

I will record in my pages here what little I recall of his words: "*If I were awaiting my Judgment, I would feel no pain.*" I chose to read it as a revelation that he was alive.

A ship's log would be on the ocean floor and these passages were early in the notebook. After reading only that short passage of Theodore's confusion about how he survived, I lifted my face to the morning light splashing into the room from the window and told myself to let go of feeling, to read on without judgment. For I knew, somehow I sensed, that what I would read might undo me if I allowed it to do. I continued as Theodore went on sleeping. He wrote of his lack of connections, or prospects, that by rights he should have drowned and his Captain survived. And then, the sentence I will never forget: "*My Captain's wife is what keeps me from wishing I had perished.*" I could not stop reading then, and wish I had done, for I learned too quickly after those words that, yes, James gave him his cameo, his own talisman, as his ship was going down and he was sending his men overboard to swim for their lives. "*Perhaps it saved me,*" Theodore wrote. "*I'm safe ashore with her face in the palm of my hand, part of my memory from the moment I beheld her husband's likeness of her.*" I read this passage many times sitting in the chair as Theodore slept. If I believe wholly in talismans, I would have left the room, left Theodore to his illness. I know this. For, if it were a talisman, James would be in this life. All the men might have survived.

Replacing the book, my hands trembled. I could not read another word. What I feared most of all, but had dismissed when he sent me his note imploring my forgiveness for knowing who I was before he met me, was now fact.

But do I fear his love, early to bloom as it was? He had not yet seen me in the flesh those many months ago when he came to my door, before knocking, and already he knew his heart, had known it for weeks. Yes, I feared the certainty of his feeling, but I know, too, that there is nothing in it to fear.

Theodore stirred in his sleep, his breath growing ragged for a moment as he roused himself, and mumbled something from a half-waking dream. His eyes opened slowly, settling upon me and upon the book in my hands as his vision cleared. He tried to rise but gave up the effort, as if he had decided that to remove the notebook from my sight was futile. He understood that I had read its first pages. Whatever impression I had formed, he must have concluded, upon seeing me in that moment, that I would address it later or not at all.

"I should think you would flee at the sight of me after reading that," he said, a wry smile upon his lips. I drew nearer in my chair. For, though his written words confirmed something I had pushed aside these many months, at the sight of him I let it slip away.

"I am not going anywhere for the time being," I said.

Even when James took ill, which was not often, he preferred to convalesce alone and allowed only the most essential nursing from me, all of it leaving me feeling frustrated with my lack of use. I had wanted to hold James in the crook of my arm and feed him tea and broth or press cool cloths to his head, rub cures on his ailing chest, anything to show him my love, but he would have none of it, confessing once that he felt it rendered him weaker still to be fussed over so much. Perhaps it is one reason why I resisted Theodore's care of me when I learned he sat with me while I was ill. Can I have been worrying about my late husband's disapproval of my need to be ministered to, worrying as much over that as over this man at my bedside when I was at my weakest?

Theodore held me in his gaze and I had to smile. "You look as though someone dragged you around town without a saddle under you, or a horse for that matter," I said. His smile, still weak, broadened a little.

"I've never felt more like it. And I was once dragged by a horse, so I know how that feels. It's not as grave as this."

"You have only a fever and a sore throat," I told him, though he appeared more ill, far too pale, and my worry must have belied my words. "I will stay with you just a little while, long enough that the children and Lucy will not miss me. Perhaps you can take some broth? I am a great believer in it. Theodore, do not turn away. Turn to me."

He did, with the hint of a frown as he realized who governed him in that moment, though his gaze remained gentle, giving me all of what lay behind it. I placed my basket at my feet, pulling from it the crockery with the soup, and a spoon and a cloth for his chest. I moved to his side and helped him sit up straight enough to take something in without it finding an errant path and causing him to choke.

"I may be the most fortunate man in all of New England," he said, his voice faint.

"I would argue with that."

"And you would lose," he said. "You shouldn't have come, Marianne. You risk much and Mrs. Allison is a capable woman with good intentions. Even the doctor was going to come back later in the day, I think I heard him say."

"Theodore, open your mouth just a little, enough for broth to slip in but no words to escape," I said.

"I see I have little choice."

"You have no choice."

Theodore took half the portion I brought and then slipped back into sleep as I was cooling his forehead with the water and cloth in the basin by his bed. Through me surged such affection for him that I had almost put the journal out of my head.

It was while Theodore slept and I ate some of Mrs. Allison's soup, enjoying her blend of spices and feeling no remorse about eating it myself, that the book commanded my attention once more and I lifted it from the bedside table.

No matter that he had seen me do so, it was no better than common thievery to read Theodore's words further. I would be most indignant if someone had paged through my own when I had stowed it away from prying eyes. He had not expected me here, and had no reason to hide the notebook. He was too weak now to protest, and had resigned himself to my having read it once his eyes opened and saw me with the pages. No, I did not truly belong in Theodore's mind and I told myself this as I opened the thin volume to another page, hoping he would waken and have a change of interest, that he would ask me to replace it on the shelf. He did not; he slept on.

In an entry dated in early October, 1855, he wrote of feeling stronger, yet haunted by the night of the storm that took the vessels down. He wrote that James shouted, *"we must abandon our posts and fight for our lives."* He was, and perhaps still is, haunted by water and wrote that often he wakened in the instant before drowning. He added a note below, in darker ink, as if freshly scratched: "I am again a seaman, against my wish. I would rather love the land." James clung to work on land against his will, for me, and perhaps for greater gain in his eventual work for the quarry, with some months of the year at sea. I believe Theodore would choose easily to stay upon land the rest of his days, loving the sea as he stood upon its shores, not as he sailed toward them.

I closed the book and put it away. I did not, nor do I now, understand why my hands had grown cold and begun to tremble. Not for another moment did I feel comfortable in that room, brimming with questions I hardly knew how to form. I went downstairs with the remaining portion of Mrs. Allison's soup and asked for something on which to write a note. I left it with her to give to Theodore, an assurance that I would return the next day.

At home again, I was relieved to find that the house was quiet. A quick search of the children's and Lucy's rooms confirmed that they had gone on an outing. And why not? June is now well toward summer, and the spring blossoms are still in full bloom. Mill Pond Meadow would be a likely place to spend such a day.

Up in James' study the light bathes the darkest corners of the room in the mornings and by midday it shifts to the center of the room. I stood at the entryway and let my eyes adjust to the darker space before me, for though the light was generous, the sun not yet at its highest point. To my left was the small side table and, carving a brilliant path before it that traveled that side of the room to arrive just there, was a prism of color I had never noted before, for even when I had chanced to visit James in his study, if only to inquire when he might be coming to sleep or to call him to a meal, it was not my habit to come up here, by day or evening. I did not feel welcome into this space while he lived and still feel as if a hand halts me from further entrance. I wished today to move past this feeling, and did so, hardly a yard more, my heart rushing, my skin prickling.

I felt, more than heard, the side door close two floors below and left the room immediately, though I was just as likely to have moved further in still, and closed the door behind me. Neither Lucy, nor the children would have thought to come searching for me there, even if Hannah and Henry were to venture up to the cupola. As I left the room and closed the door behind me, I wondered what had drawn me up to the room and I decided that for the time being, I did not wish to know.

JUNE 7, 1856

I have resolved to visit Theodore each day, spending as much time with him as a watchful community might endure when they are about their own business. But this is where I have erred. For, today—and I will mention that Theodore sat up in bed and took a meal while I read to him—Virginia Pringle came to look in on her husband's new associate.

It was after an hour of reading to Theodore that I heard the cadence of her voice below us, not at all certain in the first moment that I knew who had called, only that the voice, muted through the door and its convey-ance up the stairs, was familiar in a most unsettling way. I stopped read-ing. Then there were steps on the way up and my hands gripped the book as Mrs. Allison knocked gently and Theodore croaked, "Please enter" before I could stop him.

"Excuse me," she said in a mercifully soft voice. "Mrs. Pringle has brought some food she would like to give you herself, Mr. Abel. Shall I show her the way up?" In her eye was a twinkle of mischief and know-ledge. Of course, she must not have understood that to bring that woman into this room with me sitting here would be an incalculable disaster. And yet I had an impractical urge to face Virginia Pringle, to let her know that my being here was in every way acceptable, that a visit to the infirm required no defense. After all, she herself had come alone, had she not? Who was to be nearby her for propriety's sake? The question need not have been asked.

244

I stood and moved toward Mrs. Allison. "May I just sit in the room across from this one, in your room, for a little while? I think she will be quick, for she does not truly admire Theodore." This was in a whisper, and I was frightened in that moment.

When Theodore cleared his throat I turned around and caught a crooked smile behind his whiskers. It was a comment I meant in irony, not in malice, and he took the former meaning, knowing it himself. I will trim those whiskers, I thought, if he will let me, and offered my own smile.

Without a word, Mrs. Allison hurried me across the hall into an empty room in which was a bed, a side table, and a washstand. She bade me sit in the window seat, a comfortable space with embroidered cushions, no doubt stitched by her hand. As she left the room, I turned the lock in the door from the inside and moved toward it for a listening advantage.

Not a moment had passed before I heard Virginia Pringle and Mrs. Allison chatting their way up the stairs toward Theodore. I pressed my ear to the door.

"I certainly hope your tenant is on the mend, Mrs. Allison. My husband is in need of his help at the quarry and if he does not recover soon, Reginald himself will be along to paddle the fever out of him." From anyone else, this might have sounded playful. From Virginia Pringle, the words had the weight of wet sand pouring from the maw of an ugly sea creature. I clutched at my dress as I heard Theodore do his best to muster some cheer for his visitor when she entered his room with the landlady.

I did not hear steps moving away and downstairs, so assumed that Mrs. Allison had remained. It was then that Mrs. Pringle, her voice louder as she must have turned to face the hallway in her address, dismissed Mrs. Allison. My heart surely beat loud enough to be heard across the hall as the kindly landlady obliged and walked with great deliberation down the steps into her kitchen, the sound of her shoes echoing through the wall against which I had pressed myself should the door be opened. She must have been wondering about me, yet I was too keen to hear what would pass between Theodore and his visitor and wished her steps would soften. Finally, I heard Mrs. Pringle speak.

"Mr. Abel, you do look well, far better than I expected. It was a good thing Dr. Wainright was available to you the other evening and that my husband and he are fond friends, for he might not have consented to leave his own comfortable house and come here for a man he does not know." *Or care to know,* I heard unspoken, recalling how she had eschewed the very idea that the good doctor would pay a visit to a man for whom she herself held little regard. Of course, I did not mention this to Theodore. Anyone who calls himself a physician and who has taken his oath would not refuse care to anyone, I wished to remind her.

"I'm very grateful to you both," Theodore managed and then asked after her, Mr. Pringle, and Thomas.

"They are all very well, thank you," came her curt reply. "Thomas had thought to pay you a visit, but I told him it was best to keep away from the ill to avoid illness himself. Of course, I am built rather more sturdily than he, yet my son's constitution is perhaps weaker than yours. That he has not succumbed to anything of late does surprise me. In fact, I thought you the hardier one."

It was the first time, though I am sure unintended, that Mrs. Pringle had ever offered anything like praise to Theodore, buried as it was in her own arrogance. I could not imagine his expression but I longed to be there to interfere with her cold stare. I had to hold fast to the bedpost to keep myself from fleeing across the hall. Seeing me would no doubt cause another fit over my association with a man not my husband, the lack of a chaperone, and the lavender sash I wore at my waist. Too much color, too little regard for my station, would be her bitter complaints. Simply thinking it, I reached for the bed, thinking I would sit, and I nearly toppled a small bowl on the night table. Quickly, I seized the vessel to silence it and the conversation across the hall ceased.

Mrs. Pringle had lowered her voice, yet her words were not quite what I feared. She had not heard my near calamity, or perhaps she heard it distantly and decided it was the sound of an old, inferior house. "You have had visitors besides me, I trust?" I scarcely pieced these words together, but the duplicity was there in her tone, like a cat stretched languidly on a window ledge, surveying the floor for prey. Even a child would know her motive, perhaps especially a child, as they are wont to divine truth in its purest form, even disguised.

"Madam, yes, excellent visitors. Mrs. Parsons' cousin Lucy and Mr. Talbot came to me with a basket the other day and Lucy and Mrs. Parsons came once, today. They remained a while and it was very pleasant."

Oh, be very careful, Theodore, I willed to him. *Too much half-truth will reveal the whole and give the woman what she wants.*

"I see. And has Mrs. Parsons been along to see you on her own? I dare say she was very distraught when she learned of your illness the other evening at our home."

"She's a kind lady," he said without a trace of anything that would draw her nearer what she hunted, for it—I—was nowhere. In fact, he sounded rather bored and even fatigued. I rejoiced in his theatrics. Yet, I puzzled over Mrs. Pringle giving him information about me that she could not have intended to give. Could she have hoped he would betray any delight? Perhaps she was offering it up in the spirit of trickery, to give her further cause to disparage him, perhaps even put an end to his new livelihood. I wonder how hard she would press her good husband to release his new protégé; I imagine she is capable of the worst kind of subterfuge, and that she would stop at nothing to bring it about if she suspected I have once been there alone with Theodore. As their conversation continued, I folded my arms to my chest and pursed my lips.

"Indeed, she is that," came her reply, wrapped in disapproval and what might have been a grudging acknowledgement, for it is true I have never wronged her.

There was, again, a most disquieting silence. And then she spoke. "Mr. Abel, I had not known you enjoyed literature."

"Oh, I do, Madam. I enjoy it most when I'm read to." Theodore coughed, briefly, seemed to be able to stop himself and then went into a spasm of coughing. I wanted to run into the room, but forced myself hard to the spot.

"Oh, dear," Mrs. Pringle said after a moment during which she must have stood there and not known what to do with herself as Theodore let his fit go on. It was then I moved to the door, ready to turn the key and reveal myself, to aid Theodore, for it did not sound as if his visitor were doing anything of the sort. "You ought to take more rest, Mr. Abel" she said over his coughing. "My, you are not at all well. I will fetch your land-lady. She will know what to do." There was an inkling of concern in her voice that I did not want to acknowledge and then I heard her brisk steps going away and down, followed in short order by a few words between the women. At last, mercifully, a door below me closed. In the next mo-ment, as Theodore's coughing spasm calmed, Mrs. Allison had ascended the stairs to tell me, through the door that divided me from her, that Mrs. Pringle was gone away. I turned the key, and dashed across the hall.

When I entered, Theodore was sitting on his bed, his blanket wrapped around him, his face red. He was laughing, which was not helping his cough.

"What is so amusing, Mr. Abel?" I tried for a stern tone and failed abjectly.

"You must ask me, kind lady?" There was that word again, ascribed to me. I would attach the same to him.

Instead, I scolded him. "You are a trickster then. I give you full credit for being the consummate pretender. But you must not tax yourself even with pretense or you will bring up a real fit with the one you feigned and then where will you be?"

"I'll be here, with you, reading to me, feeding me your home-made broths, your biscuits, with your gentleness and care."

I moved just a step closer to his side and reached for his hand. I let his touch run through me like warm syrup before I turned to leave. He did not look well after that fit, but he was calm and had pressed himself back into his pillow, his eyes hardly open, but still on me as I turned to leave.

"Tomorrow I will groom your beard," I said over one shoulder as I pulled the door closed.

"You aren't fond of my whiskers?" He asked just as the door would click. I opened it again, but stood outside the room.

"I am, Theodore. Quite. But they must not overwhelm you. You are beginning to look like a common—"

"But I am that. I've always been a fisherman, a man of labor." He sighed and I felt the flush of shame in my face. "As you say," he finished.

In his pale brown muslin night shirt and loose britches, he bowed his head to me as if he wore all the finery Thomas Pringle is accustomed to donning each day of the week and more so on Sundays; still, this man with his rope-scarred palms and wind bitten cheeks held my heart the way Thomas never will.

Had James held my heart, I thought as I wandered home. Yes, but his grip had come looser in the past many weeks.

JUNE 8, 1856

Last night after a nourishing supper with Lucy, Hannah, Henry, and even Mr. Talbot whom Lucy has asked me to invite to join us each night—and I have consented, for he is, after all, trying with all his decorous might to find ways to hover near my cousin—I took myself off to bed immediately after seeing to the children's comfort.

Once alone, it was my first inclination to think of my latest visit with Theodore, of the near encounter with Mrs. Pringle in his room, of the pleasure I feel in his company. It is no use foreswearing the fact.

Unbraiding my hair, my nightgown fell open at the throat, its ties loose. The skin at my throat was bare and I had the urge to touch it. As a girl of thirteen, I had tripped and fallen into a thorny bush. The thorns were pulled loose quickly enough, yet the one sharp branch poking from the bush scraped hard against the flesh at my throat and left a harsh mark after healing. I have always covered this unsightly mark, yet found myself wondering last evening, as I made ready for bed, if Theodore would look away from this as James had the first time he spied it. It is a bite taken from otherwise smooth flesh. The memory moved me to fasten the button of my gown to hide the mark even from myself.

Sleep came in its own good time. I drifted away from the familiar touch of my bedclothes and fell immediately into water, cold and depthless. I looked up at the surface and saw the hull of a ship and knew, somehow, that I had just left that vessel, leaping into the ocean after James. As with an earlier dream, I found him at the bottom, yet he was not trapped there as before. He simply sat in an armchair, the very one he favored that sits in the parlor. It is a raw silk of midnight blue woven through with thin threads of gold and green. He looked up at me, his pipe between his lips, a book in his hands, and he crooked a finger for me to come near. I swam to him and embraced him. He held me without words, kissed my neck and face and pulled me to him. As I realized the air was leaving me, I tried to pull away. He clutched more firmly until I was horrified to discover that he meant to hold me there. My lungs felt as if they would burst and I twisted from him, moved away and up, my eyes closed tight against the bubbles I made as it seemed my last breath left me. Below, James held his arms wide to catch me even as I struggled upward. I found I was directly beneath the ship's great hull again, my hands scratching at it, looking for its corners and a way up around them, and finding none.

I awoke gasping, twisted in my bedclothes. It was late in the still of those hours when, most nights, I stare at the wallpaper and how its design tricks the eye in a room half-lit by the moon. As my breath steadied itself, I heard a noise, a scratching of the sort an animal makes when tunneling its way from one place to another. Its rhythm was steady and determined, even at times frantic. It kept me company through the rest of the night, though I did not dream again of a vessel's unyielding hull, or my dead husband's unyielding embrace. In fact, I did not sleep. I simply read until first light and fought an unnamable need and a truth that tugged at me. I cannot continue to need James and cannot possibly set my hopes on Theodore. Even as I write of the dream and recall the feeling of James' grip on me, his wish to keep me from breathing my own air, I wish to be free of the need of any man. Yet, how can I place a lock on my heart? I am young. My child has no father now and I have let another take up residence in my thoughts in a way that suggests to me he is not leaving soon, unless I banish him altogether.

250   When I finally left my bed, brushed and pinned my hair, and dressed, I went to Mr. Talbot to ask him to search the attic, the flues of all the chimneys, even the chimney pots themselves, and that if he should find a creature, that he must free it if it is unharmed. If it cannot walk, I will leave it to Mr. Talbot to decide. James would have wrung its neck as an act of mercy if it were injured, and I would have turned away.

Mr. Talbot will no doubt do as his master had done, the right thing, the kind thing to do for a suffering animal, yet a thing I cannot bring myself to attempt. I hoped it would be a matter tended to quickly.

Recalling those few instances of James ending an injured creature's worthless life, an act that was in itself a kindness, I could not look upon him, could not enjoy his touch, not for days, perhaps a week. For, it was with each day that the memory of the violence I had conjured even without looking at the act, was diminished.

Mr. Talbot found the prowling creature within an hour. It was nothing more than a chickadee trapped in the first floor eaves below my window. He set it free with a broom, brushing it first one way then another, with Henry looking on a safe distance from the window and saying, "go, birdie, fly, birdie!"

And it did fly, high and far away from my boy whose wondering eyes were wide, his mouth round with interest.

JUNE 9, 1856

When I visited a much improved Theodore today, I decided to ask him if I might read more from his notebook about the horror that took my husband, so many others, and not Theodore. His face registered surprise for only an instant, yet memory took its place, for he had seen me read from it. Then he surprised me by offering it to me whole, to keep for my own understanding. I argued that I should not be its owner and did not make a move toward the shelf where I had found and then replaced it the other day, though not as snugly as it had been there before.

"I've nothing to hide from you. Satisfy yourself. I don't want it back." I did not make a move and the matter was put aside. I was just as glad for the time being and he seemed quite content to have me read some Hawthorne to him, *Tales of the White Mountains.* I read and read, hardly stopping to speak to him between pages. When I finished the chapter, I looked up to meet his steady gaze. His complexion was smooth and he looked young, if pale.

He had shaved his beard clean off and when I first arrived I nearly turned around to leave, for I had grown accustomed to his whiskers.

Without them, he looked quite like another man! I would not have removed them altogether, for they framed his face well, as if to cup it, yet I had been unable to go to Mrs. Allison's yesterday. I was needed at home. Henry seemed too much for poor Lucy to handle with his penchant for running, a thing she cannot do in her advanced years. Hannah is able, yet she was doing her lessons, as commanded by her parents during this extended stay. Her mother sends them to her each week, with sweet notes encouraging her to keep learning. I did not have the heart to leave Lucy to her huffing and puffing after my son, so sent a note to Mrs. Allison asking that she beg my pardon for not coming around. I had thought to send it directly to Theodore, and promptly reconsidered. The day, of course, crawled as slowly as it might for a woman watching the clock's hours pass, yearning for the day to turn to night and then to day again.

This morning, a closer look at Theodore's face when I looked up from the book I had been reading to him revealed that he had nicked his left cheek above the beard line, and another tiny gash was hidden just at the joint of his left jaw. Seeing the small, angry wounds, my hand went to his face. Theodore pressed his palm over my hand and I felt its roughness. I felt, too, the warmth of his cheek, and his breath at my wrist.

"Why did you take them off altogether?"

"The truth is a disgrace," he said. "It will amuse you."

"No, of course not. I can hardly laugh at the truth," I told him, and I did mean what I professed, for I have always found truth to be somewhat sobering.

"Well, I've never had whiskers for quite so long or as full as those and as I was aiming for a more gentlemanly appearance. I failed. It was such a poor job, I looked as though I'd been attacked by a very large, vicious mackerel."

At this, I did laugh against my own will, imagining such a thing. Of course, the very thought of Theodore's struggle to appear a gentleman when he has a more admirable nature than most men of privilege, saddened me, putting an end to my laughter.

I resumed reading, having little to say in response to his comment, and again when I looked up, I found his eyes were settled on my face.

"Theodore, have you been listening?"

"Of course," he protested and laughed. "But don't ask me to repeat what you've read."

"You are fortunate not to have Hannah here, or she would do just that. She will make some impish lad sorry for his wandering mind when she has her turn."

"Why did you stop reading? Are you needed at home?"

"I am not rushing away. It is only…" I could not bring the words forward. Theodore leaned toward me.

"Marianne." In the utterance of my name, his plea was gentle and earnest. I do not know what he thought I might have to say, but it could not have been what I did say.

"It is your notebook, Theodore. The one you now offer me as if I have a right to it. I am ashamed to have read it at all, but there are things I must understand." I stood and walked around his bed to the shelf and looked for the notebook, found it was not there, and then turned to face him.

"Have you removed it? Of course, you have. You are more troubled than you let on that I should have seen it. Oh, I am a poor friend for looking at it. I was sneaky as a child."

"No, I haven't touched it." He looked toward the shelf and frowned as if trying to recall where he might have placed it. "Never mind, I imagine I put it amongst my other things. I'd read it some after you had. I might have left it elsewhere." He moved toward a small trunk, searched its contents, and drew up again, empty-handed. "Marianne, there's nothing in that notebook I wish to hide from you." He said this so softly that I felt rather than heard the words. "Only truths I should have shared long ago and didn't." I turned from him and reached for the light shawl I had brought and put aside. I felt it best to leave and Theodore did not try to prevent me. He draped it over my shoulders and took my hands. "I can only think what your horror might have been, what your confusion must be."

"Yes, I admit to confusion," I said. "But not horror. Not now. Perhaps not ever."

"I'm not a messenger sent by your husband to care for you, to do his final bidding. How could I, in his name rather than my own?" He had spoken to my question, of course.

"Is it not very warm in the room?" I asked and he laughed, a small rumble in his throat, and watched me as I moved toward the window to lift it and let in the June air. Below was the bustle of merchants and children, of lives being lived in the most ordinary way, on School Street, an ordinary street of homes and shops, with people who have known one another their entire lives. I wanted none of it in that instant and turned my back to the window. Theodore was now, I could see, somewhat uncomfortable in the moment we had created.

I went to him. His arms came around me and I stood against him, the thud of his hammering heart in my ear, his breathing unsteady. We remained this way for many moments until his heart's rhythm slowed and his arms found the most comfortable place around the curves of my waist. I felt his hands move, felt his fingers spread over my back as he and I both tried very hard to be still. We failed. For, in the next moment I pulled away to look at him, and he brought his face down to mine, placing his mouth to mine. It was a different kiss than the one he stole that day in my parlor.

I would like to say that it was as if I had come home, as it had been with James when he first embraced me. James' kiss is the only one I have ever had, so a kiss ought to feel like a kind of coming home if the feeling between the two people is very tender.

But it was not home. I was, in that wondrous kiss, removed from all that felt familiar. There is no cherry tobacco on Theodore's breath, nor any tobacco, for he does not take a pipe. He kissed me in such a way that I felt something inside me, something beneath my corset, leap and yell, as a child might when she runs up and down the surf, the water licking at her feet. She runs into it and then dashes away. So it was in Theodore's embrace. We stood there a very long time, his lips grazing my ear, lingering upon the scar at my neck, his hands around my waist, his heat rushing through the fabric of my blouse, my skirt.

The knock at the door was gentle and, though Mrs. Allison's voice came softly, we started and moved apart.

"Mrs. Parsons," she whispered, though I cannot think why except perhaps that she thought Theodore was slumbering through his fever. But at the sound of my accustomed name I moved away from him.

"Too soon," I whispered, my hand at my forehead as I grasped at the wall nearest me to steady myself. Despite how it must have sounded to Theodore who was silent and watchful, I was not thinking of a widow's propriety but that the visit had come to an end too, too soon. Yes, that was what I meant. Oh, and I was grateful and miserable all at once to have the intrusion of his landlady.

Mrs. Allison had come to tell me that Lucy was downstairs in her little parlor, with the children. Hastening my parting with Theodore who tried to kiss me again, playful as a boy as I moved just out of his reach and told him to get back into bed, I joined Mrs. Allison in the hallway. She peered at me and had the decency not to ask after what she might have noticed, then led me down to Lucy. My cousin reported that Henry is lately in the habit of plundering the pantry and tipping over bins of flour and cornmeal so that she had to get him out of the house and end the mischief. We hurried home, as it was near enough to dinner, and I helped her clean up while Hannah busied my naughty boy. All the while flour dust rose up in a cloud around us at my every sigh and Lucy was left to wonder very little at my distracted state. She could only shake her knowing head, with hardly an inkling of what I had still to tell her.

It is evening and the nights are growing shorter even as they seem endless. I still feel Theodore's lips upon mine, tender and searching at my throat, grazing back and forth across that scar. Mrs. Allison could not have known the good she did me this afternoon with her knock at the door.

June 10, 1856

A letter arrived today by messenger, one of the Pringle household's cowed staff. I placed it on the hall table and opened it after walking past it several times throughout the day, expecting the usual rebuke from Virginia Pringle for what she may have surmised about my visits to

Theodore. As I read this letter, it was worse than I imagined!

Dear Mrs. Parsons,

I will not waste words on what might be proper or gentle behavior for you, knowing I have gleaned my facts from a source not belonging to me. I will simply say that what I now understand vindicates me with its very truth. You see, my young friend, I am faced with having to tell you of a discovery concerning my husband's newest employee and your friend, Mr. Abel. It would seem that he has had designs on you from very early on in his association with your husband, that he knew of you, knew well of you, from a cameo with your likeness that your husband shared with him whilst at sea. I have come to know, after his survival of the wreck that took your beloved husband, that Mr. Abel sought your acquaintance with premature affection for you. It is my belief that Mr. Abel's intention is to undo your standing in this community and that of your future marriage prospects, not to mention your son's legacy as his father's heir.

It is my belief that if you do not sever ties with this Mr. Abel, whose name might not even be his own, whose provenance continues to be an unsettling question, that you will bring shame upon your father's family name, your own fine name, and upon Rockport itself. I cannot urge you strongly enough to heed my counsel or I shall be forced to bring this matter directly to your parents for consideration. As it is, I act in their interests for you. A man with such questionable motives behind his acquaintance with you has no place in a town of honorable citizens. You can be certain that it will take little to convince my husband to relieve Mr. Abel of any further service to him.

Your concerned neighbor and guardian,
Mrs. Reginald Pringle

Immediately, I showed the letter to Lucy whose fury blazed as hot as mine. We two sat in my parlor, Jack nosing about for biscuit crumbs, the children drawing at the dining room table one room away, and said nothing. For, in the face of such treachery as that wrought by Virginia Pringle, I could think of nothing to say. Dear Lucy, always insightful where my sensitivities are concerned, did not try to prompt or soothe me. I sat quietly and recalled my visit to Theodore the day before. And I saw it clearly. Mrs. Pringle must have pilfered Theodore's journal during his coughing fit. Yes, it must not have been tucked into its shelf, and sat visible, a curiosity in how its appearance differed from other books around it. She must have taken her opportunity on impulse, though she could hardly have come expecting such good luck.

Looking half-blind out the window at Mr. Talbot busying himself with laying a flower bed, I imagined Theodore sorting through his trunk, eyeing his bookshelf, perplexed as to where his notebook might have gone. He might even be entertaining the notion that I took it. Truly, I cannot bring myself to tell him anything, and must deal with that thieving woman myself.

JUNE 11, 1856

Theodore is well enough now to take a stroll and so we did, with Lucy and Mr. Talbot not far behind and Henry trotting up ahead with Hannah. I cannot any longer bring myself to care if we encounter any one of the Pringles when we move about. I am bored of her tirade, and more worried what Theodore must think of where his journal has gone than what the dour Virginia Pringle imagines now that she has read it.

We took to Mill Pond Meadow and sat on the bench, watched an old man brush his palette and then his bright white canvas with colors that rivaled the vibrancy of the subjects themselves. He painted the mossy banks opposite him, the clusters of periwinkle hugging those banks, the pond itself and all that was mirrored there, the brilliance of the sky, the clouds, the gulls drifting over our heads, the ducklings paddling after their mother.

Henry approached the man as he painted and stood with remarkable stillness watching, the back of his head moving just enough for me to know that he was following the motion of the old man's paintbrush.

Hannah called out to him and he turned toward her voice. She was behind where we sat, sitting in the grass, her hands filled with buttercups and dandelions, devil's paintbrush and sweet William. He ran to her and sat down, plucking the flowers from her hands one by one, listening to her name them, and trying to form the sounds with Hannah's help.

Theodore had said very little other than to remark upon the warm air, the faint chill behind it that blew in off the bay. I was glad of it, grateful for the quiet between us, and for its ease. I wanted him to rest and, indeed, when I turned to look at him, his head was tilted back to the sun, his eyes closed, his breathing quiet and slow. Lucy and Mr. Talbot were walking along the banks, their forms slightly inclined toward one another, though still not near enough to touch.

What I wanted most in that moment that was more perfect than any I have experienced since before losing James, was to draw it out like taffy and watch it grow and change shape. I wanted to taste and linger in its sweetness. I will let the memory of it drift to the back of my throat, down into my chest where it burns a little, a tang that has caught me by surprise.

JUNE 12, 1856

I have wrestled with this all night, and finally rested on the notion that it is better to tell Theodore that his diary is in the hands of that treacherous woman, for he does not appear to want to approach me about it. It is possible he forgot it was missing.

I cannot figure how, if Virginia Pringle claims to be a guardian, a position that implies unimpeachable trust and morality, she can justify thievery. It seems to me her act renders her dishonorable even if her intention is cloaked in the pretense of honor for my parents' sake and so, presumably, for mine. Now she will use Theodore's tender words against him! If I am to tell him, it must be gently, free of the rancor I feel for Virginia Pringle.

So, I have invited him to tea for tomorrow and since it is a Sunday, tea might turn into supper, an early one, and then I will tell him as he leaves so that his distress at such a betrayal will not be so apparent to the children, wondering children in the most ordinary of circumstances. Need I mention here that he has accepted my invitation and that at the very thought of having him near, I am faint?

JUNE 13, 1856

I will forgo the details of the afternoon and evening except to say that
Theodore came to the house wearing a new shirt, tailored it would seem,
just for his size. His clothes looked pressed and the wounds he had in-
flicted upon himself from shaving had faded to faint scratches. He looked
younger and in better health so soon after his illness than when I first saw
him at my door so many months ago.

We took tea on the side porch with the limbs of the linden shading us
from the afternoon sun. The children held forth with songs and even a
story Hannah had created and taught to Henry, which they performed
for us. Henry's sense of theatrical timing was no doubt a source of some
frustration for Hannah. He would often utter her lines, or so it seemed
when she would open her mouth to speak and it was he who bellowed the
words. Theodore, Lucy, and I could not help but laugh at my son's antics
and we clapped mightily for Hannah's efforts.

Supper was just as lively, with Theodore telling us of his days at the
quarry and how one particularly hot afternoon some weeks ago, he encountered an old man hunkered under a great rock just below the lip of
the quarry, on a ledge, hidden from anyone who might see him. How
Theodore had spotted him was owing, he said, to where he sat in the office that sat back from the quarry but had a view of it. No one was there
but Theodore that afternoon, and he ran to beg the man from the ledge.
He learned that the unfortunate man had once worked in the quarry
himself and had lost his livelihood when he broke his hand the year before. He had lost his wife to an infection of the lung and his only child,
a son, had run off to California to find gold. Theodore had taken the old
man to Mrs. Allison, bade her feed him a meal and then taken the man
home to his little two-room cottage in Pigeon Cove, promising
he would talk to Mr. Pringle about finding suitable employment
within the quarry office or somewhere else. The man's face, he
said, was mapped with veins as prominent as those in a slab of granite.
Theodore did not doubt the man took too much rum, perhaps drinking
that and nothing else. He might have been fifty or nearer eighty years old,
Theodore said. He does not know what became of the man who has since

not been seen about town and whose home is abandoned, a fact which Theodore verified when he looked in upon him the very next day and the next, keeping on for a fortnight until he heard from Reginald Pringle himself that the man had been found dead in Gloucester, a demijohn of spirits near him. I should mention that the children had gone into the house by this time or I would have asked our friend to forestall the telling of such a sad tale.

Since our closeness the other day, when no one is about Theodore gazes at me with his own brand of shyness, though not as shy as I have become in his presence. I turn my blazing face from him when I catch his eye, knowing I have been caught with like sentiments lying just below the surface of what I have lost hope is a serene expression. There is no calm in my gaze, for my heart gallops at the sight of him. It is difficult to write these words for the truth they imply, and yet so easy, so very natural.

When Lucy and I had tucked the children in, Lucy had retired to the pantry to clean up the supper dishes, brooking not even the insincere protest I offered when I told her to leave them for me to do later. She simply leveled one of her knowing looks at me, and turned me by the shoulders toward the parlor and the side door. I joined Theodore on the side porch again and we looked up at the moon, bathed as we were in its generous light even as it was two weeks into waning. Mr. Talbot was in the stable. It was late for him, although he had told me he needed to see to one of the horses' hooves and to the carriage which had a loose axel he feared might prove dangerous. I wondered if perhaps he lingered more to be nearer Lucy. A pathway and two rooms are all that separate them when he is at his work and she, in the kitchen, tends to hers. I imagine them imagining each other fondly.

There we sat, Theodore and I, and I was grateful for the presence of others nearby but not hovering, with Mrs. Pringle's vigilance now at its height.

"It has been a lovely day. Thank you for asking me here. I thought you might try to stay away after that moment before Mrs. Allison—"

I could not imagine staying away, a sentiment I did not utter, yet he seemed to hear it. I turned to him, keeping proper space between us.

"I must tell you something and you will not like it one bit."

"Are you ill?" He asked and took my hands, which I took back, fearing watchful eyes. It had occurred to me some months ago that the Pringles' home, which sits on a rise three blocks southwest of my home, has an upper floor with a window that could ogle the rear side of my own house and certainly this porch in daylight. The linden tree hid us well as long as there was not a stiff breeze to shift its boughs, and my porch had little enough light in the dark of evening other than from the moon.

"No, no. I am not ill," I reassured him, and hoped this would stick. So much resided in that kiss. I have much to lose, and I have begun to wonder how much this matters to me. I was unprepared to discuss any of it. "The volume I read and that I should not have touched while you slept is no longer in your possession." Confusion turned his mouth down as I watched him search his memory for how such a thing might have happened.

"You only had to ask me if I'd part with it," he said.

"Theodore, I did not take it away from you," I said, too quickly, with the shame that visited me all over again for reading his journal at all. And now it is shame and worry, too, for what if wretched Mrs. Pringle is correct about Theodore?

"Ah," he said. "I hope you won't...that you don't think..." I watched him closely, noting how frustration and the first inkling of hopelessness came and quickly left his face. Such an expressive gaze he has. What sat with us as surely as if it were a person in the room was the specter of Mrs. Pringle's damning words, harsh words he did not yet know, could scarcely imagine. "Oh, hang it" was all he could manage.

"I do not hold a single word against you, Theodore. It is Virginia Pringle who does so," I assured him, and myself.

It took only a moment for this to settle around him and as it did, I saw the workings of his mind and the dawning that when a particular woman paid a visit to his sick bed, he was burgled. 261

"And I thought myself so clever working up a coughing fit to be rid of the woman!" He said, clearly disappointed in himself.

"I would like to get it back for you. She has no use for it other than to use it against you. She spoke of having your position at the quarry taken from you and I fear she will soil your name in this town."

"She will soil yours worse than mine, my good lady. I don't want harm to come to you and your son through your association with me." He wrung his hands, turned away and looked skyward as if to implore every celestial body overhead to aid him in making a decision. "Marianne, don't place your efforts in getting something of so little worth back to me. The words I wrote are still present in my head, the truth as clear as I'm standing before you, even if she burns the pages."

"Oh, she is not likely to do that!" In fact, I imagined her parceling the notebook off to Mother.

"I must go away for a time. I was to be voyaging abroad and now it seems the timing of such a trip can't be better. Reginald Pringle would like me to make further contacts in England. It will be good for you if I'm gone."

"How can you say such a thing?" I said, wanting to shake him. "I can do what I must where Virginia Pringle is concerned and she is slow to act, trying to read your intentions. If we remain civil without too much discourse and keep little company, it will pass."

"We've done that much before now and she still preyed upon you, and now more directly upon me. I'm assigned to go and, more than before, to keep favor, I must. The voyage is brief, altogether a month, and it will pass along with her appetite for undoing me. I'll be home as soon as early July and we can enjoy the summer as friends of our kind do, with your son and with Lucy. We'll be beyond reproach. Come," he said, his hand reaching for mine which I held to my waist, crossed tightly over my body, the other hand behind my back as if I held a posy of flowers there like the one Theodore brought me when he first arrived today; redolent pink and orange blossoms he had picked from a meadow near the quarry.

262

And in that instant, I had made a decision of my own, the certainty of it striking me with a force that made me move away from Theodore.

"If you go to England, when you return, you will not be welcome in my home."

I felt his eyes on me for a long moment. "You would keep me away?" He asked, his disbelief a whisper, yet clear as the bell over the Rockport Congregational Church that I seldom attend.

"I must protect my heart, Theodore, and that of my son. You are a thinking man and you know what I have lost, what it has cost me. You will understand and not argue this point, I know."

"No," he said with a great sigh. "I can't argue," he said. "You aren't wrong to shelter yourself, even as I can assure you that no such sorrow will visit you again."

"You can no more assure me of that than I can assure you that Virginia Pringle will not drive you out of Rockport and even Gloucester altogether."

He turned to leave, just a few steps, then came back and guided me toward a chair, knelt before me, and took my hands in his.

"If I'm never to see you again, then I'll tell you this, Marianne. I would etch my affection for you on every tablet in every schoolhouse in every county in New England. I would want everyone to see it. If Mrs. Pringle will hold love up to a harsh light and find it punishable, she's cold indeed. You do what you must where she's concerned. Only please don't try to belittle my words. I've loved you from the moment I saw your likeness in the palm of your late husband's hand and if that's my sin, to have loved you before truly understanding your nature, then I'm as guilty in life as I will be afterward. I regret nothing."

With that, he leaned closer, placing one hand at my cheek and bringing me to him under the canopy of the linden tree. His kiss was long and filled with the words he had spoken. I watched him walk toward Mill Pond Meadow where he would take the path along the pond and toward High Street and home to his little room, then out to sea and away.

June 14, 1856

This morning, I reached under the bed for the mahogany box I had forgotten was stowed there and held it in my lap on the quilt. I shook the box again as if to satisfy myself that there is still something in there, even if it is foreign to me now, even as I long for whatever is in it not to exist. I could not bring myself to open its latch, so I replaced it once again. One day, the hour will come for me to face its contents.

Oh, it is this endless folly spilling from my mind that keeps me wakeful. My mind is a spiteful thing. If it cannot rest, it sees no reason why I, its keeper, should do!

JUNE 15, 1856

In need of cheer, I have gone to Hannah Jumper for some mending of a dress I found in my wardrobe that fit me well before I had my son. It is a shade of geranium pink with pale blue piping at the throat and cuffs, a dress Theodore would admire if he were ever to behold it. But of course, he will not, so I do it for myself and for the expectations of wearing such things more regularly by summer's end. Perhaps the good Miss Jumper will find some extra fabric in its folds to let out to make the wearing easy, for my waist is just a bit thicker than it was when I was nineteen and not yet with child. As Miss Jumper stitched and pinned, I heard two other women in the next room, abuzz with complaint about their husbands' tippling and what sounded like a conspiratorial tone, but their voices had lowered and I could no longer make out their words. I looked down at Hannah Jumper's steady hands and the straightness of her form, and knew the bitter complaints of her customers' ire over the great consumption of spirituous drink in Rockport were what she bore all her days at work. I have heard the complaint more of late when I am in town. One woman after another; fisherman's wife, merchant's wife, perhaps even banker's wife, for Emily McCutcheon's husband's indulging in spirits drove her away. They must bring their sad, angry tales to Miss Jumper's spare and clean room, relying upon her listening, sympathetic ear. I wonder as I write this what they think an old woman can do for them?

Standing there today, I imagined my young cousin Hannah as a seamstress bent over other women's clothing, her more delicate posture ruined after years of it, her head addled with unhappy tales of others' lives, and in my own heart felt the first true stirrings of what Lucy felt toward Timothy.

Hannah Jumper is well into her seventies and lives a Spartan life, her quarters very bare. Miss Jumper has never married. She is a very capable woman, her fingers aged but nimble, her back strong despite all the bending she does for her work. She is as tall as a man and she can, without straining, reach the drying plants dangling from the wooden rafters overhead in her two small rooms in the upper floors of the house where she lives.

When I visited her, she chided me for not letting her know if the herbs I had purchased from her for Henry's cure when he was ill had done their work. Despite her scolding, Miss Jumper is kind, and really says very little as she works. I could only offer apology and then she offered me a licorice tea that was very strong and sweet and helps to ease one's digestion. I drank it as she had me stand. She pinned, snipped, and pulled at the dress I wore that was far too snug for me these nearly five years after I last wore it. For a moment, I doubted my decision to tailor it, but after some time spent doing whatever she does so well and that I have never hoped to master, the task was complete.

Leaving her home, I wondered if she had ever known love, the kind a man and a woman share, or if she had ever sought it out. Perhaps it had come to her door and she had turned it away. I had heard men praise her for her cures, and seen a man now and again bearing seasonal vegetables to her door, yet she really is always alone when she does not have customers seeking her cures and mending. As I let my mind wander into her singular life, I realize as I write these things that my curiosity is getting the better of me. Who am I to wonder of such intimacies that should not concern me in the least?

The days are warm early, the sun reluctant to set each day, the lilies beginning to open each morning earlier in the season than they might, and I feel this need to revisit a time when I wore a frock that spoke of no worry, no sorrow, no misgiving. I might just wear that pink one about town before my mourning year is up.

265

JUNE 16, 1856
I dread it, yet it must be done. I have written a note to Mrs. Pringle asking her to tea tomorrow. I invited Thomas and Mr. Pringle along as well,

though she will say they are occupied with matters of business because she will want to face me alone, to cow me into believing all she holds true about Theodore. I will set her straight. A part of me wishes for their presence, knowing her husband in particular will have a calming effect on his wife should she lose her composure, but it is I who will need calming. I will not betray myself. She may call me young Mrs. Parsons, and may be my elder in a way that prevents me from censuring her as she would me, yet I will hold to what I know is true about this man regardless of whether I have turned him away.

JUNE 18, 1856

Today, I hold in my hands nothing with which to build my hopes for Theodore's livelihood. This afternoon, with Lucy tending expertly to our needs as if she were born to service, and the children out in the sunshine of the side yard tending to the garden with Mr. Talbot, I sat with a very stalwart Virginia Pringle in my home, asked after her husband and her son, and treated her to a spread I do not normally enjoy myself. I had planned for more cakes and scones than sandwiches with our tea, and even cherry cordial waited in its decanter for us. I had picked some lilies and placed them in two vases, one on the china cabinet, the other on the little table between the two chairs in the parlor where we sat. If I were a guest entering this room, I would have smiled at the brightness of the blossoms, the sweetness on the tea cart. Virginia Pringle only offered a tart greeting.

"Lucy has made her lemon scones and oatmeal cake," I said, a little chirp in my voice I could not prevent. I hoped it sounded more welcoming than anxious.

"I am afraid lemon gives me mouth sores and oatmeal binds me," she said rather more frankly than I might have expected.

"I do have butter cookies."

She nodded and I went in to Lucy to ask for a plate of them along with the other delights she would bring. Lucy arched her high brow at me, her thoughts my own, though she uttered nothing as she gave me what I requested.

As we sat, my guest remarked favorably upon my black dress, the black bow that fastened my bun. It was, to my recollection, the first kind word she has offered me, though her mouth was drawn as if she had indeed eaten a lemon tart. She liked, she said, the miniature grey florets at the bodice and around the waist of my frock. Yes, I had dressed for her.

"I hoped for a daughter," she confided, as if we had been conversing of matters that prompted this comment. "And I did lose a child, a girl, when Thomas was ten years of age. He never knew I had carried her, for I was somewhat rounder in those days and could hide my girth under larger skirts. It was the midwife who told me I had given birth to a girl, though she was not fully formed. After that, I had no strength to carry another child and was instructed not to weaken my heart with attempts to try."

I heard each word and measured them for meaning. Was she hinting she wished I were her daughter? Or perhaps she was admitting to another weakness in her constitution besides what food provoked. I found myself wondering how any man, though this one had been her physician, had managed to solicit her will or offer his affections and ardor and in that same moment, knew Virginia Pringle was a mother who would want to live for the child she had.

I poured our tea and gave her my best teacup, a delicate bell-shaped piece with green on the inside and white edged with roses on the outside. She did not admire the cup, though she seemed to enjoy the tea.

"Mrs. Pringle," I began after a moment when she was busy nibbling and seemed more relaxed. "I must beg your indulgence."

"Do, then," she said, and offered me a thin smile, her best, I believe.

"It is of a delicate nature, the thing I must ask of you. I hope you will hear me before you issue your rebuke."

Her eyebrow went up at this, as if to say, *I would rebuke?*

I gathered my courage. "You have in your possession a thin volume of no consequence to anyone but its author," I said. She looked about to speak and then thought the better of it, I imagine, after my request. "I understand from your letter to me that Mr. Abel may seem to you to have questionable motives. However, I have come to know him…" and here she put down her teacup with too much force and it clattered in its saucer before I righted it. "I have come to know him as an individual of pure motives, a heart that seeks friendship and acceptance, a life that has known loneliness. He does not pretend at anything and, though he was not formally schooled, has read a great deal of literature I know you would find in your own library. His speech and comportment are testament to the knowledge he has gleaned through books. He speaks well of his captain, my beloved late husband, and he is decent in all ways, kind to my child, my cousin, and her granddaughter. I would ask that you please address your own heart's motives and, in doing so, see that bringing shame to Mr. Abel can bring you no satisfaction and bring him only suffering. He has done nothing to earn your scorn other than to spend time with me. This is no crime, for he is a companion to me. What he lacks in all we know of propriety, he makes up for in goodness." I did not want to overstate my case, so I took a breath and rested my cold hands in my lap to keep them from trembling. She did not speak for a full moment.

"Have you said all you must, Mrs. Parsons?"

I nodded, my eyes level on her face, divining her affect for any sign of compassion. She was no more readable than hieroglyphs on the wall of an ancient cave. And then she spoke, ending the mystery, and taking my breath away as quickly as a blow to the stomach.

"I disagree with your assessment of Mr. Abel as having the purest motives. He states very expressly in his diary that he adored you before he knew you, and this is indecent. It is neither Christian nor in any way acceptable within our society that he should have felt an inkling of desire for another man's wife, particularly his captain's wife."

"But it was not desire!" I protested, knowing differently, and forgiving it, for Theodore knew me for only moments as James' wife before James went to his death.

268   "I did not interrupt you. I ask the same courtesy." Just then Lucy peered in and asked if we wanted anything more, though I know her; she timed her appearance to rescue me as I had asked her to, and now it was too plain that there was no rescue. I had set this stage and it would play out to the end. I looked at her and shook my head. She retreated, a furrow in her brow that bespoke her worry.

"Your Mr. Abel will be sailing to England and, because I cannot shake my husband's interest in him, upon his return to Rockport he will take up residence elsewhere, minding the interests of the quarry. You will not see him socially, and if he should appear at your threshold again, you will turn him away with the full understanding that if you do not, his reputation with my husband as a hard worker, what meager name he has to support himself, and any livelihood he hopes to purse on Cape Ann will be snuffed out. I will see to it."

"But you have no right!"

"Indeed, as your elder and the emissary of your good parents, I have every right. I am making a great compromise in allowing him any further tenure with my husband's business, for I do not trust him for one moment." She stood and straightened her skirt and I stood with her, not to be looked down upon in my own house, though her height made quick work of that. "You may have your own designs on this man whose origins are so vague as not to exist, but you know no better thing for yourself in your grief than a young girl lost in the woods. You cannot be trusted much more than he to exercise shrewd judgment."

I thought in a rush of heat and fury what Thomas had told me about his mother's own heartbreak and I sat down again, heavily, placing my face in my hands. I should not have revealed my weakness to her, for she came near then and put a stiff hand on my shoulder as if to comfort me. She might have laid a cold, dead piece of fish on me and I would not have known the difference.

"When you have collected your wits, my dear, you will see that not only am I correct about Mr. Abel, but I have always held your interests near. Perhaps we might not be friends, yet if the day should ever come that my son should court your fancy, I would not turn you away. Because your parents are dear to me, I would welcome you to my family as 269 my own. You have a child and it is hard for a woman with a child to wed again in her accustomed society without a helping hand. Do think of that and let it satisfy you that a possibility for your happiness and that of your son awaits you."

I looked up at her. "Good day, Mrs. Pringle," I said. "My cousin will see you out."

After she left, I sat a moment. When I rose to leave, I spied Theodore's diary in the place where Virginia Pringle had been. I took it, clutched it to my chest and began to write my parents an impassioned plea, which, after the first paragraph entreating them to see Theodore as only good, I abandoned. For I realized, even as Mrs. Pringle had delivered this hateful message in her own words, with her own motives besides, that it had come from Mother as surely as if she had issued the decree from her own lips. I would, I decided, appeal first to Father and it would require a visit.

JUNE 20, 1856

Today as I sat in the parlor reading, trying with every ounce of might to steer my thoughts away from missing Theodore, I was startled when Henry's little hand stole into my lap and placed the mahogany box there. It had a fine coat of dust over it that paled the wood's dark gloss. It is a lovely piece of wood, inlaid with mother of pearl and with a silver latch on it, tarnished now after so many months under my bed.

"Mama, here," he said, pressing it to me. "Open."

"Where did you find it?" Of course, I did not have to ask this. Mischievous boys do not avoid the undersides of beds.

"Under your bed," came his frank reply. I wanted right there to scold him for it, yet it was not any more trouble than he usually finds and in this, perhaps, he had done me a service. He has also told me the truth. Left to me, the box would have stayed unopened. I have always been disinclined to surprises but for the most benign, such as a birthday token or a posy of flowers, perhaps even a visit from a bosom friend, the likes of which seem scarce these days as Irene is not yet home and Emily seems finally to have severed her ties to Rockport.

"Well, then, you be the one to open it," I told him. "There," I pointed to the latch. His strong little fingers pried it away from its catch and he flung open the lid to reveal a smaller box of velvet and an envelope, still sealed. It was James' seal.

Henry reached for the smaller box and opened it. Within was a strand of perfect pearls. My son closed them in his palms, shook them, delighted. I asked him to help me fasten them around my neck and he obliged, though he was unable and let me do it. The moment I felt their cool perfection against my skin, I took them off and replaced them in the box, sending the boy to play.

I sit here now at my writing table, my hand moving almost as if it wills itself, my eyes fixed on this page, turned away from the letter I have finally read and which is now propped next to my bed.

Dearest Marianne,

You will fight me on this, for in your eyes lately I often see a storm. You do not understand that I do it all for you, that every hour I toil and every day I am gone, each and every one of them that separates me from you and our son, is all for you.

Yes, you will rail and say that you know it, that your mother taught you well and that even as you know all you must do as a wife and mother, even standing by as I seem to be less mindful of what goes on in our very own home—our son growing bigger each day, you growing more beautiful— that you cannot tolerate any longer this absence I have imposed. My earnest hope is that you will see that it has all been for good. Do we not now live as well as any? Perhaps not yet as well as those Pringles you seem to enjoy disliking, though that will soon change with the guidance of Reginald Pringle. He is a good sort, even if his wife is vinegar-like in her affect.

The pearls are from Malaga, Spain by way of England, from an old world I have never visited but where I will someday take you. It was Reginald who procured the pearls for me on one of his voyages. We will travel to many lands in Europe and our son will grow to know many languages and you, my darling, will always have me at your side.

I must go now, for I have a voyage to prepare for, paperwork to prepare for Reginald and for my journey. He has commissioned me, for my first duty, to survey the need for granite on other parts of our very own continent. You will not enjoy my absence, yet I believe that when you see all that I have brought us through this new commerce, you will fret far less. I will give this to you upon my return as a promise of it all.

> *Your loving husband,*
> *James*

I am undone! There is no date on the letter and yet I distinctly recall that the package came to the house shortly before James made a mackerel trip in late August of last year. He then returned home from that trip on my birthday and gave me my mother of pearl treasure, even as these pearls were hidden away in the house. Why did he not give me this lovely strand of pearls then, or this letter? Now I take them from a cold hand. He was such a foolish man to want so much more than his own comfortable life provided! That the possibility of landing his fortune beyond our own shore so preoccupied him and that he was brought down right here in his own harbor is a trick of the cruelest kind. I cannot wear these pearls, for they have been given to me by a dead man. They must remain in the dark of their velvet tomb.

JUNE 21, 1856

Mother and Father will receive me. Their note, penned by Mother, was short and to the point. I will visit with them after Hannah leaves us, for the note below will tell all about the imminence of this unfortunate event.

This afternoon, a letter also arrived for Hannah from her father. When she opened it, her face darkened to a most anguished place, the likes of which I have never seen in the girl. I knew the news had to relate to being summoned home. She showed me the letter without my needing to ask, so I will offer a short account of it. Timothy let her know that her mother will come in a fortnight, stay a week, and then they will make for home. He wrote that he had decided her formal schooling would come to end in a year's time and that she will begin her sewing trade at her mother's side. He did not sign off with affection, or an understanding of Hannah's heart as she prepares to separate herself from her grandmother and from her family to whom she had formed attachments. Perhaps he had not observed this when he was here, nor I suppose had he listened with great interest when Hannah was in his midst to how at home she felt among us. I imagine she made her visit here by virtue of wearing him down, that he allowed this visit—lengthy, yes, to his credit—out of a sense of frustration with his daughter's dogged requests to return. This is mostly conjecture, yet it does come together for me this way knowing Lucy's feelings for him and having heard bits from Hannah when she first arrived.

Hannah crumpled the note, made a noise I can only liken to an angry feline, which sent Jack whimpering under the side table in the front hall, and then she fled to her bedroom.

"But what's the fuss?" Lucy came in from the kitchen, wiping her hands on her apron. She has taken up her life here with such enthusiasm that I cannot begrudge her her love of cooking virtually every meal, for we are all the better fed for it. "Was it Hannah I heard just now? What can be the matter?"

I handed her the note and as she read it, the color left her full cheeks, her plump little shoulders sloped more deeply, and she looked to me. "That man hasn't a speck of affection in his heart for the child he calls his own. Only after his own interest, he is. She's a bright thing, far brighter than her mother, with a gift she shouldn't waste on thimbles and ladies' hems." And she straightened her shoulders with a resolve I could see overcoming her. "I'll have a word with her mother when she arrives."

"I believe half a fortnight has already passed since the letter was sent. She must be due here in a week, Lucy."

"Cousin! I can't let the child go back. I know by rights the place she might call her home is by her parents' side. I *do* know this," she said to me as if I might have challenged her. And perhaps I had, for in her words I heard her lack of conviction and my expression must have revealed this. "Still, she won't come to much if she remains in her father's home."

Of course, a child belonged with her parents and there was nothing wrong with this fundamental truth, except that Hannah herself was so reluctant to return home that it caused not just Lucy, but me as well, to doubt that her true happiness was in the home where she was born. Before long, she will reach marriageable age and her work 273 as a seamstress will age her further. She possesses a talent to teach young children and can draw a very pretty portrait, all skills which Mother would relegate to the leisurely parlor hours a married woman keeps with and without her children, though a school or a governess can take over the teaching in Mother's estimation of a life. Yet, Hannah is not to marry a man whose house boasts a parlor that will be host to a crowd much disposed to quiet pursuits such as embroidery, playing piano, reading books or painting pictures. No, Hannah will toil her entire life. It is the way in which her parents are raising her. It is her circumstance and, though nothing shameful, a life I would not choose for her.

Mr. Talbot was digging around the garden and lingered by the window nearest the parlor window I had opened to let in the fast-warming morning air. He looked as if he had just taken up the spade and his profile was serene, for he liked to till and plant; he has brought new glory to my tulips in spring and my roses this season, though they are mostly fading now as others flourish in their turn. I looked out and caught his eye, spied him peering in at us. I smiled, seeing his plain concern for Lucy carved on either side of his kindly mouth and around his eyes. Then I turned away, my own tears on the way down at the thought that Hannah must leave us once more.

JUNE 22, 1856

Henry can recite his alphabet and I am a dismal mother for having missed the journey that got him there. I know Hannah has guided him expertly these past many weeks, that I have been in a world of my own, a place in my life that has kept me at a remove from true involvement. In this way, I remind myself of James in his last months. I can only hope my son has not felt this shortcoming in me, for with darling Hannah and with Lucy as his very able elder, I am at ease and the boy does seem content.

Today I planted some impatiens. Henry and Hannah helped, kneeling in the moist, cool soil and digging their little fingers through it, my son coming up with great, long earthworms that he held before me with satisfaction. As we dug, I thought of Theodore. I felt the harshness of my decision to banish him if he journeyed to England. What have I done? I could no more have banished James for making a livelihood and felt the lack of reason in my words to Theodore. As I blindly shoveled earth in a heap before me, I looked ahead to the unthinkable, that he might one day vanish at sea as James had. With this image, my resolve returned, rooting itself as firmly in the bedrock of my heart as the seeds I planted with the children. These seeds are annuals; they will die and not grow again unless we choose to plant them next year.

JUNE 19, 1856

A note from Father:

> Dearest Marianne,
>
> Your Mother is in the parlor with a gaggle of her lady friends reading poetry, so I thought it a good moment to steal and write to say in my own way, that, yes, we would quite enjoy a visit from you when you can manage it. We have not seen our grandson in too long. You and I can take our strolls as we used to do and your Mother can show off the boy to her circle. I have a touch of a cold and do not want to infect you or Henry, so being out of doors will lessen that risk.
>
> With love,
Father

JUNE 23, 1856

Even as I think it a horrid compromise after our last encounter that I should cross that woman's threshold at her bidding, I will do so. Her note came the day before yesterday after I had recorded my day. It is an invitation with nothing more to tempt me than the promise that Irene would also be there. It was all I needed and could not refuse the invitation. I feel altogether powerless where Mrs. Pringle is concerned since our dreadful conversation last week. I still do not know if Theodore has sailed for England, other than the certainty that he will sail. I will not ask after him and it will take all I have. I am afraid to inquire (whom would I trust with such a question other than Lucy? I will not ask her to be my messenger in this).

Hannah and I went to the Pringles' home yesterday afternoon and Irene was, in fact, there, but without her daughters. So was Thomas, and he looked to be in better humor. I was so glad to be in Irene's company, I quite forgot to entertain Hannah, but I need not have worried, for Thomas took to her right away, and she to him. The two, like merry thieves, snuck into the conservatory where Thomas showed her the instruments he could play and explained the paintings on the walls that were of the various and some long dead ancestors on his father's side, except for the one painting of a young Virginia Pringle. I have been in this room and seen the paintings, but the light was dimmer for me, sconce-lit rather than in daylight. I had not allowed my curiosity to move my eyes to linger on the paintings of these ancestors or to discern any one remarkable likeness in them to Reginald or Virginia Pringle. (On the way home, Hannah reported that she cannot believe how handsome Mrs. Pringle once was, that it was as if she were looking at another woman from another family. True to the reference the woman made of herself in my parlor as having once been rounder, Hannah later described our hostess as rosy in her portrait, a fact I still cannot reconcile with who Virginia Pringle has become).

When Thomas returned Hannah to tea, he sat down next to his mother and immediately began to talk to her in a way I had witnessed before, quite like he had some say in matters of the house.

"Mother, you really ought to air out the conservatory more often and let me breathe more life into that pianoforte."

"Oh, it's a pretty pianoforte, Mrs. Pringle. Do you play it?" Hannah asked and it was immediately clear to me that in her address, Hannah was attempting to soften the woman. It seemed to do the trick, for almost immediately, our hostess's expression changed. It looked as if a child had drawn a thin line with the afterthought of a slight upward curve at either end in imitation of a smile, yet behind it was a trace of something else, of memory, and it did soften her eyes.

"I did once, child."

"And you don't like to play now?"

"Hannah," I warned with a gentle push at her knee with mine.

"No, I do not," she answered perfunctorily, restored to her usual severity. "However, Thomas does enjoy it and I hope he will play for all of us after our tea."

I could see that even she was trying to affect a cheer for all of our sakes, and Irene, too, peered at Mrs. Pringle and then at me, as if something was amiss.

It was a far more cheerful afternoon than I expected it would be, though I spoke very little to my hostess other than to inquire after her husband and to compliment her on her dress, a dark red with a black ribbon at the waist and cuffs. Irene spoke to Hannah at length about her schooling, telling her all about her own daughters whom she said would be home soon as they were on the mend from an illness and had had to be away from home to properly recover. Hannah, to her credit, did not riddle Irene with questions about her daughters, asking only if either of them liked to stitch or draw and receiving the most satisfying reply that, yes, they did, immensely.

Thomas then beckoned us to the conservatory and we took our seats.

There he sat at the pianoforte, found the music he wanted, and announced he would play Chopin's Ocean Étude Opus 25, No. 12. He began with no further preamble, his entire form seeming at once to loom and retreat, his slender hands moving rapidly left and right as if to create a stir in the sea with the music. I could not keep the vision of a frothing angry sea from my mind as he played. Hannah sat back in her seat and moved closer to me, shrinking a little from the power of Thomas' might at the keys. When he rose from the pianoforte, his first gaze and bow was to his mother who looked shocked.

"You have never played this way, Thomas," she said, visibly stirred.

He said nothing and bowed lightly to the rest of us. The housemaid, Mary, was near, for she had passed by with the tea cart and lingered near the door. When her employer caught her idle, she gave her a flick of the head and hissed the order to "be gone, Mary." I could not have been the only one to see or hear it.

By the end of the afternoon, Irene had invited Hannah and me to her own home for a luncheon the following week. Hannah, looking up at me with eager eyes, curtsied when she understood from my own smile that Irene is a most wonderful woman to know. Of course, I told her, we would go for a visit and realized, too late, that Hannah would be gone by then unless we planned carefully.

I am struck still by how reticent Mrs. Pringle was today, almost concili-atory, particularly given our recent encounter. I had been quite prepared for an altogether unfriendly demeanor. Yet, she seemed most content to watch Hannah, Thomas, Irene and me speak and laugh and enjoy the afternoon. On one occasion her son held forth with a story of a three-legged dog who had followed a man to the quarry each day until at last the man had to surrender and take the dog into his little house where she now lived as if she had always done and who they called Peg (because she is a female and has no peg at all for the missing leg). As we giggled over the story, Mrs. Pringle tried again to smile, yet the muscles of her face would not comply and she looked more forlorn than amused. Of course, she has likely heard this tale before.

My parting thought is that while the invitation to Irene's home tempts me, the more pressing destination is to Newburyport to see Mother and Father. Oh, but that will have to wait as it is, for Rose is due here on the 26th to take her daughter home and that, of course, truly does mean that Hannah will not be visiting Irene at all, unless I can arrange for her to do so while her mother visits. I will send Irene a note inquiring into the possibility.

JUNE 24, 1856
I have received a letter from Irene with an apology that we will not be lunching with her after all, the reason so shocking and marvelous I have pressed her letter here. She leaves Rockport as I read this letter.

June 23, 1856

Dear Marianne,

It was the perfect diversion to see you today at tea. I was very taken with your young cousin; she and my daughters will get along well when they return. Will Hannah be staying on much longer?

I have spent too many weeks brooding and fretting over my daughters and have finally brought my heartache to Peter. We spoke at length after I returned from the Pringles and I made a strong case for being near them. I told him that if they cannot convalesce closer to their home, then I, their mother, must go to them, and that it would be criminal to deny them the love and care a mother can and must offer. My husband resisted me harshly at first, and then I made my final plea: If he would not consent to my going to stay near their sanatorium, I would go without his consent and he could either divorce me and risk the scandal of that upon his family, or I would divorce him if he denied me further, risking similar scandal, the worse for me as a woman.

He must then have seen something in his otherwise peaceful wife, for he sat down, put his pipe on the table, and looked at me as if seeing me anew. Very well, he had said. If it is this you want and so badly that you would risk our name and the comforts that come with it, your place in society, then do what you will.

I confess to shock that he should have needed so much convincing, that he could not see for himself that I must be with our children, and that surely I would forswear not only my status, but trade my life for theirs in an instant.

Thank you, my friend, for seeing clearly what I could not, would not, for fear of this very situation. Seeing Hannah the other day inspired me to resolute action and, while an ultimatum is not something I would have preferred, I was desperate enough to feel it was entirely warranted and would have acted upon it. I have spent sleepless nights since my daughters' leave-taking and with every letter I receive from them, even as it promised they were healthy enough to write to us at all, I would convince myself that they were on the point of fading until another letter would arrive to convince me otherwise.

I leave for Clifton Springs tomorrow morning and will write to you of progress made once settled there.

Be good to your heart, Marianne. I see the clouds gathered in your eyes and hope that whatever you long for, or miss, will find you once more.

> Your loyal friend,
> Irene Jamieson

JUNE 26, 1856

Rose has arrived, and looks not at all the way I remember her.
She is thinner, for one. Her hair is paler, the burgundy shine
gone out of it. The shock of this change in her brought Hannah's
words back to me, though I wondered if her mother was simply ill from
a long journey on what might be a bumpy course.

I let Lucy show her to her room, settle her in, and then Lucy came down alone. "She is not well," she said, looking over her shoulder for Hannah who had not known her mother was here, as she and Henry were in the stable helping Mr. Talbot feed the horses. Hannah had lately taken an interest in this and my son followed her everywhere she went. I would likely find both of them happily grooming the mares.

We let Rose sleep the entire afternoon. She woke and came down before supper, a blanket wrapped around her traveling clothes, and sat at the little table in the parlor with a cup of tea Lucy had brought her. The rest had done her well, but there was a deep furrow at her brow and lines on either side of her mouth that I am not sure were there when I first met her only months before.

"Timothy will be here in a week's time if I've not already left to bring our Hannah home," she said, her voice high and brittle. "I don't wish to go back to my husband. He doesn't know this, though it can't be a surprise. But I won't be leaving Rockport and if he chooses, he can hitch me up to a coach and drag me back. I won't go on my own and would ask that if something should happen, if I should be harmed or…" and here she stopped and placed a hand over her eyes. "If I should be unable to care for my daughter, I ask that you, Mother and Marianne, be her guardians."

I placed my hands on her shoulders, shocked that I could feel so much of her frame through the cloth of her blouse, and said only what I hoped my hands conveyed with their touch, that I would be any help to her that I could, but that I did not think it would come to this. It was then that Hannah, who had waited patiently all afternoon for her mother to waken, wandered into the parlor and, seeing her mother, flew into her arms and sat with her head pressed to her bosom. Rose stroked her daughter's long plaits, her face bowed into Hannah's crown so that neither Lucy nor I could see it. I imagine Lucy noticed the quiver in her daughter's shoulders and we left the two alone. I went to my son who was up in his room building with his blocks. Lucy, I suppose, went off to see to supper, always most at peace when she putters about in the kitchen. By the end of supper, Rose's mood had picked up, though her daughter cast a worried look toward her now and then. It was, but for Henry, a company of fond women. My son did, for just a moment, look about him and seem not only to see this, but to enjoy it.

June 27, 1856

Before I woke this morning, Theodore appeared in my dreams alongside James. The two stood side by side, Theodore looking large and healthy, glowing in the sun, smiling at me. James appeared worn and tired. I went to him and touched his face. As my fingers came near, his eyes darkened and he moved away, angry and unreachable. Theodore stood his ground and waited for me to see what was plain before me, but I could not join him. In my dream I could not. What message is in this?

Now I am awake in the middle of this moonless night, upstairs in the cupola where I can see the stars pinpointing the ocean's calm surface and I do not know how to find my way back, to bed or to a life I can take comfort in knowing will cause no pain.

June 29, 1856

Hannah, Lucy and Rose have spent the past days since Rose's arrival as if they are on holiday. I suppose they are, for they have only just become acquainted as a trinity of women. I confess I felt left behind at first, but they have welcomed me when I happen upon them and when I am with any one of them we are also happily together. In Hannah's eyes I see hope and when her mother is near her, I see it in Rose's eyes, too. She is a woman not unlike Lucy, though they have been apart for most of Rose's adult life. She is quick to take up a task, always deferring to me as if I governed her, yet she is also possessed of a wisdom and strength that has emerged since her arrival. It makes for a beautiful woman in Rose. Lucy has bestowed her best attributes upon her daughter even as they have been apart.

I know that Lucy's life was vastly different, that she did not have the benefit of Rose's father to help raise her, for her parents did not see the man who made her with child as a benefit to anyone. Lucy might, by her own admission, have played at mothering her daughter for she was but sixteen and her parents were caring for both in their way, which was to make certain that both were fed and clothed and raised as if they were sisters. Rose has never called Lucy *Mother*, though Lucy would wish it.

Hannah plays with Henry each morning when he wakens and they frolic in the surf on balmier days now that the sun warms the water. It is one of my favorite activities to sit under a canopy on a blanket and watch them. Rose looks on, and Lucy, too, when she is not busy in the house. I have continued to insist that we must share its upkeep and have taken some of the duties from her this week. "Be with your women," I tell her, batting lightly at her backside with my wooden spoon.

It was Mr. Talbot who informed me of Hannah's intentions. I found him cleaning the horse's stalls when I went out to the garden and thought to pluck some weeds along the stable walls, weeds that persisted so and which I knew would overtake the garden entirely.

He saw me as he came out of the stable with the wood barrels he would put on the coach and take to the granary for a supply of oats. "Mrs. Parsons," he said by way of greeting, dipping his head to me and stopping as if he would assist me in some way.

"Mr. Talbot, hello!"

"Do you need to go to town, Missus?"

"No…" I began. "But I must ask you for a confidence."

He put down his pails and drew back some, signaling me to follow, so that we were in the shade of the barn door, removed from a view of the house.

"I do not know how to begin."

"Is there something the matter, Missus? Is someone ill? Is Lucy ill?" His concern grew with every question, his kindly face blooming with it, his gray eyes wide. I put him at ease and asked him finally what it was I needed to know, which is whether he knew what it could be that Rose fears in returning home.

Mr. Talbot's relief that his Lucy was well seemed to breathe new life into him. He spoke in a torrent the likes of which I have not heard from him, for he is a reserved man at his most polite. I suppose I have not really seen him agitated until today.

"Rose has lived with her husband in a way that suits the community but it's been a true hardship for her and for their daughter," he explained. "She seeks to be even the slightest bit free of him, but he won't loose her from their home by day except to visit the ladies whose dresses she stitches. The only condition that allowed Rose to come for Hannah was that if she didn't return in one week's time, he would come and bring them home himself, and not too gently either. Hannah with her gifts for learning and drawing besides has upset his vision for her, his plan to keep her in the home until she marries a man *he* chooses for her." I knew most of this from Hannah's letter, yet still found it hard to believe. Logic and experience countered the surprise of it, for still clear was the memory of that hard glint in Timothy's eye that had greeted me when he brought his wife and child to Rockport in the winter. Yes, now I see what I had missed then. His gaze told me, *we may be here, but we are only here at my say*. And Hannah had snapped to at his authority. Rose had been quiet, too quiet.

I am worried for both of them, for the week is nearly up and I have not seen their happiness together subside and ebb into anything like resignation that the end of these lovely days draws nearer. They behave as if they have forever ahead of them.

"Thank you," I told Mr. Talbot. You were right to tell me." This last I added, knowing he might feel he betrayed a trust by sharing this with me. Yet, busy as we have all been, in constant motion around one another, I know my cousin would have gotten around to it eventually, for I am to her, and she to me, what sisters might be, even with these twenty or more years between us. I like to imagine it is not a very different relationship than what she might have known as a mother to the young Rose, though I am a woman and not a girl.

June 30, 1856
Tomorrow, Rose must leave with Hannah and this knowledge
has finally caught up with them. Even Henry seems less playful,
and is perplexed by the line between Hannah's brows, placing his hands
over her forehead and pressing there to smooth it. "Go 'way," he orders
the furrows as he tries to banish them with his sturdy little fingers.

"I *am* going away," Hannah said to him, looking affronted, misunderstanding. But his meaning was very clear to me, for not too long ago, this is what he did when he saw me grieving, often enough trying and failing to hide my sadness.

"No," he whimpered and held fast to his cousin. "No! Stay with me!"

"I can't, Henry. My papa needs me."

"Papa?" My son sat back from her, his gray eyes wide with curiosity and the sound of something familiar. I could see it in his face, hear it in his voice as he turned to me and said, again, "Papa? Where my Papa?"

It was the first time he had asked the question. I gathered him up, big as he is now, and he began a campaign of screaming and kicking, which smarts now that he is not a baby any longer but well enough past three and stronger each day. "Papaaaa!" He screamed and I could not stand there with him in Hannah's room, but had to take him downstairs, out into the afternoon air to distract him. By the time we reached the garden my eyes were hot with tears.

JULY 1, 1856

They have gone without lingering, their satchels packed into the coach that arrived just before dawn for the day's journey, sent by Timothy as an act of faithlessness that they would make their own arrangements, a challenge perhaps. Our goodbyes were brief, as if to prolong them would shatter the fragility of the moment. Lucy, holding tightly to her daughter and to Hannah, was swallowing her grief that these two were truly leaving this most comfortable home to go back to a man whose only true interest seemed to lie in exercising his will upon them. The reminder, his smug reiteration of his power over whether they would remain longer or do his bidding, arrived just yesterday, casting a pall on their final day here, and I caught Lucy putting it into the woodstove she had lit, it would seem, for that express purpose.

So, off they went, and Hannah leaned out the coach window until she was a little, pale dot blending with the trees and houses and sky.

Lucy now drifts about the house on this first day of their leave-taking as if there were ghosts in every room. It is at it was for her in February when Hannah left, and far worse, for she is now convinced that she will not see her daughter and granddaughter again for a very long time.

JULY 2, 1856

In the late afternoon, a letter arrived from Irene:

June 28, 1856

My Dear Friend,

I arrived in Clifton Springs the day before yesterday, a long and tiring journey. I traveled some by coach and also by steam engine, and then another coach to my destination. I am sorry I did not say goodbye to you, yet I know you will understand. I knew that as soon as Peter gave his consent to go, I would be a fool to linger, so I packed my satchel and took advantage of his more charitable nature. Are you familiar with the Sandersons of Pigeon Cove? They attend the First Union Church with Peter, our girls and me. They have a grown daughter who lives with her family in Philadelphia and offered to have me along in their coach for part of the first leg of the journey. Mrs. Sanderson is a kindly woman who loves to chat and giggles at everything her husband says, which I find endearing if only because I do not laugh at anything Peter says.

I have at last been to see my daughters. They have both grown in spite of their illness. Pauline, my eldest, has begun ever so slightly to fill out her dress! Eleanor, still very much a little girl in ways your cousin Hannah is no longer, is not recovering as well as her sister, so it is right that I have come even as I cannot forgive myself for waiting so long to take a stand. I shall remain here until they no longer need the administering to that the nurses here must do. They do it well. For all of his difficulty, my husband did choose a fine sanatorium. I am only chagrined that I had no voice in the matter until now, for surely there must be somewhere nearer home for them to take a cure. Hannah Jumper would have been my choice and had I been asked or heard, I would have seen to that. It is revealing of my husband's lack of care that they are so far away, even as it bespeaks great discernment in the choice.

This is a small place, this part of the country. After my first day with my daughters I took a stroll just to think in the quiet of the approaching evening. I return to them before they went to sleep. I have already greeted every individual in the town at least twice and I am here only two days! It is my hope that we will be home in a month's time and then you will meet my fine daughters.

I know that Hannah has had to leave, that Lucy must be languishing over this, that you must be lonesome for her, too, but please take heart in knowing that she will be well, for she is a girl of great inner fortitude—this is apparent even in the gentleness she offers to those who meet her—and will one day be a woman of considerable strength of character who will be a credit and a complement to any man.

I must end this letter now to go and visit my daughters. I will pick some flowers from the patch of meadow behind the little hotel I am residing in, the only one in the town, though I must admit the meadow behind it is the comeliest part of this establishment!

With affection,
Irene Jamieson

I am glad for Irene. A month's time seems far off, but she will take pleasure in nursing her daughters, and the eldest, Pauline, must improve with her mother near.

This morning, Henry, Lucy and I made the trip to Newburyport. At every turn, my son cried, "Mama, look!" though often enough he had simply spied just another house along the road, its field behind it. Or there might have been another coach passing by with people in it who returned his eager greetings. Of course, some stared ahead with fixed or dour expressions and this was very alarming to my son who yelled out to them, "Hello! Hello! Say hello!" We spied a grandfather of a tree, a great maple, next to one house that even Lucy and I exclaimed over. It was a lovely little journey, made sweeter by Henry's sweeping gaze taking it in. Though he has seen a tree, a house, a coach before, it has been in the usual places for him, always within a few paces of our own home. It occurred to me then as we clopped along the dirt road, that I had kept my son very close to his own nest, much the way Mother and Father had with me, and I turned to Lucy with this.

"I must venture beyond Rockport more often. I have not been to my parents' home in nearly a year!" She nodded in recognition, though she has been with me but a half-year.

"Yes, a young man must learn to navigate both land and sea," she said. Of course this struck me as something Mother would say and I frowned. Yet, she did seem to be preoccupied, likely thinking of Rose and Hannah, and even of Mr. Talbot who did not look at all happy to see her off for these several days. She, too, looked chagrined, though not as much. It was the stoic Lucy I encountered as we left and she did not but wave a hand to her admiring friend.

"I hope my son does not choose the sea," I said. "I will try to open other ideas to him if I can, if he will listen." And we both regarded the boy with some amusement as he sat up on his knees and pressed his face to the window to see beyond our little confines. "I can already see he has the spirit of an adventurer. He might well choose what his father has," I said and crossed my arms over my chest, pulling my shawl tight around me despite the warm summer air. "How can I tether the boy to me? He will go where he is bound and no doubt the pull will be to the ocean."

We arrived soon before supper, having left somewhat later than planned. Mother whisked us into the house and bade her housemaid Bridget take our things to our room. Of course, Lucy immediately seemed more comfortable taking up similar duties to the ones she performs for me, but Mother would not have it. "You are my family," she reprimanded her. "We have Bridget to help." And that was that, for Lucy would not arch her back at Mother, sensing it would not be worth the fuss.

"Think of yourself as on holiday," I whispered to her when Mother had bustled off ahead of us into her parlor, leading Henry by the hand. And he went as willingly as if Mother had cast a spell. I suspect he was worn from his ongoing thrill of looking out the window of the coach. He had been wide-eye for most of the journey.

I now write from my childhood bedroom where I spent years, then months, and at last days dreaming of my life with James be- 287 fore we wed. It is true I was a dreamer as a girl, most often letting my thoughts drift so far beyond my walls and windows that Father or Mother coming upon me gave me a start. Mother would chide me for losing myself to fancy, as pleased as she was at the match with Mr. Parsons' son. In every way, it could not have been more perfect.

Henry sleeps in a small bed near mine and Lucy sleeps in a room with Bridget who seems kindly and glad enough to have the company. She did not work for Mother and Father while I lived in the house and is considerably older than the maid employed during those years. She is older than Lucy and moves rather more slowly than I imagine Mother might tolerate. When I asked her why she keeps Bridget on, she explained rather perfunctorily that the poor woman simply has no where to go, and that she had needed to find a replacement for her predecessor who had become less interested in doing the work of the house than dawdling about with Mr. Ferguson, who keeps the stables and grounds. She keeps him on because he treats her horses well, keeps her gardens growing well, and, but for his penchant for comely young ladies, is devoted to doing good work. The thing to do, she told me, was to rid him of the distraction. In this story was revealed Mother's unflinching pragmatism and, where Bridget is concerned, a compassion Mother does not wear upon her sleeve. It is most gratifying to catch this when she is least aware of conveying it.

JULY 3, 1856

Father and I took our first stroll this morning. I explained everything to him, revealing that I had read Theodore's diary, that it had at first shocked me until I reminded myself how fine he truly is, how honorable. Of course, I spoke with open contempt for what Virginia Pringle had done and Father looked sideways at me. Yes, I said, with some annoyance, it was not commendable of me to have read something not meant for my eyes, yet for her to take it and use it against Theodore was by far the more shameful of the two crimes, loathsome in fact.

The rest of the day was easily spent entertaining Henry, playing in the yard where Father has had Mr. Ferguson hang a swing and which Henry did not tire of enjoying. As soon as Father came upon us, after an hour of my being the one to push my son back and forth on the swing, I gave him the grandfatherly pleasure of pushing the boy who began to ask to be pushed higher. This would not do, for I worried he would fall to the ground. After a time, both Father and I told Henry it was time for a nap and he obliged by climbing off the swing when we had stilled it, and telling his grandfather to take a turn. Humoring the boy, Father sat upon the broad plank of wood and let Henry push him until, even with small pats to his grandfather's back to get him to move, Henry was knocked down and began to cry. Not truly hurt, he calmed easily enough and then did not resist a rest.

JULY 4, 1856

This morning before we took our leave, Father and I took a little stroll before we got on the coach. He was very quiet and, even as I had made an apology to him the other day for my abruptness, he wore a forlorn smile.

"You are a headstrong one, like your mother," he told me. I thought to argue the point, but understood a protest to be of little use, for I have often lately recognized that quality in myself. Father, the more amenable between them, seldom takes a stand. I have witnessed it perhaps twice in my life and each time, his conviction was uprooted in short order by Mother.

"Careful, Father, for if you would compare me to her too closely, you would suggest I cannot discern between a man of dubious and a man of sterling character. And you would suggest it of her too."

"Come along, Marianne Elizabeth, and let me tell you something you do not know about your old Papa." He took my arm and put it through his. I looked back at the house and on its great front porch sat Mother and Lucy, with Henry between them. Mother had been kind to Lucy this visit, though it has been a short stay, paying her more respect than when she came last to Rockport. Bridget, too, took a liking to Lucy, grateful for any help she offered, so I was left to myself quite a bit more than even I might have opted for, though it had freed me to consider my future, to write here, and to walk. I have almost come to an understanding with myself, a reckoning.

289

Father and I had reached a path that would take us in one of two directions, water or meadow. I chose the meadow, this one with no pond like our little park, and we continued on until we reached a great willow where we sat under its shading boughs.

"I love your Mother very much, even if she drives me to tipple on occasion," he began and I laughed. When I feel as I have this visit, Father masterfully lures me from my tendency to worry and brood. "I have loved her almost from the day we married," he continued and this won my attention. "Why so surprised? You were a very lucky lass indeed, winning the heart of that fine man long before you married." His voice grew deeper and scratched a bit. He waited a moment and went on.

"Marianne, your mother and I do not want to see you lose your small, but significant, fortune, to a man about whom the world knows nothing. You are a generous one, and perhaps you are mistaking friendship with Mr. Abel for something else that portends great sacrifice. Think first of your son if you will not think of yourself."

"My son adores Mr. Abel. And I keep James' memory alive every day. We look at his picture and I speak of him, of how Henry is so like his father. He is, truly!"

"It is not my business to ask, but I wonder if you have received any improper attention from Mr. Abel."

"I have not," I said and felt the flush that came with my lie. I did not confess to my banishing Theodore.

"If this is so, then it is not too late to save your reputation from being further sullied by association with him."

Again, I lost my patience with my beloved father. "You are as quick to cast Mr. Abel to the wolves as Mother and that insufferable Mrs. Pringle! Only Reginald Pringle seems to be of the opinion that Mr. Abel is beyond reproach. And there was James, of course, and Lucy and I. Your grandson is very fond of him. Are these not excellent sources of regard?"

"Reginald has written to me, yes, endorsing Mr. Abel's character. He has said his new employee possesses everything he would ask for in a man who would represent him in business, except prior recommendation." I heaved a great, relieved sigh and lay back in the grass.

"You see, Father? A man of sterling character in my very own community, a man whose judgment you trust, speaks well of my friend!"

"He did express a misgiving."

"What was it?" I did not truly want to know.

"He cannot reconcile Mr. Abel's obvious good qualities with what he knows of him through the words his wife shared with him, the things she read."

I sat up. "Is he to be flogged for his candor? Is there no shelter for a man, for anyone, who has private thoughts and a place to put them? I keep a diary and it is meant for no one but me, or perhaps after I am gone, long after, another who will read it for their own amusement."

"Did you not read his words without his knowledge, Marianne?"

It was a gentle rebuke, a reminder of how insincere I sounded.

"I did, Father. And given the chance, I would do differently. I judge myself harshly for it, yet Theodore knew what I had done and not only did he forgive me, he said he had nothing to hide and was prepared to have me read more. So, you see, if he has nothing to hide from me, why would he be the sort to hold himself aloof from others in the community? He stands only to lose by being truthful and he is now well aware of it in the contempt Mrs. Pringle offers." I thought again, as I had often since saying it those weeks ago on my porch, how I may well have thrust Theodore as far from my life as the seagoing vessel that now conveyed him home from England. For even if he returns and I learn of it, he is of no more use to me, for he did make his final choice.

"I can only tell you that when you decide to marry again, and I believe you will, for Henry needs a father and you a companion, choose wisely. Choose a man who can take care of you and not the other way, for you will lose respect for him if he is always to be under your thumb."

"I do not rule in my household even now, Father. Lucy and Henry are quite in command of late." I knew this to be a weak statement, an avoidance of his truth.

"I believe you hear me clear as a bell, my Lassie. Marry as well as you ought and you will always know where you stand in the community."

"Father, did you marry Mother for her money?"

"I married her for her fortitude, if you must know. My mother was a strong woman and I wanted one for myself. Though she is not so gentle as my mother was, she is still with a great heart and a keen mind."

"You are happy enough, I see."

"Far happier than that, and you will be too, again." He kissed my forehead and we walked back to the house.

Later that morning, we boarded our coach and Mother embraced me for a long while, quite out of character for her. "Go carefully, my dear," she whispered to me and I saw a tear creep from her eye.

I had purposefully avoided the conversation with her about Theodore, and what I had imagined was her harsh judgment conveyed through Virginia Pringle. After all, she might not have been the voice behind Virginia Pringle's contemptible actions. Mother, in her turn, had not pressed me to speak of it with her, had not approached any conversation with a trace of her usual instruction. More than I had ever seen her, she seemed content to be in the company of a woman her age, her cousin Lucy. Not wishing to open the subject as long as Mother did not open it herself, I have reasoned that Father has taken this matter in hand with her blessing, and that his opinion speaks for them both. It is a new age, and I welcome it.

Father lifted his grandson high in the air, wrinkled his brow as his back took the strain of such a growing boy, and put him in the coach. Lucy and Bridget said a friendly, sweet goodbye as new friends, and Mother paid the same to Lucy, extending an invitation to her to come along on her own for a visit so that they might become better acquainted. And, as we pulled away, Father reached for my hand, squeezed it a moment, and smiled, not a trace of the forlorn lingering there.

Perhaps, I thought as we made toward the main road, their understanding of me is better than I imagine and why, after all, should it not be so?

We arrived home to two letters, one from Hannah that she had arrived safely, the other from Theodore, postmarked from Gloucester, and dated June 15, 1856, the day he should have boarded his vessel. It is my belief that it is a letter of farewell. Because I do not wish to appear too eager even to myself within these pages, I will say with some pride that I saved Theodore's letter for last. Hannah's letter is pressed to these pages first.

July 2, 1856

Dear Grandmother, Cousin Marianne and Henry,

Mama and I arrived safely and I didn't get to sit down and write to you until just today. I was set right to work as an apprentice to Mama, at Papa's instructions. For even as I'm not finished my studies and have another year of school to go, he felt I should begin with the work I'm to do after school comes to an end so that I have a name to recommend me.

I don't want it to end. I want to become a teacher and this means I should go to school until I'm sixteen, yet Papa feels strongly and has said so many times, some of them very loudly when Mama protests (which I wish she wouldn't because quiet is so much better), that the work I'll do with Mama will improve our standing.

I miss all of you and I miss having a room that faces the ocean. My room at home looks out upon the town and the ocean is nowhere near. I hear all sorts of yelling and clop-clopping from early in the morning until well after the sun sets. It's enough to keep a girl from growing, all this noise that keeps me awake late into the night. Mama has said we'll move into a house further from the center of town, though not so far as to make it difficult for the ladies for whom she sews to reach us. Papa's smithy is attached to the house, behind it, so he'll have to build another one if we do find a different house, an idea which makes him laugh in a way that makes Mama look anxious.

How is Henry? Is he reading books yet? I know I left only a few days ago and that he's only three, but he's a smart little boy and I know he'll read soon. I was reading books when I was almost four years of age, Mama tells me, and she's proud of me for it. Even Papa is proud of this, though he is discouraging me lately, wanting me to spend more time practicing my stitching for the piecework I do.

Mama says to send you all much love and to thank cousin Marianne again for her generosity. Mama also says to tell you that she hopes we'll see you soon, very, very soon.

With warmest wishes,

Your Hannah

293

When Lucy read the letter aloud to me, she was in a state of constant movement, and I reached across the table where we were sitting in the kitchen, where I found her when the post came, and tried to still her. Henry was sitting at the table pounding his fists into bread dough that Lucy had given him to keep busy, for he is all about now, looking for things to tip and rock, hold and toss, and we are ever on the alert for falling objects. I have put Mother's best China, given to James and me as a wedding gift, in a very high cupboard and as I see things, I place them up there, far from my son's curiosity.

After she read the letter, Lucy lowered it, took the small spectacles from her nose, and pursed her lips.

"Do you see now how it is for them with that tyrant? I had no notion until Hannah spoke before they left, and even then I was willing to admit that girls are prone to fancy, that her mother was miserable as all that. But there are clues here in this letter, Cousin, and I don't know what to do. I'm helpless to make any change in this girl's life. For Rose I can do nothing. She was a grown woman when she chose to marry Timothy and she was bent upon it, for he made a practical living and was very fond of her. But Hannah has no need to live this way, to see her mother wither and let her own interests be ignored."

What could I do but keep her hand in mine and tell her that it was good that Hannah and Rose went back as they were expected, that if they had not, Timothy might be unwilling to allow another visit? This, even with its implicit gloominess, seemed to relax her some and we set about preparing supper to which I had invited Mr. Talbot. He told me he had something he wished to say.

As for Theodore's letter, it is here.

June 14, 1856

Dearest Marianne,

I've posted this letter before I've made a decision to sail or not. My ship sails in two days' time and I am still uncertain whether I should be on it, doing Mr. Pringle's bidding or answering to the call of my heart, which is you. One action promises to see me comfortably established with work that will support a family, should I wish for one. The other, you, tethers me to land where, if I remain, I may keep you as a companion, though certainly never a wife, yet lose what livelihood is offered to me. If I refuse to sail,

Mr. Pringle has every right to relieve me of my position and then who will have me? I will, I think, return to the sea as a fisherman, easy enough work to come by most seasons, but it will be away from here where the name of Jonah can't follow me.

I can't begrudge you your first duty. How can you accept a poor fisherman, even turned to commerce, yet with no origins, no legacy to offer you? I can't ask it of you. In this, your guardians are wise. So, I'm faced with a quandary. Perhaps when you read this letter, you may see that from either choice, I shall lose. I place my hope in your understanding of what I must do to hold fast to a fighting chance for you in either case.

Your Theodore

He has written this letter before his decision and I do not know if he is in Rockport or Gloucester, for he has sent me no other missive. With considerable and unaccustomed restraint—for I did wish to know in the weeks before we went to visit Mother and Father if Theodore was still ashore—I have not inquired. Whom might I have asked? I do not keep company with Mr. Pringle and Thomas has been keeping very much to himself. That Virginia Pringle has not offered the confirmation in a gloating moment perplexes me, for even if he is still in her husband's employ, he is also as far away from me as it is possible to be. I would expect her to gloat if Theodore had sailed, even if it were on orders from her husband to perform duties for the quarry, even without her knowledge of the banishment I imposed upon him were he to sail. If Thomas had imagined I wanted to know, he might have mentioned it when we went to tea that afternoon a fortnight ago, yet he was in an altogether different frame of mind, hardly attuned to me at all.

I dread learning of Theodore's decision, for if he has chosen to sail to England, then he has decided against a continued friendship with me and, if we dared, a later courtship. Yet, if he chose to remain, he will have fallen from a loftier professional standing than I believe he has ever held and it will be my selfishness that brought him down. There is nothing for me to do but to wait for the day of his return to see if he has sailed. I must then decide for myself and for my son what is the best course.

Part IV

Under the Linden Tree

Supper was lovely last night, with a sourdough loaf that Henry had a hand in preparing with his expert pummeling, and a Beef Wellington prepared by Lucy that melted on the tongue. I prepared the vegetables and a lemon meringue pie and it was while we ate dessert that Mr. Talbot stood at table, raised his glass of port, and took Lucy's hand.

"I would like to announce to you that this lovely woman and I are to be wed near the end of the summer, on September fifth." He turned to Lucy then, whose eyes had spilled over, but who stood beside him and clasped his arm with her two hands.

"We'll invite Hannah, Rose and Timothy, too, if they'll come." Of course, in this last mention, there was abundant hope that Timothy would not, but that he would send the two most beloved to Lucy.

Mr. Talbot kissed Lucy's hand and I wished Theodore could be present to share in this moment, to shake hands and make a merry toast with us. Henry stood on his chair and with a serious face, an outthrust arm, and a mouth full of bread said his congratulations. He is a comical little man and a quick study.

After supper, Lucy, Mr. Talbot, my son, and I sat on the back porch with the band of sun a brilliant light on the horizon. We did not rush to Pigeon Cove or to the town center to see the fireworks. Instead, we watched from the porch and saw it well enough, and did not have to stuff our ears. A year has passed so quickly since the last Independence holiday when Henry and I sat huddled in James' embrace and watched the firelight erupt and fall over our heads. I cannot fathom how time passes, how people we love disappear. I can hardly sit with my decision to force Theodore from my life. Though he is, for now, absent, I am more certain than ever that these people with whom I spend my days are as beloved as any I have known. I managed to put Theodore out of mind for a full quarter hour.

It is hours later, near dawn, and I cannot sleep, which has brought me to these pages to make something of my restlessness. Again, I am aware that as I drift away from wakefulness I am not alone and then, when I open my eyes and look about, I find I am quite alone after all.

Earlier last evening, even before our momentous supper, and the fireworks, Henry ran around the house, laughing and saying, "find me, find me!" and tucking himself into corners and shadows just as I came upon his heels, which I did very slowly, for if I truly gave chase I would pass him. Each time I found him, he would point at me and say, "found you!" and we would both run away from each other. He was not to be beat. Finally, I said that I would count to ten, which he is learning to do and does well for a young one, reaching six and then jumbling the numbers from that point. As I counted with my face to a corner in the parlor, I heard his feet stomping up the steep stairs to the second floor and rushed my counting. Then I heard more climbing and I began to climb, too.

First I searched the second floor, making a great show of stepping into all the rooms and tapping on closet doors before opening them, peeking under beds and finding no boy.

I called out to him, worried that he had gone too high, for I do not want him to climb to the third floor and then to the cupola, not alone. The stairs to that highest perch are too steep and, of course, the third floor just below it has James' study. It was there I went, this time with some stealth. I did not want Henry to know I was coming, for he might try to run too close to the stairs going down or flee to the cupola and if he were startled by my approach when too near the stairs, he might lose his balance. Even now, I dare not think of the harm he might easily do himself.

You see how I worry so! Lucy is trying to cure me of it when she catches me wringing my hands. Still, it is hard to disavow one's own nature. My concern for my son frightens me into a state of chill and gooseflesh.

I crept up the stairs and found myself standing at the threshold of James' study, again hesitant to enter, intent on finding my boy, yes, though something kept me on the spot. Then I heard a whisper.

"Find me!" Came his voice, too gruff for a young one, and I reached for the door, about to close it on the room, certain that what I heard was not my son, but his father. As I pulled the door to me, my son shrieked gleefully, "Mama, find me!" Oh, but I felt the fool as my limbs nearly gave out beneath me. Of course, it was my boy whispering. Of course. I still could not see him.

Pushing the door open again, its progress was stopped and Henry peered out at me from behind it.

"Darling, we must not be in here," I chided him, and asked myself why I should not enter. I have held myself away from James' study for too long. It is my home and I have the right to enter every room within it. I heard these words escape my lips, realizing they were not just thoughts, and in that realization I spied the small table once more. It sat just behind the door, and Henry sat beneath that table. I had not opened the drawers before and think that perhaps I have thought them sacred. Yet as I recalled how I spent the years married to James, seldom cross-ing the threshold of his study for fear I would invade it, I felt an indignation growing and the greatest urge rose up in me to defy my former inclination. I pulled hard on a drawer and it yielded to me too easily. I was prepared for a struggle, perhaps wanting one, uncomfortable with my urge to flout an unspoken rule that had existed when James lived.

I am a silly woman for even expecting to be reprimanded for choosing against the deference I had always shown. Who, but I, would have anything more to say about it?

In the drawer were four envelopes, all of them unopened and bearing James' wax seal, a pair of sails flying high above James' own vessel, the *Marianne Elizabeth*, her initials etched across the hull.

Henry was pulling at my dress, his hands wound through the fabric, and he wanted to be picked up. I reached down for him and, clutching him to my hip, I held the letters in my free hand and fled the room.

Lucy was not about, for she had gone with Mr. Talbot on his errands for me, and I did not expect her back until after three o'clock when we would begin preparations for supper. It was just my son and I in a very quiet house. I have not noticed its quiet before; the kind that reminds one of the people who have left the house.

With time I did not know how best to use as Henry played and I sat in a chair and watched, I held the letters, the names of their intended readers etched in James' elegant hand across the grain of the fine paper on which he chose to write them. One letter was meant for me, one for our son, one for Mr. Pringle and—this was the most curious of all—one for Theodore.

Below his name, on our son's envelope were the words, "To be read when you have reached the mature age of twelve years." On Mr. Pringle's and Theodore's was written below their names, "To be read in the event of my premature death." And the envelope meant for me said, "My beloved wife, Marianne—to be read in the event of my premature death."

The weight of each was different in my hand. My letter was light, as if one page were tucked in containing all James ever meant to say from beyond his grave. His son's was even lighter, if that is possible, which must imply that his is one page, mine two. I chided myself for this calculation. That I should vie with my son for the attentions of his deceased father was folly and I shook my head to free myself of the thought, fancying I could see it fall to the floor and scuttle away like a hermit crab of the sort that Henry had lately taken to catching and setting free again, at my urging.

Theodore's and Mr. Pringle's letters were of equal heft to Henry's letter. I did not know what to do. I knew I would keep ours and give the other letters to Mr. Pringle at the first opportunity. Yet turning them over in my hands, feeling the raised ink, the wax seal, the seams in the envelopes, I did not understand what he had to say to Theodore, a man he did not know for very long. I brought mine to my lips and breathed in, hoping for the lingering scent of whatever James might have been thinking or feeling, the pipe tobacco he was using that day. I smelled only the red cedar cabinet in which these letters had hid for nearly a year.

I could not open my own letter any more than I could imagine nearly nine years passing, nor what our lives would resemble at the end of those years, nor even the passing of one more year from today. If the past nearly ten months are any measure of what can occur in a life, I dare not imagine the changes awaiting us. A part of me wishes for a calm heart and a quiet mind.

Taking a great breath and holding it until behind my eyes I saw celestial bodies, I steadied my hands, took a final look at the intact seal, and broke it.

April 22, 1855

My Dearest Wife,

I have long known that I might go before you. How could I not, with so many days at sea, so many often perilous days away from you? I cannot ask you to forgive me. I only ask for your understanding. You have been my best support, my truest ally since you were a wee girl it seems, since you spoke your first word, and such was my delight when you one day spoke my very own name! I, a boy of barely eight years, felt certain I would hear my name on your lips as music for the rest of my days. For you were such a spirited one, even as a babe, and though you seemed to have tamed this aspect of yourself as you grew to be a woman and my wife, I hope that in time it will re-surface, that you will give to the world the same often mischievous, free-thinking woman you offered me at barely three years of age.

I may not be there to enjoy you in this way. In fact, as I write this, the force of my truth is bluntly made to you: upon reading this letter, you will have lost me and I will have lost you and our son, our life together.

Theodore Abel, my first mate, is a man of sound reason and judgment, though lacking in formal education. If he should survive what I have not, do make him at home in Rockport. Do make of him a friend. Perhaps he will establish a connection that lifts him from the impoverished life he led before he took to the fisheries and find a suitable woman with whom to make a life. He has been a tireless worker on board my vessel and a devoted fisherman, taking to it as if he were born to it when, from what he has told me, he was born to a family of tinsmiths, forced early to labor on his own behalf when his parents were killed.

I am leaving the most important truth for last and it is that I adore you, Marianne, even from where you cannot hope to reach me, hold me, or see me. I will not haunt your days and you must prevent me from doing so if it seems I am, for I want only your happiness. Yet, I beg of you to make a good choice for the future of our son and for you. There is no doubt that a young, lovely woman such as you will not want for a suitor after you have mourned for the formal year. I do not want you to mourn me well into your life, yet I do ask that you do not choose hastily whom you will wed as the years pass. Choose a man who can provide for you. Think not too long on those who will impose their sensibilities upon you, for they will always be about. Virginia Pringle will, we both know, prove herself a vociferous presence. Your Mother, dear woman that she is, will in her way, guide you where she thinks best. But it is you, your voice and where it leads you with which you must make peace. Think of our son.

And now, I suppose I cannot forestall what I began with in this letter. My darling, please understand that you are first in my heart and first in my thoughts as they drift toward you from where I now sit, as far from you as I will ever, forever be.

Marianne Elizabeth, my heart's wonder, mother of my sweet, mischievous boy who cannot be so very little if you have found this much later than I think you will, remember me, take me along in your dreams now and then, and love whom you will. I will try to stand quietly by and accept him.

Your Adoring James

It is mid-afternoon and no one is about, for Lucy, sensing my preoccupation and shorter patience, has taken Henry for a much-needed walk to
expend some of his energy. In such heat as this, there is nowhere comfortable to sit but with a fan under the shade of the linden. Theodore has not
returned to the house, nor has he written since his letter about his choices.
Of course, if he is taking my decree to heart, I have no reason to hope that
he will write again if he has voyaged to the Continent, for he is honorable
and will not press me after that unfortunate choice I have forced upon
him. It will be up to me to turn the tide between us if he has had to go.
And yet, I crave the satisfaction of knowing he is safe, on either shore, far
away or near. I have avoided mention of it even to Lucy who is busy with
the planning of her new life with Mr. Talbot.

Now it is evening and the house is quiet once more. This afternoon,
restless as Henry, I finally decided to take myself for a walk, and found
my steps leading me to town. I chanced to meet Thomas at the Bedford's
mercantile and heard him speak of things that mattered little to me—his
mother's flowerbeds wilting in the heat, his pianoforte out of tune—and
then he caught my attention when he mentioned that his father had sent
Theodore to England. Yes, he had gone to England after all.

My disappointment was so great that I dropped the sack of flour I held
and it burst open, sending a white cloud rising up around us both. Oh,
why should I have expected that he would choose to remain ashore? He
is a seaman, as much one as James ever was, and he will always choose
the sea, its pull too great to rest long on land with any woman except for
when the seasons leave little choice.

Thomas was alarmed by my shock and tried to temper his news. "Well,
the truth of it is, Marianne, Theodore did not see this coming
and my father was also acting with some urgency to send him."

I chanced sharing a thought. "Thomas, what is your estimation
of Theodore? And please do not consider the influence of anyone else's
opinion of him."

"You mean, Mother, I presume?"

"You presume well." At this I almost smiled, for his question need not have been uttered.

"If I tell you that when I first met the man, I thought him quite possibly a cad and a tippler, I am turned around in my view, for I have yet to get a whiff of the rum on him and he seems, if you must know, devoted only to one woman."

My heart dropped from its place. "He is devoted to another?"

"You silly thing," Thomas whispered, steering me away from the heap of flour. "It is you who lights his eye. Scarcely do I mention your name then he lifts his head and smiles."

"Then, you do not regard him as a cad?"

"Not at all. I do worry, though. He seems to come from…"

"Nowhere."

"Quite, my dear friend. How can he be trusted?"

"You bear a likeness to my elders and their opinion," I said.

"Think of it, Marianne. If you were to choose a man who had a past, even a past with dubious chapters and a nefarious family, at the very least, one would know his standing and could make a decision. To be very frank on the matter, Mother detests him because he is as beyond reproach as he is beyond explanation. She does not like things without a resolution, without a beginning, middle and an end. Such things lacking this reliable configuration earn her distrust. I cannot fault her for this, given what her life was like before my father, Reginald, came along when I was a boy."

"Your father, he admires Theodore or he would not have taken him on and given him such a good position. Is it unreasonable of me to assume this?"

"Marianne, you are not an unreasonable woman. It is one of the things I adore about you. You are at once headstrong and filled with a kind of whimsy that has likely followed you about all your life. Of course, my father is a shrewd judge but even he is perplexed, for how can a man, after all, have no one from whom to trace himself before his parents, no relations after them anywhere? It is a reasonable question."

"Perhaps, but I have decided to be satisfied with it. There are people so unfortunate as to be quite alone in the world. Even Mr. Talbot professes to have no family."

"Well, then, whatever you do, use your reasonable mind to choose with whom you spend the coming years. I would vote myself in, if you would have me, though I suspect I am not what you seek."

"You will do any woman proud, Thomas, but you cannot fool me. I know who draws your eye. I know you are not having an easy time of it." I sighed as I stood to dust the flour from my skirt. "And, yet, you have a point about us," I yielded, half-believing the words that came next. "That we two are hopeless about those whose favor in our families is utterly unattainable may mean we ought to join our own two hands someday just to quiet them all."

Thomas' demeanor changed in an instant, from casual and friendly to something more like shy, even humble, qualities I had not seen in him for months.

"Marianne, you would truly give my mother such satisfaction by giving into her wish to take me as a suitor after your mourning ends?" I could not recant here, and nodded, swallowing hard. "Then you have my word that for such a good friend as you, I would give up my own foolish heart's desire, my silly Mary, and have you. You need never imagine yourself and your son alone, dear friend."

He took my hands in his, both our palms dry and dusted white, and kissed the back of one, leaving a faint impression from his moist lips.

"Thomas, you care too much for me."

"Oh, Marianne, the trouble really is that I care not enough, not nearly enough to make you as happy as our friend Theodore would do. Happier than we two would be our mothers. Whatever it is that haunts you about others' opinions of him, you must push it away and act on your own behalf."

And with that, he left the mercantile, left me standing with surprise coloring my cheeks and gratitude warming me. I hardly felt Mr. Bedford gently move me aside as he swept up the rest of the mess we had made.

Even Lucy's kind ministrations, which I know are heartfelt in spite of her own lingering melancholy over Hannah's and Rose's absence, set me somewhat on edge, for I am angry with myself for toppling into my own doldrums. I do not mean to snap at her when she asks me what the trouble is, yet all of her kindness offers little comfort.

And I have given Lucy cause to fret as well, for my seething over Mrs. Pringle has irked Lucy more than it used to do. In fact, she is as grumpy as I of late, and she is a bride-to-be! This evening after I tucked Henry into his bed, Lucy and I sat on the side porch amid a display of fireflies borne on the still, close evening air. I had found a bottle of Port in the back of my china cabinet and poured her a small glass. I cupped some chamomile tea in my hands. It relaxes me in a way I did not appreciate even when James would be at sea for days, sometimes weeks at a stretch.

The air has been far more fragrant this week than I recall from other years living in this house James built, surrounded by the heavy, sweet perfume of the peonies he had Mr. Talbot plant on either side of the house. Their perfume follows me as I follow my own footpath through the garden and in the evenings it seems even headier with every breath. I filled my lungs with the sweet air as Lucy took her seat next to mine.

"Where is Mr. Talbot tonight?"

Lucy sighed and then turned to me, the look of a lovesick girl belying her years.

"He's working, Cousin. You should know this. You employ him to do the things he does and he's worked very hard indeed since our betrothal." It was an accusation, to be sure, though I cannot think of anything more that I have knowingly added to his duties. Well, perhaps he has gone more often to town, but I do not think it a function of my needs. I believe, though I will not say so, that whatever occupies him more, it is owing to his wedding my cousin.

306

"Lucy, he has never complained. You have yet to complain about his labors taking him away from you and now you do so bitterly. What is really the matter?"

She let a silence sit between us until I turned away and then had to look upon her again to see if she had fallen into the garden or into dreams.

"My granddaughter," she finally said. "She's written that she'd like to bring her mother and come to live here, with us, with Mr. Talbot and me when we're wed and can offer them space in our home."

The gravity of this struck me as it had her and I leaned closer, held her hand.

"Timothy will never allow it, of course. Not as long as he lives," she said. In this, I heard just a shred of wishful thinking in Lucy's busy head.

"And Hannah's fancies, are they matched by her mother? We cannot know this, I am certain. Rose would be a fool to confide to her child any dream of leaving." Yet, even as I said this, I wondered if the day would ever come and hoped someday it would, and wished no harm would come to even Timothy's steely heart. In fact, I wished more for his reform and that happiness should be restored to all of them that they might remain a family.

Lucy rubbed her shoulders and pulled her shawl tight around her, then seemed to shake her thoughts away into the evening air.

"Have you heard from Mr. Abel?"

"You know the answer as well as I do," I said, taking my turn at being the petulant child.

"Well, I thought, perhaps..."

I have told myself each day that I am not as bothered as I was the night before last, or the night before that one, and so on, and so I answered according to this refrain. "It is not for me to worry over, Lucy. He is not my husband, or anyone of any significance to me or to my son. Were he to disappear from Rockport forever, I would not be the poorer for it." And I stood and smoothed my skirt as if to leave, my eyes turned away from Lucy's studious gaze, then sat down again and felt the welcome press of my cousin's firm and reassuring hand at my back.

307

JULY 9, 1856

There has been a startling violence in Rockport and its leader was none other than the woman I have long thought one of the most peaceful in the village! Hannah Jumper, already well advanced in years, a woman raised on a farm and known to be a healer (I have used her cures and recorded their use here!) led two hundred women through town yesterday morning on a rampage to rid all shops and establishments of rum or anything else spirituous. It comes out in the eyewitness accounts that the men's tippling has been the cause of much disgruntlement among the womenfolk whose husbands spend many months freely drinking, bringing home less and less of their pay. At sea, between voyages, and especially during the off-season for fisherman, there is a great consumption of rum and other liquors that have robbed families of a proper living. So, it would seem that many of Miss Jumper's customers have complained to her over the months and, bent at their hems and peering close at their necklines, she has not only listened to them, but offered vociferous agreement. The women used hatchets, a frightening thing to imagine. I had Lucy and Mr. Talbot lock the doors and windows before we four (Henry too) rushed up to the topmost part of the house and looked down on Dock Square to see a cluster of women swinging hatchets at demijohns and barrels of rum, spilling it in the street. As it happens, we did not know exactly what we spied from so far up, but there were some women running down the street toward the commotion, and some bore hatchets. Rather than follow the riot, we thought it best to remain indoors, not understanding fully what caused it or whom the rioters sought with their weapons.

Had I been listening, I would have heard nothing in town during my visits, for the secret of this rampage was secured among the few men who knew and complied, and among the many women who swore them to secrecy as they plotted. I have stowed what little liquor I do have in my pantry behind sacks of cornmeal and flower, adding that bottle of Port I found in my cabinet the other evening, yet I do not think it is what the women were after. Not such a small, harmless lot as mine.

I will look differently upon Hannah Jumper now—with admiration, of course, for she was brave and a natural leader. I believe she will live on for more than the cures that hang drying from her rafters.

July 11, 1856

As I scribble, I listen for the sounds of Henry sleeping soundly in his bed, in his room across from mine. The great weight of all of these months of telling myself that Theodore means less to me than I am willing to accept presses upon me with a question, causes me wonder if I am the kind of woman I would want to know.

Oh! I cannot even answer that! In my dreams, it is Theodore who comes to me, his hands held toward mine, his smiling mouth so lovely and full of the sound of my name, calling to me. Yet, when I awaken, it is James' presence I feel, as if he has been in the room. Now it is a cool, reproving stare that follows me from within the frame I once held to my breast each night before bed, each night before I could even rest my eyes, and every morning, my lips upon the glass, pining in vain for any lingering essence of him. Was I mad in a way? Perhaps I am mad now. No, it was grief most profound, and it lingers in its newer form. Yet, even for a moment, I can see it now as having been just a step away from a kind of insanity. Losing someone so dear to me, how could a kind of madness not take hold? Had Theodore not come into my life, would madness have taken root? I like to think I had gathered my wits by the time he arrived.

Where shall I begin then? With the afternoon at the Pringles, or the letter? Yes, the letter! I have already read it a thousand times and it is creased almost beyond repair, though it has been just a day and a night since its arrival.

Or, beginning with Virginia Pringle might be the more practical thing.

No! I shall lead off with Theodore Ethan Abel.

His letter arrived just this morning and Lucy took it in. She crept toward me like a round kitten, still light on her feet but difficult not to notice. Holding the letter out to me, she pressed it into my palm and told me she and Henry were to take a walk around to visit a friend of hers, a Mrs. Paterson with whom she had been spending some time lately. She is a kindly older woman who is well suited in her even temper to Lucy whom I have come to observe is prone to a flash of hot-headedness lately with which I, in my own brooding temperament, am not much help. With my distractedness I hardly fault her for seeking other companionship, glad as I am that someone could provide it. And Mrs. Paterson adores my son, gives him pencils and tablets of paper for drawing, bakes him the most scrumptious lemon biscuits.

Theodore's letter, decorated with markings of England's sovereign, the Queen Victoria, and rumpled from its travels across the ocean, was all things to me, filled with hope and despair in the same way the other letter he wrote contained. Yet, what I learned within his newsy phrases angered me so. It would seem that Theodore believes Thomas to be my suitor or, when the time is deemed proper, my first marriage prospect, that he has been all but promised to me, and that I have agreed to such an arrangement!

He wrote, "If you choose to marry Thomas, I will take it as your duty to both your parents and your son, for he can provide you all you need to live, whereas I'm currently unable to provide for much more than myself. I'm best leaving Rockport if that should come to pass and ask you to understand with a clear mind that it's my only choice." This sent me from one end of the parlor to the other and I heard a kind of choked cry come from my own throat. I was relieved to be alone in the house.

How could he have thought this? Surely Thomas himself had not waved him off to England with this false notion; he bears him no ill will, nor, despite his generous offer in the Bedfords' Mercantile the other day, does he harbor any hope with me. And even with the answers revealed to me today at the Pringles' home, where I went fresh from my dither, I had just the fleeting sense that Thomas might, after the man I had come to know, have chosen to stand taller, let his voice be heard above that of his meddling mother. I could no more brook her opinion of Theodore than I could swallow my suspicion that she was responsible for Theodore being sent away in despair over me.

I do not believe he would have revealed this despair of which he writes so plainly in his letter to me, for he does not wish to burden me any further. Oh, but how can he think his presence a burden! How can he imagine that I would want to marry Thomas or that Thomas would vie for me? Do they not speak of these things? No, I suppose they would not, for Theodore may not feel at ease with Thomas, may not feel his equal, strong as he stands beside him. It is, after all, about money.

Perhaps it is better that I demurred Mr. Talbot's offer to convey me to the Pringles by carriage, for hot as it was, the minutes I spent metering my steps and my thoughts as I breathed the fragrant air had the effect of a calming hand on my shoulder. I had thought to put that woman in her place once and for blessed all and I wished to do it in the way Mother might, with intelligence and control.

And then Virginia Pringle surprised me by opening the door wide when I pulled the bell. There was no servant in sight. "My girl is ill," she said, as if reading my thoughts, though perhaps anyone would appear as surprised to see her greet her guest before they were fully welcomed and settled in the sitting room by her maid. Mrs. Pringle requires ceremony, I have observed.

"What ails her?" I asked of the maidservant, Mary. I recall her as shy and very pretty, and had a memory of her melancholy affect when she was near Thomas, her timidity every other time.

"She is abed. I do not think she will return to service with me."

I could not understand such cool-running blood as ran through Virginia Pringle's veins, for when she spoke of Mary, it was as if she were the one inconvenienced by this girl's ailment.

I could not leave it alone. "Did she take a fall?"

She ignored my question. "Dear Mrs. Parsons, please do not linger on the step. Come in. We were about to sit down to tea. You must not worry yourself over trivial matters. The girl was careless to begin with and the young man responsible has left her alone, rebuked by his family for consorting with a servant girl."

My eyes grew wide.

"Oh, come! Enough!" She scolded me as if I were hers to scold. Then her voice softened and she attempted a smile. I glimpsed the ghost of the happier woman she professed once to have been. "She will recover and I will help her to find another situation. Your concern for her is very sweet, very like I imagine your Father to be, for I know your Mother is a more sensible woman."

I nearly turned heel and left for home. And then I snuffed out the notion. Henry was not there to nag me out the door, nor was Lucy along to distract me, for she has not once been asked to tea, the lucky thing. But I heard in my head the sound of my husband's voice, chiding me lightly for caring too much what this woman would think. I heard Thomas' words of the other day. Calm again, I stayed and allowed myself to be led into the sunlit parlor where, at a little table laden with a fine linen cloth on which were a delicious variety of sandwiches and cakes, biscuits and preserves, sat Thomas. It was almost as if they expected me, though they are avid about their teatime and its elegant spread.

My friend looked uncomfortable, like a boy in too-stiff britches, and I smiled and gave him my hand. He kissed it, yet would not meet my eye. He simply rose from his seat to pull out a chair for me, nodding just enough to leave me wondering if it were indeed a nod at all or if he had only just looked down at the floor for a lost pocket watch. I tried again to catch his eye, to let him know I came as his friend, and what did he do but look past me at a rather imposing philodendron in a clay pot near my seat. Oh, poor Thomas, I could not divine his thoughts, and wanted very much to take his hands in mine and tell him to *stiffen up, stiffen up, friend, and be upright in your family!*

Of course, this would have been a catastrophe. I held my tongue.

"Please, Mrs. Parsons, do have some preserve," Mrs. Pringle said, placing it by my plate and beginning to lift the little spoon heaped with the sun-colored jelly. I held my scone toward her and then took rather a large mouthful, enjoying the tartness mingling with the butter.

As I tried to work all I had bitten off into my cheeks, Mrs. Pringle began to speak. "I have heard that your new friend, Mrs. Jamieson, will be coming home with her daughters."

I nodded, swallowing, before I said, "I am as glad as I can be, both that I will enjoy her company once again and that her daughters have recovered fully. They ought to be home by week's end."

"The kumquats this season are quite fair," Thomas added as he spooned some onto his scone. Both his mother and I turned to him, her teaspoon poised in the air between cup and cream pitcher.

And she did a lovely thing, engaging her son in normal discourse.

"Thomas has been tending to the fruit. Reginald is terribly busy of late, taking more trips than he might. I believe this is because he can, now that he has a protégé, a successor to the kind of work he did not particularly enjoy. He is grooming his new liaison well and he is a quick enough study." This was the first time I had ever heard a kind word about Theodore from that woman's mouth and I was certain she had been poisoned. I began to wonder if something were not stirred into the jelly on the sly, perhaps by Thomas.

"I am apparently not much more than the keeper of the kumquat," Thomas said, playing at levity, but a frown belied it.

"Thomas, you must not say such things," she chided. "You have your skills and they are fine and enviable, making you ill-suited to business or the travel it involves. You play the piano well enough to entertain royalty and you are an excellent nursemaid to this crop of strange fruit that, I must say, yielded a tasty treat."

I was dumbstruck. Virginia Pringle did not strike me as the soothing type; no, she has never betrayed any gentleness in her nature. And today, as if she had something to gain from it, she brimmed with it, certainly compared to the dour sort I have long understood her to be. Of course, it was not the kind of believable sweetness that Irene Jamieson possesses, but I could see that Mrs. Pringle was doing her best to please someone, perhaps me.

"Mrs. Parsons, how is your boy? The last I saw, he had a gleam of mischief in his eye that perfectly suited him. He looks very like his father, does he not?"

"Yes," I agreed, thinking that I would rather have her call me something else. Marianne felt too familiar, yet the name Mrs. Parsons, which I continue to be, unsettles me on her tongue, for she uses my name as if it were very much the way I should experience it with James living.

I regarded Thomas again who had turned his attention to the buttonhole of his suit that was nearest his waistcoat and the gilt chain that dangled from his pocket watch. He made the chain swing in tiny arcs to and fro, and seemed entranced. Perhaps feeling my stare, he looked up, whisked his hands back together, clasped across one folded knee, and offered me such a charming, genuine smile belonging much more to the Thomas I had come to know that I really did see for the first time what a handsome man he is and wondered why his parents had not tried to match him to me before I married James.

Of course, this is merely a wonder and not a wish, for I still find Thomas' tendencies sometimes a little off-putting, namely what flies from his moist lips when he is too near as he speaks. I only wonder that he has not been paired to some comely thing here in Rockport or a town beyond in all these years. He is a man of twenty-six already.

"I imagine *my* child might have looked very much like me, were he a boy. Mother, do you not think so? And his mother would have been proud of him, as she is a proud young thing herself."

Mrs. Pringle rose taller even as she sat and her lips pressed tightly together, turning them white.

"Thomas, you must not speak of this. The matter is finished. You have no hope there, none, and it is folly to have imagined otherwise. Your father and I would have discovered sooner than later what you and this fool child were planning and your funds would have been cut clean."

The blood in my veins chilled me as I realized what Virginia Pringle was saying. A servant girl had no hope of winning the favor of a man like Thomas from such a fine family. And it did not surprise me that Mrs. Pringle would rule with an iron will any decision regarding her son and his future, in particular with a lowly housemaid being out of the question.

And yet, here was a man, not advanced in years but growing older in his heart, whose mother would deny him happiness. She would, if she had her druthers, keep him all to herself as I imagine she has done since losing her first husband, even as she has a fine husband in Reginald.

Thomas had begun to shift in his seat, his brow gathering, his hand returned to fretting with his pocket watch. Then he stood so suddenly that he toppled the tea cart and the teapot wobbled and tipped, making a frightening clatter before Thomas himself reached for it and righted it again. Its spout was chipped and Mrs. Pringle frowned at the injury done to her fine china. Thomas moved to the window of the greenhouse and then he turned on his heel and left the room, stopping only briefly to nod to me and take my hand to kiss.

"I regret that I am unable to finish the afternoon with you and Mother," he said as I looked up at him, entreating his troubled eyes to meet mine. My heart cracked a little for my friend and his unfortunate choice. Virginia Pringle had other plans for him and I still had not discovered if they involved me.

"Mrs. Pringle, I must get home to my son. Thank you for your kindness despite my unannounced visit. You do not need to see me out. Your son will do so," I said and turned to him, "If it is no bother."

As he took my hand and put it through his arm, I felt his sadness. Out in the entranceway, I whispered to him. "So, it is not you and I who are intended, but you and Mary?" His laugh, when it came, was filled with the irony of unfortunate knowledge.

"Intended," he said, as if the word meant nothing. "Marianne, I was a fool, a boy caught in a girl's gaze, in her youth. Mary will find a man better suited to her. Mother is right."

"No, Thomas, she could not be more *in*correct," I whispered. "Your young love will marry a man perhaps older than you but who must work very hard all day and then come home expecting his wife to pander to his needs and bear him a passel of children, all the while thrusting his hands at her, pulling her this way and that, likely tippling their money in rum that Hannah Jumper and her gang did not find, and they will live in squalor. Is this what you want for Mary?"

Thomas' eyes were narrowing as I spoke, as if all I said were the gospel truth, aware as I was that I wove facts from my own imagination into what seemed perfectly logical. When I had finished, he took my hands in his as if he had just discovered something, and said, "no. It is the farthest thing from what I want." And he opened the door and we two left the house. At the end of the path, he walked his way toward a part of town where Mary lived, and I mine.

Chancing to look back toward the house's front garden where her topiaries nearly hid her, I spied Mrs. Pringle hovering there where she might have a view of us, but when I looked directly toward her, she was gone.

July 12, 1856

I am awake again between the nightingale's and the lark's song and it is no place to be. The quiet is too loud at my temples and my longing has found its name. Now that I have sat awake these many nights wondering at it, staring at it and it at me from opposite corners of the room as we inch toward one another, it speaks its name.

July 14, 1856

My son has taken a fall and his little wrist is bound up now, held against his chest. He does not like this one little bit and the only thing keeping him from running away from me when I try to keep him from running at all is that it hurts him. Lucy had been clutching at the railing to keep up with my son as they came downstairs yesterday morning and down he spilled, down on his right side, the poor love. Doctor Wainright administered laudanum as he had for me so that he could set the wrist right again, and left a tonic to help my son sleep at night after the effects of the medicine ebbed. I spent the night at the edge of sleep, watching Henry who lay next to me, passing my hand over his tiny, already barrel, chest every hour or so to feel his breath. It is only a fracture, I realize, but after that bee sting last summer, it is his first bout of persistent pain and I cannot abide it even as I am helpless to have prevented or to heal it. Lucy blames herself, of course, as I blame myself and we continued to cluck and console each other at supper tonight as Henry slept deeply for the first time since yesterday.

"What," I asked her, "is a woman ever to do when her beloved child or her charge suffers pain? She must suffer as well." We both sighed into our teacups and when I chanced to look up at her over the rim of mine, she smiled at me, reached over the table and patted my hand.

"You are dear, Cousin," she said. "Too dear, the both of you." A tear swelled and spilled as she rose from the table to place our dishes on the cart and begin the work of cleaning them, with me right at her heels, for I was not to be left to my own thoughts.

JULY 15, 1856

I awoke this morning to a flurry of voices and bustling below. It took a moment for me to understand that it was coming from downstairs and had begun to move toward me. Lucy was at my bedside almost before my eyes opened, letting in a thin, brilliant stream of lamplight and my excited cousin, bathed in its glow. "Marianne, come down to the kitchen as soon as you can dress. There is something I must show you."

"But it is hardly dawn," I yawned at her and stretched until my toes had separated and my muscles, every inch of me, had let in the morning. I curled into a comfortable ball, resisting her. "Is Henry awake?"

"No, but if you do not move yourself quickly, he will be. Now, out of bed you get!"

I had never seen her so strident. She was flushed and anxious.

Her mood infected me. I hurried into my dressing gown, ran a brush down my hair for only a few strokes, because she thrust this brush toward me and would not let me leave until I had done so, and then she poured water into the basin at my washing table, handed me a cloth and towel, and urged me to wash my face which, having little choice, I did directly. Then she led me from my bedroom and down the stairs.

And there he was, in my parlor, his face turned to the window, his hands looking for a place of comfort along his tall, strong body, his dark curls gold-tipped, surely from weeks under the open sky. I stood a moment watching him and felt the light pat of Lucy's hands at my shoulders as she tiptoed off to the kitchen from where there wafted the smell of something most delicious, a bread pudding. But my appetite was absent.

He turned to me, hearing something, a step, a breath, mine as I caught it, and his eyes caught me as I tried to move toward him and then stopped, spoke, and spoiled the moment.

"You are here to stay?" I asked.

"You may banish me," he said. "If you say so once more, I'll know your mind too well and not insult you further by remaining."

"Oh, no, do not go one step. But must you go to sea before too long? It is not easy for me to bear that."

"Nor is it easy for me, for I had hoped for a longer reprieve, but Mr.

Pringle will have me off on another of his campaigns soon enough. You look well. Lovely, really. Quite awake for so early in the morning." His smile was shy and he tucked his face away into my hair, for at last we stood close.

I let myself lean into him, placed my cheek against his heart and felt the drumming there. His hands moved up my back and into my hair, twining it round his fingers and bringing it to his lips, his face. We two stood there, listening to the birds waking, to the unnecessary clatter of Lucy in the kitchen, and to the sound of our breath.

I looked up at him. "Theodore," I whispered. "Stay. Stay for breakfast."

"I will stay for that, and for dinner, and supper, too, if you will tolerate me that much longer." There was the crook of a smile in his words, on his lips and he brought his mouth down toward me then, placing it so softly over mine it was almost as if just the kiss of air had passed over them.

"Stay only for breakfast," I said, against my will. "Then come again for supper and stay on as long as you can after Henry and Lucy go to bed."

If I were a religious woman I would live in fear of divine retribution for what I was inviting with this man not my husband. Yet, the thought of letting Theodore out of my life has shaken me and now there is no going back to any prim or girlish pretense that he never belonged here at all.

JUNE 5, 1857

She is very small, with tiny, balled fists. Her face, even in sleep, is pink from the fitful feeding she took only an hour ago. Mother has continued to insist that I employ a wet nurse to feed the child, and she is barely a week old! As often as Mother insists, as earnest her need to let me know what she considers best for me and for the baby, I will stand firm. I did not have a wet nurse for my son and will not for my daughter.

Lily Amelia's presence has offered me a life I thought I might never know again, filled with joy and hope. Her lovely skein of silken black hair wrapped around such a fragile head, the heart shape of her cheeks and that dimple in her chin so like her father's. In her eyes, slightly upturned like little brown almonds, shaped like her brother's lighter ones, is wisdom in one so very small and new.

Virginia Pringle has been to the house twice today already, which has been a mercy of a sort. She occupies Mother in ways I know Lucy cannot, for Lucy, nearly a year married, is still by turns caught up in her reverie over being Mrs. Richard Talbot and in being a nursemaid to me. And with Hannah as her charge for the few months we have her each half-year, she is perfectly diverted. Lucy is here today laundering sheets and preparing meals that will see me through to the next century. She is a dear cousin and friend and I will not imagine a life without her.

Peering at my new baby girl as she sleeps against me, her cheek pressed to my breast, I have thought at odd moments that traces of James are there, for she favors her brother's lovely curved lips and intelligent eyes that were so like his father's. But, no, she does not resemble James so much as her living, breathing, affectionate big brother, and Theodore, her father.

Lily will be a comely thing, though I will have her concentrate less upon her own reflection and more upon her lessons. Hannah, approaching fourteen and a splendid teacher for one so young, has taught Henry, now past four, to read. He is a quick one. If his sister is anything like me, she will spend many days dreaming and mooning over the garden and the sea and pay less heed to her lessons. I will help her to strike a fine balance between the two pursuits, for even as

I do love to rhapsodize over what my eye captures beyond the windows, beyond the threshold of my house from up in the cupola or simply sitting under the linden tree, I also believe firmly in learning to read and write with a proficiency that will allow my children to converse comfortably in sophisticated company. There is nothing worse than a vacant-headed young lady. I should like to think myself the opposite.

I have had no end of well-wishing notes for Lily's birth. One, in particular, has come from a very long way, from England. I have been unable to open it and it does not bear an address on the outside. It is just as I felt with the package. I did not wish to be surprised.

Lucy bade me open the letter, post-marked mid-May, hardly a month from today, and here is what it said:

My Dearest Marianne,

How lucky is a man who wins the woman he loves? I won't dare count my blessings, for if I do there's every possibility that I'll lose count and come up missing one, or take too many in the counting and be punished for being greedy.

When you receive this letter, I'll be home again, with you and our soon-to-be born child, with Henry and Hannah, with Lucy and Mr. Talbot. I can't think of a place I'd rather spend my days and nights and defy any seagoing vessel to tempt me away. Even as I say this, Mr. Pringle will want to ready me for another voyage before the summer ends, but I've made a decision and won't regret it once spoken:

I'm never again sailing for open waters. Before sailing for England this trip, I gave Mr. Pringle my notice and he gave me his word, so long as I stay on at the quarry, that he won't ask me to board another ship. The only thing to push me toward open water is you, should you have a change of heart, and I hardly think that's in the stars.

One gift I have to give you that I have never imagined being able to is a life free of worry. Let this be your gift from me, for my family. For us.

Your loving husband,
Theodore

Just a fortnight ago, the day before Lily was born, and just a few days after Theodore's arrival from his last voyage, I heard a sound on the upper floor directly above my bedroom. Lucy had been up to visit me while I rested, bringing me tea. She had left only moments before. Theodore had brought me a clutch of peonies, his presence and their sweet perfume a balm as I worried over the days before the birth. I was very tired most of each day and could hardly climb the stairs anymore. My best moments were spent asleep.

And as I drifted off, I heard a sound, a soft fall of feet, of limbs, something that bespoke a restrained step, its weight heavier than quiet would allow. When I opened my eyes, it stopped. I heaved my round middle from my bed, knowing it would be a cumbersome journey from my room to the floor above, but in my state, with James' troubled face drifting in and out of my mind as I rested, I could not remain. He had once written, in that last letter meant for me to see after his death, that he would not haunt me, yet he has done, and with a certain skill. For I have not dreamed of him for nearly a year until now. It is as if in finding my heart with Theodore, James has finally let me go. So, why does his face return now? Why did I feel drawn to the upper floors when I ought to have stayed still in my ripe, uncomfortable state?

At the bottom of the landing I looked up to the third floor. Oh, those stairs, all ten of them, and my great, round middle going before me with not much of me to hold me steady. Not with child, I am a clumsy woman when fatigued, so it was with great concentration that I grabbed hold of the newel post and took each step in its turn. It was a long time before I reached the top. And when I had done, I turned to James' study and moved inside its long afternoon shadows.

I had intended all along to keep this room as it was, but soon after Theodore returned from his voyage to England last July and I gave him my whole heart, I made a decision. This study, with its compass, its telescope, its maps and books, shelves and desk would become a place where Henry, Hannah, and now one day Lily, too, could *321* call a room of their own, a place to pretend and dream and frolic, teach themselves about new worlds, and Theodore and I would be here with them when they tolerated us, absorbing their contentment and wonder. It still contains the table James used, and the table behind the door remains there. The maps have been put away, the books shelved in other rooms of the house, and Theodore has moved the telescope to the cupola.

I began with the table behind the door, not knowing, or remembering if I ought to know, what urge I should possess to do such a thing. It was a small enough table that it moved easily, and behind it was a loose panel. I removed that easily enough and found a flat cedar box there. Inside it was a sheaf of papers, all of them small maps, faded either from disuse or overuse I could not be sure, though on most of them were names of places I knew James to have gone on his vessel, places such as Georges Bank, the Isle of Shoals, and other rich fishing grounds up and down the coast.

Taking the papers in my hands I moved to the chair where he once sat and with some struggle I hoisted myself up into it, hooking my slippered feet onto the rung for support and clutching at one of the chair's arms.

I looked at the maps again, recalling these places, his often thrilling description of them it seems a lifetime ago, before he retired into an unyielding reticence about the nature of his days at sea. He once spoke to me with real excitement of the rocks in the Shoals that nearly tore a hole in his hull, the collision he avoided with another vessel on approach to Georges Bank, as if the other vessel would thwart anyone else with its progress, as if, he said, the captain on that other vessel had rights to all the bounty in those waters and would prevent the other schooners' approach.

The wind outside beat a furious tempo at the windows and one of them was opened, for which I could only fault myself, recalling that I had asked Lucy herself to open them and air the room and then forgotten to ask her to close them. Yet, I realized as the curtain blew wildly into the room, tangling itself around the window crank, that there were no leaves or anything else on the window ledge that would have resulted from having left it open too long, that of course she would have closed it without need of a reminder. *Oh, come,* I chided myself. *Can she not forget something occasionally?* But I knew in that moment there was a different answer, far less ordinary, and looked quickly away from the window, feeling my skin prickle.

Looking about the room, I knew that something was different. The baby kicked and rolled inside me so that I cupped the underside of my belly and cooed, as if that would still the activity. But it only grew and I shifted in my seat and very nearly spilled off, gripping the table ledge to right myself.

As I crooned a lullaby, I beheld my surroundings, not altogether familiar to me to begin with, and realized that the faint smell of cherry tobacco hung in the air, as if a pipe had been smoked earlier in the day. Theodore has never taken to the pipe, though I have offered many kinds of tobacco, except cherry, and he has turned them down, saying he dislikes the burn and bitter taste at the back of his throat. It cannot have been Lucy, nor Hannah.

Stop. Stop this nonsense, I chided myself again, this time aloud. *Go back to bed and do not come up here alone again.* I resolved to ask Mr. Talbot to apply a new coat of fresh paint, pale yellow and blue to cheer the room, and I left, the sheaf of papers clutched in my hand.

As I made steps toward the door, the window banged shut so loudly that the pane of glass cracked down the center and I beat a retreat as quick as a woman with a belly the size of a ripe pumpkin could, grabbing hold of the wall and the rail to keep from pitching forward.

In my bed again, I looked through the pages in my lap and understood nothing except that James was clearly making his trips worthwhile, sailing more in our last year together than he had in all the years I knew him as a girl. And this was not surprising to me. I was unaware, fretting, and utterly mystified as to why he chose to spend so much time away from his wife and child. I did not need a reminder of his inclination away from us.

As these thoughts hardened in me, I felt some lingering sadness for the life we might have had and then I put the papers in the drawer of the bedside table. As I did so, Theodore came into our bedroom, his smile warm and loving, his hands already reaching toward me.

"Darling," he said, his palm across my middle, his cheek now resting there, too. I let my fingers comb through his hair. I have missed my Theodore this past year, for even as he sojourned more at home than at sea, his trips out were too long for me to sit comfortably with in any state, least of all with child. I know Reginald does well by him and, by extension, us. There will be no more seagoing vessels in our lives.

Thomas has stuck by his father and apprenticed Theodore in commerce. The two men have taken to this partnership rather well, Thomas not begrudging his father's need for Theodore's skills, understanding his own limitations within the realm his father has so comfortably functioned for so many years. Thomas has his own gifts and applies them to where he is needed, namely to Mary and their child, and to the nursery he has fashioned in his own house. For Theodore he is the perfect foil; part friend, part helpmate where a particular kind of written language is needed to communicate with merchants abroad.

"Now that I'm not a seaman, you'll want to put me out now and then," Theodore murmured into the tiny pocket of air between us, his face alongside mine, his eyes filled with the ardor that has been there since the first day he came to my door, and which I did wish to see.

"You will have to mistreat me for this to happen," I whispered into the curls at his temples.

He moved his lips to mine and, as we embraced, there rolled through me such a wave of longing for him that I began to remove my nightgown just as he moved to push it gently from my shoulders, covering them with whisker-rough kisses, roaming my neck and my bosom with his hungry mouth, a hunger we have not had the luxury of indulging in this first year of our marriage in the way we began, for our child took root in me almost from the first week after our wedding and I took ill in the months to follow, well into winter. As I have grown larger and clumsier still, it has been most difficult to welcome my new husband.

We lay in our bed, our arms wrapped tightly round one another, his breath warm and ragged, our shared desire coming fast and warm in my ear, and then I laughed.

He raised himself up to peer at me, perhaps hurt that I should giggle during this tender moment.

"Oh, Theodore, it is not you. It is us, it is this!" I said, pointing at my great big middle. "I adore every inch of you and would like to give you every inch of me. I am impatient to have my lover and my husband back and it makes me laugh. If I did not laugh, I would weep."

He wrapped both hands around my thickened waist even as I lay sideways, one of his hands wedged tightly between me and the fabric of our bed, and he kissed me, deeply, exploring all parts of my mouth. "Marianne," he said. "For you, I will wait forever."

September 1, 1860

Dearest Marianne,

You are where you should be in your life. I have left it, unwillingly, and have had little choice in the matter. I found myself on an unfamiliar shore, my clothes mostly torn from me, my name a mystery to myself, and even when kind strangers took me in and tried to help me recall who I was and whence I came, it was too late by the time my memory was restored. When at last it was, I made a decision that sealed where I do not now belong. I write this to you in the more distant wake of my discoveries from that day and do not imagine you will ever see my letter, for there are those who love and will protect you from this truth.

I made my way back to Cape Ann in the late summer of 1859, with whiskers and hair too long for anyone to know me. My clothes were not those of a captain, but of a man who knew not a single thing to do with his new life—I wore plain clothes that would not have distinguished me. I visited the cemetery and saw where you buried me. You did what a dutiful wife must do. I tried not to then, and still dare not, imagine your grief. My legs took me toward our home, uncertain what I would discover. Hardly was I two or three houses from ours, when I saw children in the yard, one of them hardly a child at all, but an older girl of about fifteen or sixteen whom I did not recognize, and a small child of perhaps two, who bore a remarkable likeness to Henry and to you. I believe that even from my vantage point across the street, I saw a resemblance in that tiny, sweet-faced girl to a man I knew, and admired for his integrity; yes, she resembled Theodore. Just then, it was Henry, so big and able on his feet, and speaking a stream of words I could almost hear, who came bounding around from the rear of the house, saw me without recognition, waved, and went toward his tiny sister. He took her gently by the hand, and led her into the house, with a small, hurried tug in the last few steps as he looked over his shoulder at the man standing across the street. The older girl remained outside, sitting in a chair on the porch under the linden. She appeared to be reading. I did not know who she was until I heard your voice call her from just inside the door. "Hannah," you said. "Will you please help me with Lily's lunch?" I still do not know who Hannah is, but imagine she must be a relation and not a housemaid, comfortable as she looked and in finer clothes. Is it possible you, too, looked out the window at being told by Henry that an odd-looking man was simply standing there, and decided the

326

girl must come in? I will never know if this is the truth of that lovely yard emptying within a moment of my nearing it. But in she went, this Hannah. Those few words out of your mouth, though you were inside and I could not see you, brought you back to me after four years of neither seeing your face, nor being able to conjure your voice in the thick fog where my lost self seemed to drift, anchorless. Who I was that day reminded me sharply of those men I lost when they took the dory out.

Not long after that day I saw you and your family, and my son, I sent Reginald Pringle a letter describing the situation and asked him, in strictest confidence, to find a man of law to draw up a legal document that would sever your tie with me in the eyes of God and of the United States so that your marriage to Theodore, a good choice, my dearest, would be whole and true and your daughter would not know dishonor in her name.

If you have found this letter, and a devoted part of me hopes you will not, it is my farewell in a way I hoped never to have to convey; not in this way, not in any way, not twice. We cannot choose our end, and I have two demises I would not have chosen, with a third and final one awaiting me that should have been my only end. It is a cruelty I wish upon no one, nor upon those they love.

Marianne, my once-wife, my forever beloved, you need never look over your shoulder and wonder if I am near. After delivering this note to Reginald Pringle whom I asked to deliver, at his discretion, to Theodore, I will go far away and not return. I promised I would not haunt your days and I shall forever keep my word.

My love and good wishes to you always,
James

END

About the Author

M. J. Cohen

Cassandra Krivy Hirsch, born and raised in Toronto, Canada, was a freelance writer of essays, travel, and lifestyle articles for many years while raising her family and writing fiction.

She currently teaches at Drexel University, has published fiction in *Philadelphia Stories,* and received a Pushcart Prize nomination for memoir in 2007. With her youngest daughter, she lives today in the Philadelphia suburbs in a town notable for its nineteenth century sensibility.

Under the Linden Tree is her first novel.

encompass
E D I T I O N S

ENCOMPASS EDITIONS is a young publishing house, founded in 2009 and based in Kingston, Ontario, Canada but dedicated to providing access to traditional publishing to a wider spectrum of writers than is often the case—writers in the United States, Canada, the United Kingdom and the European Union.

Although Encompass does not accept unsolicited manuscripts, the company relies upon several agents who work closely with writers at every level of experience. This policy permits Encompass to focus on what it does best: publish books good to read.

You can visit the Encompass website at www.EncompassEditions.com or contact editor Robert Buckland at words@encompasseditions.com